THE ROAD TO
MASADA

THE ROAD TO
MASADA

ROGER ELWOOD

MOODY PRESS
CHICAGO

ISBN: 0-8024-7938-3

1 3 5 7 9 10 8 6 4 2

Printed in the United States of America

To my beloved parents
for raising me to believe

CONTENTS

AUTHOR'S NOTE

Years ago, I went to Jerusalem with a group of evangelical leaders I had organized. Stopping at Gordon's Calvary was the singular time of greatest impact during the trip. Since then, I have wanted to return to that place and spend more time.

The Road to Masada is my way of doing so.

It is, in fact, my first biblical novel, coming after tackling scenarios in time periods that ranged from the Civil War to World War II, to the future in outer space. Getting a chance to create a story, with historical validity, that is anchored in the events during and directly after the death, burial, and resurrection of Jesus Christ is paramount among blessings for any Christian novelist.

Many of the characters in *The Road to Masada* are actual people, as evidenced by such names as Pontius Pilatus, Nicodaemus, Simon Peter, Saul of Tarsus, and, after them, various kings, martyrs, and others. Every attempt will be made to hold to characterizations that are accurate and supported by records from the period.

Some characters will be fictitious, but even here they will be written in a manner that is true to the times being depicted.

One other word of explanation. Rarely will there be a deliberate attempt to capture the speech patterns and such of the historical period. Often, a zealous dedication to this sort of thing leads to parody and obfuscation. In the interests of clarity, it may be necessary to elevate the level of speech beyond what was actually true of, say, Roman legionnaires. But I think the greater goal is that of presenting clear, verbalized thoughts, showing what a character means, rather than trapping that character in what might seem to us, today, well-nigh indecipherable utterances.

The Road to Masada is my longest book to date and, for me, one of the most rewarding from an edificational point of view.

I hope you agree.

PREFACE

M<i>asada . . .</i>
  The events surrounding this historic spot in the bleak Judean wilderness marked a hastening decline of the Jewish people that would cause many of them to think that they, as a people, were doomed.

Today, Masada is no longer assaulted by Roman legions but, rather, by tourists who make the long trek from Jerusalem to spend time at a site that has become nearly a holy shrine for Jews from all over the world.

The physical specifications of Masada are impressive in themselves. From north to south it measures 1,900 feet, and about a third of that from east to west. The mountain upon which it rests is some 1,400 feet high.

The Jewish leader Jonathan established the fortress itself during the Hasmonean Revolt in 167–142 B.C. This was the period during which the Jews won independence from Syria but then lost it less than a hundred years later when the Romans became the latest oppressors to gain control of the whole of Judea from the Jews themselves.

In 40 B.C., Herod the Great was appointed king of what was considered an outpost region. He proceeded to make extensive reinforcements to the fortress begun by Jonathan and added to the strictly military buildings what would prove to be two extraordinarily beautiful palaces on the same site.

During the years to follow, Jewish passions built up against the Romans. Insurrections broke out periodically, only to be quelled by the inherently superior forces of the occupying nation.

The Road to Masada in its entirety takes place during this chaotic and memorable period from A.D. 33 to A.D. 73.

That Roman soldiers could have had such a famed fortress wrested from their legendary control by an irregular army of zealots proved to be a monumental embarrassment to Rome in general and, in particular, to Emperor Titus Flavius Vespasianus, who had succeeded Nero after the burning of Rome. He knew that something had to be done to take back Masada, or else Rome's prestige would be significantly damaged, which could not be allowed on top of the excesses of his predecessor.

11

So Vespasianus ordered an all-out assault, one that was to go on for years, causing yet more difficulty, since it had been the conventional wisdom of the day that the Romans would accomplish the task in a few weeks!

The resulting scenes of bravery during warfare and their tragic outcome form a memorable climax toward which a long series of events had been heading: the death, burial, and resurrection of Jesus the Christ; the joy and majesty of the Day of Pentecost; the arduous but fruitful missionary journeys of Paul the apostle; the eventual burning of Rome, though it was not started, as was once believed, by a deranged Nero. These epochal happenings are all covered within the pages of *The Road to Masada*.

And then there is that most momentous of historical conclusions: the defense of Masada by zealots who had captured it in A.D. 66. They were called Sicarii, those brave men whose numbers seemed almost laughably limited when compared to the massive fighting power of the Roman Empire.

The Road to Masada covers a sweep of just forty years, not much time in the flow of the history of Planet Earth but truly an era unlike any other in its impact upon the history of the human race from that time onward.

No one who visits what remains of Masada and who realizes all that it symbolizes comes away from that bleak spot without being profoundly affected on both the emotional and the spiritual level. For the Jews, Masada represents in a figurative and perhaps a literal sense as well the last nail in their coffin, for only many centuries later after the horrors of The Holocaust were they able to return to their homeland.

For Christians everywhere, the defense of Masada came nearly at the close of the apostolic period, with those who had been closest to Christ all dead by martyrdom by that time; but Christ had set in motion that which would never end, the God-ordained growth of Christianity itself, that growth continuing today as a vibrant demonstration of the Great Commission as mandated by Christ Himself.

There are many characters in this book in whose lives the reader will become involved: Decimus Paetus, the legionnaire who, at Calvary, thrust a spear into the side of Jesus, an act which would haunt him; Pontius Pilatus, the proconsul of Judea who washed his hands of the blood of this innocent Man, after a sincere effort to free the Nazarene, but who could never quiet the conscience of his wife Procula; Mary Magdalene, once a harlot, now one of the most devout followers of this man called Jesus, before and after His death; Simon Peter, a tall, tough man who would never quite let go of his guilt over three denials that he ever knew

Jesus; Severus Accius, Marcus Vibenna, and Fabius Scipio—the three other Roman legionnaires who, along with their comrade Decimus, would be drawn into a decades-long drama that would change their lives for time and eternity.

Looming ahead of them is the coming battle at Masada and the impact it would have on each one.

CHARACTERS AND OTHER CONSIDERATIONS

Characters

Severus Accius—Roman legionnaire.

Claudius Crassus Inrigillensis Sabinus Appius—Cofounder, with Fabius Scipio and Publius Carnelius Dolabella, of the first Christian hospice.

Pollio Ausonius—Captain of a seafaring vessel.

Barabbas—Insurrectionist who was freed instead of Jesus the Christ, who becomes a Christian years later.

Caligula—Emperor of Rome.

Claudius—Emperor of Rome after Caligula; often sided with the Jews against the Alexandrians and others; was tolerant of Christianity.

Ummidius Nasica Corculum—Outspoken critic of the reign of emperor Nero, who delivered a stirring speech to the Roman Senate.

Publius Cornelius Dolabella—The third cofounder of the first Christian hospice, partner in this with Appius and Scipio.

Gaius Gallienus—Wealthy Roman Christian.

Tullio Gallienus—Wife of Gaius Gallienus.

Quintus Egnatius Javolenus Tidus Germanicus—A convert to Jesus the Christ and benefactor of Fabius Scipio.

John—Apostle of Jesus the Christ.

Joseph of Arimathea—Friend of Nicodaemus.

Lydia—An elderly woman who experiences a great miracle.

Lysimmachus—Wise old wayfarer.

Matthew—Former tax-gatherer, now an apostle of Jesus the Christ.

Mary Magdalene—Prostitute forgiven by Jesus the Christ, now a follower.

Nahum—Befriended by Scipio.

Lucius Dimitius Abenobarbrus Nero—Emperor of Rome after Claudius.

Nicodaemus—Jewish businessman, friend of Jesus.

Onesimus—Chariot driver for Joseph of Arimathea.

Decimus Paetus—Veteran Roman legionnaire.

Paul—Apostle of Jesus the Christ.

Simon Peter—Fisherman, apostle of Jesus the Christ.

Pontius Pilatus—Roman proconsul-governor of Judea.

Procula Pilatus—Wife of Pontius.

Lucius Annaeus Seneca—Famed Roman poet, playwright, and tutor to Nero; later a brave critic of the emperor.

Berneices Scipio—Mother of Fabius Scipio.

Fabius Scipio—Youthful legionnaire and second cofounder of the first Christian hospice..

Livius Scipio—Father of Fabius Scipio.

Flavius Silva—Commander of the Roman forces arrayed around Masada.

Tiberius—Emperor of Rome.

Marcus Vibenna—Veteran legionnaire nearing retirement.

Eleazar ben Ya'ir—Leader of the zealots at Masada.

Zedekiah—Crippled beggar.

The Jewish Calendar

Tishri—Mid-September through mid-October.

Marchesvan—The rest of October, through mid-November.

Kislev—The rest of November through mid-December.

Tevet—The rest of December through mid-January.

Shevat—The rest of January through mid-February.

Adar—The rest of February through mid-March.

Nisan—The rest of March through mid-April.

Iyvar—The rest of April through mid-May.

Sivan—The rest of May through mid-June.

Tammuz—The rest of June through mid-July.

Av—The rest of July through mid-August.

Elul—The rest of August through the first half of September.

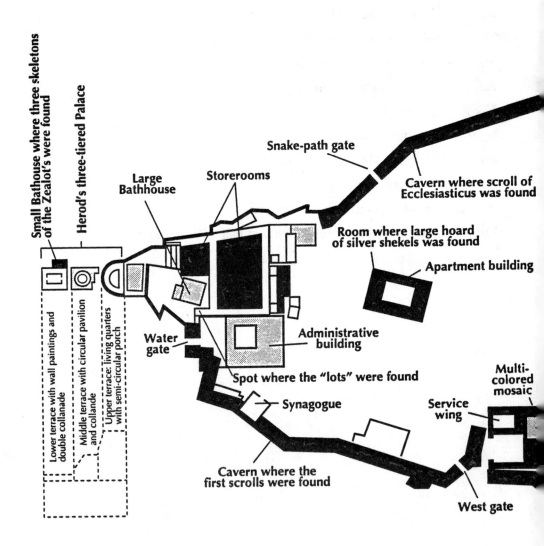

Small Bathhouse where three skeletons of the Zealot's were found

Herod's three-tiered Palace

Snake-path gate

Storerooms

Large Bathhouse

Cavern where scroll of Ecclesiasticus was found

Room where large hoard of silver shekels was found

Apartment building

Lower terrace with wall paintings and double collanade

Middle terrace with circular pavilion and collande

Upper terrace: living quarters with semi-circular porch

Water gate

Administrative building

Multi-colored mosaic

Spot where the "lots" were found

Synagogue

Service wing

Cavern where the first scrolls were found

West gate

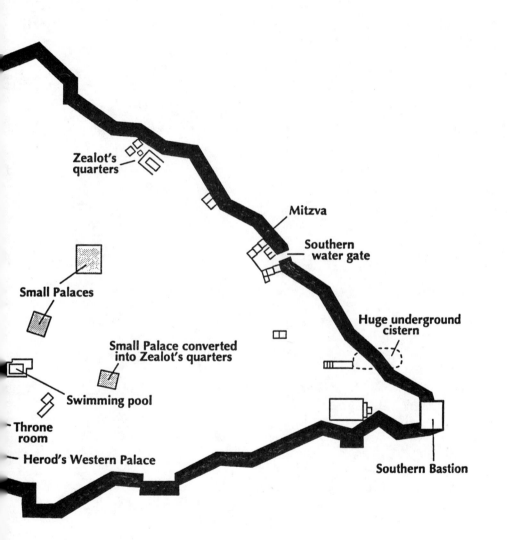

Zealot's
quarters

Mitzva

Southern
water gate

Small Palaces

Huge underground
cistern

Small Palace converted
into Zealot's quarters

Swimming pool

Throne
room

Herod's Western Palace

Southern Bastion

Part I

I

Legionnaire Decimus Paetus, handpicked by proconsul Pontius Pilatus, then-governor of the ancient land of Judea, as one of the Roman guards to be stationed at the site of the latest crucifixion atop a hill called Golgotha by the Jews, somehow could not manage to get all of the blood off the sandpapery skin of his large, scarred hands.

When I punctured the criminal's side, so much blood and . . . and water gushed out, Paetus, trembling, thought as he looked back over the past several dark and ugly hours. *I have never seen such an amount flow from a corpse.*

Much of his rock-hard Roman soldier's upper torso seemed to be covered with it, and he became uncustomarily faint, not from the sight of spilled blood, for he had seen that often in battle, but because there was something altogether different about this one condemned man, and Paetus had had to brace himself against the base of the cross.

His comrades, learning of this, ridiculed him, but he took no offense, for that was their way, emblematic of the danger-forged closeness between them, men who had fought together in campaign after campaign, victorious each time, though increasingly bearing the physical scars that became as much of an indication of bravery and loyalty to the empire as the medals bestowed upon them by any centurion or, even, the emperor himself.

The way I acted, I truly did deserve their scorn, he told himself. *How could I be angry with them?*

It was part of the code of conduct for every Roman legionnaire. Quite simply, they should never reveal their human feelings before a conquered populace. They were to be as little more than dumb machines, machines required to follow the will of Claudius Tiberius, who had been emperor for nearly twenty years, and those to whom he had chosen, in his wisdom, to delegate authority, such as Pilatus.

By appearing to be weak, Paetus had committed a breach of that code, and if the worst that came his way as a result was the temporary derision of his regular comrades, he was to be considered fortunate indeed. A less well-liked legionnaire would have been brought to the attention of a centurion.

Hours later, the crucifixion accomplished, he held his hands out in front of him as he sat in the middle of a stream bordered by a clump of olive trees just outside Jerusalem. His palms, especially, seemed as clean as they had ever been. And yet—

"I feel so dirty," he said out loud. "Shall I ever be clean again?"

Paetus had excused himself from the other soldiers, who were eating their dinners around a campfire just outside the massive main gates to Jerusalem a few hours after the three dead bodies had been taken from their respective crosses, two of those to be thrown in a mass paupers' grave, and the third, that of a man who had stirred great controversy, to be taken by friends to a site quite near the place of his death.

Paetus headed straight for that stream, isolated as it was, but well known to many of the men because it was a place where they sometimes took their women. He hoped that he would be alone, that—

The blood would wash away.

Physically it did, and he could no longer see it. But images remained, accusing, insolent images of that crimson flow gushing out of the side that he had violated with the lance he had been assigned, the kind that had come into heavy use just a few years earlier. Called a *pilum*, it lacked the thrusting power of other heavier such weapons, but it remained popular with the legions because it was comparatively lightweight.

Which meant that Paetus, in order to pierce the side, had to thrust upward and in with extra force, causing greater damage to the tissues, something he might not have had to do had he used a *pompeii*, for example, the design of which allowed for quick, destructive penetration and retrieval.

People from the crowd that had gathered from the very first hour were shouting at him to cut into the body in other places, their blood-lust appalling even to a veteran legionnaire such as himself.

"He healed others," the coarse voices yelled, "now let Him demonstrate that He can do the same with himself. Perhaps He can climb down from the cross this very moment and make fools of us all!"

Paetus wanted to turn from that pathetic body hanging just above his head and rush into the mass of onlookers and slash away at them with the various weapons he wore until he had silenced their bestial comments and shown them a measure of the pain the condemned man had experienced during the hours it took for Him to die.

Later, at the stream, Paetus clamped his hands to his ears, trying to shut off that recollection, as though it had just then materialized externally, and not from within, the same hands that had raised the blade and jabbed it into that hapless side.

Why should it matter to anyone like that? This condemned one, a humble carpenter on the surface, was actually a craven beast under that guise, an insurrectionist, worse than Barabbas because He seemed quite different from that thug, so much quieter and unassuming, a gentle man who would be king.

Paetus' eyes opened wider as another aspect of what he had seen hit him in every part of his body, nerves tingling with the realization.

He did not fight back. He claimed followers and yet no one tried to defend him. Thousands listened to his sermons and were fed, it was said, miraculously by Him and His apostles—wealthy, powerful senators and the aimless poor side-by-side; religious rulers and those blind beggars who had claimed to be healed as well as others; so many interested in His words during His life but none willing to lift a hand to stave off His death.

Except Nicodaemus.

This rich, old man contested with the various members of the Jewish ruling council. But they were more concerned with their status as respected members of the Judaic community, a status that the doomed criminal had assailed any number of times, particularly the afternoon when He confronted them and called them "whited sepulchers on the outside, all clean and proper, and yet full of the bones of dead men inside . . . hypocrites each and every one!" Though Nicodaemus ultimately failed in what he had hoped to accomplish, at least he tried, which no others seemed willing to do.

And one follower even denied him altogether—the fisherman! Paetus remembered. *What does it say about a leader that those professing their loyalty to Him turn away when He needs them most desperately?*

Paetus thought back over an encounter some months earlier with this very man, Simon Peter, a hulking individual with a scraggly beard and long, unkempt hair. The group of so-called apostles who hung around with the carpenter stopped at the camp where he and other legionnaires were eating roast pork, goat's milk-cheese, and some sour wine—the latter primarily because drinking water was not often pure for any but the rich and privileged, who could afford the proper filtration methods. All of the soldiers yearned to be back in Rome or any of the Italian seaside encampments where they could lounge in bathhouses or sample the temple whores. He liked the pleasures of such times as much as any man!

We were grumbling, he remembered. *We were grumbling quite loudly about the food, and the thirteen of them stopped and offered us some of what they had.*

The soldiers accepted the olives, raw beans, and figs with appreciation.

I asked this Peter why they were being so thoughtful to the conquerors of their land. He told me: "Because our Lord commanded it."

24

Some minutes later, after they had consumed the unexpected gifts, the soldiers engaged in the often obscene conversation that was typical of them as they relaxed. Rome no longer objected to lasciviousness. In fact, the pornographic drawings on temple walls and other public places at Pompeii coupled with tolerance of lewd behavior made that location a favorite one for legionnaires on leave, and they brought back with them the latest vile language, humor, and whatever else they picked up.

But Paetus was strangely less interested than usual that particular evening, and he approached Peter, who, with the rest of those in his group, had been eating on the other side of the ancient dirt road, near an area where shepherds kept many flocks of sheep, the night air laced with the odor of piles of dung.

"You seem so peaceful, fisherman," Paetus remarked after some minutes of idle conversation that made them both feel more at ease with one another.

"Oh, we are not," Peter admitted. "We are often the most tempestuous of men. We still have within us the natures common to all. But there are times—"

The large man cut himself off briefly.

"Are you ill?" Paetus asked.

Peter waved his hand in front of him as he shook his head.

"No," he said finally. "I am not ill. I just see, in moments of great clarity, what I am like without Jesus the Christ, and it saddens me. At the same time I wonder how He can possibly waste His time with the likes of us."

"Who are the others?" Paetus asked.

"A tax collector, other fishermen, ordinary . . ."

Paetus's mind wandered for a moment. He realized how hated tax collectors were in that land. They were drawn from among the local population in a given district, and other Jews considered them traitors, men whose loyalties could be bought by the enemy. The job of tax collector could be a profitable one, as those serving Rome in this manner were authorized to collect double what was owed and keep half of the overall amount for their own pockets. Some men, sniffing the scent of abundant lucre, paid for the position.

. . . a tax-collector, other fishermen, ordinary laborers.

"Hardly an army!" Paetus said, snapping off that reverie.

"And yet we are more and more being accused of insurrection."

Paetus had heard such stories. One of these claimed that the followers of Jesus were nothing more than puppets of the insurrectionist Barabbas, that they were softening up the populace for the more violent onslaughts of that rabble-rouser.

Further, it was said that Barabbas, in turn, wanted to be the successor to Spartacus, the courageous former slave of the previous century who had come closer to thwarting the will of Imperial Rome than anyone could have suspected.

I could scarcely admit to my fellow legionnaires that the story of Spartacus had always been appealing to me, he thought. *I saw in him bravery and integrity that was missing from the legions of Rome. They fought because they were required by law to do so but Spartacus fought against that very law. He claimed Imperial Rome would become more and more evil as the years passed. Already, in his time, the cruelties abounded.*

"I see no threat in any of you," Paetus said in a kindly manner. "You and the others do not seem successors to Spartacus."

Peter burst out laughing at what he thought was the intended sardonic humor of that comment.

"Yet some in Rome and elsewhere might disagree with you," he said after getting himself under control.

"Spurred on by your detractors, no doubt," Paetus offered. "The politicians claim to be in touch with the people, and yet I have found they are in touch only with their own needs, let the people hang."

Peter looked at him, a suggestion of tears in his eyes.

"You are an uncommon soldier," he said.

"You see me only now," Paetus replied, blushing.

"Would you like to meet this Jesus of whom I spoke?"

Paetus hesitated, for he had no interest in seeing the man, but Peter's manner was so sincere, so tender, that he decided to accept the fisherman's invitation.

"Just for a moment," he said.

"Follow me," Peter told him.

They passed by the other apostles and approached someone who was kneeling a few hundred yards away from them, near a tall, wide clump of bushes with scarlet flowers dangling from them.

"Lord?" Peter asked tentatively. "May I introduce you to someone?"

Paetus noticed that, at first, the man whose back was turned to them did not react at all, as though he had not heard Peter speak.

"Perhaps you should tell Him again," he suggested.

"He knows we are here," Peter assured him. "He will join us when He finishes communing with the heavenly Father."

The man fell forward, on His face, His body shaking.

"He suffers a fit," Paetus whispered, with some concern. "Perhaps we should see if he needs help of some kind."

"It is not what you think," the fisherman replied. "He is in agony over this once unspoiled world that Satan has corrupted."

Paetus started to turn away, not interested in what he considered to be lame religious dogma or idle fantasy.

That was when the man stood suddenly and called to him.

Paetus stopped, just as quickly, his legs frozen.

That voice! he recalled. *I had never heard one like it. Until I did, I wondered how a crowd of thousands would willingly stand before Him, on a hillside, under a hot sun, listening to His words as though they had come directly from the gods themselves.*

Paetus turned and faced Jesus.

He seemed so much more than I had expected, not the lowly carpenter from Galilee, but a tall man, with shoulders as broad as those of the strongest Roman soldier, much more so than mine, and yet I am not a tiny individual.

And those eyes!

Rich blue, the blue of the ancient Mediterranean on a clear, quiet afternoon in July perhaps, eyes that gave the impression of at least equal depth, reaching through to the very center of his being.

I felt some sense of age, as though he was far, far older than his physical frame indicated, a man not of thirty-odd years but someone who—

Paetus shook that thought out of his head, hoping that the rest of that perplexing memory would be soon forgotten. But that did not happen, the vision of those eyes and that voice lingering despite his best efforts to quell everything connected with that evening, not merely because of the way Jesus looked, or how He sounded, or what it was that He had said during the later moments.

It is what I had to do to Him, it is the awfulness of standing before the instrument of His hours-long torture and then His death; and doing nothing but holding the multitudes at bay, then driving my lance into that side to make sure that He was truly dead, not just in a momentary faint . . . and the blood, the water, all over me, clinging to me long after I had washed every drop of it physically from me.

Most disturbing was what Jesus the Christ had said a short while before the last second of life left Him in a sigh, leaving His battered body nothing more than an empty shell.

"Father, forgive them, for they know not what they do." The words came from lips barely able to move, a voice broken and strained.

How could he say such a thing? Paetus asked himself as he sat beside that little creek. *How could he forgive his executioners as well as those who had fled from him?*

Reasonable questions for someone such as Decimus Paetus, who could not forgive himself.

II

Finally, Paetus stood, dried himself, and put his military garb back on—minus the armor that was supposed to be reasonably lightweight but which he found cumbersome at best and wore as little as he could manage. Now he had donned just a corselet of bronzed *squamae* dropped over an arming doublet with a single layer kilt, his upper arms reinforced by *pteruges* made of leather.

Due to the dangers occasioned by increased activity from roving ragtag groups of revolutionaries commanded by the likes of Barabbas and others in infamy, Paetus kept his *pilum* in its leather-sheathed *cingulum militare* at his right side, and his heavier, ivory-handled *pompeii* in another sheath at his left.

Strapped to the middle of his athletic body was a *dolabra* in a holder decorated with blue beads, the pickax a more efficient weapon in certain circumstances than any sword he had ever used. Beside it was a *pugio*, a dagger of Spanish origin that was distinguished by an ornate decoration of gold edged by a thin line of silver around its circumference, with enameled inlay on the scabbard and the hilt as well.

How many heads have I split open with such weapons as these? he mused as he considered this hardware. *How many hapless limbs have I separated from their bodies? How often have my adversaries on the battlefield held up their hands in supplication, begging for mercy as I stood over them?*

Paetus looked at a reflection of himself in the stream, his image distorted by the movement of the gently running water.

He had long ago lost the almost girlish-features of his youth. Weathered, heavily pockmarked skin was stretched tightly over large cheek bones, and his forehead was crisscrossed with wrinkles, some quite deep.

A scar started at the bridge of his broad nose and ran down to the nostrils. He touched his eyes—blue but not like those of Jesus the Christ —eyes that had seen what no human being should.

Service for legionnaires lasted twenty-five years. Paetus had joined when he was eighteen. That was more than a decade ago, all of his adult life, time to a great extent spent in battle.

He never questioned the wisdom of those governing Imperial Rome, for which he was every bit as willing to die as his comrades.

Furthermore, Paetus had encountered many other executions of criminals, knowing full well that Caesar did not send a man to his death for idle reasons, and yet the number of those doomed seemed to be increasing as restlessness in the conquered countries of the empire was on the increase.

I have seen so much horror, he thought. *Another naked criminal hanging from a cross should not drive me to this state of anxiety in which I find myself.*

"But that is what You are doing," Paetus screamed to the clear night, his left hand in a fist that he held up above his head and shook with a mixture of defiance and frustration, "as You somehow cling to this tortured mind that wants to shut you out. You will not be gone! Nor can I go to you and shake that frail body of Yours and demand an explanation, because You are now forever beyond my reach."

He spoke to me that night about a peace that passes all understanding.

I tried to tell Him that I had as much peace as I possibly could ever expect. My comrades and I would be together for many more years, and we were well taken care of by Rome. We had quite few worries at heart except the central one of life and death—and was not that the concern of every mortal man?

If we were not killed in battle, we would die of some disease or of old age—but whatever the cause, die we would.

How important, then, could the means of the death of any of us be?

For me, that part of it was unimportant. I had clothes on my back and sufficient food in my stomach and big-breasted women whenever I felt any kind of need for them. What more could I—could anyone—expect?

He told me that all this of which I spoke would pass away, and I replied that, yes, of course, I knew that would occur, which would be followed by an abyss of nothingness, the utter and final end for every living being, unless the gods had a surprise in store. He said that there were no gods, there was only one, and that life did go on.

I looked at Him, thinking how calm He was, how serene, His words not the ravings of some deluded mind.

"Who are You?" I asked quite directly.

He smiled slightly as He replied, "Whom do you think Me to be?"

"My thoughts are unimportant," I told him. "What say You?"

"Before this world began, I am . . ."

Paetus could not believe what he had just heard!

A man of flesh and blood and bones claimed to have existed before the bare and very dry ground on which they sat had come into being. Paetus was beginning to see the danger in this Jesus the Christ. Anyone with such a delusion *could* come to think, in time, that he was above Caesar!

29

* * *

As soon as Paetus returned to the legionnaires' camp, short, slim, even bony-looking, but astonishingly strong Severus Accius, who had joined the Roman Army at the same time fifteen years before, greeted him with a nervous hello.

"Thank the gods that you are back, Decimus!" he exclaimed.

Paetus smiled despite his own anxiety, because this small man, nearly too short to have been accepted as a legionnaire in the first place but blessed with a remarkably strong frame that got him through the training regimen, seemed to be perennially on the verge of an emotional collapse for one reason or another.

"I wondered if Barabbas, now that he has been freed, got ahold of you, and kidnapped you," Accius went on, perspiration beaded on his forehead and trickling down his cheeks. "What happened?"

"I needed to be by myself," Paetus replied.

"I can understand that. You haven't been the same since you were at Golgotha a few hours ago."

Accius turned in the direction of that hill. It was not far away from their camp. If he squinted, he could see the faint, skull-shaped outline against the clear, starlit sky.

"You will have to go back now," Accius said a bit solemnly.

"Go back? What do you mean? Speak sense."

"The grave of that chief offender."

"What about it, Severus?"

"Pilatus is concerned that followers of the man will steal His body and then claim that He rose from the dead."

Paetus felt a chill then. He had been impressed by the genuine simplicity of Jesus that one night weeks before and by the words of forgiveness He had uttered as He hung from the cross. Now, so soon after his death, the politicians, the plotters, and the planners and others were starting to complicate His simple memory by rearranging the facts with no regard for any kind of truth except that which they declared to be so.

"What does that have to do with me?" he asked slowly, dreading any kind of response his friend might have.

"You have been selected as one of the four who will stand guard for the next three days and nights—"

"Why *three?*"

"The Jews claim that this Jesus said that after three days he would be raised from the dead."

"So Pilatus wants to avoid the possibility that some who were apostles of this Jesus would feign a resurrection."

"Yes, *yes!*" the other man said with such impatience that he stamped his sandal-clad foot on the ground.

"Then I must go if Pilatus orders it," Paetus acknowledged.

"I will take you there," Accius offered, relieved. "I suspect that the others are already at the site."

As the two men started the quite short walk to Golgotha, Paetus glanced at his friend and stated, "You also are one of the guards Pilatus wanted, are you not?"

"I am," Accius admitted sheepishly.

"Why did you wait for me? Friendship is one thing. But you should not have risked what could have been a harsh reprimand."

Obeying orders had been a central part of the structure of the legions of Imperial Rome since the beginning. No alternative was tolerated. Infractions were dealt with harshly. At that period in the history of the empire, desertions proved largely unknown.

"I was worried about you, Decimus," Accius acknowledged.

Paetus reached out and grabbed the other man around the back of the neck.

"I would give my life for you, Severus," he said.

"And I for you, Decimus," the other man replied.

As the two of them approached Golgotha, Paetus saw that the crosses already had been taken down.

"So quickly . . . ," he muttered.

"Apparently Pilatus thought it unwise to rub the noses of the Jews in the surpassing might of Imperial Rome. He *could* have let the crosses stand. Another governor might have done that very thing, as a lesson. But not this man—he feels, I suspect, some regret for being pushed into the decision he made."

Pilatus stood before the screaming mob, one of his aides holding a large bowl of water in front of him.

"I have done what you wanted," he said, with ill-disguised loathing, after he had ordered them to quiet down. "Now I wash my hands of the blood of this innocent man. May His death be on your consciences, not mine!"

Paetus grew pale and stopped walking for a moment as that recollection rose fresh in his mind.

"*Might* have done the same thing . . . as a lesson?" he remarked. "An accused insurrectionist and two common thieves? What power did their executions take?"

"You bark at me too much this night. Just idle conversation, friend. Not some pronouncement from the seat of Caesar himself!"

Paetus regretted the sharpness of his voice. Accius had saved his life again and again on one battlefield or another. The man deserved better behavior.

"Ignore my manner, if you can," he said.

"I pay it no heed."

"Pilatus and I share much the same problem. Symbolically he washed his hands of the blood that he caused to be shed, but I would wager that, since that public demonstration on his part he has not found it so easy as he thought, at least by that simple act. I wonder how often he is reminded of his wife's dream?"

"Is that it, Decimus?" Accius asked. "The blood of this Jesus lingers in your mind, if not on your body."

"I drove the *pilum* into His side! Not Pilatus. Not you. Not the ones who thrust a crown of thorns on His forehead. No one else but me!"

. . . a crown of thorns on His forehead.

Paetus winced at the recollection, at the fact that Jesus did not even let out a single cry of pain—not then, not when they stripped Him of His clothes and whipped His back until the blood covered it from shoulder to waist.

"Yet He was dead by then, Decimus, my dear friend. Besides, after you met the man that evening sometime ago, you came back and told me that, indeed, He might be dangerous after all, that He could one day go as far as placing Himself above even the eternal Caesar."

"Yes, you are correct. That was my impression a fortnight ago."

"Have you changed your mind?"

"It—it—," Paetus uncharacteristically stammered. "It had to do with something He said minutes before He died."

"Whatever words could a vagrant utter that would affect you as deeply as this?" Accius asked of him.

Paetus thought that tears would flow from his eyes in an instant and turned away as he answered the other man. "Forgiveness, Severus. He spoke of forgiveness. This hapless wanderer said, 'Father, forgive them, for they know not what they do.'"

"But to whom was He speaking? Do you think a mistake could have been made? Could He have been the son of a senator, or even a member of the household of Caesar?"

"I think," Paetus spoke slowly, "that it was none of those. I think He was speaking to one of the gods."

"Then He was uttering blasphemy. On that we must surely be in agreement with the Jews for a change!"

"Perhaps so," Paetus said, shrugging his shoulders with a diffidence that was scarcely more than skin-deep.

Animals could be heard against the cover of night, howling or scampering through the brush on either side of them.

"It is so bare in this place," Accius remarked. "So many miles of desert—dry, dead land, unyielding in its barrenness . . . there seems to be little else. I am told it was once worse. There were no green spots whatever. But the Jews took at least part of the land and made it come alive. Now I see an abundance of acacia trees and myrtle, some fir and pine, terebinth and poplar.

"And yet even with these, as welcome as they are, there are such vast deserts and plains that were once the beds of large lakes. When it does rain, it is usually in fall or winter, when temperatures have dropped from the shriveling heat of summer, and the cold drops make everything all the more unpleasant and dreary.

"You act as though, despite yourself, you are beginning to find something of interest about this land," Paetus said.

"You should realize as well as I how boring it is here, with no battles to fight and only an occasional band of rebels to round up. I choose to learn as much as I can about where I am being kept by order of Rome. Perhaps, one day, some part of this knowledge will be helpful in a way I could not possibly predict."

Paetus clapped as he and his friend walked.

"Well-spoken, Severus," he remarked, genuinely impressed by his friend's outlook. "I wish I had your discipline. I would much rather be a-whoring."

"Knowledge in one hand and lust in the other," Accius said, smiling broadly. "Now *that* is a rare and wonderful combination!"

In another few minutes, they were at the foot of Golgotha.

"Birds are nesting in one of the eyes," Accius remarked. "Look, Decimus!"

It was as his friend said. On the front of the hill were two hollow cavelike indentations, with a small ridge of rock between them. A mother lark had started a small nest back a few inches from the edge. She looked at the two of them with obvious apprehension, wondering if they were a threat and ready to call to her mate for assistance.

"The cave is to the left a few hundred yards, right in the side of the hill," Accius told him. "Let me offer an explanation."

"I am quite capable of speaking for myself, old friend," Paetus protested.

"But your very manner speaks of transgression. Please, let me do this. Besides, I am a much better liar than you could ever be!"

Paetus smiled as he said, "Have your way. Convince them that Jupiter himself took me away for a while and has only now returned me to this world."

"I was scarcely thinking of anything as bizarre as that, Decimus!" Accius said, enjoying the humor.

They approached the two other legionnaires, who were seated around a small campfire, a common scene at night in an occupied country such as Israel.

Accius introduced himself.

"And this is my friend Paetus," he said. "He had the rare privilege of making sure that the criminal Jesus was dead."

The others were quite excited about that.

"Paetus is late because he was speaking with some Jews of all people," Accius told them. "They were thanking him for his help in ridding them of such an irritant. The man probably welcomed death in the end. Neither Romans nor His own kind had any love for Him. He was an outcast. It almost makes you pity the poor devil."

"But all your friend did was pierce a dead man's side," one of the men retorted with some sarcasm. "Of how much praise is *that* worthy?"

"You know the Jews as well as Decimus and I do," Accius added quickly. "They can tear open all the sheep and other animals they wish in their mindless sacrifices and also smear blood on their doors once a year. But when it comes to a man's blood, even a dead one, the swine show how cowardly they are!"

The one who had spoken so brusquely stepped forward, smiling.

"You need explain nothing. I know Decimus Paetus. He and I are not strangers at all!"

The two men embraced.

"It has been long," Paetus remarked. "I remember every battle we ever fought together."

"And I remember a great deal more than that," Vibenna told him. "How many women have we shown the *real* power of Rome?"

Vibenna roared lustily, but Paetus seemed only embarrassed.

After the other legionnaire—a younger, rather handsome, considerably less experienced man named Fabius Scipio—had introduced himself, both pointed to the large round stone that rested at the entrance to the tomb.

"The stone was already here, part of what the owners, two men named Joseph and Nicodaemus, planned for this grave," Vibenna told the newcomers. "But even that failed to satisfy Pilatus. He issued issued a special edict, at the behest of the Sanhedrin, no doubt. They wanted to be certain that no scraggly followers of Jesus would be able to retrieve His body under any circumstances. So that is why we have been stationed here."

He looked with some scorn at both of them.

"We must hurry. It should have been in place hours ago. But we four could not roll it across the entrance by ourselves. That thing weighs nearly a ton!"

His eyes shot opened wide, and he turned to Accius.

"You have told us about Decimus here," he pointed out, "but you were late as well. What is *your* story?"

"Because of his absence, I had to take his place at guard duty," Accius commented as casually as he could manage.

"If you say so," Vibenna replied.

"I can see what you meant," Paetus agreed, as he approached the stone. "It may be that we will need help, that even the four of us will not be able to do this."

He examined it in awe, against the flickering flames of their fire, pressing his body against the side, and grunting as he did so.

"No skinny Jews will be able to move this once we get it into place!" he declared.

Vibenna walked up to him.

"That may be the problem," he said. "Not all of them are quite so malnourished and small of stature and strength. We may be preparing ourselves for the wrong enemy. I've seen some of these people who could be every bit a match for any of us, especially the ones who do hard manual labor outside. After all, how weak could they be if the Egyptians used them to help build one of those ancient tombs?"

Paetus remembered the fisherman again.

"You may be right," he admitted genially. "But, still, the stone and our presence seem adequate to ward off any attempts to create a fraud here. I doubt that they would risk the anger of Pilatus or any other powerful Roman for one dead body, no matter who they suspect the man to have been!"

"We will get to know each other well before we go on to other duty after this one," Vibenna assured him. "None of us will be allowed to leave this spot, according to our orders. Food will be brought to us. I, for one, plan to celebrate quite wildly with the extra leave we have been promised as a reward."

Paetus had not heard about that bonus. But it was obvious good news to him. He had become quite tired over the past months, feeling very much like some common riffraff as his comrades and he moved from place to place. Spending some duty with Pilatus in a stationary assignment proved a welcome respite by contrast, taking his shift during the day and sleeping with other legionnaires at night.

His parents lived in one of the seaside villages. It would be nice to see them for a while, shedding his military clothes and hardware for a time of rest.

"But, first, we need to get this stone across the entrance," Vibenna's voice intruded upon his thoughts.

The four of them approached the massive object and started exchanging ideas about how to get the job done.

Paetus glanced inside for a moment and saw the body covered by a gauzelike wrapping, a spot of red at one side.

He sucked in his breath at the sight.

That is where I pierced His side, he thought. *His benefactors were not able to remove all the blood in their haste to bury Him by sundown.*

Paetus could smell the odors of spices and ointments that had been rubbed onto the still body to retard decay.

"I am going inside for a moment," he told the others.

Paetus stepped within the tomb, walked over to that still form, reached out in a tentative manner and slowly lifted the wrapping at His head, and fell back, for a moment, as he saw not an expression of pain, not a look of frozen anguish, but—

"Decimus, Decimus, come on out," Accius's voice summoned him. "It is getting late. We should get this task over with."

He placed the thin, semitransparent material back over the face and left the tomb.

"We cut a trough in front of the tomb's entrance," Vibenna said a minute or two later. "The owner never thought of that. I think it is the best—"

With hardly better timing, a voice interrupted him.

"A very good idea!" they heard someone exclaim.

All four legionnaires turned around abruptly and saw a silver-haired, dignified-looking man standing just behind them.

"I am sorry to have startled you," he said. "My name is Joseph. I am the owner of whom you speak."

The legionnaires relaxed, glad that he had come to that spot because he might be helpful to them.

"How did you get it here in the first place?" Paetus asked, feeling oddly relaxed in the man's presence.

"A combination of mules and men," Joseph replied. "It took a long while. The quarry where it originated is many miles away."

"Why would you go to so much trouble for an ordinary grave site?"

"I cannot say with any absolute certainty, but I do only suspect that Jehovah knew better than I did and was guiding me from the beginning so that this place would be ready for His blessed Son."

The legionnaires glanced at one another.

Vibenna spoke up with a surprising admission.

"I was thinking that it did seem as though almost everything was spelled out in advance long years ago," he said, self-consciously clearing his throat and suddenly looking like a man who wished he had kept his mouth shut.

"Would you—," Joseph started to say, nervous over something.

"Speak your mind," Paetus said in a kindly manner. "Whatever you say will not go beyond the four of us. You have our word on that."

"I would like to roll the stone across," Joseph went on, "if you would let me."

Vibenna chuckled for a moment despite himself, then flushed red, regretting this.

"I know what you are thinking," the aged Jew told them, "and you may be right, but I would like to try."

Paetus stepped forward, placing a hand on the man's shoulder.

"You would only injure yourself," he replied. "How could any one of us stand by and let that happen?"

Joseph looked at him with an appreciative expression.

"It is rare that I see a Roman soldier caring in any way about an old Jew such as myself. If it seems that I have to strain too much, I will stop. Please, though this must seem like a peculiar delusion on my part, allow me to indulge it for a moment."

Paetus glanced at the others. They said nothing. He stepped aside, as he said, "Go ahead. Try it if you must."

Joseph thanked him and walked forward to the entrance of the tomb, eyeing the large, round stone cautiously. Then he put the palms of his hands on the left edge and pushed, groaning even with that initial effort.

The stone did not move.

He tried again.

Still nothing.

"You must stop now!" Paetus protested. "We cannot permit—"

As he was speaking, Joseph had started to try again, perspiration drenching his body even in the midst of that cold dusk.

Vibenna gasped.

This time, the stone started to roll forward, a fraction of an inch, then another, then—

"It cannot be!" exclaimed Paetus.

But the stone *was* rolling, slowly, inch-by-inch, until it was halfway across the tomb's entrance. And finally it was completely in front.

Joseph fell back against the flat side, catching his breath.

The legionnaires could not speak.

"It was almost as though Someone else was beside me," he told them. "I could feel a Presence. My strength was so little."

Joseph smiled at them before starting up the little path away from the tomb.

"Remember what has happened this night," he said. "Miracles can come from God in many forms."

He bowed slightly before each one and then left.

★ ★ ★

Later, when his shift at duty beside the tomb was over, Decimus Paetus discovered that he could not simply close his eyes and comfortably drift off. For his comrades, new and old, it had been little more than an ordinary day, no overwhelming experiences to ruminate over, or, if unpleasant, try to let go of, not even that extraordinary period of darkness in the midst of the crucifixion, though Vibenna had, an hour before, at least referred to it.

"Seemed strange, yes," he had remarked in passing. "But then this has always been a strange land, would you not agree? The weather certainly must be as odd as the people who live here and the numerous customs by which they conduct their lives."

"They hate us," Paetus offered, "but they have learned to love the money that we spend while we are here. They smile to our faces, take our *denarii*, and spit on the ground behind us as we walk away."

The Romans were the latest in a series of conquerors who had overrun that ancient land. And the Jews were more and more in a rebellious mood, despite, or perhaps because of, the coziness of the Sanhedrin with the Roman hierarchy. Common, everyday people viewed the religious leaders with far less respect as a result, Romans' control over the populace becoming less and less certain as the years passed.

The legionnaire knew this from personal experience. He had nearly beaten to death more than one careless Jew who had not waited long enough before spitting, and, thus, Paetus had been able to see this contemptuous action.

They thought they could vent their disgust and I would not notice. How wrong they were, how many broken bones they suffered!

"Greed is at the center of everything they do," Vibenna added. "Look at what they have done to worship in their temples."

"I am new to this assignment. Tell me what you mean."

"Oh, it is their sacrifices to this god they call Jehovah that I have in mind, Decimus, my new friend. The animals are sold to worshipers at a very large profit. This is in addition to what the priests exhort them to *donate* in order to sustain their various religious activities. I suspect it does not end there, either."

The two of them were standing away from the tomb, around the side of Golgotha, at the very front, the part of the hill that had been responsible for earning it the renowned description of "place of the skull."

Vibenna looked up at the flat top where the trio of crosses had stood earlier that day.

"I met this one from Nazareth once, you know," he said, as though guilty about the very admission.

"The one who was called Jesus the Christ?"

"I met Him as He was single-handedly throwing the greedy profiteers out of the temple one afternoon."

"You were called in by the Jews?"

"I was. They asked me to take Him into custody for disturbing the peace and whatever other regulation I could use to justify my action."

"What did you do?" Paetus asked, quite fascinated.

"When he left the temple I went up to Him," Vibenna recalled. "As soon as we were far enough away from the grounds that we could not be overheard by any of the priests or their spies, I admitted to Him how much I agreed with the action He had taken."

Paetus cleared his throat and told the other man about his own encounter with Jesus the Christ.

"Why was this atrocity allowed to happen?" Vibenna speculated after he had finished. "That man did no harm to anyone. You feel He might have had pretensions to overshadow Caesar, but there is no way of being certain of that."

Paetus fell into silence for a moment. Vibenna let him alone with his thoughts without interrupting.

"I think the Sanhedrin considered Him a threat," Paetus spoke finally. "The more people listened to *Him*, the less heed they would have paid to that group of hypocritical and conniving old men."

Vibenna sighed wearily.

"Enough of this for both of us," he said. "We should be getting some sleep. My turn to take over the watch begins in two hours, and yours right after mine."

They left the front of Golgotha and returned to the tomb.

As Paetus stretched out on the ground, he glanced briefly over at the round stone covering the entrance and thought, *What was Your purpose in this life? What did the gods have in mind for You? How could it be that they failed so miserably?*

He shivered at that thought.

. . . the gods failing.

If they were so fallible, no wiser in some respects than mortal man, what was the point of worshiping in their temples?

No answer forthcoming, he surrendered to the wave of sleep that washed over him, so welcome it was after the perplexing events of that uncertain day.

III

No attempt was made to steal the body that first night nor during the day following. Paetus, Accius, Vibenna, and Scipio spent their time standing at guard or sitting and talking, trading often ribald stories, eating spartan meals, and dealing with the occasional visitors who approached the spot.

Including Nicodaemus, a man of short physical stature but with an impeccable reputation among Romans and Jews alike.

Paetus had noticed him the day before, at the scene of the crucifixion, the only man dressed in the garb of the rich who dared to stand close, the others from the Sanhedrin preferring instead to be at a much greater distance lest, somehow, they receive some kind of contamination. None of the other legionnaires had any reason to recognize Nicodaemus.

I want to talk with him, Paetus told himself. *I want to find out more about this Jesus. I want to prove for myself that He was nothing more than a good man misunderstood by Rome and fed into the collective maw of a mob of slobbering Jews.*

But Vibenna approached Nicodaemus first.

"You are not allowed to be here for the next two days," the legionnaire told him rather brusquely.

"But you are wrong," Nicodaemus replied.

"How is it that you can say what you do and believe such words when you know them to be wrong?"

Nicodaemus smiled.

"You sound like a student practicing some newly acquired skills of speech," he said, though not in an unfriendly manner.

Vibenna blushed with embarrassment.

"Show me some reason why I should not send you immediately from this spot," he stated with exaggerated firmness.

"My friend Joseph and I *own* this spot."

Vibenna had no words in response. He just stood where he did, resting the fingers of his left hand on the sword at his belt.

"Forgive me for approaching you in this manner," Nicodaemus said. "I have a reason to enter the tomb. Would you please roll back the stone for me?"

40

Vibenna shook his head adamantly.

"We have the strictest of orders, orders that surely forbid—"

Nicodaemus handed him a small parchment, which Vibenna unrolled.

A note from Pilatus himself.

Vibenna read it, nodded, then handed it back to the other man.

"No, please, keep it," Nicodaemus told him. "That will protect you if anyone should question you about this."

"Thank you for your concern."

"I am concerned about injustice in any form, whether that injustice be a major issue affecting a nation or a much smaller one involving four Roman solders."

Vibenna shook his hand.

"You are most unusual, sir," he said.

"You mean, a most unusual *Jew*, do you not?"

Again, Vibenna's face was red.

"Forgive me," Nicodaemus asked. "Unfortunately, I am more bold now than I was earlier, when it mattered much, much more, and the risk was far greater."

Vibenna stepped aside and let him pass.

Nicodemus knelt before the stone, his head bowed. Paetus, Accius, Vibenna, and Scipio could hear his words as he spoke softly.

"You told me that I must be born again," he said sorrowfully. "Yet, now, You lie there in this tomb which belongs to Joseph and myself, as cold and dead as any man who has passed from life. When I die, my body shall be placed opposite Your own, and that is where it all ends, both of us in the same grave.

"What is the difference between us, then, Jesus called the Christ? My body will decay as will Yours and become the food of worms. How can You talk with any honesty of a resurrection when there is nothing of the sort?"

After a few minutes, Vibenna tapped him on the shoulder.

"Do you want the stone rolled away now?" he asked politely.

Nicodaemus shook his head as he stood, his shoulders slumped in discouragement, and replied, "No use, I see now. It is what it is, all of this that has happened. There is no place for idle dreams."

Vibenna spoke then, oddly feeling sorry for the man.

"But even Pontius Pilatus half-believes," he said.

"Pilatus *half*-believes nothing of the sort," Nicodaemus shot back. "He *fully* believes the possibility of a plot by zealots of one sort or another, men who would take the words of this Jesus and use these to foster a charade, a deception, to the embarrassment of Rome. For if it were to appear that Jesus did arise from the dead, then it would be obvious to everyone that the might of Rome was no match for the simple God of this simple man. If the empire cannot kill such a man, so that he stays dead, then all the budding insurrectionists over the entire empire would surely find out someday and feel emboldened to challenge Rome whenever and wherever they wished, even more vigorously than they may be planning at present. For them, Jesus would become an entirely new kind of martyr."

Nicodaemus was relieving himself of some theories along with emotions that he had kept to himself until he could no longer do so and not have a breakdown.

"Pilatus is little else other than a hypocrite," he added. "He appears so anguished as he washes his hands of the blood of Jesus, and yet he is already making plans to minimize the political consequences of giving permission for the crucifixion to begin!"

"You may be wrong," Paetus interjected.

Nicodaemus turned, saw him.

"The one who used his lance to—," he started to say.

"You are right," Paetus cut him off.

"I was in Pilatus's personal guard after coming off several battlefront engagements over the past two years. It was only a temporary post, but I observed much. You give him too little credit for a conscience."

Nicodemus studied this brash legionnaire's face.

"How can you be so sure that he has one?"

"I saw him with his wife," Paetus recalled. "She had had a dream about Jesus. She begged him to set the man free and not be captive to the cries of a mob."

"But he obviously chose to ignore her entreaties," Nicodaemus pointed out. "Where is the conscience in that?"

"Not at first. That he wavered at all raises the possibility of conscience, if only a compromised one."

Nicodaemus looked admiringly at Paetus.

"My opinion of the Roman hordes has been elevated several notches," he said. "May I bring you some tidbits at dinnertime? Would you like a hefty bowl of raisins, along with a helping of parched corn and perhaps some fig cakes? I could bring some charoseth sauce, as well, and a large loaf of spelt bread to dip into it."

Paetus glanced toward Vibenna standing nearby and Accius who was with him. They both had overheard and were nodding.

"Your offer is accepted but we are four. I could not eat without having some for my comrades here."

"Understood, Paetus, there shall be quite enough."

Nicodaemus took leave of him and waved to the others.

After he was gone, Vibenna walked over to Paetus and congratulated him.

"You have a way with the natives," he said.

"At least I did not jab a spear into his side!" Paetus remarked forlornly.

"I think you had best let go of that burden, my friend. It could drag you down to some awful depths."

"I cannot avoid the truth."

"The truth is that you were doing what was prescribed. How can that be so wrong? You had little choice. You did not *kill* the man. Even if you had, he would be one of *many* that you could have notched on your belt, if you were inclined toward anything like that. You are serving Imperial Rome, helping to keep the empire intact. Making sure a dead man is dead should not be something to disturb you in this manner."

Vibenna put one hand on each shoulder and spoke to Paetus with the emotions and the words of a brother.

"We have known one another for the briefest period of time," he acknowledged. "But I like you, Decimus. You are indeed intelligent and very brave, as Severus tells me. Do not throw everything away on a ridiculous man who deserves so little of your time and your thought. He was a liar, an impostor, a rabble-rouser, a deceiver or whatever the case may be. Jesus is merely dirt under our feet. He—"

"You have forgotten what you told me about your meeting with Him," Paetus reminded him. "You had a much higher opinion of Him just a few hours ago as you were relating the circumstances."

"But not high enough to tolerate His impact upon a good man such as yourself! I see only that right now."

"I also do not care any longer about idle speculation of this sort," Vibenna moaned as he shrugged wearily. "It is dreary at best. I am tired. I need to rest. We all do. And when this duty is over, I shall be content to take a bath in the little creek near here, washing away all this Jewish dirt. Perhaps you will join me. You know the spot?"

"Yes, I know it."

"Good. Now, let us stop all nonsense about this simple carpenter and do our best to wait out the rest of this pointless and stupid assignment as patiently as possible under the circumstances!"

IV

O*thers came, after that first day, to stand worshipfully at what they deemed a sensible distance or, more boldly, to approach the sealed-off entrance of the tomb, but the four legionnaires made these brash intruders leave, as they had been assigned to do by Pilatus. Only Nicodaemus was treated any differently. And one other—the fisherman.*

Simon Peter was six feet tall, with a beard that was fully half a foot thick. He had been a man of the sea for more than twenty years and counted himself someone with fierce loyalties. But that one morning, early, before the Crucifixion at Golgotha, he had denied Jesus the Christ three times, just as his Friend had predicted.

Thus this fisherman was drawn to the tomb, drawn so strongly that he seemed immediately prepared to strike down, if possible, any of the four legionnaires who stood in his way. They had Roman swords, pickaxes, and short-bladed knives, but he had his considerable size and strength and the sharp determination to stand before the body of Jesus and weep as he confessed his shame to a corpse.

Vibenna, who had the watch that first morning, noticed him as soon as he set foot on the narrow path leading down into the tomb area, so narrow in fact that the fisherman had to place his feet on either side of it as he walked.

"I will need help!" Vibenna said, summoning the others from sleep.

They did not know what was wrong until they saw Simon Peter lumbering toward them.

"You cannot go any further," Vibenna demanded just before Peter grabbed him around both wrists and flung him to one side.

Peter continued toward the giant round stone.

Accius tried to stop him but ended up near Vibenna. Scipio swung at Peter with an ax, but the fisherman grabbed the handle in midair with one hand and roughly forced Scipio's arm down.

Only Paetus was left, standing directly in front of the stone.

"Let me past!" the fisherman cried.

"You cannot move it, man," Paetus told him. "It took the four of us here to do that. One man cannot."

"Do you not understand why it must be so? I want to stand by His body. I *must* stand by His body!"

"It is nothing, this corpse of His or that of any man's, nothing but a useless piece of dead flesh."

Peter raised his left hand and started to swing it at Paetus, who stood without moving or trying to defend himself.

"He spoke so eloquently of peace, your Jesus did," the legionnaire said hastily. "Yet you cut off someone's ear in the Garden of Gethsemane. This man you professed to love encouraged devotion so strong that it would cause you and the others to leave each one's father, mother, brother, and sister to be one of His own. Yet He is arrested and all you could do afterward is deny Him. Now you want to strike out at me in your anger, which is nothing more than your shame in pathetic masquerade."

Peter dropped his hand by his side and opened his mouth wide as he let out a cry of utter anguish.

"How do you know these things?" he asked some seconds later, desperation in his strained voice.

"I have heard many stories from the streets of Bethlehem and Jerusalem and Nazareth," Paetus told him. "Stories that were being passed along by whispers, from legionnaire to legionnaire, from crippled beggars as well as those once blind now with the ability to see, from their kind and others, stories so numerous that they were, for me and soldiers like me, impossible to ignore, yet just as impossible to believe fully."

"But it is true, what you have said," Peter told him. "The blind do have their sight returned to them. The lame ones walk as lithe young men. The demon-possessed maniacs are normal once again, like the rest of us, their minds functioning with clarity. There is more, you know. Think of the rest: A few loaves and fish feed five thousand and—"

"What you say simply is not rational," Paetus, interrupting, countered. "Except I see the reality of these claims with my eyes and know them to be true, how could you expect me—any of us—to accept what we know to be Jewish delusions?"

"But these eyes have *witnessed* everything!" Peter went on.

"You saw what you wanted to see, and that is all, I am afraid. You needed to believe all this and convinced yourself that you actually did."

Peter looked at him without saying anything for a few seconds.

"Go now," Paetus told him, "and I will see to it that no charges are brought against you for what has occurred here."

Vibenna had gotten to his feet and was protesting.

"You cannot do that!" he said stridently. "You do not have the authority."

"But I have the ear of Pilatus," Paetus reminded him.

"It cannot be that easy, Decimus. No one challenges the authority of Rome as he has done and not feel the lash. What do we say to our superiors?"

"We give them some lie."

"For what reason? We owe this Jew no favors."

"But we owe the one Peter served better than He got."

"You are right," Scipio spoke up.

Everyone turned in the direction of this young Scipio, dark-haired, handsome, quite somber, by far the quiet one of that little group who had said little during the brief period of time thus far that they had been spending together. He made the others seem even more like the veteran warriors they were, for he had been in the legions for less than a year, a fraction of the length of their own service.

"Before I was shipped here, I lived on a Greek isle with my brother. We heard stories of the followers of Jesus dispersing beyond just this area of Israel to spread His message to as many countries as they could."

"To turn the conquered people against the empire!" Vibenna exclaimed, his wrinkled countenance looking more grizzled than ever.

"Not that, as I understand it," Scipio contradicted him. "His message was one of a kingdom beyond this world, a place called heaven."

"Such nonsense. I am sorry I wasted any time with this crazy man," Vibenna said, remembering the earlier encounter.

"They healed in every region they went," Scipio told them. "One of His men rid my brother of leprosy."

At the sound of that word, the rest of them stepped back.

"No, no, I was not in contact at all with my brother after it became dangerous for that," he assured them. "He took up living on an isolated section of the island, bordered by towering mountains on all sides, except for a narrow pathway running through them on toward the east. My brother stayed with other poor ones like himself. No one dared to visit, of course, either him or anyone else in that colony of lepers.

"Then one of the followers of Jesus—I cannot remember who it was—learned about the colony and determined to find it. He said he wanted to prove the power of Almighty God by healing every one of them. My friends and I all laughed at him.

"Perhaps a fortnight passed. We forgot about the silly claims of this eager man, though we had to admit that we could respect him for wanting to do something to take away their constant and terrible pain."

Vibenna spoke up at this point, his impatience readily apparent to the others. "Get on with it, Fabius, what are you leading up to?"

Scipio was pacing as he talked.

"My brother is well today because of this follower of Jesus!" he declared, aware that the others would tend to laugh at him.

"I find that hard to believe," Vibenna said, "but if it happens to be true, you have already mentioned that to us. He took one man out of a colony of lepers and healed him. Fine, wonderful, we here are very pleased for you."

Scipio swung around and faced the three of them.

"The entire group, my comrades!" he exclaimed with great energy. "Every man and woman was made normal again. They woke up the next morning their sores gone, their pain along with it. And—"

He had to force the words out, past his emotions.

"Those whose limbs were rotting away found they had new fingers, new feet, their skin fresh and healthy once again. Some who were close to death revived completely. Their minds had been gone, ravaged by what they had experienced, but now they were laughing, talking normally, sitting and praying with joy."

Paetus, Vibenna, and Accius did not know what to make of their young comrade Scipio's strange tale.

Though young, he had seemed to them levelheaded, intelligent. Now he was talking like someone possessed!

He saw their expressions and acknowledged that his tale seemed quite unbelievable, but he went on. "It *is* true. I was there as as they approached the village. Everyone was spellbound by what they witnessed. Some had relatives among the lepers. They saw their loved ones suddenly whole, with normal limbs and faces unscarred!"

Scipio cleared his throat and added, "I could not have suspected that I would be guarding the tomb of the one that this disciple claimed gave him the power to do what he had done. I owe my brother's life to him!

Vibenna approached Scipio and stared directly into his eyes.

"There is no jesting in your words, is there?" he asked pointedly, studying the other man's reactions.

"None, Marcus. I have not exaggerated any detail. There must have been more than a score of people for whom leprosy was no longer a curse. *They had been freed from it!*"

Vibenna turned to the others.

"I wonder what kind of man died yesterday," he said.

"But you yourself called Him an impostor, a deceiver," Paetus was quick to remind the legionnaire. "The rest of us had been inclined to agree with you, Vibenna. Now what is it that you are suggesting?"

As he glanced one more time at the stone, Vibenna replied, "I cannot be certain. I am not a prophet."

"That is not an answer," Paetus said.

Shrugging his shoulders, Vibenna added, a touch of exasperation in his voice, "Perhaps we shall learn the truth by tomorrow."

V

The fisherman was the only visitor who gave them any real difficulty. He was followed by Mary Magdalene.

Vibenna recognized her, for good reason.

"You are looking well," he said, acknowledging her as she slowly walked down the narrow path.

The woman blushed as he said that.

"How are you, Marcus?" she asked.

"Very fine. Why are you here? It is a peculiar place for you, Mary Magdalene. I thought you had set up shop at only that one address."

"My life has changed."

"You mean you are traveling these days."

"I am no longer a whore," she said, her eyes wide.

"When in the name of the gods did you stop?" Vibenna asked. "What a waste of voluptuous flesh if it is as you say."

She was standing in front of him now and placed a finger on his lips.

"I speak in the name of no gods but one," she told him, smiling warmly.

"It is a joke, what you say," Vibenna remarked, still incredulous. "Please, Mary Magdalene, we have with us now a very young but hearty legionnaire. His name is Fabius Scipio. We could excuse him for a few minutes. There are some nice large rocks and a few bushes here. We promise not to look!"

He turned from the woman and gestured toward Scipio, who was polishing his helmet at that moment.

"My friend, my friend, Mary Magdalene wants to meet you!" Vibenna said loudly, gesturing for him to join them. "She has slept with everyone here but you. Trying out a fresh, firm young body should interest her greatly."

. . . she has slept with everyone here but you.

It was true. Paetus, Vibenna, and Accius all had been in her bed at least once. Vibenna, in fact, had seen her regularly for a time. But then she seemed to have disappeared. He had asked for her at the place where had lived but the woman in charge simply shrugged her shoulders and said that she had no idea where the she was.

"Marcus . . ." Mary Magdalene's voice was soft, kind.

He glanced at her.

"What is it?" he asked.

"I no longer sell my body," she told him. "Do you not know what happened?"

Vibenna shook his head.

"The Sanhedrin brought charges against me," Mary Magdalene recalled. "I was led to the center of Jerusalem, and a crowd had picked up stones and they were about to—"

"Those hypocrites!" Vibenna interrupted, his face reddening in anger. "How can they cast stones at you and ignore the filth in their own lives?"

"That is what *He* said, Marcus."

He was genuinely puzzled.

"What are you saying to me, woman?" Vibenna asked, not without some tenderness in his voice.

"Jesus the Christ told them, 'He who is without sin should cast the first stone.' They looked at one another, then at Him, and lastly, at me. One by one they tossed those stones in a common pile and walked away, grumbling."

"Simple words from this carpenter stopped them?" Vibenna asked, incredulous.

"Simple words, Marcus, but words that cut through to their souls —that hit *me* hard as well. I was with Him much of the time after that."

"You traveled with His band of tax collectors and the rest?"

"Often, yes."

"And you did not provide them with your services?"

She smiled as she replied, "They did not ask. Nor would I have done so if they had."

Vibenna pulled away from her and started laughing. The others had heard as well, and all joined in except Paetus.

Paetus walked over to Mary Magdalene.

"I was at the cross with Him," he told her. "His blood covered my hands."

"Yes," she replied. "I know."

Paetus stepped back, not believing that he could have heard her say that.

"But I did not see you nearby," he said. "I was the only one at the very foot of His cross. What do you mean by what you have now said?"

"I was there—with His mother and several other of the women —and we saw what happened when you pierced His side with the sword. And now I await His resurrection, Decimus. It will be glorious. All heaven will join in. That is why I came here, late in the day. I was hoping that it had happened already."

"That is nothing but a fable," Paetus insisted, "a fable born from the pathetic wishful thinking of a bunch of senile old Jews unable to concede that they have lost the power to govern themselves. How could you believe anything so absurd? When we die, that is it, unless the gods choose to intercede. No mere man—"

"But Jesus was more than mortal flesh."

Paetus was tempted to slap the woman, hoping that that would jar her out of what he considered to be her mental stupor.

She was looking up at the darkening sky.

"Angels are poised tonight," she said, with utter conviction. "They will swoop down on this place and roll the rock aside, and Jesus' resurrected body will come forth."

"You seem so certain," Paetus pointed out, "but others, including the fisherman and Nicodaemus, have been here and displayed hardly a measure of your earnestness."

"Those forgiven the most should have the most gratitude and the greatest awe," she said. "Peter and the rest never considered themselves such sinners as I have been. Except for Matthew, they sought to make a living in what could only be called an honorable manner.

"Yet I had been mired in lust and its utter shame and decadence most of my life, even from my youngest years. I allowed my body to be abused for the satisfaction of those who paid me. And I did this often. For me, it was the sin of illicit intercourse often in league with blasphemy."

"You speak with the cultivation of someone learned," Paetus observed, "and yet you are a product of the streets. Did this Jesus aid you in that way also?"

"He did," she replied, her eyes luminous. "He cleansed my mind as well as my soul. He spoke with great precision. He taught with great joy that which is the beauty of language, not vulgar, debased talk. It is little enough that I follow His example."

All four legionnaires had been listening to her for some minutes and witnessing the extraordinary transformation of a woman whom they had known carnally.

"I have to go now," she told them. "But before I do, will you permit me to kneel before that great rock and pray briefly?"

They stepped aside without hesitation.

Mary Magdalene walked up to the sealed tomb entrance and knelt as she spoke, her voice just above a whisper.

"You called Lazarus forth," she said. "When will the heavenly Father bring Your body from this grave, O Lord?"

The five men waited respectfully for her to finish. After saying, "Your broken and humble servant offers this prayer to Thee with the wish that she could be here when the angels descend upon this spot tonight . . . Amen." Mary Magdalene stood and turned in their direction.

"Look at her face!" Scipio said.

But the others already had seen the glow on it, the absolute and total peace.

. . . those forgiven the most should have the most gratitude and the greatest awe.

She was smiling as she walked past them.

"You are an intelligent woman," Vibenna called after her. "How can you hope for these angels to come? They are creatures of imagination, nothing more."

At the top of the walkway, Mary Magdalene turned, glanced at him for a moment, and said only, "Tell me this in the morning, Marcus Vibenna . . . if you can," before she walked away into the gathering night.

VI

Decimus Paetus awoke past midnight.

His watch was not for another three hours.

Normally he slept quite soundly. But his experience at the cross of Jesus the Christ just two nights earlier had made a full and refreshing rest something he no longer took for granted. Then there was all that talk, that infantile talk of healing and redemption and whatever else, from a fisherman as well as a member of the Sanhedrin plus a whore with which he had slept three times—and a fellow legionnaire!

Pactus stood, expecting to see Severus Accius standing in front of the large rock or, at least, quite nearby. His friend was not anywhere to be found, while the two other legionnaires remained asleep.

Paetus walked quietly around the side of Golgotha and, at first, still could not find the other man.

He was about to give up and let a growing sense of alarm overtake him when he happened to glance upward, at the top where the crosses had been that Friday afternoon.

Accius!

He was standing directly in front of where Jesus the Christ had been crucified. His head was tilted back, and he was crying.

Paetus climbed up the side of the hill, using the crude steps that had been chiseled out of the western side, the same steps that had presented such an awkward path for the so-called Messiah days before. Once Jesus the Christ had tripped and opened a gash on His left knee. Even the strong, tall black man named Simon of Cyrene who had been carrying the cross for Him did the same thing and nearly dropped the heavy piece of wood joined together from two crossbeams, its weight a burden that would have been altogether impossible for a less muscular individual to bear for very long.

Accius had now fallen forward onto his stomach, sobs tearing through his body which shook fitfully.

"What is it, friend?" Paetus asked, rushing to his side.

"I do not know," Accius said, barely able to talk. "I do not know why I am here. I scarce remember even coming to this spot now."

"Calm down. Explain more clearly, Severus. I cannot understand what you are trying to tell me."

"I thought I heard someone crying from the top of Golgotha. I had no idea what or who it was. It was an awful sound, Decimus. I cannot describe it. Like the cries of demons from some nether world."

"Hush!" Paetus said. "Listen!"

"I hear nothing. I—"

And then the sound reached his ears as well.

"Wings!" he exclaimed. "Some giant bird!"

But not just one pair. A dozen, a hundred, perhaps a thousand, perhaps ten thousand times ten thousand, the number increasing with each blink of their eyes.

And then the night sky seemed to open up.

Light poured forth over Golgotha.

And they saw a multitude of iridescent creatures with transparent wings coming in a vast wave!

Golgotha and the land for miles all around them were filled with countless numbers of these beings until the scene was like that of daylight, bright almost to the point of blinding the two legionnaires.

Then came the voices, the most beautiful that Paetus and Accius had heard in their lives, voices so sweet, yet so thrilling that the two of them could barely stand as they listened, their legs suddenly weak, their hearts beating faster.

As the two men reached the bottom of the hewn steps, both of them realized that they had been crying.

Paetus and Accius stumbled toward the little tomb, their vision blurred by their continuing tears.

The other men were awake also and, stupidly, had gripped their weapons, thinking that some kind of enemy was attacking them.

Suddenly the light and the beautiful voices ceased, and the four legionnaires were plunged into darkness.

"What in the name of the gods—?" Marcus Vibenna started to say but never got to finish that sentence.

In an instant, the stone at the entrance to the tomb was rolled to one side as though it had been made of papyrus and, from within, a blinding light shone forth. Their eyes affected, none of the legionnaires could see, for a moment or two, anything but vague shapes distorted into indistinct blurs.

One larger shape, radiant, surrounded by a myriad of others.

Paetus' vision returned first. Then Vibenna's, followed by the others.

And they dropped to their knees.

They saw the carpenter, the one who had been crucified earlier, the one proclaimed to be the Messiah for whom the Jews had been waiting, not by the respected and powerful religious rulers of Israel but by His small band of followers, the very ones who had largely deserted Him the moment His mortality seemed to be proven.

No one else had believed the message He had been sending forth, as far as any of the legionnaires knew. But then no one had seen the sight that was playing itself out before them in colors of silver, gold, white, and traces of crimson.

Jesus the Christ stood before them but He was not alone. A multitude of those shining, translucent beings formed an outline around him.

Scipio walked forward, though Vibenna tried to stop him.

As the young legionnaire fell to his knees, Jesus the Christ reached out and touched him on the crown of his head.

Scipio fell forward on the ground and stayed there without moving.

Vibenna's eyes opened wide as the Figure took his head in his hands and looked straight into his very soul, or so it seemed. Then Vibenna crumpled to the ground not far from Scipio.

One by one, the legionnaires fell without injury, Jesus the Christ walking past them, still surrounded by those extraordinary beings, even the sound of their wings like music in the still night air.

And then He came to Decimus Paetus.

"Give me your hands," He said.

Paetus thrust them forward without hesitation.

"I see no longer any blood on them," spoke Jesus the Christ. "You are free. You have been cleansed, for now, for eternity."

Paetus burst out crying again.

Jesus the Christ took the sleeve of His garment and wiped the tears from his eyes and from his cheeks.

"Save them, beloved Decimus," He said. "Save them for the end of your days when they will be felt more deeply."

"Are you the one they call the Messiah?" Paetus asked, his voice trembling with the emotion of that moment.

"I am whom you say but only of those who believe," that voice, as those words were spoken, radiating not through Paetus's ears only but every inch of his body.

"But what do you want me to do?" Paetus asked. "I know nothing but the will of Imperial Rome, no commander but Caesar."

"From this moment on, you will listen to Almighty God," Jesus the Christ told him.

"And my comrades?"

"They will be with you for part of the way; but for the rest, you will know only the company of the Jews."

"The *Jews!*"

"Yes, Decimus Paetus, you will die with them, your enemy surrounding you, your comrades' bodies on every side, when you are very old and there is no one else left, for you will be the last."

"How can I do this? I am a simple man."

"Take My hand."

Paetus did this.

"Feel the mark of the nail?"

"I do. Yes, I—"

Jesus the Christ held out His other hand.

"And in this one as well?"

"I do! I do feel the mark of the nail."

"My feet. Touch each foot."

Paetus quickly got down on his knees and placed his fingers in the mark of the nail in each one.

"Yes, yes," he agreed, "I feel them."

"My side now," Jesus the Christ said. "Place your hand into My side."

"Please, not that!" Paetus begged. "I cannot do what You want of me. It was my lance that . . . that was thrust. . . . that I—"

Paetus was sobbing now to the point of hysteria.

"I know what You did," that voice rammed its way into his ears and straight to his brain. "Do what I ask, Decimus Paetus, and I will give you such peace that you could not comprehend it possible before now."

"If only I could . . . Lord," Paetus said, almost in spite of himself, though uncomfortable with the use of that title, since he had been doing little but disputing the validity of the Nazarene's claims.

"If I am Lord, then I must be Lord from this moment on. Do what I ask. Do it now, my beloved Decimus. Do what your Lord asks of you."

. . . my beloved Decimus.

Paetus felt those words touch the very pit of his soul.

He looked up into the face of Jesus the Christ.

"How can You call me beloved?" he asked with awe. "How can You forgive those who mocked you, who beat You, who were responsible for crucifying You, along with the one pierced who Your side as ordered by Pontius Pilatus."

"Because that is why I died."

Paetus began to raise his right hand, pulled aside that shimmering garment, touched that ravaged side and thrust not a blade up into it but his hand.

"My Lord, my Lord, my holy Lord," he said.

"That first moment was to certify My death," Jesus the Christ spoke for the final time that night. "This now witnesses to your eternal life, Decimus Paetus."

The legionnaire fell to his elbows.

He did not want to stop looking at the beauty, the majesty, that he now saw with full comprehension. One of the wondrous winged beings came to him and bent over him and touched his eyes. In an instant he was asleep, before the night became dark again.

VII

Pontius Pilatus had slept but little since the crucifixion, especially in view of how his wife Procula never seemed to lose an opportunity to remind him that he had condemned a good and innocent man.

"I dreamed about this man, this Jesus some call the Christ," she said earlier. "A strange and terrible dream, my husband."

"What could be so strange and terrible about a vagrant carpenter who fancies Himself a messiah of some sort?" Pilatus replied, finding her protestation quite beguiling, since she was dressed in a golden-hued, rather flimsy-looking nightgown and he was wearing little more than a thick tan-colored fur robe he had wrapped around his body. He had to fight the temptation to make love to her at that very moment, the thought of her taking his mind for the moment off the pressure entailed in deciding what to do about the Nazarene.

Procula had been in bed then, and he had been standing on the large balcony adjacent to their grandly appointed bedroom, having come in late after meeting with the Sanhedrin and not yet ready to join her.

"It happened while I was waiting for you, dear Pontius," she continued earnestly that particular night. "I fell asleep and, in a dream unlike any I had experienced before, saw this man sitting on a throne. You were there in front of Him, and so was I, by your side. We both were being pronounced condemned for eternity and were soon to be cast into a place of unrelenting heat and pain.

"I begged Jesus to tell us why, to tell us what we had done to cause this kind of punishment. Then He stood—very slowly, majestically, I must admit—and turned His back to me, and I saw open sores festering on it. He held out His hands, and there was an ugly hole in each one and, likewise, in His feet."

"Nonsense, Procula, your madness is—!" Pilatus exclaimed, regretting that, regretting that he now reminded her that Caesar's own physician thought she was doomed, that she would never pull back from the brink of losing her mind.

Then she had confessed to him that this had occurred not that night but during the day, for she felt quite exhausted somehow and had lain back, her eyes closing, sleep coming quickly, and then the dream. At its end, Procula continued, she had awakened and felt compelled to hurry on to the place where Jesus was being held. She had gotten those legionnaires who were abusing him to stop before they had intended.

"But why?" Pilatus asked. "He was a criminal. Rome's will cannot be thwarted because of anyone's silly dream."

"Pontius, this man was someone the Jews *said* was a criminal. How often have you believed them in other instances?"

"Little . . ." he had had to admit.

"I stood before the Nazarene," she continued, "after I had dismissed the men, and I tried to find out for myself."

"You failed, did you not?"

"I suppose I did."

"How can you suppose? Did you or did you not fail?"

"I indeed failed to find out anything but the fact that He was more gentle than I could have imagined."

"Some thought Him to be a coward, my dear Procula. Surely you have heard this as well as I. He never once struck back."

"Coward, Pontius, or simply a man who saw that resistance would do no good? He could not possibly escape. He could only drive the soldiers on to even more barbaric torture if He did anything to anger them."

"You may be right," he grudgingly admitted.

"You met with Him only prior to your men doing their worst with His body. You never allowed yourself to see what was left of Him just before He was crucified. His back was a mass of ribbons of flesh, some hanging loose, the bones showing through in a few spots. The legionnaires feared, at one point, that He might die before they could get Him along the Via Dolorosa to Golgotha, and so they called a physician to stop the bleeding and gave Him a little wine for his pain, along with a few pieces of bread."

Pilatus smiled sardonically.

"Since when did you concern yourself with the treatment accorded common criminals by Rome's legionnaires?" he asked.

"This man was neither a criminal nor common, in any imaginable way, my husband. You caught some of His manner yourself or you would not have tried as hard as you did to gain His release!"

Pilatus said nothing in response, accustomed over the years to his wife's unpredictable outbursts.

"If your men had been just a bit more harsh," she went on bitingly, angered even more by this indifferent silence, "you would have saved yourself the later public spectacle. Why was that part of this foul business so important?"

"As a lesson to the Jews," he did say this time.

58

"To them, my husband, or to Caesar, whom you perceive to be wavering in his opinion of your capabilities?"

"What in the name of the gods we hold dear could I ever be proving to Caesar by such an act, Procula?" Pilatus spoke, trying to conceal the fact that she indeed had found a sore spot in his outlook.

"That you were not an inept has-been. You know, for you have told me so, that there have been stories."

How well I understand that, he thought, not surprised at the woman's astuteness because he had seen innumerable flashes of it over the years of their marriage. *How keenly you understand that of which I myself am only vaguely aware.*

"To sacrifice an innocent man's life for the sake of my image in Rome? How can you think that of me?"

They had been standing on the massive whitewashed balcony adjacent to their bedroom. Procula stepped back a foot or two from her husband, anger flashing for an instant across her eyes.

"Then you *did* believe that He was far from being the guilty man your sentence proclaimed Him to be! You executed someone you should have sheltered instead, someone perhaps the two of us could have learned from!"

"A citizen of Rome, a member of the Senate, an officer in the Imperial Army learning from an itinerant carpenter with delusions of kingship? You *are* tottering on the edge of losing your mind, Procula!"

I know it is true, my husband, she said to herself. *I feel the mad night lapping at me more and more often now. I find it ever harder to deal with the clutching phantoms that are pulling at me . . .*

Seconds after he had spoken, Procula gasped as she looked out beyond the edge of the balcony, toward Golgotha.

Pilatus turned quickly in that direction and his gasp followed her own.

"The sky, Pontius. *That stream of light!*" she said in a half-scream.

Beams of light shone from the dark night sky directly onto the Place of the Skull, and nowhere else.

"Only there," Procula pointed out. "Only at the spot where He died!"

"I must go," he said. "I must—"

"We both will go, Pontius," she insisted. "I *must* know! I must know what is happening at that spot."

VIII

Pilatus decided to travel by way of one of the wadis near his house, those deep canyons with bottoms that were sandy, which would keep him out of view of the general populace. The one he selected ended less than a mile from the crucifixion site.

The sound of owls could be heard on either side of the wadi, probably as the birds clung to nearby acacia trees or perhaps one of the terebinths prevalent in and around Israel, the latter certainly a tree of some legendary status in that land, its huge crown and dense shadow making it suitable for tired travelers who were attempting to shield themselves momentarily from the heat of the day.

From what he heard, Pilatus guessed that the sounds were from an eagle owl, the largest of the species, with the loudest call, though he preferred listening to the scops owl, which was rather small, the sound of it considerably more pleasant.

They could hear other indications of nightlife, hints of scampering feet, possibly foxes or jackals moving about in the darkness.

When they arrived, driven in a carriage by a guard Pilatus had awakened, the dazzling light had disappeared. They found that all four legionnaires were asleep and that the stone had been rolled away.

Pilatus was stunned.

"The Jews have gone ahead and done what I suspected, what I wanted to prevent!" he said, bitterly angry as he stepped from the carriage, went around to the other side, and helped his wife out. "They have committed this theft of the body of this Jesus, and now they will proclaim His resurrection."

The proconsul strode directly over to Decimus Paetus and kicked him hard in the small of his back.

"Idiot!" he screamed as the legionnaire's eyes opened abruptly.

Paetus jumped to his feet, avoiding Pilatus's eyes as he did so. The others were awakening now, the noise jolting them out of their sleep. When they realized who the visitor was, they stood immediately.

"You allowed what I had expressly forbidden!" Pilatus roared, walking up to Marcus Vibenna and slapping him across the cheek, an insult reeking of the profoundest shame. "You are supposed to be the veteran, are you not? But you failed me, you failed me and the divine Caesar and the whole of Imperial Rome. You all shall be beaten for this. I will not be bothered even slightly if any of you succumb!"

He returned to Paetus.

"And you! The one I trusted most, from my own palace guard. I asked that you go, and you recommended Accius who chose Vibenna and the rest. I wanted you here. I thought you would see to it that my order would be obeyed."

He was about to slap Paetus as well, but naive young Scipio ran up to him, and held his wrist and begged him to listen.

"Any man who does that must have a good reason," Pilatus said, his face reddened by rage. "Speak now, and speak well, or you may regret that action until the day you die!"

Scipio, halting in his speech, nevertheless managed to get across to Pilatus what had happened as soon as that brilliant light had started to shine down on them from the sky.

Pilatus's first reaction was to laugh rather hysterically, his anger gone, cast aside by the sheer absurdity of what this young man had related. After regaining control of himself, he looked at Paetus.

"Tell me every bit of the truth that you can," he demanded sternly. "Your young friend's little gambit succeeded, I admit, but only for the moment. Believe me when I assure you that I am still disturbed by what I have seen here."

"He exaggerated no details," Paetus commented, fear nearly freezing the words in his throat. "We saw the stone being rolled aside."

"By beams of light," Pilatus repeated disbelievingly. "How can that be? Do you not see the absurdity of it?"

"Pardon me, sir," Paetus said, trying not to speak in what could be considered a presumptuous manner. "I too saw creatures that looked like beams of light. But then Jesus the Christ emerged from the tomb with a flesh-and-blood form. He was surrounded by the others, as though they were His guardians."

"How do you know that your eyes were not being deluded?"

"Because when He asked me to touch the print of the nails I did so, on his hands as well as his feet. And I thrust my own hand into his side."

Pilatus winced at that.

"The side that was pierced at the cross?"

"Yes, sir, the same side."

"And there was a hole in it."

"From his front and out his back. My hand went straight through, sir."

Pilatus was silent for a moment, studying Paetus, then glancing at the other men, who seemed quite terrified as they considered their prospects.

"I cannot explain what you have told me," he said finally, "nor can I doubt the sincerity of at least two of you. If the others make the same claims, then I must not question any of you, or be prepared to cast you all into the dungeon!"

Pilatus conferred with each one privately, at a distance from the tomb, summoning one, then another, until he had spoken to the rest.

"I have decided that, whatever happened, it was something over which you had no control," he said finally, standing before the legionnaires as his wife continued to sit in the carriage that brought them. "But the only way we can make this work is to claim that a Jew pretended to befriend you and gave you all something to drink. In it was some drug of which you were not aware. That soon caused you to fall asleep.

"Then a band of the Nazarene's followers, with some beasts of burden, managed to pull the stone aside and left with the cold body of their dead leader. Immediately they began to circulate the lie that this Jesus the Christ had actually arisen of His own power from the tomb, thereby fulfilling the ancient prophecies."

He grimaced as he finished and added, "Yes, I know, Caesar has encouraged only the telling of truth. He has decreed that this be done *if at all possible*. But should we do so now, should we agree with that small group of zealots that tagged along with Jesus, and confirm such truth, then we are setting the stage for the eventual downfall of the empire itself, for we will have shown that, indeed—"

Pilatus hesitated, perspiration on his forehead and trickling down the back of his patrician neck.

"—the laws of Rome, the will of the divine emperor himself can be thwarted by a vagrant carpenter from Nazareth of all places!" he continued. "The lie has to be set in place before any Jews come upon the truth."

As he pointed to the open entrance directly in front of them, Pilatus added, "Our proof will be what everyone will see for themselves. If Jesus did not arise—and few rational men will take that utterly bizarre notion in any way seriously—then it had to have been that the Nazarene's body *was stolen*, and therein will be seen the duplicity of those treacherous people claiming to be His devoted followers!"

Pilatus ordered only Fabius Scipio and Decimus Paetus to stay on with him, while he sent the two other men back to the location where they were being stationed for their period of service in Israel.

The two remaining legionnaires joined Pilatus and his wife for the return to the proconsul's residence on the outskirts of Jerusalem.

"Such a desolate land!" Pilatus sighed. "I could be in the midst of Rome right now, which is, whatever its shortcomings, at least *civilized!*

Caesaria can be very pleasant, but in no way is it a worthy substitute for what we knew earlier."

Procula nodded at that. She had hated the idea of Israel from the moment she learned what her husband's assignment was.

"An outpost," she told him before they had left Rome. "We are being sent to an outpost with only snakes and Jews to keep us company."

"Herod too," he replied cynically.

"That overstuffed toad!" she bellowed. "I would almost prefer the Jews."

"We get them both, Procula!"

She knew she had to go along. Women in Imperial Rome had little choice but what their men dictated. And yet she manifested a much more independent spirit than was typical of the times. She had even thought of appealing directly to Caesar.

"On what grounds?" Pilatus had asked.

"That we deserve to be treated far better than the way we are now. Blame it on bureaucratic bungling!"

"If we do the latter, it will mean that the emperor himself was the chief bungler, since he signed the order personally. As for better treatment, Procula, are we wise to put ourselves in the position of being unwilling to sacrifice for the cause of the empire when so many others like us go without protest? Will we not be viewed with some apprehension and mistrust from that moment on?"

She hesitated after he had spoken, holding in her left hand a rare vase that had been part of the booty from Syria, a priceless item indeed.

"I have *everything* here," she said. "My family, my friends, so many *places* that I cherish. We will have to leave so much behind. Who will take care of our treasures, Pontius, like this vase? I doubt that it can be packed well enough to withstand the journey. I could not bear to find it broken—what a frightful thought."

"Is all that we have comprised of *things?*" he asked. "Is there no more depth to our lives that that, the things that we possess?"

She was embarrassed by his words.

"We have one another," she said, reaching out for him.

"But you need more, Procula," he told her. "You need us plus status plus parties plus the convenience of living in Rome."

The parties—ah, yes—those remarkable feasts in which anyone of status indulged with shameless frequency! That was done for what were called "business reasons." The guest lists were comprised mainly of *patroni*, the most powerful individuals in Roman society, including senators and other political figures as well as those who were financial power centers.

A large group of slaves waited on the guests the instant they arrived until they were leaving, often many hours later. The shoes of every individual, male and female, who attended were removed just after they entered, with sandals supplied by the host, which were to be worn instead. On humid evenings, slaves were stationed with the guests, to keep them cool by waving peacock feather fans in front of them, movement that was also intended to keep flies off the food. As each course was finished, other slaves would bring earthen bowls of perfumed water so that patrician hands would not have to suffer the indignity of dirty hands for more than a few seconds.

Along with the *patronis*, or guests of stature, Pilatus was obliged by the social conventions of the time also to have *clientes* in attendance, younger politicians, artists, or lawyers without a job. The very rich thus mingled with wannabes. If Pilatus found any of them to be too threadbare, an embarrassment to the other guests, he would give them food in a *sportula* and they would leave, thus freeing him of any further social obligation to them.

And memorable *coenas* they had enjoyed, that main entrée of each day so grandiose that it could easily generate the beginnings of a banquet if there were enough guests and exactly the right combination of other foods, as they sat on their sloping couches around square tables piled high with hors d'oeuvres, three entrées, two roasts, and the dessert. The appetizer was always eggs and honey mixed with wine, the dessert generally something spicy that made host and guests alike thirsty for more wine.

With perfume in the air to please the nostrils and carefully chosen delicacies for the stomach, the *look* of the more important feasts was not forgotten either. A wild pig, though delicious to the taste, was hardly a pleasing sight for the eyes, so in order to soften the grotesque look of the stuffed, cooked carcass usually placed on a large, flat tray, it would often be joined by a number of little sweet cakes that had been molded and baked in the form of suckling pigs.

Even all of this attention to detail at a feast did not guarantee that the guests would escape boredom, so Procula and Pontius Pilatus worked together with considerable ingenuity to sprinkle surprising little moments throughout the evening. One idea that proved successful was serving a boar whole, then opening up the belly and extracting some live nightingales from it. Immediately afterward, Pilatus was applauded for this little trick.

With wine in abundance, drunkenness became something of a problem, as well as overeating, which led to frequent bouts with nausea among the guests. Certain of Pilatus's slaves were given the sole task of cleaning up after them. The bigger the guest list, the busier they were.

Pilatus was fond of being a matchmaker between single men and women or for those spouse-swapping for the evening and beyond. To encourage this, he engaged in a custom that was prevalent at each occasion, the hanging of a rose from the ceiling at certain spots in the banquet hall. This was to symbolize romance—or lust, it mattered not for such Romans as Pilatus or others of his station—but also a code of silence, with *sub rosa,* under the rose, guaranteeing that whatever was said or done beneath the flower was to be kept in the strictest confidence.

In addition to the feasts, Procula seemed to find the various local pastimes to be treasured integral aspects of the life she had been leading in Rome. She enjoyed playing *trochus,* or one of the dice-oriented variations nicknamed "petty thieves" games by the women of that period. Her husband had usually gone off on his own to bet on a particular bird at one of the cockfights that were prevalent in and around Rome, or to play *trigon* at the baths or perhaps *harpastum.*

"How can we survive," Pilatus added, "a man and a woman such as we are, Procula, when so much of what you require will have been ripped from your grasp."

Her eyes widened at the thought. Trembling, nervous, she dropped the vase, and it shattered on the hard floor of the room where they had entertained countless numbers of Rome's social and military elite.

"It has already started, Pontius," she said, tears welling up in her eyes. "Please, my husband, I need your arms around me. I need your strength."

He obliged her, without reminding her that *his* world was being shaken as well, that his expectations were shattered, at least for the next half-dozen years.

And now my friends are Jewish high priests and a few women from the market, she thought as her mind returned to the present.

Pilatus closed his hand around her arm.

"Not in this place," she whispered, "not in front of—"

"Two men who are hardly of our station in life, is that not it?" Pilatus answered. "Is this how we are to conduct ourselves until that much future day when we finally pack up and leave this place?"

He snorted with irritation long dormant but now surfacing.

"Are we to keep around us this invisible wall, if I may refer to it as that, pretending that it is necessary to preserve our status—the gods forbid that we mingle with the common people—while being unwilling to admit that it does nothing but ensure our loneliness, heightening the exiled state in which we find ourselves?"

Lapsing into silence, Pontius Pilatus recalled some moments—quite unforgettable if he were honest with himself—that he had spent alone with the Nazarene before the terrible toll wrought by the admitted abuse of the legionnaires who "prepared" the man for the crucifixion that would take place in a few hours.

"This is no pretense with you, is it?" Pilatus had said. "As far as you are concerned, your claims are not based upon some concocted deception but are actually quite literally honest. You have not lied to me, to others in any respect, is that not the case, as far as You are concerned? Is there truth in my words, Nazarene?"

"It is as you say," Jesus the Christ replied simply.

"If You be a king, why are Your subjects not rushing this building to free you? Are they cowards in the face of Imperial Rome?"

"My kingdom is not of this world, Pontius Pilatus."

"Where is it then?" Pilatus asked, laughing heartily, as they stood in the courtyard, all others ordered from it so that he could confront the accused and draw his own conclusions without the biases of some angry members of the Sanhedrin and their motley group of patently false accusers. "Is it beyond the clouds? And if that be so, how do we get to it, Jesus? Do the gods reach down and pull us up?"

He was doubled over with laughter by then.

But when his gaze met that of the Nazarene's, his amusement was cut short. He stood up straight and frowned.

"You do not see the absurdity in all of this?" he asked.

"The only absurdity, Pontius Pilatus, is that you speak of the *gods* reaching down to mortals. There are no gods above, for only from the pit of hell do their kind come, and they are but demons *posing* as your ancient deities, in allegiance to the same master of darkness that you serve so well—Satan himself."

Pilatus reached out and slapped the Nazarene across the face.

"Did You not feel that?" he asked when there was no reaction. "Did they give You a drug to kill the pain?"

"I feel pain. I feel the pain of your hand across My cheek. I feel the pain of their lashes across My back. I feel the pain of your sins, and theirs, and the sins of this entire world, for already have I started to take such sin upon My very self, that with My death, all of it may be forgiven and forgotten by Almighty God."

Pilatus's mouth dropped open.

"You *are* a madman!" he said, genuinely astonished. "I shall not waste any more time with you!"

Pilatus turned and strode from the courtyard, which seemed deceptively pretty even at that dreary time of year, with its bright green climbing vines bedecked with fragrant and colorful flowers, some of which were peculiar to that region, others having been brought from Rome specifically at his request.

66

For a moment, when Pilatus—ruler of Judah and appointed by Imperial Rome's emperor—reached the doorway leading into the main building, he turned and glanced almost reluctantly at this strange man, this Jesus called the Christ, who had bowed His head and was obviously engaging in a quiet prayer.

"Even now You cling to Your fantasies," Pilatus spoke softly, a curious touch of admiration sprinkled amid the pity he also felt.

As that memory faded—though only for a while, for surely it was so strong that it would rise up again when he least wanted to be reminded of it—Pilatus realized that he could hardly scorn the carpenter about His delusions when, in fact, though a Roman citizen, he himself was tangled up in those peculiarly his own.

I have become ensnared by feeble assurances from Rome that my career has not taken a turn for the worse, he reminded himself as the outline of his residence against the star-filled sky could be seen less than a mile ahead now, *that this is only a temporary assignment out of sheer necessity or whatever other specious words I was told. What if I never leave Israel? What if any hope for a better station is as pointless, as futile as the Nazarene's protestations about some kind of heavenly kingdom not of this world?*

He shifted his gaze for a moment to the two legionnaires. Moments ago, he had berated them for falling victim to idle imaginings.

Poor fools, he told himself as the hint of a single tear appeared in his left eye and then was gone.

IX

Paetus and Scipio slept in special guest quarters at Pilatus's Jerusalem residence, considered the second most luxurious of the ones he maintained throughout that country, the first being the one at Caesarea.

After they had awakened and bathed in the mineral springs adjacent to the main house, they were given a most hearty breakfast.

And then Pilatus joined them for a walk around his estate.

"I can scarce wait until the almond trees start to blossom in another month," Pilatus said as he sniffed in the clear air of that morning. "It is such a useful plant. The flowers are quite lovely the nuts are among the foods we consume regularly, and my wife adores the oil to help keep her skin young!"

He stopped for a moment and raised one hand.

"Do you smell that?" he asked.

"Myrtle, yes," Paetus replied. "A sweet scent indeed."

"It is something else that my dear Procula likes about this land. Perfume made from those small, white blooms ranks among her favorites from any land in the empire, better than even jasmine, in fact."

"What is her feeling about the willow?" Scipio asked.

"Very pleasant," Pilatus told him, "especially its shade during a particularly warm day. She also likes the sound of a gentle breeze weaving through it."

They stopped abruptly as they were confronted by a peacock, its tail feathers spread out in full glory.

"She will not allow those feathers to be plucked prematurely," Pilatus chuckled, "so I have a servant going around this property for the better part of a day, scooping up those that have dropped naturally. We have a dozen of these fine birds here and, in fact, several at each of my other residences."

A bit further on, they saw a brood of partridges.

"She will permit only their eggs to be taken," he added. "The birds themselves are not to be harmed."

"Were those partridge eggs that we had for breakfast?" Paetus asked, recalling how tasty they were, with a loaf of large, gritty Cicilian bread divided up between Scipio and himself, topped off with thin, very crisp wafers that included wine, pepper, and milk among the ingredients, dipped in goat's milk, the latter normally reserved for a *prandium* or midday snack and a special treat at any other time of the day, especially breakfast.

"No others are allowed, by Procula's direct orders. Your pleasure is my reward for serving them."

A high, stone wall surrounded the property.

"As you know, Paetus," Pilatus commented, "Rome can have all the might it wants, but that alone does not guarantee our safety. We still need walls to keep out whatever enemy we might have in whatever land we have conquered. Once we show any weakness, any loss of resolve whatever, forces now at bay will no longer be held back."

"A hundred Barabbases barking at the gates," Paetus said.

"Well put, Decimus. Which reminds me: I have heard through my sources that, in recent years, you have contributed more than just your battlefield prowess with swords and lances and the like."

"I am not sure what you mean, sir."

"Come now, modesty has its place, I might agree, but hardly where your own abilities are concerned."

"The defenses, sir? Is that what you mean?"

"Precisely those, yes!"

Paetus had been able to devise some defenses for Roman fortresses on the European continent, each of which had had an ingredient or a design not used before he had suggested it to the particular commander at the time.

"Thank you, sir. I enjoy coming up with that sort of thing."

"And you do it exceptionally well. Congratulations and much encouragement are in order, whatever that modesty of yours might be telling you. It could be that Rome might have special uses for a man of your ingenuity."

They sat down on three separate benches, the trio of these finely wrought from local oak trees.

"Oak is such a superb wood," observed Pilatus. "It has no pretensions. It is what it is—strong, reliable, easy to work with. Do you not agree?"

Both legionnaires nodded, and Scipio added, "My father's hobby is working with wood, sir. He has been chosen by Caesar himself more than once to provide exquisite items for the grand palace in Rome."

"And it is only a hobby with him?" Pilatus asked.

"He can do little else, I am afraid. He is blind, sir."

"Blind and yet it is as though he can see!"

"Every figure is perfect, even the delicate wings of the figure of a small bird."

"Your father could not have been blind since birth then."

"He was injured in combat, sir. Blindness occurred slowly, over a period of months, his sight fading in stages."

"You were very young when that happened?" Pilatus said knowingly.

"I was. It was a terrible time for my family and me."

"Please tell me the details, young man."

"Thank you for being kind enough to ask, sir, but these cannot be important to someone such as yourself."

"They *are* important here, now, because I have made them such. Do tell me about how this father of yours coped with blindness."

"Badly at first. And this was in part because he thought that his usefulness to Rome was ended. Service on the battlefield had been his life. And when that was taken from him, my father wanted to die."

"You stopped your father from going as far as committing suicide, did you not?" Pilatus offered.

"I did. But how could you have known that, sir?"

"I have what some might call special powers of perception. I am considered an unsurpassed judge of human nature."

Pilatus lapsed into silence just then, his mind going back to that morning when he washed his hands of the blood of the Nazarene.

He held those hands out in front of him.

"They look so clean, do they not?" he asked.

The two legionnaires agreed quickly but were not certain what he was actually talking about, or the connection with Scipio's story.

"I judged this Jesus to be a good man," he spoke softly. "I looked into His eyes and I could see no hatred, no deception, no submerged violence waiting to gush forth—indeed, none of that of which He was accused."

"But, sir, why—?" Scipio started to ask but cut himself off when he saw Paetus's expression of warning.

"Please, go ahead," Pilatus assured him. "There is no punishment here. You ask whatever you wish. I pledge that I shall not have your head for it!"

Scipio cleared his throat nervously.

"Why did you send Him to Golgotha then?" he asked.

"I have been wrestling with that for the days and the nights since," Pilatus admitted. "And I come up only with reasons that are shameful."

Paetus and Scipio were startled by the candor of the man.

"Your expressions reveal your feelings," Pilatus commented. "But to be quite frank, I can hardly blame either of you. You see, the way I am feeling has been a surprise to me perhaps most of all."

"Sir, you wanted me to tell you about my father," Scipio reminded him.

"Yes, yes, please go on."

"But I would like to say something about my brother, who was a leper."

"Was a leper?" Pilatus said, not prepared for the past tense.

"That is correct, sir. He no longer is. My brother and an entire colony of others like him were healed by one of the followers of the Nazarene."

Pilatus stood suddenly and started pacing.

"That is, I believe, the same ability to heal that is reported Jesus himself had!" he exclaimed.

"I do not know about the truth of the rest of it, but I can confirm my own witness concerning my brother and a score of others. Yet even my parents thought me mad when I wrote to them about what had happened."

Realization came to Pilatus and the blood drained from his face. Feeling wobbly, the proconsul needed to sit down again.

"Can we help?" Paetus asked, genuinely concerned.

"No one can help," Pilatus replied with some weariness. "What I feel is a job for the gods themselves, but I can no longer be so deluded as to suppose that they exist at all, so I shall be forced to carry the burden quite alone."

Some time passed, the three of them just sitting there, quietly, only the occasional sounds of a nearby raven or a disagreeable donkey heard.

"Sir?" Paetus ventured. "I could not get my hands or the rest of my body free of His blood, no matter how I tried."

"You would wash your hands again, and again, and again, and still the blood would cling to your skin?" Pilatus asked, his head bowed, his words coming slowly as though he disliked the very speaking of them.

"There is a stream near our camp," Paetus continued. "I covered my entire body with the water, and yet I could never feel less than unclean, the memory of that blood, the smell of it strong without letup."

"You are free now, though, the way you talk of it?"

"I am."

"But how?"

"Through what happened at the tomb. Jesus the Christ washed everything away, my guilt, my shame, His blood from my body."

"You were healed of the spirit, is that it, young man?"

"That is a good way of expressing what happened, yes, sir."

Slowly, Pilatus stood again, with some anger, they thought, but his words told them otherwise.

"I want us to disguise ourselves," he said.

"Sir?" Paetus asked. "What are you saying? I do not understand."

"I am not certain that I understand it at all myself," Pilatus acknowledged with a bit of reluctance. "I want the three of us to walk among the common Jews of this area, but not the Sanhedrin, not those snobs and fools and wretched hypocrites. I have been forced to play a variety of silly games of intrigue with them, but they have not earned my respect for a single moment, not one, only my continuing contempt."

He faced them with an expression of anticipation.

"I want to meet the followers of this Jesus," Pilatus declared, "those who were healed by Him, who ate the loaves and the fishes I am told He was supposed to have provided in some miraculous manner."

"It would be easy for *us* to do this, but how would you keep from being recognized?" Paetus asked.

"I doubt that they have paid very much attention to me, nor have I given them much opportunity, frankly. I have stayed within my residence here or one of the others, especially at Caesaria. Procula has more than once expressed her dislike of mixing with the common folk, particularly those Jews whom she detests.

"We shall do what I have just stated in not more than two weeks from this moment. None of the three of us shall shave, so that we will look less like smooth-cheeked Romans. I will have servants buy clothes that these people wear.

"We study as much as we can about them. We will learn enough, in this week I have commanded, to pretend to be able to move among them without undue suspicion."

X

During those two weeks decreed by Pontius Pilatus, legionnaires Decimus Paetus and Fabius Scipio studied all that they could from whatever scrolls happened to be available. They also were allowed to go out on informational forays of their own once their faces had become sufficiently adorned by scraggly beard growth. They, as well as Pilatus himself, realized that this was scarcely a guarantee that they would be accepted as Jews, but that was not as important as forestalling any suspicion that they were Romans. Better a Gentile than a Roman, it seemed. The only justification for secrecy by Romans would be to go among them as spies.

Spies the two of them were, but for an entirely different reason than any of the Jews might suspect.

Paetus and Scipio soon became aware of where the disciples of Jesus the Christ had a habit of staying. One of those places was a large room on the second floor of a building in the midst of Jerusalem.

The inn keeper was paid a few denarii and, as a result, allowed the two disguised legionnaires upstairs.

"How could it matter?" he said. "That band has no hold on the place. But please hurry. I understand that they may be returning tonight. There is a ceremony of some sort that one of them said the group wanted to perform."

In the center was a long table. On top were empty goblets and a ladle with some bread crumbs remaining.

"Thirteen cushions," Scipio said. "Twelve disciples plus Jesus Himself!"

"You speak of Him with reverence now," Paetus pointed out.

"And do you not *think* of Him in such a manner?" the young legionnaire retorted. "You called Him *Lord, Lord* only days ago, did you not?"

Paetus smiled at his friend's spunk.

"Yes, I did, I did. But what we saw was nearly two weeks ago, Fabius. Can we be so sure that our minds were not deceiving us and, therefore, our eyes as well?"

"Did it not seem real at the time?"

"Yes, it did. . . ."

Paetus hesitated at that. He had had his sight affected, his emotions stirred mightily. But memories derived from seeing and feelings themselves all were transitory at best. Nothing lingered of that moment as far as he, Decimus Paetus, was concerned, while Scipio had the advantage having witnessed his brother's healing in person, something that was capable of reinforcing his experience literally every minute of every hour of every day.

And yet his Roman skepticism could not resist trying to find some explanation that had no physical foundation to it.

"So you supposedly witnessed that remarkable sight of your brother and many lepers suddenly whole again, without a trace of their former condition."

"I am not given to flights of unrestrained imagination," the younger man protested.

"And so I am going to assume that such healings are around every corner and in every nook and cranny, is that what you are suggesting?"

"Am I wrong, comrade?"

"You are *very* wrong!"

They searched the room, which had cabinets attached to the walls, then stopped before a small alcove with a bare wood stool in front of it.

Some scrolls were on the floor next to the alcove, tucked into that corner of the room.

Scipio picked these up, handing a few over to Paetus and reading through several that he kept.

"Blessed are the meek," Paetus said out loud. "Where would we be if we were meek, Fabius? But then you have seen little combat thus far. You may not realize the absurdity of that statement as much as I do."

"But if the enemy had been meek," Scipio suggested, "there might be no wars."

"How right you are. If *they* were meek, they'd be easier to kill, and we would have fewer opponents!"

Scipio put all but one scroll back where he had found them.

"You retain just that single scroll," Paetus noted. "What does it say?"

"In it, this Jesus talks about heaven."

"How would *He* know anything about a place that only the gods can speak of, if they and it exist at all, I should say!"

"Jesus claims that He took human form to be among us."

Paetus threw the scrolls he had been holding back in the corner and tore that final one out of the young legionnaire's grasp.

"You do not want to listen because everything you have thought important until now would be endangered," Scipio told him pointedly, then walked over to the table, sat down on one of the long benches in front of it, and bowed his head.

Paetus politely waited until he was finished.

"You act as though you yourself were a follower of the Nazarene," he observed. "Were you praying to this Jehovah they have been talking about?"

Scipio looked up at him, tears trickling down his cheeks.

"Yes. . . ."

Paetus was not pleased.

"I thought you more intelligent than that," he said. "I thought you more loyal to Rome, Fabius."

"I have no wish to betray anyone or anything and certainly not Caesar," Scipio tried to assure him. "But I have *every* wish to pursue the freedom to worship as I please. The empire guarantees that, you know."

"Tolerates is the better word, my friend. But never at the expense of what Caesar deems necessary to maintain control of all conquered lands."

"How is my simple prayer colliding with the will of Imperial Rome?"

Paetus softened his manner as he sat down next to the young legionnaire.

"Mere words alone, short of outright sedition, cannot be the difficulty. It is what they portend that is the root of what worries me."

He put his arm around Scipio.

"My young friend, let me ask you something, please?"

"Anything you like."

"If ordered to do so, would you round up the remaining disciples of Jesus the Christ and execute them by your own hand?"

"That is too hypothetical, Decimus. It is a foolish question. Nothing like that would ever happen."

"Would you?" Paetus persisted.

"I would—," Scipio started to say, then turned his head away so that the other man could not see the expression on his face.

"Would what, Fabius? Finish what you were just now going to tell me."

"I would not shed the blood . . of a brother in Christ . . . whatever the circumstances might be. I would rather put myself in his place and die for him."

"Very noble but very dangerous. No one else should hear you speak in any manner such as that."

"Are you going to tell anyone, Decimus?"

"I may not be a brother in Christ, as you say, but I am not someone who would hand a friend over to Pilatus or anyone else with the authority to sentence him to death."

They had not noted the passage of time. Light was dimming, the sun's rays retreating from the two small windows side by side in the room.

"We must be getting back," Paetus said.

"I cannot go," Scipio told him.

"You are talking from your emotions. Not going back would mean that you had deserted, and you would be executed as soon as you were found. I will forget that you said anything about not going back with me."

"But you must go alone, friend Decimus," Scipio persisted. "Forget my words or not, I can *never* return."

"You are acting like a—"

Paetus was interrupted by sounds coming from the street outside. He rushed to the windows, which faced in the same direction, and peered through them.

"The disciples of Jesus!" he exclaimed nervously after a moment. "The whole motley group of them is here now."

"We have nothing to fear from these men," Scipio tried to convince him. "I, for one, am bound together with them now in a spirit of love, and that same spirit could be yours so easily, Decimus!"

"Fear has nothing to do with it, my young comrade. I know, with the might of Rome supporting us, that we do not have to cower before any riffraff like them. I merely want to hear what these people talk about when they are alone with one another.

"We either learn some of what Pilatus has assigned us to learn, or we find out that perhaps they are just ordinary insurrectionists in disguise, and then we will have no choice but to expose this duplicitous bunch for what they have always been—liars to the core. In the process, if any of that is true, we are certain to receive special commendations from the hand of the divine Caesar himself!"

"But, Decimus, Caesar is not—"

"Stop jabbering, Fabius. We will hide in the pottery closet over there. Hopefully they will not be gathered here for a very long time. When they have left, we ourselves will go. That is an order. *Understood?*"

Scipio nodded obediently.

It was only a few seconds after the two legionnaires had carefully shut the door behind them and crouched down on the floor that the remaining disciples of the Nazarene entered that upper room.

XI

The eleven of them went through a ceremony that had been performed the day before Jesus had been arrested by Pilatus. Paetus and Scipio listened to every word, from the eating of the bread in commemoration of the broken body of the Nazarene to the drinking of wine from a single goblet as a testimony to His shed blood.

Paetus became a little weak as the ceremony reached that point. His reaction to piercing the side of Jesus came back to him.

I only wanted to wash the blood away, he thought, *and here these men are intent on drinking wine as a symbol of that very blood!*

"Are you all right?" Scipio whispered into his ear.

Paetus nodded, although if it were not so dark in the pottery closet it would be clear that the pale, almost sickly pallor of his face seemed to contradict his words.

They heard conversation after the ceremony, talk about the miracles of Jesus and how much He was missed by each of the men.

And then words spoken about something else, an earlier visitation by one they were calling the risen Christ.

"*Jesus!*" one had cried apparently. "You are *alive!*"

"Oh, Jesus, Jesus," another had called out. "If I could but believe that it was you!"

"Thomas, my dear friend," Jesus had said, "put your hands into the print of the nails in My hands. And put your fingers into the print of the nails in My feet."

Thomas had protested, but Jesus stopped him. "No, Thomas, take your hand and place it into My side and be sure it is I before you this very moment."

Thomas had dropped to his knees, then cried out, awestruck, "Jesus . . . my Savior, my Lord."

The disciples stopped the recollection, exhausted by it as they had been when the events first occurred.

There was silence for several minutes, then the sound of someone gasping.

A voice. A voice like the one at the tomb, so rich and strong that it could not be mistaken for other than what it was.

Paetus fell back against a row of pottery.

"What was that sound?" somebody said. "Listen!"

"At the closet over there!"

Paetus could not help himself. Someone else had been asked to do what he himself had done just days earlier.

"Decimus, Decimus," Scipio begged, becoming increasingly frantic. "What is wrong? Are you having a—?"

His words were interrupted as the door to the pottery closet was flung open, and they found themselves looking at the resurrected body of Jesus the Christ.

Decimus Paetus had not forgotten one second of the encounter at the tomb. It was doubtful that any man could have. But his life had not changed since then because, he rationalized, those moments were just a few out of a lifetime, with little lasting impact, making up only a small percentage of the years he had spent in service to Rome.

Paetus had been looking forward to his coming retirement, which was when the government would give him—as it did in the case of each and every legionnaire who completed a full term of enlistment—a generous parcel of land as a gift, encouraging him to farm it and bring it to a high level of productivity and allowing him to earn enough money to support himself and the family he surely would have by then.

After the first few heady years of excitement felt by most legionnaires, the years of exaltation that came from knowing what they represented, Paetus had settled down into a routine of waiting, waiting for a centurion to come to him, give him his papers, shake his hand, and wish him the very best.

He had fancied that moment many times, anticipating those final decades of his life being spent in a satisfyingly quiet existence, with some farm animals and some crops, and a lusty woman as his wife.

But now he was on his knees, as before, and looking up into a face that possessed eyes that cut through to the very depths of his soul.

"Decimus, Decimus, I told you before that you were special among men," that rich, kind, deep voice spoke. "This is true, and it is not something you can turn your back on, nor will you do so."

Paetus wanted to object, wanted to say again and again that he was not special, that he was an ordinary man, like any other legionnaire embodying the might of Imperial Rome, one among tens of thousands.

He did not say any of this, thinking the words only, and yet Jesus the Christ knew them as though they had been shouted from the Forum in Rome before a gathered multitude.

The Nazarene spoke with a voice of such clarity as none of them had ever before heard. "You will be forgotten by the generations to come after you. No man will speak your name. No scroll will contain it. Yet

Decimus Paetus, some forty years from this moment, nine hundred and sixty human beings, on a high and isolated place in the midst of the wilderness, will accept you as a brother and friend because you will have chosen to devote the remainder of your days to the cause for which each and every one of them will be giving their lives.

"You will be to a handful an instrument of righteousness since you are to bring a message of redemption so strong and so beautiful that, at the end of their mortal lives, some of them will turn to you, Decimus Paetus, for the hope of eternity, and you will give forth the very truth that will free them from the flesh-and-blood domination they fought so hard to overthrow."

"I know not of what You speak, sir," Paetus confessed. "I—"

Now also on his knees, Scipio interrupted joyously, "I think I see. Oh, I think I see what is to be!"

He reached up both hands toward Jesus the Christ.

"Touch me . . . Lord," he asked.

Which Jesus did, taking Scipio's young hands and folding His own around them.

"You are *real*," the legionnaire gasped. "I do not imagine You. You were dead, but now You are alive!"

"And you, Fabius Scipio, will be in Rome the day in burns," Jesus told him. "You will save the lives of many."

"Rome burning?" It was Paetus's turn to interrupt. "How could that be?"

Jesus then spoke of a madman who would view the Roman Empire as his own personal plaything, someone who would horrify the known world with his actions.

"And *I* will help?" repeated Scipio uncertainly. "Decimus here will stand with a thousand souls and be God's instrument for salvation for those who believe, and I will save hundreds in the midst of a burning Rome?"

Jesus nodded.

"Thousands will live to tell their children of you, Fabius, unto generations far removed from this day."

"But, surely, no one will of me, good sir?" Paetus spoke, not entirely pleased with that turn of events.

Jesus bent down and cupped His hands lovingly around the veteran legionnaire's weathered cheeks.

"Do not be like the religious hypocrites, with their public prayers, to be heard by all within the reach of their voices," He said. "Do not seek to do your good deeds in the center of the public square. There is but one witness of consequence—your heavenly Father. None other shall ever truly matter."

"Will I die in Your service?" Paetus asked.

"Yes, Decimus. But you shall also is also decreed that you shall join Me past the gates of heaven, as the angels raise their voices in welcome."

"And my friend Fabius here?"

"He will be waiting for you, along with the other two."

Paetus' eyes widened.

"We will be reunited?"

"Forever."

It was then that the two legionnaires were given, in a single moment, a glimpse of heaven, and ten thousand angels singing a triumphant hallelujah chorus.

A glimpse which the disciples of Jesus shared.

And now everyone in that upper room, Jew and Roman alike, immediately fell forward on their faces.

Cries of "Savior and Lord!" rose from the lips of the thirteen there.

Then Jesus the Christ was gone from that place, but not yet from their lives.

XII

Decimus Paetus and Fabius Scipio did not return that afternoon to report anything to Pontius Pilatus.

Nor the day after that.

Until a full week had passed since they left on their mission, and there was as yet no word from either of the legionnaires.

"Have Paetus and young Scipio betrayed me?" he reluctantly suggested to Procula on the evening of the eighth day.

The two were having dinner by themselves, no guests at the long, hand-carved cherry wood table, only servants coming in to leave another course or to take a previous one that had been consumed.

Pilatus glanced around the pillared room for a moment, looking at the familiar statues of Zeus, Diana, Neptune, and other gods, each set in a white marbled alcove.

"From cold stone they came," he mused mournfully, "and cold stone is all that they shall ever be."

"Blasphemy!" Procula said in mock offense.

"Truth, my dear wife. Some imaginative individual had a self-inflicted vision many centuries ago, and then someone else during another period following it, and so on, and so on, and, thus, shall we say, the magnificent gods who are worshiped daily by Romans and their subjects were born."

"Are you suggesting that we have no gods after all, Pontius?" Procula said in a slow, calculated manner.

"Not gods, only delusions to which we cling in desperation."

"But why are they necessary at all in light of the majesty, the power of this empire that you serve so well?"

"So well? Ah, but some would disagree with that."

"You did not answer my question, Pontius."

"Perhaps because I did not want to, Procula."

"And why would that be so?"

"You must examine your own self to provide the answer, my love."

He studied Procula for a moment: a woman with delicate features, a face one of the more artful sculptors could have designed only on his very best day of creativity. Although other women of Rome's elite class would don wigs that used either blonde hair from the Germans or red hair from the barbarians in the north, Procula found this affectation quite unnecessary and more than a bit offensive.

But, then, my dear, he thought, *your hair is so magnificent that no wig could improve upon its crowning touch.*

Indeed, Procula had a great deal of hair, the lightest brown imaginable, almost blonde in its subtle shade, which her *ornatrix* braided for her in a manner that no wig could ever match. Since her face was long and delicate-looking, she had had the part placed into the middle of her forehead, with the strands framing her cheeks. If her face had been round, she would have put a knot on top, and uncovered her ears.

Procula did give in to ostentation, however, with a comb of tortoise shell attached to the hair on the left side of her head, and little vials of perfume hanging at intervals from the top, the right side, and the long, flowing sweep of hair down her back. For some women, similar vials would contain very effective poison instead, just in case they tired of whoever their male companion happened to be at the time and saw no other way to extricate themselves from the suddenly banal relationship. The effect of the poison simulated, or perhaps produced, a heart attack and was quite undetectable.

But not those dyes, like so many other women, Pilatus reminded himself, with a bit of pride surfacing. *I have become quite tired of seeing other beautiful creatures crowned with red so intense that it seems their heads are on fire! I am very glad that yellows and blues are taboo, except for the courtesans.*

A sad thought rose up.

So beautiful, so sensual, yet always one step closer to madness . . .

He knew there had been clues since the beginning of their relationship, emotional highs and lows coming sometimes scarcely within minutes of one another. When she learned of the transfer from Rome to Judea, she was at first delighted, then deeply melancholic, and had remained in the latter state, with the slightest mild variations, ever since.

Procula, once she had settled in Caesaria or one of the other residences, would go on redecorating sprees, spending sums well beyond her allowance. Tiberius liked her very much—there were rumors that the two had had an affair before she and Pilatus had married—and continually gave her husband increases to cover her excesses.

But still she would end up depressed. Not all the silk curtains or marble walkways or sumptuous beds with stuffed pillows from Egypt could give her what she missed in her life, an inner core of peace.

Pilatus had found none of this coveted peace himself but he dealt with the existing vacuum in quite different ways from Procula. He administered Roman law. He engaged in intrigues with the Jewish leaders.

He kept his finger on the pulse of what was happening back in Rome. He devised campaigns to thwart the intentions of the insurrectionists. And he dedicated himself to being a source of strength and stability to the woman he had loved with great intensity for a very long time.

Yet for troubled Procula Pilatus, there seemed little long-term hope—until the Nazarene entered their lives.

Increasingly, she had been focusing her attention on the Nazarene, this Jesus whom some also called the Christ, the prophesied so-called Messiah of the Jewish people. She had come to see and to hear Him at first as merely an object of curiosity, with no intellectual or spiritual pretensions attached to her action, though later that was not the case.

She would lose herself in the crowds that followed Jesus wherever He went, sitting or standing often for hours with the rest of the listeners, transfixed by every word this remarkable teacher uttered and taking these back with her, to recall and study again and again after she returned to Caesaria or Jerusalem, but afraid to tell Pilatus for fear he would think it all was part of the process of an accelerating breakdown and because of that perhaps ship her back to Rome where she would be forced to live in glorified seclusion like some kind of mental leper.

I could not endure that, she had reasoned. *I could not endure the whispers of other women, the sideward glances, the look of condescension on their faces when they were no longer able to avoid contact with me. I should think my mind would deteriorate further, rather than be healed of its supposed maladies, and I would soon walk the halls of even a gilded palace in Rome, screaming incoherently . . .*

"I shall have to go after them," Pilatus's quite somber voice intruded upon that moment of reflection. "They may have been murdered by Barabbas or perhaps the vengeful disciples of the Nazarene Himself."

"Not the disciples, if those men *are* dead," she said quickly, perhaps too quickly. "It could never be one of them, Pontius."

He looked at her, noticing that anxious interjection.

"How can you say that, Procula," he observed, "at least with the kind of certainty your voice betrays?"

"They are dedicated to salvation, not destruction."

"You have heard words only. Talk is very easy . . . a rather mechanical exercise, in fact. Words alone offer no assurances, at least from strangers."

"You suggest that they are lying, these dedicated men?"

"I suggest that that is a possibility, my love."

"Then those words you just uttered . . . my love . . . I can assume that they mean nothing then, that they never have."

"It is not the same. You are hardly a stranger, my dearest."

"But they are hardly liars because they are strangers," she retorted, with some anger in her voice.

Pilatus chuckled heartily.

"Would you expect less of me?" Procula asked, offended by his manner, which suggested that it was unusual for a mere woman to be so quick-witted.

"I would not."

"Then why do you mock me with your laughter?"

"I was appreciating your forthrightness, not mocking your impetuosity. There is a difference, Procula."

Her face turned red as she realized how rash she had been.

"When do you start your search?" she asked, thinking it best to try to change the direction of the conversation.

"In the morning."

"Would you delay it one day?"

"Why?"

"I should like to see what I can learn."

"From the Nazarene's followers?"

"Yes."

"So, that is why you tried to get me to release Him," Pilatus said, "rather than send the man to die at Golgotha!"

"You make it sound like a conspiracy."

"That thought did occur to me, Procula."

"I have never spoken with any of them."

"But in my absence, you joined the crowds that followed them everywhere. Or am I mistaken, dearest?"

"Yes, I did that, Pontius."

He fell back against the leather-strung chair in which he had been sitting.

"I must admit," he spoke after a moment, "that if you can find anyone or anything undetected, it would be considerably better than doing so through dozens of my legionnaires searching them out."

"I have your permission then?" Procula dutifully asked, reflecting the social conventions of that era.

"You do, but then why are you seeking it now? Not having it does not seem to have perplexed you before."

She had no answer.

"Never mind," Pilatus said. "You have a day. Please, be careful. I could not bear to lose you, my dear."

As she looked at him, a single tear trickled down her right cheek.

"Do not seem so surprised," he told her uncomfortably.

"Otherwise you would not have put up with me for so long?"

"I did not say that."

"I love you for it, Pontius, I love you so much indeed."

"Go! Make your preparations. Take Sabina and—"

"Alone, my dear Pontius," insisted Procula. "Having an entourage would raise suspicions from the start."

"But you have seldom been anywhere alone," he reminded her, not without kindness in his manner.

Procula knew that he was right. Even when she went on those earlier occasions and listened to the words of Jesus, she had not less than two servants with her.

"This can be a dangerous country, and we are in a uncertain era now. It could be risky, what you are suggesting, especially for the wife of the governor of Judea. We do, after all, represent a conquering nation."

"All the more reason not to draw attention to myself."

He sighed, knowing when his wife had won an argument, and reached across the table, taking both her hands in his own.

"If I were a Jew or one of those so devoted to the Nazarene, I probably would say at this point that I shall pray for your safety."

"But you cannot pray to empty air, Pontius."

She had touched a nerve with that remark.

"That is why I shall indicate only that my greatest wish is for your safety tomorrow and always."

"Pontius, I—," Procula started to say, then stopped, biting her lower lip, her discomfort apparent.

"Is there anything wrong?" he asked.

She stood quickly, and turned away so that he could not see the tears coming more freely down both cheeks.

Lord, I cannot tell my husband as yet what I have done, she thought. *Forgive me for my reticence, forgive me, blessed Savior.*

XIII

Procula Pilatus left her husband's presence and prepared for her journey into Jerusalem. She had not told him that for months she had been forming links with Jews close to the band of followers who had been tagging along with Jesus virtually everywhere He went, merchants who gave that group food and money and sometimes clothing, as well as landlords willing to turn over spare rooms to them for a night.

What impressed her was that they seemed to be dependent solely upon the generosity of others.

How could that be? she asked herself. *To go from place to place, with no income assured, with no clear-cut destination in mind, drifting only?*

And yet, she had heard, Jesus and His men did not consider their travels to be mere idle wanderings from village to village throughout Judea. They claimed that wherever they went was in fact ordained by the God they purported to be serving, and they were simply being attentive to His leading in their lives.

But they also believed something else, something that she had dismissed as ludicrous when she first learned of it.

That Jesus Himself was—

Her throat constricted at the thought, for it was so preposterous and yet so audacious at the same time.

—the Son of the living God, and there proved to be continuous direct communication between Father and Son!

Procula's hand trembled in the simple process of wiping makeup off her face—she had decided that it would be wiser to go into the city with a plainer look, so as not to draw attention to herself—as she considered the significance of that statement, which seemed so arrogant, and yet if it were true!

She dropped the piece of moist cotton she had been using and tried to steady both hands now.

"If it is true, as I feel in my very soul that it is, then Pontius sanctioned the blasphemous execution of . . . divinity!" she exclaimed, realizing that she could afford this moment of candor since she was alone and could not be overheard. "And if that were the case, then all those stories about a resurrection on the third day, together with what Pontius and I had found at the tomb . . . it means that—"

She realized that she had become a Christian without understanding everything about what that meant. At some point she felt she was simply affirming her belief in His goodness and the resulting injustice of His death.

Lord, I cannot tell my husband as yet what I have done, she thought. *Forgive me for my reticence, forgive me, blessed Savior.*

Even when she had prayed in that manner such a short while ago, it was scarcely clear to her exactly what she was doing, the implications of those passionate words.

Savior . . .

She had always thought Rome had played that role in her life, and so did many of the others who served the empire.

"We look to Rome for the satisfaction of all our needs and the fulfillment of all our desires," she whispered.

Rome gave her the man she loved. Rome gave her the emperor she was supposed to be worshiping.

I have slept with a god, she thought, with a bit of sarcasm, *but my husband proved to be a far better lover. And now there is this Jesus.*

She found him to be an attractive man, tall, strong-looking, with a long, lean face that betrayed large cheekbones and a jutting, dimpled chin.

But curiously she felt no sexual attraction, though such a man ordinarily would have stirred erotic desire within her.

When I saw Him, I was moved by Him but with feelings of a much different sort, she recalled. *And then that day, when He looked into my eyes and seemed to know every thought in my mind, every emotion in my—*

She held her hand out in front of her.

He took my hand, and I felt something quite wonderful radiate throughout my body. But then His expression turned sad. I asked Him why He seemed to be on the verge of tears, and He chose not to answer but turned away. I was prepared to do anything for Him, call Him any name He desired, for He had only to ask whatever He wished of me.

She remembered how the two female servants had reacted, thinking that Jesus had put some kind of spell over her.

"Sorcery!" one of them protested. "This Jesus of Nazareth is nothing more than a common sorcerer!"

Procula had shaken her head in reaction to those words of doubt.

"No, it is something else," she said firmly but with no tone of reprimand in her voice. "I have a clear head this day. I do not feel myself at all controlled by this man. It is something I cannot explain."

The two women with her were not convinced.

"You should tell your husband," the other one offered. "He can take you to a doctor who might be able to deal with whatever this Jesus has done to you."

"Jesus has done nothing *to* me," Procula asserted. "I think, yea, I think He has done something *for* me!"

Both servants stared at her, at the expression on her face.

"There is a look about your eyes," the first one acknowledged grudgingly, well-familiar after long service with the various depressive states into which Procula would often sink and not come out of for a number of hours, sometimes days.

"What do you see now?"

"I cannot say."

This servant, who had been with her since the early days in Rome, was clearly becoming uncomfortable.

"Please try," Procula insisted.

The woman bowed her head, blushing.

"What is it?" Procula asked.

"You seem more at peace," she said, with obvious difficulty, "and suddenly so. I have not noticed this to be the case with you before now."

"Seconds ago, you felt this was a spell cast upon me by a magician."

The servant started to cry.

"Please forgive me," she begged.

Both women fell to their knees in front of her.

"Do not do this," Procula urged. "You must not bow before me as though in worship or fear. Please stand . . . please stand now!"

They obeyed her.

"If this Jesus be a sorcerer," Procula told them, "then I shall indeed need help, and I hope you will remain at my side as always. But I cannot find in me any basis for believing that He is. I perceive no threat from Him. I harbor no fear in my heart. Can either of you, searching your heart, feel differently?"

The two servant women glanced at one another.

"Should we not go after Jesus then," both blurted out at once.

"We cannot linger away from the residence any longer," Procula advised them, "for my husband will grow concerned."

Yet, after hesitating for a moment, torn between the wisdom of what she had said and a very real urge to follow after the Nazarene wherever He was going, the three of them embraced as they stood in the middle of that dusty, continually busy main road outside Jerusalem, not knowing exactly what was happening in their suddenly confused lives but willing to submit themselves to it at least for some while longer.

XIV

Being alone in the midst of a crowd was a new experience for Procula Pilatus.

One of the realities of having an influential husband was all the attention that went with such a prestigious appointment in those days, even though her husband suspected that his post had far more to do with getting him out of Rome-based politics where he could become a threat to one group or the other.

Whatever the case, position and power were treated in godlike fashion in the Rome that existed then, and Pontius Pilatus had both. But that also meant that people were hanging around Procula incessantly, waiting on her, responding to the slightest command.

And I am so unworthy, she thought, as a carriage driver dropped her off near the main gate leading into Jerusalem. *They do this fawning only because it is expected of them, for there is no respect that I have earned, there is only, beneath the surface civility, a loathing. I am a woman, not a goddess, and yet their women must treat me with nearly as much deference, and they hate me for this, especially since they have but one God, and they come close to blasphemy by according me the treatment Roman laws mandate.*

"I will return in two hours as you have directed," the driver told her.

"That is fine," she replied. "I expect to be here, waiting for you."

She approached the tall, wide, carved stone archway and smelled immediately the odors of that ancient city.

They do not keep it as clean as Rome, she observed. *This place is horrid —it smells like a tomb.*

The narrow, cobblestoned streets that passed between two and three story buildings where thousands of people lived in dreary one or two room residences were crowded with monkeys and camels, passersby as well as merchants standing just outside their shops trying to sell linens and trinkets and food stuffs and whatever else.

There was no plumbing in all of Jerusalem. Water was always obtained from wells available to the public at large. Open gutters provided the only means of draining waste materials away from homes.

The odors throughout the city were pungent, to put it mildly. As Procula walked past window after window, in addition to the sewerage outside, she caught whiffs of burning oil, which came from earthenware lamps inside, a stale, spoiled, fatty odor added to all the others that drenched ancient Jerusalem.

Scattered piles of animal dung had to be avoided, as did the sprawled bodies of beggars who had passed out from hunger or illness. Those still alert, many of them blind, reached out with their little cups, raspy voices calling out for mercy.

Usually, in the past, when she ventured into Jerusalem, it was to do shopping. She had been allocated 400 denarii a day for luxuries, which was a handsome sum, especially when just one denarius would have been considered ample pay for a common laborer.

In addition, she had a very large budget for various foodstocks, and she ended up spending much time in a single part of Jerusalem that had been named the Street of Butchers, which was where fresh meat was bought, most of it sold by scribes and teachers who considered butchery a trade.

Suddenly Procula heard noises directly ahead of her, many people screaming, carts being overturned, animals adding to the cacophony as they were startled by whatever it was that was going on.

"Leper! Leper!" the words rose like a tornado, ripping through the crowds filling the crammed streets.

Procula flattened herself against the nearest wall, other women as well as men on either side of her.

The leper was young, a teenager, in fact. He appeared to her right and started to stumble past her on feet where his condition had eaten away all the toes. Most of his fingers were gone also, and his face had become quite grotesque, large growths all over it, several of those in the area of his left eye, closing it altogether.

He stopped for a moment in front of her. His gaze met hers, and he started to open his mouth as though to say something.

Procula saw on that tortured face of his, with its one visible, blood-shot eye, the most anguish she had ever witnessed in another human being. All the years of his progressive malady seemed crystallized for her in those two or three seconds.

She reached into a pocket of the black robelike garment she was wearing, and took out a small coin.

The young leper smiled, grabbed it quickly with the two remaining fingers of that one hand, for an instant his flesh almost touching hers, and then he was gone up the street as a pair of legionnaires came running after him.

Procula was tempted to step out in front of them and order the two to let the poor teenager go on his way, but she resisted the impulse, fearing that if he would continue to stay within the close confines of Jerusalem his disease could be spread in an epidemic there throughout the citizenry and later, the entire country.

Through no fault of her own, even such a highbred woman proved to be a captive of the prevailing medical ignorance that characterized his condition, having no more insight than anyone else, though she never went so far as to accept as valid the wild tales that lepers were riffraff who had allowed themselves to become demon-possessed, the demon in each case changing the sufferer's physical into that of its own hideous image.

Finally, the momentary terror of the throng that had frozen everyone where they stood subsided and people started to mill about again.

Shaken, Procula managed to continue on her way, toward the large bazaar area in the center of Jerusalem, where she had seen Jesus speak on more than one occasion. She was hoping that perhaps she might find one of His disciples there or at least someone who would know where they might be.

Abruptly she felt quite faint, not able so quickly to shake the troubling impression her brief encounter had left with her.

"May I help you?" she heard someone say.

She looked up, saw a very large man standing in front of her.

"The fisherman!" she exclaimed.

"Yes, that is what some call me," he acknowledged. "I must say that you yourself look familiar."

"I spend much time here," she replied, bending the truth only somewhat.

"Your face is so white. You seemed to be on the verge of falling a moment ago."

"I have not been well lately."

Inadvertently emphasizing this, another dizzy spell gripped her, and she fell into the strong arms of Simon Peter, who smelled of fish oil.

He picked her up and carried her into a nearby building where he put her down on a simple straw bed.

"I shall fetch you some wine," he said. "Perhaps your stomach is upset."

The thought of cheap Jewish wine in her mouth and coursing down her throat made Procula protest.

"Is there nothing else?" she asked plaintively. "Surely, poor wine can do me more harm than good."

"This is not my residence. It happens to be that of a friend. He is not here now. I cannot say if there is anything other than the wine available."

Reluctantly Procula agreed to take the wine because she knew she had to have something or she would lose consciousness altogether.

The fisherman brought it to her in a large earthen scoop, lifting her head up gently and putting the edge to her lips, the taste a pleasant surprise.

"I think I *have* seen you before," he said as he sat down on a stone slab next to the bed. "Were you not at various places where the Master spoke?"

She nodded weakly.

"Are you one of those who believe that He is the Messiah?" Peter asked, his manner surprisingly gentle, given the bulk of the man.

Procula hesitated. She wanted to say yes, but the reason for her journey in the first place was to find out what all this meant.

"I have called him Savior," she said.

Peter broke out into a broad smile.

"That is wonderful to hear," he replied.

"But I do not understand what I have done," Procula added.

The fisherman turned serious then.

"You have heard some of His teachings," he remarked, "a few insights here and there, but you have no idea how these may fit together, is that it?"

It was Procula's turn to smile, just a bit, in appreciation of how perceptive this supposedly common man was.

"You speak well," she told him.

"And you are surprised at that?"

"I must say that I am."

"My friends and I owe that to Jesus as well."

"Did He teach you?"

"He did. Jesus gave all of us knowledge. And He spoke what He did more perfectly than any other man."

Procula chuckled a bit at that.

"More so than the most learned scholars?" she jested.

"They merely discover knowledge that He had before the world began."

If Peter had not been so firm, seemingly so clearheaded when he said that, she would have burst out laughing.

"This Jesus was still a young man when He died," she pointed out. "And the world has been in existence for so many years. How can you say what you have?"

"Jesus is alive, not dead," Peter told her.

"I was at the tomb. I saw the empty grave. But that proves nothing."

"Then why do you go so far as you do? Why do you call Him Savior and yet not know whereof you speak?"

Procula thought about that. Yes, there had been something in the presence of Jesus when He spoke . . . and also that brief meeting after He had been scourged and mocked prior to His crucifixion.

Sorrow.

Not hatred or a desire for vengeance, only deep anguish over the actions of those around Him.

"'For they know not what they do . . .'" Procula said out loud.

"You heard Him?" Peter asked.

Procula had tried to block that image from her mind, those words of unfathomable forgiveness. Facing Him earlier, just after He had been beaten so badly by several of her husband's legionnaires, was deeply disturbing, but then, as she stood near that middle cross and saw the Nazarene hanging from it, a crown of thorns resting on top of His head, the sharp points pressed into His skin, moans of pain escaping His lips every few seconds, she thought she herself would die on that very spot, believing Him to be innocent, and fearing the wrathful judgment of the Roman gods for this despicable act.

"Yes, I was there," she told the fisherman.

"I hid in shame," he admitted. "because I had protested three times that I did not know this Man. I betrayed His trust, and I could not face seeing Him like that."

"You feared the Romans?"

There was no answer.

Peter started to speak but turned away, his shoulders sagging.

"I want to learn more," Procula stated. "Will you help me, fisherman?"

This very large man whispered his answer, so low, so filled with guilt that it was barely discernible to her ears.

"Yes . . ." he said. "Yes, I will help you."

* * *

Pontius Pilatus held the gold and ruby chain admiringly in front of him. It had been offered as a gift from a tribal leader in Ethiopia.

Not to me, he thought. *Its intended recipient is Procula. She is known to be beautiful. Men of every region want to give to her whatever is allowed. Some would like to go beyond that, but they fear the retribution of Rome.*

But Procula had left that morning. She could not take the chain personally, so he interceded and convinced the chieftain that it should be left in temporary possession of the proconsul of Judea.

"This chain is, I fear, sadly unworthy of your wife, sir," the tall, colorfully garbed Ethiopian said through an interpreter, "but it is the finest example of handcrafted work that we have in our country. I trust that she will not be too offended by it."

Pilatus smiled with appreciation and thanked him.

"You are kind," he said. "I know that my wife Procula will be much honored by your gracious act."

The Ethiopian and his entourage bowed as protocol required and quickly left. A moment later, Pilatus retired to his bedroom quarters.

"We have treasures, you and I," he said out loud, "and how very beautiful they all are, gathered here before me."

He was thinking of other gifts—silks and furs and gold and other jewels as well as hand-carved ivory and wood items—all of which had been given by representatives of conquered nations, allies of Rome as well as others more interested in maintaining cordial relations than any show of noble generosity.

A whole large room full of these, Pilatus thought. *Procula would enter it periodically and select a bit of fur to wrap around her or perhaps a bauble to slip onto her finger, or just stand there, in the midst of all that wealth.*

He had found her doing so a few months earlier and surprised her by a quiet entry and a gentle tap on the shoulder.

Procula swung around and faced her husband, and he saw that she had been crying, her cheeks moist.

"What is wrong, my love?" he asked, concerned.

"This is all we have," she said.

"But what bothers you about that, Procula? Are these not beautiful things to feast one's eyes upon?"

"That is truly what they are, Pontius, mere *things!*"

"What else is there?"

"I cannot say. I feel so empty at the center of my being. And nothing seems to help, nothing gives me peace."

"Could it not be your—?" he started to say, then stopped, regretting going even that far, for he knew what would follow from her lips.

"My mind?" she added for him. "My troubled mind that always seems wreathed in darkness? You were going to say something like that, were you not, husband? I have guessed the truth with great accuracy—admit, Pontius!"

He kept quiet, not wishing to fuel the display of madness that seemed unstoppable, then and on previous occasions.

"These adorn but our outer selves and are only a facade, you know," she said as she walked over to an ornately carved chest of solid gold that contained pure-black pearls from one of the Mediterranean provinces. "We wear them in public, along with our finest attire, and we have our ready smiles, and the masses adore us."

94

She stood quietly for a moment before saying, "But what are we like inside, my dear Pontius? If we were happier, kinder; if we put aside these trappings and eschewed all the power of Rome, would that not be wonderful?"

"Without the power of Rome, as you call it, in our lives, we would be little better than the masses of which you speak," he reminded her.

"And what is wrong with *them?*" she asked pointedly.

"Their kind are without learning, their culture is abysmally crude, if you can call what they have culture in the first place, and they seem more like brute beasts than sophisticated, intelligent human beings."

Procula sighed as she said, "To them, *we* seem vain, we worship make-believe gods, we indulge our passions without restraint, we—"

Pilatus slapped her, instantly regretting such an impetuous act, and wrapped his arms around that slender body.

"Please, please forgive me," he implored.

"Oh, I do, Pontius," she told him. "We are what we are, and I can scarce condemn the man I truly, truly love as much as life itself."

While holding Procula and instinctively sensing the gulf that was increasing between them, quite beyond his apparent control, Pontius Pilatus wondered how much longer the two of them would remain together. Months after that singular incident, as he awaited her return, the same dark thought would enter his mind.

She wanted to go out there alone, he reminded himself. *Yet I could never have allowed any such caprice on her part, whatever the impression I may have given her to the contrary. After she left, my orders were that she was to be followed wherever she went. And I was to be given a report several times a day. I could hardly let dear, mad Procula disappear into a sea of Jews and perhaps never return to me.*

XV

The tomb at the base of Calvary was no longer being guarded. Virtually everyone in the whole of Judea would soon hear the stories being passed about, together with all the futile and self-serving denials that were being regularly issued by the high priests, anxious that their authority not be undermined and their complicity in the brutal death of the Nazarene not become a posthumous dagger struck at their hearts wielded by the duped masses who had blindly followed their instigation.

But none of this was, for the moment, important to the remaining apostles of Jesus the Christ as they stood in front of the opening, their heads bowed.

"Oh, Jesus, Jesus, dear Savior . . ." John, the youngest of the men, started to pray out loud, but the emotion he felt interrupted him as he tried to deal with the tears that were flowing down his cheeks.

Peter placed a large hand on John's shoulder, suddenly a father to him, rather than simply a comrade.

"We miss You so, Lord, and some of us find it difficult to deal with our grief," the fisherman continued. "We know that You are still here, and when You choose, You are able to stand among us, as You have done already. But it is not the same as before, and we realize it can never be the same for us any longer. We just do not know how we can let go, Lord, how it will be for the group of us when You go back to be with the blessed Father in heaven, and we are left with nothing, are not reassured even by the brief appearances You have made to comfort us."

Decimus Paetus had joined them, standing to one side, his head bowed. Every so often, he would glance up, half-expecting the Nazarene Himself to walk without warning into the midst of the group.

Decimus Paetus, some forty years from this moment, nine hundred and sixty human beings, on a high and isolated place in the midst of the wilderness, will accept you as a brother and as a friend because you will have chosen to devote the remainder of your life to them.

You will be to a handful an instrument of righteousness since you are to bring a message of redemption so strong and so beautiful that, at the end of their days, some of them will turn to you, Decimus Paetus, for the hope of eternity, and you will give forth the very truth that will free them from the flesh-and-blood domination they fought so hard to overthrow.

"Jesus . . ." he blurted, without thinking, surprising everyone there. "I do not know why You should find me worthy of Your attention. I am he who inflicted the wound to Your side. I still see before me the gaping wound, the blood pouring forth."

Paetus found it difficult to go on but he knew he had to confess in order to receive forgiveness and cleansing.

"I cannot endure what I have done, Lord," he continued. "I have tried to hide behind all of the years of conditioning bestowed upon me by Rome, my previous master, but that does not work any longer, because I have no peace of heart. I turn this wretched self, which is all I have to offer, entirely over to You."

Paetus fell to his knees on the rocky ground but without paying heed to the fleeting pain that jabbed through his legs and up to his hips.

"Now, I say in humble dedication that You, O Lord Jesus, are the only Master of my life I can or will ever acknowledge henceforth . . . through whatever time remains . . . until the end of my days," he added, his voice trembling. "And I shall serve You with all my mind, all my heart, all my soul, now and throughout eternity."

★ ★ ★

Those whose limbs were rotting away found they had new fingers, new feet, their skin fresh and healthy once again. Some, who were close to death, revived completely. Their minds had been gone, ravaged by what they had experienced, but now they were laughing, talking normally, sitting and praying with joy.

Atop Calvary itself, kneeling at the hole in the hard rock where the middle cross had been placed, Fabius Scipio struggled with that memory, struggled with the reality of what had happened at that spot so few days before, a man put to death whose only crimes were healing the sick and speaking of a kingdom that was not of the physical, material world, so much of which was ruled by Rome.

He felt a woman's hand gently touch his shoulder, and he looked up at her.

"They do not yet know who you are, do they?" he asked.

She shook her head.

"Your husband represents all that the people of this land have hated about Rome," he added, "and you wonder if they will turn their backs on you when you tell them or they find out otherwise, is that not it?"

"You are perceptive for one so young," she said without offense.

"There are some things in life so obvious that only the blind could not see them."

"I have felt greater peace here than at any other time in my life," she confessed, with little discomfort. "I do not have a palace around me. There are no servants taking care of my every need."

"Some needs exist that no mortal can satisfy," Scipio pointed out, surprised at the wisdom of the words flowing from his mouth. "You can have a chestful of jewels; a tall cabinet the shelves of which hold the finest linens; imported foods on your table, to be eaten any time of the day and night; and yet the emptiness inside you continues."

He stood now. The woman and he looked intently at each other.

"I know well the truth of what you speak," she told him. "I know what it is to get up each morning and look at what is physical around me—the marble floors, the hand-carved statues, the dozen human beings who stand ready to do whatever I wish, for if they were to disobey, my husband could bring upon them whatever judgment he wished—to look at all this and wonder how I can spend the time ahead of me without going mad."

She knew that her husband considered her mad already, his pragmatism colliding with the emotional upheaval that, at various times in her life, she either foisted upon herself or which pure circumstance brought about, quite beyond her control. He had been lovingly patient for years, but as her behavior seemingly deteriorated, so it seemed that his tolerance of her growing eccentricities grew more and more limited.

"I know what it is to cherish the night," Procula went on, "to get into bed and wait for sleep to overtake me. Only then can I hope to find relief unless it is that my dreams assault me with their visions of despair.

"I awaken to find the new morning that confronts me every bit the same as the one before it, and doubtless, all those that are yet to come. And I have come to think that only death itself will end my misery."

"But death is not the end," Scipio offered, though nervously at the prospect of someone of his youth lecturing a woman of her maturity and social station. "Jesus has proved that. He suffered, He died, He was put in a tomb, yet He arose. We all here have seen Him."

"However, I have not," she reminded him. "I hear what you say, and I know that for you, it is a reality. Yet I have encountered nothing but your words, however sincere."

"And His words as well?" Scipio reminded her.

"While He was alive, yes!" she declared. "And I admit that they were filled with wisdom unlike anything I had heard before in my life, words that pierced through into my very heart, it seemed, spoken by a man with such authority that He seemed the most extraordinary human being I had ever encountered."

"Not only that. Remember what else? Let me remind you: You accepted this man as your Lord."

"I once accepted the diverse gods of Rome as my own," she said, "yet how real have any of *them* proven to be?"

"Jesus was alive, then dead, then alive again—and that does not convince you?" probed Scipio."

"It is what I have been told. But where is the proof?"

Procula had turned from him, unable to endure his questioning gaze. After a moment, detecting only silence, she asked the question again, still without facing the legionnaire, and once more without receiving a reply.

"Where is the pr—?" she started to say yet a third time as she turned to find out what might be wrong.

A gasp escaped the lips of Procula Pilatus as she saw the beautiful figure standing front of her, an iridescent form of such splendor that it seemed all the treasures she had ever seen or possessed could not compare.

The legionnaire was on his knees, his eyes wide, his attention transfixed as, now, hers would be also.

"Do not offer me worship, but listen to what I will tell you," the iridescent being said. "Soon it will be given to you to witness an event that many after you gladly would sacrifice a great deal to see, if they could." The words entered her mind; whether they be spoken or otherwise, she could not be sure. "But only you, the apostles of Jesus the Christ, and certain of His disciples will share that moment."

The figure was gone, in an instant, the space in front of them as dark, as forlornly empty as it had been seconds earlier.

XVI

Procula Pilatus was not accustomed to spending the night in a stable. To give her some privacy, the apostles decided to relinquish modest space that someone sympathetic to the ministry of the Nazarene had provided and were sleeping outside instead, as they had done often during the past three years.

They are so tired, so sad, these men, she thought, *and yet they did this for me. I came from a palace to this humble place, and yet I feel more honored here than when a dozen servants provide for me whatever it is that I can ever ask. But they do so out of mere necessity while, for these men, it was an act of love.*

Instead of air laced with the scent of lavender, there was the odor of horse dung mixed with dry hay.

And I do not mind it, she admitted. *It is natural, it is real, it is far, far removed from what only wealth and power can maintain.*

She thought of that figure seen less than three hours earlier. While appearing in the shape of a man, it nevertheless had no material substance whatever, shimmering like a thousand transparent diamonds.

And wings!

Yes, it had wings, long and thick and so powerful-looking that they seemed capable of carrying the being to the ends of the earth and far, far beyond if need be.

That voice . . .

Deep, a voice commanding full attention but not upsetting to her, simply unlike any voice she had heard previously—and yet it seemed to speak not through her ears but directly into her mind.

Soon it will be given to you to witness an event that many after you gladly would sacrifice a great deal in order to see, if they could.

The words still there, repeating themselves, reminding Procula again and again of what had been said, of whatever was ahead of her, something so extraordinary that they all had to be prepared for it by this waiting period of growing anticipation.

She had no idea what that event might be. After the legionnaire told the apostles of the Nazarene what had happened, they became very excited, the whole gathering of them, their gloom dissipating, at least for awhile, though none were able to articulate what it was that they sensed was going to happen.

Later, Procula had approached John, who was sitting inside the tomb on the slab opposite the one where the body of the Nazarene had lain.

"Do you know more than you are telling?" she asked.

He shook his head.

"I am sorry to say that I do not," he told her. "But we have come to the certainty that it shall be important, and we can scarce wait for that moment."

"How will you know when it arrives?"

"I cannot tell you that either, but I know we will, all of us, even you and the legionnaires, I suspect."

Procula sat down beside him.

"Why did you love Him?" she inquired.

"You have heard Him speak?"

"Yes, I have."

"The authority of His words?"

Procula hesitated, remembering once as Jesus was speaking of the kingdom of heaven, He had turned and looked at her, His countenance unwavering.

"This man we are discussing now saw right into the innermost part of myself, where only the gods—"

She cut herself off, comprehending a truth then.

"He is a god!" she exclaimed.

John was smiling.

"Jesus is not *a* god," he contradicted her. "He is *the* God; He is God wrapped in human flesh, walking amongst us."

"Incarnate deity . . ." Procula whispered.

She began to shiver.

"I used to pray to Rome's gods, while never feeling that they were my gods," she said, "while never being sure that they were ever there in the first place. I would ask one or the other to do this or that for me, and nothing came, there was no response. I had only the emptiness in front of me and inside me as a response."

. . . only the emptiness.

Color drained from her face.

"There has seldom been more than that throughout the whole of my unfortunate life until this moment," she recalled, with a wave of great melancholy deepening the wrinkles of her years. "I have never known the slightest hunger as a child or an adult, but I see more joy on the faces of those walking the streets, with precious little food to eat from day to day. How can that be? Please tell me, if you possibly can."

"They are depending on a source beyond themselves, beyond even this flesh-and-blood existence," John replied. "You look to Rome. You look to a man, your husband. You look to bins bulging with food not your own."

"It *is* my own, it *is* my husband's, it *is*, above all, the food of Rome itself," she said, with more than a little anger.

"Food not from your own hand in this province is food taken from those whom Rome oppresses, taken as tribute, stolen from the storehouses of countless thousands who loathe the very presence of a power not of their choosing."

Though naive in manner and hardly more than a teenage boy in appearance, John had spoken with authority that astounded her.

"We guard these people from the conquering hordes of their long history, and yet they show us no gratitude?" she said.

"You took over their land as a conquering horde," he reminded her. "Your taxes bleed them. The temples you have built to your false gods mock the synagogues erected to honor Jehovah, the one and true God."

"But they do their own mocking by turning places of worship into centers of commerce!" she proclaimed.

"Which Jesus Himself recognized, of course. For isn't that why He resorted to throwing the money changers out?"

She became silent.

With her husband, there were virtually no such discussions. Pilatus did not at any time accept Procula as an intellectual equal, preferring to indulge in that sort of exercise with men who had the capacity to do so. Mere women were simply incapable of keeping up with him, with any man short of a primitive savage. Women could fulfill certain of the needs of men, could add some beauty to life, some charm, to be sure, but beyond that, they had little to offer to men of his stature.

"You asked why I love Him," John's words, spoken with that boyish voice of his, interrupted her thoughts.

"I did," she replied absentmindedly.

"I love Him because He first showed me love without reservation. I could give Him nothing at the same time He could give me everything. His love is undeserved. It comes to me freely, and it is eternal."

"Even for the fisherman?" Procula asked with some cynicism.

"Especially for Peter!" John declared with obvious excitement. "Do you not see the beauty in this?"

"I do not."

"The less deserving a man, the greater the love that swallows him up in forgiveness. Is it so noble if we love only those who *deserve* our love? That is not transforming love. The love Jesus has given is unconditional, and it transforms us."

Eternal love undeserved and unlimited . . .

Procula was hugging herself tightly as she stared at the cold, empty slab directly in front of her.

"Would He accept even me?" she inquired uncertainly.

"You have already called Him Lord without knowing why," John responded as gently as he knew how. "Could you find yourself calling Him anything less than that if suddenly the answer were clear?"

She had stopped shivering.

"Would you let me be here alone for some few moments?" Procula asked suddenly, without a demanding tone.

"I will leave, but still you will not be alone," John assured her as he stood and turned toward the entrance.

Somehow, she did not feel the need to ask him what he meant.

★ ★ ★

The nervous young legionnaire obviously wished he was not the one to give Pontius Pilatus the message that circumstances had mandated.

"She apparently has become a follower of the Nazarene," he said tremulously.

Pilatus showed no outward reaction. To have given display to his emotions in front of a common soldier would be an admission of weakness before a subordinate that was not allowed someone of Pilatus's stature.

So the proconsul-governor of Judea simply sat impassively in the leather chair in the elaborate room where he received all visitors, a room filled with imported potted ferns that gave it a warmth that the marble walls, floors, and columns needed. Double carved, thick, mahogany doors at the opposite end were wide open, cool air flooding the interior from the open veranda.

"Shall I close the doors, sir?" the legionnaire inquired. "A sudden wind must have caught them."

Pilatus dismissed the question with a wave of his hand, thankful for the coolness, for it helped to keep his body heat momentarily in check as he fought against showing the rising red-hot temper that was threatening to erupt.

"You know exactly where my wife is?" he asked sternly.

"We do," the legionnaire replied.

"And where is that?"

"She has been in the general area of Jerusalem ever since you asked us to keep track of her. For the past several nights, she has slept in a stable."

That one almost defeated Pilatus' attempt to keep himself under control.

Procula sleeping on straw, with animals as her companions, he thought. *The woman surely has succumbed to her demons!*

"Sir?" the legionnaire spoke.

"Yes?"

"There was talk of something happening today."

"Something? What do you mean?"

"At what the Jews call the Mount of Olives. All of that band of followers so devoted to the Nazarene will be there."

"And my wife presumably?"

"Yes, sir, your wife plans to join them, along with the legionnaires named Decimus Paetus and Fabius Scipio."

"What?" Pilatus blurted out, despite himself.

The young man started to repeat what he had just said, thinking that he had not spoken as clearly as he had intended the first time.

"I heard you," Pilatus interrupted. "I want to go there."

"To the Mount of Olives, sir?"

"Yes, exactly. It is good to know that I can still elucidate properly!"

The legionnaire blushed, his palms sweaty as he realized that he had done what he hoped he would not—irritate a man who could have him reprimanded in any severe fashion he wished, if the mood struck him to do that.

Pilatus regretted the flaring up of the nasty streak to which he was given from time-to-time, especially with those below his station.

"As you can imagine, I am most interested in my wife's welfare," he said half-apologetically. "We will need enough men to overpower the Nazarene's disciples, if necessary, and take into custody Paetus and Scipio."

"It will be as you ask," the legionnaire replied.

"I shall join the men in one hour," Pilatus told him.

The legionnaire saluted and left.

Pilatus could scarcely move, his limbs acting as though they were gripped by paralysis, his mind having lost all control over them.

Procula! That same mind screamed because his mouth seemed gripped as well by the malady, and he could not open it and proclaim to the emptiness of that room the depth of his feelings about this woman. *You have no more control over your actions where you are now than I do at this very moment.*

He fell forward onto the hard, black, marble floor, banging his chin.

I cannot let these awful men take you and—

As he pushed himself to a sitting position, he cut that thought off, the truth so stark and yet so awkward for him to admit that he tried not to think of it at all and concentrated instead on getting to his feet.

He could not.

The room swung dizzily in his vision.

I cannot let these—

He swallowed several times.

Suddenly he saw what he hated to see.

"I can no longer consider them any more awful than Procula seemingly does," he said out loud, his mouth able to move at last. "I never wanted to let the Nazarene go through what He did, for I perceived that He deserved not an instant of pain. Yet His own people demanded this sentence of me."

He thought of those apostles that he had seen—the fisherman, the tax collector, the very young one, the others.

"Not even this Jesus' death has tempered the devotion of those who followed Him!" he declared. "What kind of man did I send to the gods?"

Pilatus's body was covered with perspiration.

"The mob ruled me rather than the other way around," he went on, his fury unabated. "They brought me under *their* control. The armies of our enemies have not been able to do that for decades, but a smelly, ill-kempt, illiterate horde of near-crazed Jews—!"

His body surged as adrenaline pumped through it. Feeling returned to his limbs. And his mind seemed as sharply focused as it had ever been.

It is a pity that the battle ahead seems so limited, so unworthy of my true capabilities, he told himself with some irony, *for now I feel as though I am prepared for one much greater.*

Pontius Pilatus jumped to his feet, determined to pursue a course of action that he would have scoffed at a mere few weeks before, but unaware that his final conduct would be altogether different from anything he envisioned in that moment of overpowering rage.

XVII

Procula had passed by the Mount of Olives innumerable times. For some reason it fascinated her, though it was hardly different from any other mountain she had seen, with Sinai at nearly seventy-five hundred feet being especially spectacular, reducing any other in Judea to a mere hill by comparison.

Why did it capture my attention from the beginning? she asked herself. *Did I have some sense of foretelling about it?*

Called Jabal At-Tur by the Arabs and Har Ha-Zetim by the Jews, it was in fact one peak in a large mountain range that extended across Israel, though it was not the largest one, for that was Mount Scopus or, in the Hebrew, Har ha-Zofim, higher by forty-nine feet.

Eventually Procula was able to discover that Jabal At-Tur was considered by the Jews as the sacred spot where their so-called messiah would pronounce the commencement of the messianic age during which the nation of Israel would throw off its oppressors and emerge triumphant for all time.

It was also the preferred location among the Jews for cemetery plots. Wealthy and influential members of the community would vie for the privilege of having family members and themselves buried on its slopes.

Sometimes Procula asked to be driven to the Garden of Gethsemane, and she would walk its small, serene space, sniffing the air for the scents of flowers growing there and then leave, to stand just outside, her head turned upward toward the western side of the Mount of Olives, which overlooked that area.

"Is this but an episode in my madness, a delusion and nothing more?" she once asked out loud in that garden, as careful as she could manage to be so that no one could overheard her, without knowing that someone always was listening, her coachman or another servant perhaps, those who had been instructed by Pontius Pilatus to report about every detail of what she said and did while she was gone.

Just beyond the edge of tiny Gethsemane, the Mount of Olives loomed, perhaps a little like a giant mother hen attentive over her flock of little ones. An otherwise indistinctive mass of rock, straggly brush, and earth dried by the persistent lack of rain, it drew the wife of the governor of all of Judea again and again, for she never tired of standing there, trying to imagine what special destiny it had.

Are the gods shouting the answer that I seek, and I cannot hear their words of great profundity? she would wonder. *Am I deafened by some inner part of myself that cannot quite accept fully their role in my life?*

Procula had known for years that the Roman approach to religion denied her any kind of real fulfillment.

I stood before statues that dwarf any mortal in their magnificence. I offered passionate prayers to distant deities and received only the cold stares of carved marble and stone substitutes, mocking my need.

And now—

She shook her head.

I stand before a mountain, its bulk as impassive as man-made sculpture, waiting for that which I cannot even guess, nor do His followers truly know. They can only say that the Master asked them to be at this spot at this hour on this day.

Procula glanced around her. All the eleven remaining apostles were there: Simon Peter, James, John, Andrew, Philip, Thomas, Bartholomew, Matthew, James the son of Alphaeus, Simon Zelotes, and Judas the brother of James. Joining them were the legionnaires, Decimus Paetus and Fabius Scipio.

And the wife of the man who sent Jesus the Christ to His death!

"But that was my Father's plan, Procula Pilatus," a clear, deep voice took Procula from her thoughts. "It could not be otherwise. This anguish you feel so deeply has reached the ears of Jehovah Himself."

She turned, startled, and saw the Nazarene standing just a few feet away, His eyes looking beyond her own, as though into her very soul.

"You *are* alive!" Procula exclaimed, unable at first to accept as real the image of this man that her eyes were presenting to her, but then joyous when she realized that she was not imagining His presence.

"What they have told you in love was not bred in falsehood." He spoke as he waved one arm in the direction of the thirteen men standing to one side.

She fell at His feet, sobbing.

★ ★ ★

Pilatus ordered that the group with him stop some distance from the site, intent on surprising Procula, the apostles, and the two deserters.

With just over a dozen legionnaires behind him, Pilatus led the way through a wadi and toward the side of Gethsemane opposite the Mount of Olives. The nighttime darkness provided a convenient cover for them.

107

He did not expect armed resistance, though his men were fitted with normal battlefield gear, which Rome required in any such situation. After all, the apostles had slipped away into the darkness when the Nazarene was captured, tried, sentenced, and crucified. And from what he had been told, he could safely surround them, without a fight ensuing.

They will think that I want to harm them, he thought. *I have no intention of doing that. I simply want my wife back. The others can leave, even my legionnaires, if they wish. There will be an attack only if they try to keep Procula from me.*

The squawking of several nearby birds broke the silence for a moment, as Pilatus peered through the cluster of trees at that northern end of Gethsemane, realizing that this was where Judas, paid by the high priest of Israel, had betrayed the One to whom he had been devoted for more than three years.

Judas . . .

Secretly Caiphas had brought the man to him.

I found him repugnant from the beginning, Pilatus recalled. *He seemed just the sort of individual who would make himself available to the highest bidder. I wondered why he was willing to sell out someone he adored so much.*

He snickered at that thought, never having much time for men who formed unnatural attachments, for he found them pathetic creatures, no matter what their station in life.

"This Jesus you once loved," Pilatus had said at the time, "I gather, then, He is not interested in returning that love in quite the way you had hoped."

The expression on the man's face betrayed the accuracy of that presumption.

"But what could you expect, Judas? There were eleven others always hovering nearby. When would you have supposed there to be an opportunity?"

The traitor was becoming more uncomfortable, and so, it seemed, was this true of Caiphas, a man charged with the spiritual welfare of a nation.

"How can you sanction this treachery?" Pilatus had berated Judas. "How can you accept the help of someone whose soul can be bought for thirty pieces of silver? Perhaps you are on the one who should be put on trial, not the Nazarene."

The very truth of that assertion nauseated him.

Yes, he was accustomed to the intrigues of Rome. Yes, he had been guilty of clandestine maneuverings, but never had he betrayed a close friend, never had he caused the death of anyone under such circumstances.

They are little more than beasts, these people, willing to sacrifice any-one who does not please them, or who fails to fit a rigid interpretation of their religious doctrines! What can my wife find so fascinating about them?

Pilatus decided to go around Gethsemane, rather than through it. The garden was home to a variety of rare flowers and other plants, some of which could not be seen elsewhere in that entire region. He did not want to be responsible for the clumsiness of men trained only to be brutal opponents in battle.

Several minutes passed.

He heard the sound of conversation.

A rock as tall as a man and twice as broad was just ahead of him. He approached it slowly, and peered around the edge as he reached it.

My beloved Procula! His mind shouted her name in silence, though his lips parted instinctively as well.

She stood in a large clearing between Gethsemane and the base of the Mount of Olives. Holding her hands out in front of her, she was saying, "I feel so clean, as though every sin I have ever committed has been washed away."

The men around her were smiling.

"It is as you say," someone whom Pilatus recognized as Peter the fisherman replied. "Your sins exist no more in the mind of a holy God."

Pilatus had never before seen such joy on the face of his wife.

"Where is He now?" Procula asked with great intensity. "Jesus spoke of going on to be with His Father."

"We are not sure," Peter admitted. "We do not—"

A sudden, very bright light transformed the darkness. Everyone shielded their eyes.

"Look up unto Me!" a voice of such authority that it seemed the inanimate earth itself would obey any command that were uttered, this voice as it spoke reached past their physical selves and into their very souls.

The apostles all began to weep, unable to contain their emotions. So did Pilatus, though he tried to conceal this. So did the legionnaires behind him.

Heads tilted, looking toward the Mount of Olives.

There, on the slope, was the Nazarene.

Perspiration started to trickle down Pilatus's back. He did not want to hear what he was hearing, for what he was hearing was seditious, words urging the Nazarene's followers to spread revolution throughout the Roman Empire.

Pilatus repeated those words to himself perhaps a dozen times, try-ing to find them innocent, trying to drain them of their threatening content.

He is mocking Imperial Rome, this simple carpenter, this wanderer
. . . who was raised from the dead!

The truth of that had been relegated to some neglected recess of
his mind but now came to the surface again, and he felt momentarily
faint, having to grasp the large stone by the edge in order to keep himself
from falling.

I ordered the execution myself! I carefully picked the handful of soldiers
assigned to handle it. One of them thrust a thick spear into His side to make
sure that He was dead. They sealed the tomb, they—

Pilatus ran forward, screaming.

Procula turned around, startled, as did the others. Paetus and
Scipio turned red and seemed ready to flee, given any opportunity to do
so.

"This charade must stop!" Pilatus demanded, his face covered
with perspiration, his eyes suddenly bloodshot as his emotions assumed
command of him. "Where is the impostor whose voice calls out from the
night?"

He had been out of the reach of that extraordinary light, as he was
hiding behind the large rock. Now he came within the glow of the light
and stopped.

"What is that singing I hear?" he asked, stunned by the beauty of it.

"The hosts of heaven, Pontius Pilatus." The voice of Jesus touched
his ears.

Pilatus's gaze turned toward the Figure on the slope.

"You see Me as I was, and continue to be," Jesus spoke, "and
now, can you not say with the others that it is indeed I?"

Pilatus took to the side of the mount and started to climb up, cutting his hands on sharp rocks in his frantic effort to reach the Figure.

"Are you perhaps like my own Thomas who, upon seeing Me, was
not yet satisfied and had to touch Me to quell his doubt?"

Pilatus had nearly reached the Figure when his left foot pressed
down on a loose piece of flat rock and he started to slip.

Jesus held out both hands, grabbed Pilatus by the wrists, and
pulled him up.

"You are flesh and blood!" Pilatus exclaimed. "I feel Your mortal
strength. You are not a vaporous spirit.

"You felt this earthy body that I took on over My divinity."

"*Stop!*" Pilatus demanded. "You are a mere man. Gods do not
walk this land as You have done."

Abruptly Jesus touched his eyes, closed them.

"Look beyond the darkness, Pontius Pilatus. What is it that you
see?"

Pilatus gasped, images of such beauty and purity flinging themselves across the landscape of his mind that he could not speak because the emotions he felt were choking off words.

Moments later, he opened his eyes.

"Now you see and believe?" Jesus asked.

Pilatus pulled back.

"The sorcerers can do what You have done," he said. "And yes, they brag of far greater than even this."

"Of visions and counterfeit images, yes, but how do you explain Me now, flesh and blood, which you have admitted, as I stand before you? Therefore, I am not what you could call the ethereal offspring of some wizard's spell."

"You never died," Pilatus insisted. "You swooned as though in a deep stupor, and it was from such a state that You arose, nothing more."

Pilatus saw the marks of the crown of thorns on His forehead, the deep gashes in His feet and feet, the—

"Even your wife now believes," Jesus told him. "Even she has reached through the turmoil of her mind to grab hold of—"

"Truth?" Pilatus retorted. "Is that what you were going to say, Nazarene? Jewish truth mocks the wisdom of Imperial Rome, food for pigs thrown to the resident swine of this dirty, primitive land!"

Tears came from the eyes of Jesus the Christ then, mixing with the dust of His journey to the mount.

"Oh, Pontius, Pontius," He said, His tone both tender and sad. "You who washed your hands of innocent blood just a short while ago now reject the One whose blood was shed for the redemption of mankind."

"I have my gods," Pilatus responded, "and You are not among them. How can I believe someone who is an ordinary man?"

The Nazarene sighed deeply.

"I command some portion of the many legions of Rome," Pilate retorted angrily. "I can put anyone to death that I should choose and Rome would honor any such action with all the support I need."

. . . I can put anyone to death that I choose.

Jesus smiled slightly.

"Then why am I not dead, Pontius Pilatus?"

Pilatus could feel his heart beating faster.

"I already told You what clever—"

Jesus reached out and placed His hands on the other's shoulders.

"Do you truly believe the words that you have uttered?" He asked, His eyes looking into Pilatus' own.

The governor of all of Judea tried to take those hands away but could not budge either of them.

"You are so strong," he gasped, surprised.

"And yet you cling to the emptiness that is all you ever receive from the gods of Imperial Rome."

There was silence for a few seconds.

Suddenly he heard a familiar voice.

Procula!

Pilatus turned sharply and looked down, then saw his wife struggling up the side of the mount.

"No, my love!" he yelled. "You must not. You could be hurt. You—"

She had nearly reached her husband when she slipped and hit her head against a rock, her body immediately limp.

Pilatus scrambled back down to where Procula had fallen. He leaned his head gently on her chest.

"She is dead!" he screamed. "My beloved is—!"

He put his arms around Procula, lifted her off the ground, and with great effort, carried his wife to where the Nazarene still stood, nearly stumbling back down the slope as he did so, the extra weight unbalancing him.

"It is said that You have raised the dead," Pilatus declared. "Bring life back into this dear body in my arms now."

"And then you will believe?" Jesus asked.

"Oh, *yes!* That is true, Nazarene. She is dead now. If You can give her the breath of life, truly, then, will I believe."

"And not later convince yourself that she was only swooning, as you have said about Me after My body was taken off the cross?"

"I was not there when it happened. I could not see with these my eyes but had to depend upon the perceptions of others. But I now hold my wife before You. Her heart has stopped. There is blood on the rock which her head hit. She is not breathing. I have been around death much in my life. And I know that she is—"

Jesus turned His back to them and started up toward the top, which was only a few hundred feet away.

"I asked You for mercy," Pilatus shouted after Him, "and You offend me greatly by walking away!"

He laid the body down on a large flat rock to his left and climbed up after the Nazarene, intending to grab Him and *demand* that He do what had been asked of Him.

Jesus was now at the peak. He turned toward Pilatus, the woman's still body just below and the men on the ground.

"It is not my Father's will that I be taken up tonight," He said. "That will come shortly."

Pilatus's mind was filled with an image of that familiar body leaving the ground, being lifted upward as though some invisible hand had reached down and was taking Him.

Pilatus fell prostrate on the rocks, unmindful of sharp edges cutting into the exposed flesh of his arms and legs.

"That cannot be!" he cried. "My wife's madness has infected me!"

In a moment of prophetic imagination, Pilatus saw heaven open but for that single instant, the Nazarene newly surrounded not by a mob of sweaty, dirty, common people but by a multitude of dazzling creatures of inexpressible beauty. One of these turned toward him with an expression of such beckoning love that the proconsul-governor of Judea was tempted to reach out for it and let whatever it was take him as well, if that were possible.

Over . . . it was over.

The veil between infinite heaven and finite earth fell into place again.

And he was ripped from visions of the mind back to reality, and suddenly he opened his eyes to see the Nazarene gone.

"He will come here again, as He said, and then the Father will take him past the gates of heaven," a voice spoke behind Pilatus.

Pilatus jumped to his feet and spun around.

"*Procula!*" he blurted out.

She was standing on the flat fock, moonlight sparkling off her eyes, an expression of joy on her face.

"He tried so hard to get so many to believe," she said, her voice scarcely a whisper. "And yet most turned into a mob crying for His blood."

Pilatus scrambled down to his wife's side.

"I am so glad that you regained—," he started to say.

"Regained consciousness?" Procula interrupted him. "Was that what you were going to say to me?"

She noticed the expression on his face.

"I see that I have guessed correctly. But it was not merely that. I had been *dead*, Pontius. You found no heartbeat, did you? There was no breath from my lungs. Perhaps my flesh was already becoming cold."

She put her arms around him.

"I was given back to you again, my husband," she said softly. "The Nazarene showed mercy, did He not? Can you not *now* bring yourself to accept this Jesus as the One He claimed to be?"

Look upward and see that which your very soul rejects even now.

Pilatus glanced for an instant back at the peak, but it was as it had been for so many centuries and would continue to be long after he had turned to dust.

XVIII

There was a garden at the rear of the governor's residence near Jerusalem, one that Pilatus personally tended to without the help of a everhovering servant. It was off-limits to everyone except Procula and himself.

Pilatus enjoyed the mixture of scents from four flowers that had been transplanted on the grounds upon his specific instruction, most of which he had become aware of during his early travels through Judea and whose beauty impressed him: anemone, crocus, poppy, narcissus, and yellow chrysanthemum. He likewise favored the half dozen Boswellia trees, which had tiny but quite lovely blue blossoms. But more importantly, the trees also were the source of expensive frankincense, a gum collected by peeling back the bark and cutting into the trunk. The resin gave off a sweet scent when warmed or burned, and he often used it as incense to sweeten the dry air inside each of his residences.

"It will take months for the color to come back to them," Procula said forlornly as she glimpsed the straggly plants.

"But you came back to me in just a few minutes," Pilatus told her as the two of them stood in the middle of the garden.

"Because of Jesus," she reminded him. "Without Him, I would be as dead as these plants are now."

"Jesus had nothing to do with it. You are with me now because you were merely unconscious, my love, not dead."

"You said you could not find any heartbeat."

"I am not a physician."

"But you are a military man. You have had experience on the battlefield. You have to know when someone is dead or not."

Pilatus was beginning to feel uncomfortable. There was an edge to his wife's persistence just then, an edge that he had not quite detected before.

"You seem especially disturbed now," he said. "Why is that, Procula? If it happened as you say, you were dead but now you are alive, then why are you not rejoicing this night despite my cynicism?"

Procula bit her lower lip, avoiding his eyes for a moment. Finally she looked up at him, and Pilatus saw the love that the woman had for him but something else along with it. It was this that only increased his discomfort.

"I want to shout to the world what happened back there at the Mount of Olives!" she exclaimed. "I want to tell everyone in this empire of ours that the Nazarene was not just a man but that He was much more indeed."

"Is that truly what you would announce to the world, Procula?"

"Oh, yes! It is important that people know. When they hear the different conflicting stories, they must be able to recognize the truth and ignore the sponsored lies."

"Sponsored lies? I do not understand what you mean by that."

"That the Sanhedrin have been spreading."

"And that I have encouraged, my wife."

"That was before we saw what we did."

"And what was it that we saw?"

She stepped back from him.

"We saw the Nazarene, Jesus the Christ, the Son of the living God, not the relics of our Roman past, ascending from the top of the Mount of Olives."

"Can we be sure it was not an illusion of some sort?"

"Pontius, the heavens were *opened* to us for that one beautiful moment. Can you not rejoice along with me in what we both witnessed?"

"The gods would never allow us to—"

"Who cares about the gods?" Procula shouted one of the ultimate Roman blasphemies, the other of which would have used the name of Caesar instead. "They are either nonexistent, Pontius, born of our imaginations as we stumble like blind beasts closer to the beckoning eternal night, or they are something else—darker, evil, loathsome."

"And this is some of that which you will tell anyone who cares to listen to you, my wife?" Pilatus asked.

"Just some, Pontius. There is a great deal else that our fellow Romans must be allowed to hear."

"Oh, I do not doubt that many people will listen to you, Procula, because you are the wife of a governor of one of Rome's provinces. There is in this place and elsewhere undoubtedly a ready audience. The masses and the elite alike will flock in your direction and hang on every word that you utter."

Her face opened up into the brightest smile Pilatus had ever seen on it.

"That is why I am one of those who have been chosen!" she said with great energy. "That is why I have the blessing of Almighty God. His Son, the one known to many only as the Nazarene, has asked His followers to go into all the world to tell His story of redemption and—"

"But it could hurt the empire, as you probably know, these words of yours," Pilatus interrupted without emotion, "for you will be telling the powerful and dangerous story of someone over whom even the darkness of death held no lasting claim. Surely you realize what I am saying . . . do you not?"

"I do, and it only spurs me on, Pontius. I am willing to go anywhere, yea, I shall travel to the far corners of the nations that Rome has conquered, if that be what God expects of this humble servant."

"God? Which one, Procula? Be specific, my dear."

"There is but one. Our Father in heaven—the Lord God Jehovah."

Pilatus pretended to feel a bit chilled by the passing night breezes.

"It is late," he told her. "We should go inside."

"You do oppose me in what I have been saying, do you not?" Procula inquired of this man with whom she had spent every year of her adult life. "I sense by your manner, Pontius, that you are more displeased than you would like to admit."

"We will discuss it in the morning."

She hesitated before going back into the residence with him.

"But what will the morning bring?" she asked with a tenseness she could not quite explain, examining his expression but without being able to glean anything from it.

"Who can tell, dear Procula, who can tell?" he replied.

★ ★ ★

What Pilatus had decided could not be accomplished on the spur of the moment. Even for someone such as himself, there were procedures. First, he had to write to the emperor and tell of his intentions. Not that his wishes as proconsul-governor would be overruled in so intimate a matter, but he worried that the relationship between Procula and Caesar would perhaps complicate the situation just a bit. After all, when the emperor "knew" the woman, she seemed hardly as far gone as she would become later. Was there a chance that he, Pontius Pilatus, might be viewed as the reason for her disintegration?

He decided to write as much of the truth as he possibly could, while omitting that the hallucination Procula suffered was not that at all but was in fact objective reality witnessed by the proconsul-governor himself, two of his former legionnaires, and eleven Jews.

For a moment, Pilatus thought of Decimus Paetus and Fabius Scipio. He had decided to let them go their way, in an uncharacteristically befuddled moment as he reeled from the impact of what had taken place before his eyes. Perhaps they saw that he was dazed and seized the opportunity to ask him for mercy, and he let them escape without issuing a directive that they be hunted down and arrested.

Am I to stick with my word now? he asked himself as he sat at a hand-carved ivory desk, with an inlaid teak top. *And what about the others—?*

He dropped the feathered pen that he had been holding, a cold sweat gripping him.

The guards who accompanied him to the Mount of Olives!

They had seen everything as well! So had the Nazarene's followers, but then they could be expected to concoct any sort of fantasy that would reinforce their claim of deity for the man. None of them would be regarded very seriously by people who really mattered.

A dozen legionnaires . . .

He looked at the parchment on which he had started the epistle to Claudius Tiberius, ruler of Imperial Rome, his eyes quickly rereading a certain portion: "And thus, my emperor, it seems wise to confine my dearest Procula in as isolated a location as possible, with a round-the-clock guard, and no visitors. Only servants can see her, and they too must be prevented from leaving. The legionnaires given the assignment should be told that they are to stay with my wife until they or she dies. I would not expect Procula to live to a very old age, frankly, for she is a highly nervous sort of woman, consumed of her incessant fears. Immediately after she is gone, the men must be executed so that they cannot live to tell *anyone* what they may have heard from her lips. For what she claims could become a poison coursing through the veins of the empire, in places where men are not immune to such entreaties."

. . . *the men must be executed.*

That would include even more urgently the guards with him at the site just the night before.

"I would recommend, my emperor," he continued on the scroll, "that the deaths yet in the future as well as those dozen of more immediate concern be carried out with lethal potions. Poison their rations but not all at once. Do this over a period of a week. It might be argued that Procula herself could be disposed of—"

His hand had shaken quite violently as he wrote those last eleven words, and he crossed them out, tore up the original parchment and started over.

You are mad, you are a danger to this empire which I serve, and, thus, I must act as I do and vow never to see you again once you leave this tawdry land, but I cannot be the one responsible for taking your life from you. Surely that must be an act of the gods, he thought, sighing as memories of the good years brought tears to his eyes.

Finally the epistle was finished. It would not be delivered to Tiberius for some weeks, and then an equal amount of time would have to pass, Pilatus knew, before a reply could be expected, the journey a long way for any courier in those days, with the lurking possibility that the parchment would be destroyed by bad weather, or the legionnaire bearing it might fall victim to some misfortune, but, barring either of those circumstances, the emperor would receive it, consider his pro forma request, and undoubtedly not stand in the way.

Perhaps you and my wife will have another fling in my absence, Pilatus joked to himself. *At least, my dear Tiberius, you are not someone who is likely to be corrupted by her constant harping, should you decide to spend any more time with her.*

He glanced up as he heard Procula speaking just outside, his pulse quickening, an indelible memory of heaven opening up before him every bit as clear as it would remain throughout the rest of his life and always, along with it, the sound of someone raised from the dead, someone he loved so very deeply, her sweet voice calling his name, calling his name, calling his name. . .

At least, my dear Tiberius, you are not someone who is likely to be corrupted by her constant harping, should you decide to spend any more time with her.

"Unlike me," he whispered with regret from his very soul. "Indeed . . . unlike me."

Part II

XIX

Soon after leaving the Mount of Olives, Decimus Paetus and Fabius Scipio thrust off their heavy legionnaire garb and took upon themselves the rough street clothes of the common people of that land.

They were welcomed into the Christian community with an enthusiastic embrace from each of the apostles.

"But where is the thin one?" Paetus questioned moments later, remembering clearly the rather striking countenance of one of the followers of Jesus the Christ that he happened to have noticed on occasion. "Naturally I do not know the man's name, but he seemed so very passionate, very dedicated."

The eleven remaining apostles fell silent as the group of them sat before a welcome campfire some miles from the quaint rural town of Bethlehem, that area's typical nighttime chill beaten back for the moment.

"What is it?" Paetus persisted. "Was this man arrested on order of Pontius Pilatus and never released?"

He saw their expressions.

"Is the one of which I speak . . . dead?" he asked a bit tremulously, a chill moving along his spine, despite the fire.

Peter looked at the former legionnaire, his massive, weathered face lined with an expression of the profoundest sorrow.

"You have guessed correctly, Decimus, my friend, for Judas Ischariot is dead," the fisherman spoke somberly, "and it was by his own hand that this proved to be so."

"One of you committed suicide!" Paetus replied, shocked. "How could that be? What could have driven this comrade of yours to such desperation?"

The others were silent for an hour or so.

Paetus and Scipio waited, glancing at one another, wondering what terrible revelation was being temporarily withheld from them.

Finally the entire group partook of some big-eyed fish caught earlier that day by Peter and Andrew in the Sea of Galilee. The water had been quite calm, unlike other occasions when casting the nets proved impossible in the turbulence, and the latest catch was large enough to take care of their needs.

When they all had finished, it was not Peter who dealt with the matter of the dead apostle but John, the youngest of them.

"Judas was the one who betrayed our Lord in the Garden of Gethsemane," he said, his smooth, white skin made pale-looking by moonlight.

For a moment neither Paetus or Scipio could speak.

"He conspired to murder Jesus?" the younger of the two former legionnaires ventured disbelievingly.

The eleven men nodded in unison.

Without warning, Scipio jumped to his feet and, turning his back to the rest of them, bowed his head.

"You do not have to hide how you are feeling from the rest of us," Peter spoke finally, and with great feeling. "We have had a bonding, you and I and the others. Believe that, please, *feel* the genuineness of it.

"Tears are not to be ashamed of these days, nor are they are in short supply. We all have cried great torrents. You are not less a man by letting them flow, for if that were so, we all here would be equally guilty."

Scipio swung around.

"Judas betrayed *God!*" he said. "How could he have done so? Did some evil enter his body and take over?"

"Oh, yes," Peter replied. "It was evil that did this. We felt it in the man's presence during that last day, but we had no idea with what we were dealing. Judas had always been a moody individual, keeping to himself as much as he could manage."

"But why?" Paetus asked as Scipio was sitting down again. "What could he have wanted to accomplish by such an act?"

"I can only guess," Peter went on. "I can only guess that he saw Jesus as a revolutionary, as a militant messiah who would soon cast off the Roman yoke. When he realized that this was not so, that his timetable was not to be realized by Jesus, he thought he had been betrayed, and he struck back."

"By a kiss on the cheek," dark-haired, thin-framed Andrew added. "We all thought of it at first to be an act of devotion, a reaffirmation of love."

"Betrayed by a kiss . . . ," murmured several of the other apostles, uniformly struck by the awfulness of that remembered moment.

"Our Lord had just come from prayer in an isolated corner of Gethsemane," John spoke up again, his eyes moist. "We all had fallen asleep while He was there, so tired were we by the events of that week. Jesus had asked us to stay awake and join with Him in prayer, but we could not. We had little energy left.

"Do you not see how awful such a simple matter was? We disappointed the Son of God even then. We could not obey God-in-the-flesh even then. He asked so little of us all, so very little. All He wanted was for us simply to stay awake, yes, nothing more. *It was to be Jesus' last request of any of us!*"

John bowed his head. Scipio crawled over to him, and the apostle fell against his right shoulder.

"The rest of you are so strong compared to me," John sobbed. "I feel weak before all of you now."

Gruff Matthew, once reviled as a hated tax gatherer, a small man but emboldened in the old days by the might of Rome for which he acted as a representative, stood then, and raised his hands up toward the stars and beyond.

"Savior, Savior," he said, "You are now in Your Kingdom, and we are left here in the midst of this cursed place."

He was shivering at the thought of that truth.

"We must face the emotions that Your presence raised within each of us," Matthew continued. "You have left, but the emotions remain, and to them must be added, in Your absence, a longing to see You yet again, blessed Jesus . . . to hear Your voice yet again, to walk with You along the paths of life yet again."

Matthew finished praying out loud but stayed in that position, as though continuing to say something in a more private manner, something that was intended only between Almighty God and himself.

Finally he stopped, and without addressing the others, started to go off by himself, then hesitated before saying, "It is not any of you. There is nothing wrong. I believe it was the voice of the Creator that I heard just now in my very soul."

He sighed, though not with any weariness.

"I need to be alone," he added simply.

"But it is so cold, Matthew," John said, as he stood and walked over to his friend. "Here, take another cloak, please!"

The former hated gatherer of often extortionary taxes thanked him, and then, shoulders held quite straight, disappeared into the darkness.

"Do something about this," Thomas protested. "He will come back sick. What sense is there in that?"

"If God has directed our brother to do this," Peter reminded them, "how can any of us object?"

The others mumbled agreement.

After finishing what was left of their meal, the ten apostles and the two former legionnaires bundled animal skins tightly around themselves and moved as close to the flames as they dared, before trying to fall asleep for the night.

Normally an exceptionally crowded center of Middle Eastern commerce in any event, the city of Jerusalem was even more densely packed with often boisterous throngs exactly fifty days after Passover than at other times of the year because, during that period farmers, reaching the end of the grain-harvesting season, left their parcels of land for that ancient city as their destination, a journey necessary in order for them to be able to buy food, other supplies, and various trinkets while partaking of whatever amusements they could find. It was a cherished period of needed relaxation and refreshment.

They toiled throughout the year, these hard-working Jews of that period, only to see a large percentage of the results of their labor going through the tax gatherers to their Roman conquerors as well as to greedy religious rulers and the extortionary costs of animals for sacrifice when they worshiped at the temple, the very corruption of ritual that the Nazarene had protested against so strongly.

From the month of Tishri, when the first substantial rains occurred in that region, through the period of ploughing during Marchesvan, followed by the olive harvest conducted just prior to the month of Kislev, and on to grain planting which continued through Tevet and Shevat, they were chained to the demands of the land from whose bounty they had been able to stay alive for generations. When Adar came, there was the flax harvest, and then, during Nisan and Iyvar, barley. The dry season began in the month of Sivan, which consequently marked the start of the wheat harvest.

Shavuot . . . the Festival of Weeks.

Thousands swelled the regular population of Jerusalem, tired people ready to spring loose from the captivity of their genuinely arduous labors.

The apostles among them.

Periodically the eleven plus Paetus and Scipio would pitch in to help a farm family. Though that was not what they intended whenever they stopped by to speak of Jesus the Christ, if the head of the household was polite and invited them in for some food, they would reciprocate by staying a few days and assisting in the harvest.

"I am more tired now," Scipio protested, "than when I was fighting the wars of Imperial Rome."

It was night. The thirteen men were staying in a landowner's stable. They had just finished eating a simple meal and were talking among themselves before shutting their eyes and letting sleep take away the aches and tiredness they all felt.

"We were handed everything," Paetus pointed out. "Our clothes, our food, our drink. We were told where to go and whom to fight. From morning until evening, we were Rome's own, and Rome dictated it all."

The two men had grown ample beards since they were allowed by Pontius Pilatus to leave, and they had learned as many habit patterns of itinerant Jews as possible. Surprisingly, they fit in with little difficulty.

Having a group of such men willing to accept only the payment of food and lodging was a boon to the fortunate farmers for whom the apostles worked, since efficiency was of significant importance. Harvesting the wheat meant doing so with just the right timing. Waiting even slightly too long risked the crop being overripe, which meant that the grains, now loose, would fall to the ground and become useless. It was better to be two days early, so went the wisdom of the day, than two days late.

One by one, the thirteen men had moved into the stalk-covered fields, along with the members of each farm family and any other laborers being put to work. In one coordinated movement, each man would grab a clump of stalks in one hand and with the other hand swing a scythe against the stalks, stalk after stalk, countless times an hour.

But once the grain was harvested, the job had not ended, by any means. Behind the main group always came the young helpers who gathered up the fallen wheat, bundling it together into sheaves. These were quickly taken back to the communal threshing center where the rest of the work would be completed.

Just before leaving the fields, the owner of a particular farm would signal for the gleaners to come on in.

"How sad!" Scipio exclaimed as he stood next to the towering Simon Peter.

"Why do you say that, my friend?" Peter asked.

"They exist off the scraps of a kind man's generosity."

"Why is that sad? Is it sadder than these people starving to death?"

"I know what you are saying. That is not what I meant, good Peter."

"Then explain, will you?"

"No one else cares. The high priests want nothing to do with them, for these folk cannot contribute to the temple treasury, and, thus, Caiphas and the rest of his ilk find them of no value whatsoever. Pilatus and the other Romans consider them human garbage, to be pushed aside without remorse whenever the occasion calls for it."

Peter rubbed his beard for a moment, and then responded, "But Jesus proclaimed to us and multitude after multitude that the last shall be first, and the first shall be last. How many men and women of privilege, of power, of such disdain for the lowly around them will enter the kingdom of heaven when they die?"

124

He paused, emphasizing that question, and then added, "It is true, my brother, that a camel can get through the needle's eye much more easily than the uncharitable will avoid the flames of damnation."

"Needle's eye?" Scipio repeated. "Peter, do you mean that tiny gate in the eastern wall around Jerusalem?"

"Yes, that is what I meant."

Scipio fell silent.

But Peter continued as he said, "For such men, there is to be no mercy. They claim confidence only in their material holdings, what they have accumulated from their own efforts. They turn their backs on the poor, except in a way that shows off their so-called generosity to others like themselves. It is not kindness that directs their actions in such instances but the need to be seen, to be talked about, to be complimented."

"For the farmers, it seems so different," Scipio spoke, musing about what he had seen over the past few weeks. "I can see so clearly from their manner that they experience genuine pleasure in helping the poor."

"This is because they are not so far from being poor themselves, Fabius. Except for the grace of God, there they would be also, eating from the fruits of someone else's mercy. It is the rich who are isolated from all this, and any kind feelings they might once have had dry up in time, their hearts hardened."

"Sad . . ." Scipio repeated.

"You are truly correct. The hungry are being fed even as we watch. Yet the rich will one day be hungry themselves—though not for food. They will hunger for mercy, for relief from punishment of the soul, but it will be denied by a just God. Weep for them, Fabius Scipio, not those you see before you now."

XX

After the actual harvesting was completed, there came another facet of the process of getting the wheat to market.

Threshing.

The purpose was to loosen the grain from the stalks. This could be accomplished in two ways. Farmers with few assets simply beat the grain loose by using long, wood poles. But others, the majority, in fact, were able to use threshing rollers pulled by oxen or donkeys.

The final step involved separating the wheat from the chaff, or pseudo-wheat. Called winnowing, it required a breeze that would catch the chaff as the mixture was skillfully tossed up into the air, blow the pseudo-wheat away, leaving only the genuine grain.

Then the grain was sifted, which removed any pebbles or other unwanted matter. The wheat, after this, was stored in pottery jars that the farmers had made by hand for that purpose—that is, after Rome got its share.

Tired, their cupboards dangerously low of supplies, and needing amusement as relief from their labors, the farmers and their helpers headed toward Jerusalem . . .

"Such noise!" Scipio remarked as he entered through the Damascus Gate.

All around them were a great multitude of men, women, and children; the wealthy and the almost-poor as well as the genuinely poor; and beggars who were blind or lame, or simply too lazy to work.

"And the odors," Paetus added.

Sweat, dung, grease from cooking, and other smells mingled together.

The apostles had gone in ahead of them.

Initially, Paetus and Scipio hung back, nervous over the possibility of being recognized by legionnaires who might be in Jerusalem then. Even though Pilatus's release would serve to protect the two on an official basis, individual soldiers might harbor resentment and release their feelings in a violent confrontation.

"They cannot arrest us," Paetus mused out loud, after the apostles were out of sight, feeling the tension himself but not expressing it as openly as his comrade.

"But they *can* make mockery of us," Scipio pointed out. "I doubt that I could tolerate that. I might act rashly, Decimus. I might not be able to control myself."

"We remain thankful for the absence of what could have been a greater ordeal, Fabius. We could be in prison right at this very moment. Think, my friend, of the contempt that would be heaped upon us if that had been so!"

Scipio shrugged, admitting, "It could be worse, I suppose. Yes, you are right. Forgive my insecurity."

"It is the same as my own," Paetus assured him.

The narrow streets characteristic of Jerusalem were so jammed with people that getting literally stuck was a real haphazard. People hurrying about became pressed in with others emerging from shops or living quarters, and human traffic on either side of this sudden flesh-and-blood knot backed up along that particular street all the way to the center of the city.

Shouting grew more frequent, louder.

The two former legionnaires came upon just such a pocket of congestion.

"Can we help them?" Scipio ventured.

"We should try," Paetus replied.

Which they did.

Scipio kept the crowd on his side away from those who were tangled up with one another.

Paetus surveyed the situation, and decided that he needed some lubricant.

A nearby shop owner, overhearing him speak out loud, offered some inexpensive oil for the task.

Paetus thanked the man, took the large jug.

"May I go up on your roof?" he asked.

The shop owner nodded.

Paetus entered the one story adobe-type building and climbed the single flight of stone steps to the roof. Walking over to the edge, he looked down at the knot of people.

No one could move. Bodies were twisted together, arms around arms, legs around legs, heads pressed against others. Some of the elderly had lost consciousness, but were still standing, propped up by the people on every side.

Paetus dumped the oil on them.

It may not have been the wisest thing for him to do or the most elegant, but it proved to be just what was needed.

People *slid* away from one another. Nearly all lost their anger and frustration along with what had been their growing panic from a heightened sense of agoraphobia, and turned to laughter, uproarious, uncontrollable laughter. Even those not involved in the original tight knot were drawn into the preposterous chaos of that scene.

Finally the street returned to what was a typically heavy flow of human traffic.

"Decimus! Decimus!" he heard Scipio calling to him.

Paetus hurried downstairs and outside.

His friend was holding the frail-looking body of an old woman.

"I think she is dying," Scipio said in a helpless tone. "What can we do?"

The shop owner saw this and said that they could bring her inside and rest her on a bed of straws that he himself used to take a nap on each day.

She apparently was in little pain but the skin on her quite pale face was drawn so tight against her skull that she seemed as much a skeleton as a living human being.

A thin hand reached up toward Scipio. He took it gently in his own.

"Thank you," she said, her voice weak, only barely audible. "I was in the crowd. They pressed against me. I—"

Her eyes closed, but she was still breathing. Faded lips moved slowly.

Scipio bent down close to her and stayed in that position for more than a minute. Then, as he was straightening up, the woman's eyes shot open, startling him.

"Tell your friend!" she pleaded. "Tell everyone. The stories are true. They have not been made up. Proclaim the truth everywhere."

She smiled then, and lifted herself up from the straw, to kiss Scipio on the cheek.

"God bless you, and keep you," she said, "all the days of your life."

And then she fell back, dead.

"I could feel her life just *go!*" Scipio exclaimed. "That has happened on the battlefield. But it is different somehow with this poor soul."

He continued holding her until the shop owner became impatient.

"Please, you must go now," the man said, irritated.

"But where do we put her?" Scipio asked.

"In the potter's field, with all the rest," offered Paetus, shivering as he did so.

"You do not relish the thought, do you?" the other asked.

Paetus shook his head.

"What is it about this place? I do not know it as you do."

"You will see for yourself, Fabius, especially since we will probably arrive there just as dusk comes on."

"We should wrap something around her poor body," Scipio remarked mournfully as he glanced once again at the bony figure in his arms.

Overhearing this, the shop owner, short, with a beard reaching nearly to the bare earth floor, looked at him, then at the wizened old body, and nodded, as he reached for a blanket that was spun out of pure silk.

"That is very expensive," Paetus remarked, recognizing its worth immediately. "Are you sure?"

"No one should go into a grave only in the most wretched of rags," the shop owner said, "yet too many do, day-after-day, because so few of us care about their plight anymore—we see people like her as just another homeless wreck of a woman. Yesterday it was a little boy and—"

He shoved the blanket into Paetus's hands and hurried outside, unwilling to confront strangers any longer with his emotions.

"Do you know where this place is?" Scipio asked.

"It is in a valley to the southern side of Jerusalem, just ahead of us. The area is called Hinnom."

"Odd-sounding, is it not, even for these people?"

"It has an awful history, Fabius, a history so foul that there is another name connected with it."

"Tell me more on the way there," Scipio remarked abruptly. "She weighs little but she grows heavier the longer I hold her."

Paetus smiled faintly, and walked outside, the other man following him.

If they went straight ahead, through the winding streets of the city, they could reach the southern end in less than an hour perhaps, followed a short time later by a descent into the Valley of Hinnom. So, the two of them walked as fast as they could, anxious to be done with the task they had set for themselves.

"Is that not the building where we hid in the pottery closet?" Scipio commented a few minutes later, nodding toward the two-story structure to his left.

"Yes, it is—and what is it that I hear coming from inside?" Paetus added, taken aback by the sheer magnitude of it, his legs frozen, unable to carry him forward.

A strange sound, to be sure . . . *like the onrush of a mighty wind!*

XXI

The apostles had been in prayer when the upper room in which they were meeting seemed to be lit up abruptly with a fiery light.

"*It is the end of the world!*" frightened Thomas said, crawling behind Peter, and shielding his eyes from the sudden radiance.

"I think not, poor Thomas," Peter said, smiling. "I think it is just the beginning of something altogether different, and wonderful."

Peter himself questioned how he could ever have known this, but know it he surely did, the conviction of truth in his heart every bit as certain, as real as the room itself.

For a moment, the entire building shook.

"Fire!" Matthew shouted. "Look at the fire! It—"

It came, with a sound like the roaring of a mighty windstorm. Suddenly there were tongues of fire appearing from nowhere, surrounding them, yet not burning their flesh. Instead, it seemed to enter them, every muscle touched, every nerve stimulated, the totality of each man vibrating with the sheer force of that wave of flames.

"My fear is gone!" Thomas proclaimed.

"Such joy," John spoke. "I feel as though every pain is gone, every—!"

They all stood, virtually as a single unit.

The eleven held their hands out in front of them, touching the flames, which continued like water, pouring over their bodies.

A voice.

Deep, rich, familiar.

"The Lord!" Andrew cried out. "It is the Lord Himself!"

Their minds perceived words that their ears could not hear.

Go now my beloved. . . . Go into the streets of this city, and talk to the lost. . . . Be their shepherds. . . . Gather together the flock. . . . Proclaim to them the joy you feel now, and from whence it comes. . . After you have done this, leave Jerusalem behind you and go into the provinces nearby and, later, beyond them, to other lands. . . . For you are to be the messengers of salvation to those who will heed the good news you bring with precious words of eternal redemption. . . . Take no thought for the language others might speak. . . . You have been given a special gift this day. . . . Use it with wisdom, as Almighty God intended.

Gone.

In an instant, the voice had ceased and the flames were gone.

The apostles stood in the middle of that room, looking at one another, then back at the high ceiling, confused at first, none of them knowing quite what to say or do, but feeling a curious peace that passed all understanding.

"Why do I feel as I do now?" spoke normally taciturn Thomas. "The Lord has left us. And yet . . . yet there is within me—"

He thrust his hands out before him, waving them with great excitement.

"Joy!" he shouted. "Such joy as I have never known before."

Peter straightened his shoulders, raising himself to his full height.

"Within us!" he proclaimed. "The Holy Spirit is within us. We have received Him into our very bodies!"

They heard voices outside.

"People from so many lands gathered below," Peter surmised. "They know not what has happened. They can hear only the sounds."

"Like men drunk with new wine," John said. "Yet we have not touched so much as a single drop."

The youngest apostle rushed to the window overlooking the street outside, which was wider at that point, forming a small square.

"I love you all!" he shouted out to them. "I love every one of you."

Most looked strangely puzzled, but a few listened intently.

John turned from the window.

"So many *heard* me just now," he said, frowning, "but only a few looked as though they *understood* my words. How can that be? Am I so unintelligible?"

"John, John," the fisherman replied softly, "did you not hear yourself? Are you not aware of what happened?"

"Yes, I know very well what I was—"

His mouth dropped open.

"My mind spoke the words as I have always spoken, but my lips . . . my lips!"

"And yet you did *communicate* with a few down there," Peter went on, his voice becoming more and more excited. "John, *you were able to speak in a different tongue altogether!*"

Peter rushed past the other man and stood at the window. The crowd had grown, packing every inch of that square and overflowing into the narrow street on either side.

"My friends, I want to speak to you of someone who came into the world that salvation must be yours," he proclaimed, and went on talking for at least five minutes.

By the time the fisherman finished, a dozen men and women had raised their hands above their heads, along with their voices as they shouted, "We hear you, and we understand. You have spoken in our native tongue."

One-by-one, the apostles walked to the single window in that bare, white-washed room and spoke as they were moved to do so, each one in a different language, each time a group of people from below hearing and understanding, and shouting back words of recognition and joy at the message they were being given.

"Come outside!" those in the crowd shouted as one. "Come and face us this very moment and be our teachers. Bring to our starving souls greater and greater wisdom from Almighty Jehovah Himself!"

Thomas, possessed of more energy than he had ever known before then, started toward the steps leading to the street.

"We must do what they say," he told the others. "We must go among them, and use this gift. We must talk to those from every corner of the world, and bring the good news that the Lord has given for the redemption of—"

He stopped for a moment, overcome with emotion, tears dripping down his cheeks and off his chin, onto his clothes.

"I cannot say what is happening to me," Thomas said after gaining control again. "I do not know what the future holds, for I am not a prophet as Daniel, Jeremiah, or Ezekiel, but this I can tell you: We can speak with anyone to whom we are led now. We can speak because we have the gift of tongues."

To one side, John also was succumbing to his emotions as he fell to his knees, and started babbling in a manner incoherent to the others. Peter hurried to his side, and sat down in front of him.

"What is it, John?" the fisherman asked.

"I feel such power," the young apostle replied. "I can scarce contain it, you know. I have to let it out!"

"Yes, yes, I know, John, for it is similar to the way the rest of us are reacting at this very moment. A miracle from heaven itself has been visited upon *all* of us, my brother."

John, his eyes bloodshot, looked up.

"I trust you, Peter; I love you, Peter," he said. "Let the Lord speak through you."

"Dear John, beloved John," the big man spoke with the greatest tenderness, "do not waste this gift on yourself or even the rest of us, for that is not why it has come to us this day. It was given by the Lord for *them*, for all the endless crowds of ignorant men and women we shall be meeting until the end of our days, the countless numbers who are headed for damnation. They cannot listen if they cannot understand, and they cannot understand if we merely speak as we have done since birth."

John nodded with understanding, and stood. Outside, people continued their entreaties, their voices rising louder and louder.

"They await us," Peter said, having become the leader.

The others murmured agreement, and filed down the steps after him, the crowd roaring with anticipation as they appeared outside.

From a dozen or more different locations in the known world of that day, that massive crowd of thousands had come by various modes of transportation over sea as well as land to the ancient city of Jerusalem, even from as far away as the Orient, and, though present originally for various other reasons, they soon clamored together for the attention of the men who proclaimed a risen Lord.

Despite the great mass of men, women, and children competing for the attention of the apostles, none had to be turned aside or ignored in any way, and each heard the wise and redeeming words offered by those eleven followers of Jesus the Christ, mere unlearned Galileans though these men were, yet the entire lot of them speaking in a variety of native tongues to the understanding of all.

XXII

Decimus Paetus and Fabius Scipio were able to get past the square before the crowd had packed it so tightly that moving at all would have been next-to-impossible. But they still had to battle the numbers of visitors and residents alike who were being drawn to that spot as word of what was happening spread throughout Jerusalem.

"I wish we could be there right now," Scipio said, "sharing with the others whatever it is that they are experiencing."

"We will have plenty of time when we return," Paetus replied.

Finally they reached the southern wall of the city and found a small exit to the outside. As they went through it, both detected the odors.

"What a stench!" Scipio remarked.

"Another name for the Valley of Hinnom is Gehenna!" Paetus told him.

"Gehenna? A Jewish word, is it not? What does it mean, Decimus?"

"Hell—a place of damnation."

"Smoke, Decimus. I see plumes of black smoke just ahead."

"Fires are always here, Fabius, by day and by night."

"They burn the dead?"

"They burn their rubbish here."

"A place of burial is in the same area where refuse is disposed of?"

Paetus nodded sadly as he glanced at the lifeless form in his friend's arms.

. . . where rubbish is disposed of.

The wealthy were not laid to rest in that place. Nor were the religious leaders, not even the farmers, the store-owners, or anyone of position in Jewish society—just the hapless beggars of that time, the blind, the lame; others of the homeless, including despised lepers, now mercifully dead, who were thrown by their kind onto bare wood carts drawn by donkeys slowly making their mournful way toward Gehenna.

From the north, near Gadrene, beasts carried their daily awful load of lepers and maniacs, victims of disease and madness who were

134

shunned by the rest of the populace, relegated while yet alive to a rock-strewn, isolated place where they shuffled about in caves and ate insects, rats, other creatures in order to stay alive as long as they could, though, to the contrary, many ended up starving themselves to death rather than face the miseries that were their lot for far too long.

Gehenna was the destination of the dead ones, their bodies sliding out of the carts which had been tilted at the edges of large pits in the center of the Valley of Hinnom, pits lit by bonfires that were kept burning through disposal of refuse of all kinds.

It was happening as Paetus and Scipio stood back from the edge of one such holocaust and watched, human beings entering the flames, their bodies quickly consumed.

"Sometimes the dead rise, Fabius," recalled Paetus.

"Like Jesus?" the other man responded.

"Not like the Savior, no."

"How then?"

"They are not dead after all. They have only swooned."

"We were so careful about this old woman!"

"But men assigned to Gadrene do not care, my friend. They see a body. They order it thrown onto the cart. Then they go on to the next one."

"And the whole load of them down there!" Scipio said, as he nodded toward the pit and the flames at the bottom of it.

"You look pale," Paetus observed, with some sympathy. "Let me take the body. I should have asked before now."

"Yes, you should have," Scipio said scoldingly.

As Paetus was taking the pitiable load from the younger man, he saw Scipio's gaze wander to the pit again, eyes opening wide, and heard a gasp escape his lips.

"It is happening now, Decimus—as you said! We cannot send this woman there. I could never let that poor body—"

"Such was never my intention," Paetus assured him. "It is the potter's field, not the flames for this one."

Minutes later, they had passed by the other pits.

Directly ahead they saw the old cemetery, set on a little hill, with straggly, near-dead trees around its perimeter.

And what was left of a man's body hanging from a tree.

"Oh, Decimus, look!" Scipio exclaimed as he pointed to what was left of it.

"I see. yes . . . in his left hand," Paetus said as he rested the fragile body of the old woman on the ground. "What is that?"

Scipio hesitated, and then holding his breath, he walked up close to the body and saw something grasped in that left hand. Then he returned to his friend and reported: "A small leather sack, the kind used to hold silver coins."

Slapping his forehead with his left palm, Scipio blurted, "Judas Iscariot! It must be the very one who betrayed Jesus with a simple kiss."

"He's been there for some time," Paetus remarked. "The man had no one to turn to, nowhere to go. Heaven itself rejected him."

He gripped the old woman's body a bit more tightly.

"He died, alone, near the Gehenna we have just seen. And now, Fabius, this evil man is in an eternal place of flames. What he saw in front of him here, during the final moments of his life, surely seemed a hint. Perhaps, realizing that, he started to change his mind. That could have happened, you know. But if he did, as terror got hold of him, it was too late, for he was already slipping away as the rope choked him."

Scipio hugged himself, abruptly chilled by what his friend had said, and where they were, and from whence they had come minutes earlier.

"I want to leave this place as soon as I can," he said. "I want to take off my clothes and let clean water wash over me and try to forget —oh, how I will try to do that."

He looked up for a moment and saw what he had not noticed before.

Well-dressed men and women not far away were bending down, scooping up loads of red clay, and scurrying off.

"Why are they doing that?" Scipio asked.

"Potters, my friend. They use the clay in their work. That is why this is called the potter's field."

These Israelites pointedly avoided looking to one side or the other as much as possible, closing off any glimpse of the fires and smoke to their right, and the dismal field of corpses to their left, filling their containers and then rushing off.

Finally, the two former legionnaires found a vacant spot and dug a hole that they hoped would be deep enough and gently placed the old woman's body inside.

"We have done what we can," Scipio spoke. "Surely we have no more obligation to a stranger."

"A marker," Paetus said. "We have left no marker."

"It will be gone with the first heavy rains. Please, Decimus, my spirit is weighed down with this place. Let us go. Let us be done with it now."

Paetus nodded slowly, turning only for a moment to look back at the bleak spot of red clay where the unknown woman's wretched body had been put, not far from that foul, fiery place called Gehenna.

"Good-bye . . ." he whispered.

They passed the tree where Judas Iscariot's body remained, birds once again settling on it for whatever was left to them.

"One to damnation, to the other—?" Scipio posed.

Paetus shrugged his shoulders, and then they were gone, back toward the city wall, and, soon, inside Jerusalem where they would meet up with the eleven remaining apostles of Jesus the Christ and surround themselves at last with the cleansing joy of that first Day of Pentecost.

XXIII

The aged, stooped-over widower who was owner of the modest building in which they had eaten with the Nazarene for the last time before His crucifixion offered to let the apostles live in it for as long as needed. He told them that it was nearly vacant most of the time anyway, except for the hours when he sold leather goods and molded some pottery with his own hands from the small space on the ground floor.

"Something wonderful has happened this day in these humble quarters," he told them. "If I can contribute to your lives as you all have just done to the lives of so many others during the past few hours, I would like to do so. Please, my friends, will you accept this small offer from a dying old man?"

"Dying, sir?" Peter spoke up then. "What is the cause?"

"I cannot say. I cough a great deal. Sometimes blood comes up instead of clear liquid. I can feel more weakness coming on me each morning as I awaken, and find it just a bit harder to get out of bed. Age? Disease? What can I tell you?"

Peter put his arms around the thin body in front of him.

"Jesus loves you," he whispered.

The old man pulled back.

"I have never met this man," he said. "How can it be that He would love someone such as myself?"

Peter smiled as he replied, "His Holy Spirit is with these other men and I even now. Jesus knows your heart, my friend, especially the compassion that you feel."

"My name is Abraham, you know," the other said. "Perhaps your Jesus thinks I am from the patriarch's line. I am not, you know. It is just a name, like any other."

"It has nothing to do with what you happen to be called. It is what you are that the Lord Jesus sees."

"Will I ever meet this man?" Abraham asked, a look of sudden expectancy on his bearded old face.

"Soon, I think," Peter assured him. "Soon . . ."

"How will I know when it is He?"

"You will have no doubt, Abraham, no doubt whatever."

Scratching his head, the old man turned, and walked down the stairs.

Decimus Paetus and Fabius Scipio had joined with the apostles by then.

"What happened here, in our absence?" Paetus asked, knowing quite a bit already but wanting to hear more.

As the group of thirteen sat around the table in that room, finishing some thick-crusted fresh bread that Abraham had brought up to them, Peter as well as Andrew and John proceeded to tell the two men what had transpired.

"We saw something different inside the walls upon our return," Scipio then recalled, not waiting this time for Paetus to speak first, though he normally would have done that, intimidated a bit by the veteran former legionnaire.

"What was that?" John asked, feeling a certain kinship with someone whose age was closer to his own than the others in that room. "You had some hint of what we have been telling you?"

"I now see the connection," Scipio continued. "I now know what caused people to act the way they did."

Re-entering the city had driven both Paetus and Scipio to sigh with relief. They had come from a place of death, from dreary Gehenna to boisterous Jerusalem set on a hill, like a beacon to them in the darkness.

"We saw a host of small fires burning everywhere, the only light we could find," Paetus recalled. "People were sitting around these, talking, gesturing with enthusiasm. Snatches of what they were saying came to our ears."

Virtually all of them spoke of the group of Galileans, itinerant men, by-and-large, with little learning, who existed on handouts from people either sympathetic to them or anxious to be rid of them.

"Yet they could speak with such eloquence," one man was saying, "and in whatever language necessary to be understood by whoever was listening."

"I have never seen or heard anything like it," another added. "I wonder from whence comes this miracle."

Scipio had approached this last speaker.

"Sir?" he said, with uncustomary boldness.

The man, a well-dressed merchant apparently, looked up.

"May I help you?" he asked.

"You spoke of a miracle just now," Scipio went on a bit brashly. "What is it that you meant by that?"

The man indicated an empty spot next to him.

"Please, sit down," he said.

"I have a friend . . ." Scipio pointed to Paetus.

"He can sit across from us."

When the newcomers had joined the other men around the fire, the one who had invited them identified himself as Aaron.

"I heard the followers of the Nazarene talk to that man over there, the one with the strange eyes," he said. "As you can tell, he is from the Orient, and has journeyed to Jerusalem, among other places, to dispose of his spices and some oils."

Aaron pointed to three others at the fire.

"Different languages spoken by all of them," he said, "yet the fisherman and the tax collector and all the others with them spoke as though they had been born in the various countries from which these men have come."

Paetus and Scipio exchanged glances.

"Without training, I assume, or study of any sort, they did what I have said," Aaron continued, "and each of us understood!"

His eyes betrayed his excitement.

"We understood," he said, "yea, and we *believed!*"

The two former legionnaires let the significance of this settle in, choosing to say nothing for the moment.

"You do not grasp fully what I mean," Aaron persisted. "We took their words and understood the meaning of what was said, and we . . . we now . . . are—"

Another man, sitting to his right, pulled on Aaron's cloak.

"We must be wise in this," he whispered. "We must be careful with whom we speak. We know not who these—"

Overhearing, Paetus interrupted, "My friend and I are now followers of the Nazarene ourselves. You do not have to worry, strangers. We, too, have accepted this Jesus as our Savior, our precious Lord."

At that, the half dozen men around the fire jumped to their feet, joined hands, and shouted a single name with exuberance, "Jesus! Jesus! Jesus!" Again and again they spoke it as loudly as they could, until their voices grew weary, and then they sat down once more and shared some wine to moisten their needy throats.

XXIV

In front of that little building, the crowd had dispersed for the night, retreating either to the shelter of their simple homes or to one of the campfires within the city walls and, for many more, out in the countryside.

The apostles were still in the upper room, just finishing dinner, when Paetus and Scipio entered. The two men were greeted with great enthusiasm.

"It is still very strange to us," Paetus admitted, as they sat down around the table where some fish, bread, and wine remained, "that we, so recently mere strangers, are welcomed into your lives as readily as you have allowed."

"It matters not what you were," Peter answered. "What you have *become* is a temple for the Holy Spirit."

"The Holy Spirit is in *us?*" Scipio spoke up.

"The moment you accepted Jesus as your Savior, your Lord," the fisherman assured him. "Your soul was opened up to His entrance, and He will never leave you nor forsake you, regardless of the circumstances."

"For *any* reason?" Scipio persisted, finding this new truth altogether wonderful but, as well, quite perplexing. "I could do *anything* I wanted, and the Holy Spirit would not forsake me?"

Quiet, thoughtful James spoke up then.

"What you would lose by an indecent act, an act of dishonor, would be your witness before men. You would not have your salvation taken away from you."

"James is right," Matthew said. "The *eternal* state of your relationship with God is not subject to the activity of your sin nature."

"But what if I slept with a harlot?" Paetus interjected.

"You would be chastised," the former tax gatherer observed, "but God would not cast you out."

Paetus was frowning.

"Let me put it this way, friend," James said, returning to the conversation. "If you were a father, and you saw your neighbor disown his son because of some transgression, what would your opinion of that neighbor be?"

"That he was hard-hearted, in truth, unloving and not deserving of the love or the loyalty of his son."

"Then why are you amazed when Almighty God is everything you expect your neighbor to be?" James added.

Paetus rubbed his beard as he pondered the wisdom of those words.

"You are saying that everything we want ourselves and others to be at their most noble, their kindest, their most loyal and devoted and loving, God is all of that and far more?" he mused out loud.

"Now you comprehend!" Peter exclaimed, slapping his thigh.

For the rest of the evening, prior to falling asleep, the thirteen men talked about many things, each infused with a growing wisdom that none had experienced before, a grasp of reality that they greeted as though they were children, given a new gift by loving parents, and entranced with the wonder of it.

When the hour was late and even their newfounded energies were dissipating temporarily, Paetus grew morose and went off to one side, sitting on the floor and leaning his head back against the whitewashed wall.

The others were still quite animated in their conversation and did not notice, except for Scipio, who broke away from them and sat beside his older friend.

"What is wrong, my brother?" he asked.

Paetus looked at him.

"You speak strangely, Fabius," he noted.

"In what way?"

"I cannot say, for the moment."

"I *am* concerned."

"About what?"

"You."

"I am fine."

Scipio chuckled a bit as he said, "Do I not know you well enough to sense when you are *not* feeling well?"

Paetus's shoulders slumped.

"I can hide so little these days," he confessed.

"We are no longer stoic Romans, Decimus, but emotional Christians," Scipio reminded him, smiling warmly.

"That is so very true, dear friend," Paetus agreed.

"Tell me, then, please. What bothers you?"

"The others."

"Peter, Matthew, James, the rest of the apostles? Why would *they* bother you? They are our friends, our brothers-in-Christ."

"They all speak in tongues!" Paetus blurted out, though keeping his voice low. "They can witness for Jesus to anyone they wish, because they have been given the ability to communicate in whatever language is needed."

"I do not have that gift either," Scipio pointed out.

"And it bothers you not?"

"At first, it did. I learned what had happened earlier this day, and I prayed for the same gift. How wonderful it would be to go anywhere in this world and talk to anyone and tell them the good news that it is our mission to spread."

"Your prayer was not answered, Fabius, and yet you can see the apostles blessed by God in this manner and no longer feel left out?"

"It is as you say, my brother. If God chooses not to bestow the ability which he has given to the other men, any despair on my part is the same as questioning the judgment of our Creator, the wisdom, the—"

Paetus was crying.

"Why the tears?" Scipio asked.

"I cried when I went to battle the first time and took a human life. I thought my comrades would make fun of me. But they did not. Because it had been the same with them, except for those who had no feeling at all, and there were very few of *them* around."

"But there is no battle now."

Paetus's gaze centered on his friend's face.

"There will be," he said. "We will face much bloodshed, more than you and I have seen on all the battlefields to which Rome ever sent us."

Neither of them noticed that the eleven apostles had suddenly stopped talking among themselves.

"How can you *know* this?" Scipio pressed.

"It is so clear," Paetus went on, not directly answering the other man, but tapping his forehead as he spoke. "I can see the rush of flames, naked bodies on crosses, men screaming in the night."

He started shivering.

"I see myself on a high place, looking up toward the sky, and begging God to take me so that I will not have to—"

He stopped for a moment, the images overwhelming him.

And then he turned toward John.

"You too shall see in this manner as I have," he said. "You shall see wonders of which the rest of us can only guess, John."

The rest of them had been sitting on the floor, listening, saying nothing to interrupt. But now the youngest apostle spoke, "Will you be with me, Decimus? Will we share these prophecies together?"

"You shall be alone," Paetus said with an odd mixture of sorrow and joy in his voice, "you and the Holy Spirit, communing as never before."

"And I shall die in this place?" John asked.

Paetus hugged himself, his body chilled through the flesh to every bone, it seemed.

"Yes," he replied slowly, knowing that his own place of death had been foreseen.

"Do you know the location?" John persisted a bit brashly.

"Patmos," Paetus told him. "The isle of Patmos, my brother."

"And you," John said. "What about you?"

Paetus swallowed several times before he could answer.

"Masada," he finally stated. "That is where I shall be when the Lord takes me home with Him."

The other apostles would have liked to have questioned Paetus about themselves, but they saw the paleness of his face and weakness of his manner, and knew that the time was not right for that.

"We must rest now," Peter spoke with great effort, his emotions touched by what had happened.

So they went to sleep a short while later, again in that upper room, each on his own soft patch of hay, covering themselves with lamb's wool blankets, and Decimus Paetus no longer questioned the gifts which God in His wisdom might bestow.

Part III

*S*eldom in the history of the world have a few decades been so influential, for during the forty years following the death, burial, and resurrection of Jesus the Christ, the foundation of the future of Christianity was set and nearly two thousand years of Jewish displacement from Israel commenced, the latter to be ended only after World War II.

Rome was firmly in its imperial period and seemed as powerful as ever, without the possibility of significant defeat; but the outer display of might masked a situation that was ominous. With the known world literally at their feet, upper crust Roman citizens were becoming bored. They had everything their station could bring them in an empire not yet successfully challenged to any extent on the battlefield. Increasingly they sought bizarre, often violent pursuits, ranging from bestiality to the gladiatorial conquests, this bloody, perverse trait not restrained at all by emperors such as Caligula and Nero, who themselves indulged such predilections for degeneracy.

It was a time when four Roman legionnaires, drawn together at Calvary, would each come into contact with a different person prominent during the period, ranging from Nicodaemus and Joseph of Arimathea, on to the apostle Paul, and then to Procula, the supposedly mad wife of Pontius Pilatus, along with the truly mad Nero—as well as the men destined to fight on either side at Masada, which was to become the touchstone of that period for both the Romans and the Jews.

XXV

Fabius Scipio parted from the company of Decimus Paetus just a single month less than three years after the two of them forsook their service for Rome and joined with the apostles of Jesus the Christ.

"I must return to my family, for it has been so very long since I have seen them," Fabius told the others, his emotions obviously stirred. "I want to look at my brother's smooth skin and see those hands with all the fingers in place. I want to hold him in my arms and tell him how much I love him."

Pactus understood. So did Peter and the rest of them.

"We will give you some food for the start of this journey of yours," the fisherman said, "as well as a few denarii. And we will send you away with the same love you have just now mentioned for your brother."

They were standing by the side of a dusty road outside tiny Bethlehem. The group had returned to that quaint old town and slept several nights in the very stable where Jesus had been born, all of them realizing how blessed it was that they could be there, as they tried to imagine themselves back in time to nearly forty years earlier when a virgin gave birth to the Son of God in such a humble location, wise men and shepherds alike drawn to it because of the leading of the Almighty Himself.

They went out and talked with many local people who remembered that particular day, women saying to their husbands that they could sense something going on, husbands telling their wives that they felt it also, whatever "it" was.

"Doves," one middle-aged man told them. "I had never seen so many beautiful white doves in all my life."

"Where were they?" John asked, anxious to find out more.

"Hovering directly above the same ancient stable from whence I saw you come moments ago."

"And then they were gone?"

"No, the whole lot of them stayed for quite awhile, resting on the roof, as though they did not want to leave that place."

John glanced at the other apostles, and at Paetus and Scipio.

"What was the reaction of other folks in Bethlehem?" he pressed.

148

"Some said that the doves must have smelled the odor of food coming from inside. But I pointed out to them that it was not any home where people ordinarily lived. Only the oats and such intended for the horses would have been there, and with the times as they were then, and now, not much of that either."

"What did *you* say?" John inquired pointedly.

The man, whose name they failed to obtain, turned away without answering.

"What is it, sir?" John persisted.

"Nothing . . ."

"But surely—"

The man spun around, his expression a mixture of fear and anger.

"I know who you are, the lot of you," he spat out the words. "You are that itinerant band of followers who hung around day-in and day-out with the Nazarene. It is here that He was born. I know all of this, you see. None of you are in favor in this land of my birth. The religious leaders despise you. The Romans are deeply suspicious of your motives. A humble man such as I should not be seen in your presence."

"What do *you* say?" John repeated.

"I say—," he began haltingly. "—I say that that child was our Messiah but we were too blind to acknowledge Him. Instead of helping Him, we turned on Him and made the Romans put Him to death."

His eyes were filling with tears.

"Leave me, please," he begged.

"He is not dead, my friend," John continued.

The man laughed.

"You *are* mad," he said. "I was there at the mount outside Jerusalem. I saw his poor, bleeding body hanging from the cross."

"Why did you go?" probed John.

The other man's face grew red.

"I am not under any obligation to tell you, a stranger, or anyone else, for that matter," he asserted. "I—"

The pretense was fading even as they stood, facing one another.

"Do you *know* the reason though you ask me for it?" he asked. "Do you read my mind as your leader was supposed to be able to do with anyone in His presence?"

"I do not," John admitted. "It is just that I could perceive that you would not travel such a distance for anything other than a very good cause."

"Oh, it was a *good* one, if good is the right word. I went . . . I . . . I went there because my brother was . . . was—"

He bowed his head, suddenly quite embarrassed.

"You do not have to tell me or anyone," John conceded. "It is not necessary to put yourself through this strain."

Just as abruptly, the man looked up.

"It is not something I can stop. So many nights that I scarce can count them all, as I go to sleep, the sight of my condemned brother hanging from that cross next to the Nazarene comes up so clearly in my mind, mocking me."

"Which one of the two was he?" John asked.

"The one on the right, who was supposed to be taken with this Jesus into His kingdom at the moment of death."

John's eyes widened.

"Do you believe that?" he asked.

"How *can* I?" the man admitted. "How can I believe in a man? That is all your leader was! A man as I am, as anyone."

"Oh, but he was so much more than what you say, sir," John told him. "If Jesus proclaimed that your brother would be side-by-side with Him in heaven, then, as we speak, he has been there all these years since those words were spoken!"

The man had seemed about ready to turn and leave but in an instant his manner changed altogether.

"I loved him so much," he remarked. "If what you have said is true, then at least my brother has some peace, some joy. I could never wish to take that from him, even though I shall never know it myself."

John turned to the others and asked whether they would mind if he and this man would go off by themselves for awhile.

No one protested.

★ ★ ★

More than an hour passed before John returned to their presence.

"He now has accepted Jesus as his Savior, his Lord," he told them. "I can feel the presence of the Holy Spirit."

They were rejoicing until Scipio told them of his desire to return to his family and spend time in fellowship with each member, but especially his brother, at least for a time.

"I *will* come back to you," Scipio promised with all sincerity.

"You may do that, or you may not," Peter replied.

"Yea, I will, for you all are also my brothers now," Scipio protested. "I intend to spend a few weeks there, perhaps, and then I shall head back."

Peter's eyes were filling with tears.

"If the Lord has other plans, dear Fabius, do not resist His blessed leading," he said as he hugged the young former legionnaire.

In turn the other men embraced Scipio and gave him encouragement for the journey ahead, uncertain as it was in those ancient times.

Finally it was Paetus's turn.

"We have spent only a few years together," he spoke, "mostly serving the desires of an empire we now despise because of the gods to whom it pays homage and the bloody way it has achieved its victories."

"You and I were among those who shed some of that very blood of which you speak, my brother," Scipio agreed, nodding. "We took the lives of men and—"

Memories made him hesitate, moments of women dead, their young children wandering dazedly, coming up to him, asking for help, and none would he give as he walked away, leaving them behind to become scavengers, or criminals, perhaps to die in a ditch in a land no longer their own, as a by-product of the glory that was Rome.

"I see them sometimes as I sleep," he added. "I see them become frail, thin, ridden with disease, sharing the places accorded outcasts like the lepers, digging among the rocks for worms or snails to eat and finding little."

He wiped his eyes with the back of his left hand.

"They do not know where their mothers and their fathers are buried. They cannot return to the place where they were born. And they have no place to go."

"Like the rest of us, do you not think?" Matthew asked, with the slightest touch of regret in his voice. "Like *me*, anyway."

The little man stood next to Paetus, looking up into Scipio's face.

"When I decided to make my living as a tax gatherer and could not be dissuaded from it, the earnings I would make blinding me, my mother disowned me, saying, 'You are no longer our son, you serve our conquerors, and I cannot stand the sight of you.' My father promised to kill me if he ever saw me within a hundred feet of the home in which I was born. He screamed, 'You extort money from friends, from neighbors. I too cast you out as vermin. Go crawl to the Romans who are now your only friends, but do not think that you have even their respect, for they must sneer at you behind your back.'"

Matthew threw up both hands, his brown eyes unnaturally wide as they darted from side to side.

"It is true what you said, dear Fabius," he went on. "I will never know where my parents are buried. Already they have moved on to some other location, and no one in the old neighborhood will tell me where that is. I cannot return to the place where I came into the world. And I have no real place to go.

"We share the same fate, but we share it in the knowledge that angels abound around us, for this we know from the lips of Jesus Himself, that nothing can happen to us without the knowledge and the consent of our Father. None of us can say that we are truly alone, that we have been truly forsaken. For if the Lord be with us, through the Holy Spirit, that can never, ever be. Indeed, this is a promise from Him, and if He has said it, it will stand with us until the end of our days."

. . . until the end of our days.

Scipio shivered at the very sound of those words, at the cold, forsaken, sad images they conjured up in his mind.

"I must go now," he said, with a reluctance of which none could be unaware.

One by one, they kissed him on both cheeks and stood aside as he started to walk up the road away from Bethlehem, and on toward the Mediterranean, where he hoped to get a boat on which to sail northwest toward Italy.

He turned, and shouted good-bye, waving as well, and then he set himself on a journey that, if he were honest with himself, he knew not where it would end.

XXVI

Weeks passed for Fabius Scipio as he made his circuitous way toward Puteoli, Italy where his mother, father, and brothers lived. He had to stop periodically and work as best he could in order to earn enough money to pay for the next segment of the journey. Only the wealthy could make complete arrangements all at once and then sit back lazily as they were transported to whatever destination they wished.

Yet Scipio did not consider this part of his life to be pointless or cruel. He met many people as he traveled north toward Antioch, though that had not been his preferred route because of the length of travel involved. He would rather have cast off on a vessel from Caesarea, which was much closer, sailing west toward Rhegium, on the southern tip of Italy, and then travel by land to Puteoli, which was somewhat southeast of Rome. Instead, thwarted by the lack of space on any of the boats, he went on to Ptolemais—and was disappointed once again and also at Tyre. Since Antioch offered land as well as sea routes, located as it was along the Orontes River a scant seven miles from the Mediterranean, it seemed the only alternative unless, traveling as he was so close to the waterfront, he happened to stumble upon someone with a smaller boat anchored offshore for a brief rest stop before continuing further.

Scipio stayed at inns along the roadside but occasionally residences as well, where he found himself fortunate enough to make contact only with those families that welcomed him in with great friendliness. In some instances, there were so many children present that no need existed for him to work, but instead he was simply given a thick bed of comfortable straw and as much food as he could eat because of the generous spirit he encountered.

"He who does not teach his son useful labor or a trade is bringing him up to be a thief," one father told him. "One of the greatest gifts I can give to my son is a set of tools. Another is to make certain that he does not stand by while others work in his stead."

"Your own tools or another set just for him?" Scipio had asked.

"Always another while I am alive, yes, but when I die, my own tools are passed on to him, and now he has two sets, one for his own son, and so on, and on it goes, generation after generation."

It was early summer that year when Scipio started traveling. Though the heat brought him close to collapse more than once, there always seemed to be help when he needed it the most, and he knew this was because of the Comforter that Jesus promised to send in His stead immediately after His ascension.

"You must know that I am a Roman," he told a tall, broad-shouldered man named Nahum, someone so strong looking that he would have been a match even for Peter. "How is it that you, a Jew, hold no ill-will toward me?"

"You were *born* a Roman. You have *become* a Christian. The old priests tell us to turn our backs on such as you. But my kind and I listen little to them these days. They showed their true colors with their behavior toward Jesus of Nazareth. How can we take with any respect words coming from mouths that incited a stupid mob to demand His blood?"

For the three days that he spent with that family, when it was time to retire for the night, Scipio slept with Nahum's lone lamb, right alongside the man's two very young sons in a modest stable but a few feet from where the parents had separate quarters.

At Passover, that family had managed to buy two lambs. One had been sacrificed and eaten, but the second was being kept as a pet for about six months. Toward the end of the summer, it too would have to be killed, becoming a source of food for part of the coming winter, the meat preserved in the fat that was gathered from the animal's tail. Along with this one lamb, Nahum had two goats from which the family got their milk, some of it allowed to turn sour so that goat's-milk cheese could be made.

"Your sons obviously feel great affection for their little friend," Scipio commented sympathetically.

"That they do, I know," Nahum agreed, sensing the intent of his guest's words. "It is a delightful few months for them, a time they treasure."

The two men were sitting outside the small sunbaked mud hut that the family called their home. It was one square room with an outside yard, the mud in the form of bricks twenty-one by ten by four inches, which would allow Nahum to construct additional rooms if he could get any willing neighbors together or could put together enough denarii to hire some help at modest wages.

The whole process of making the bricks could not be undertaken by just one man, and it would have been too much for his children, the oldest of whom was eight years of age. A hole had to be dug into the ground and filled with water together with chopped straw, palm fiber, and bits and pieces of sea shells and charcoal. This mixture was then trampled upon until the texture was that of thick mud. The bricks were fashioned in a wood mold and allowed to bake dry in the hot Middle Eastern sun. One by one they were placed together to form a wall, with additional mud acting as cement between them. Once the structure was finished, more mud was splashed on the walls inside to act as plaster. Any windows were tiny and set up near the ceiling to allow for cooler interior temperatures in the summer and greater warmth in the winter. Since glass was not available, animal skins pounded to a paper-thin texture were used instead.

The roof was the most expensive part of the home. Those men with more money used cypress and cedar, which lasted for many years. But Nahum and others who were poor had to depend upon wood from sycamore trees, if they were fortunate enough, or anything old, discarded, and perhaps already starting to rot if that were not the case. On top, at least one layer of a mixture of brushwood, earth, and clay was smeared by hand. It was common for grass to grow upon such a roof, and, in fact, an individual family's animals were often sent up on the roof to graze. During particularly hot nights, members of the family slept on the roof rather than inside. When the original structure had been added to, because of more children, or relatives who had moved in, and the roof space increased proportionately, neighbors could be seen dropping by and joining some sort of social occasion right up there!

"It must be a task of great difficulty for the boys when the time comes to slaughter that lamb," Scipio observed wisely while waiting for a typically modest dinner to be served. "Is this done without any sign of murmuring?"

"Ah, but those sons of mine do resist each year at the time that the act must be performed, my new friend," the other man replied. "As you must surely know, it is never easy for human nature to submit itself to the dominion of another."

"That was how I viewed the obligation of serving Rome at the beginning of my time as a legionnaire," Scipio admitted. "My self-will would tell me to go one way but my leaders often thought quite otherwise."

"So it is with everyone. So it is that when we want to serve God, we sometimes—far too often, I am afraid—end up serving the deceiver instead."

Nahum's eyes misted up with memories that came to him of the past few years.

"I have been so fortunate," he reflected. "Even when I did not obey God as I should, He never turned His back on me. I have a wife and children, and there is much love among all of us. Can there be more to life that matters?"

Scipio grinned as he spoke, "You were a man firm in your faith in Jehovah before He became flesh in the person of Jesus. Now you acknowledge a strong belief in His Son. God's blessings in your life do not surprise me since you come to Him in your poverty and ask for nothing but food, clothing, and shelter for you and your loved ones. Unlike those who flaunt their piety in public, flashing fine clothes and jewelry and livestock for all to see, you do not pretend that God is evidenced only in the possessions that people can amass. A hundred lambs are of less significance than a single prayer of thanks from a beggar's lips."

One of Nahum's sons ran outside for a moment, picked up a makeshift little toy, smiled at the two of them, and hurried back in to be with his brothers and his mother.

Scipio saw the expression on the other man's face.

"You would give your life for your family, would you not?" he observed.

"As Jesus gave His life for us!" Nahum declared.

"As I was prepared to do for Rome," Scipio said somewhat wistfully.

"Rome offers what every human being wants."

"Peace and security."

"So does our faith, Fabius. But we have to wait. We have to wait until we die to fully achieve this. Rome offers what it does immediately."

Scipio looked at the man with amazement.

"You view me strangely now?" Nahum asked, noticing the altered expression on the young man's face. "May I guess why, my friend?"

"Yes . . ." Scipio replied hesitantly, embarrassed that his reaction to Nahum's wise words was so obvious.

"In most respects, I appear to be unlearned, do I not, with no benefit of the kind of education you, as a Roman, must have had. I am quite poor in material things. My family and I would seem to have nothing that is promising in our future. And yet I speak with reasonable intelligence for someone in the position just mentioned."

"You speak *very* well," Scipio hastened to comment, glad for the opportunity to say what he was feeling.

"Thank you for that, Fabius. Anything you detect about me in this respect came about because I have been a Christian since I heard of the resurrection of Jesus the Christ. It was not a story I would have believed if it had not been true. You see, poverty bestows the outlook of a cynic upon those souls floundering in its grasp. But I saw the effect of faith on men who rushed to me with the news, men who had glimpsed the open tomb with their own eyes and come away from it with a conviction that transformed them."

Nahum indicated the hut where his family was busily preparing the evening meal, such as it was.

"Redemption has transformed my loved ones as well," he said, "for they were led to this Jesus by me minutes after I had accepted Him into my life."

His manner grew more intent.

"I realized that I wanted to be able to talk with anyone I met on as equal a level as possible, gaining their respect so that they would not ignore me or scorn me when I went on to tell them about the Savior. I determined to learn as much as I could, to gain as much knowledge as God permitted me to have and to refine my speech at the same time.

"I spread the word that this humble residence of mine was open to any weary traveler. I would show them the same love that Jesus showed the whole of humanity when He gave His life for the redemption of those who would believe and accept the truth.

"It did not take long, Fabius, my brother. Within months, men of every station stopped here. They were weary of body, yes, but some were weary of soul also. Very few were wealthy enough to have an entourage with them. But they were not poor either. They had sufficient money to have obtained an education, and in return for my hospitality, they lingered awhile, teaching me and loaning me scrolls that were quite precious to them, which I kept safely and studied until their return journey in each case.

"I felt alive then, Fabius, as I do now. Those who claim that only dullards follow in the footsteps of the Nazarene, that the faith you and I share does nothing but deaden the mind, oh, my friend, how terribly wrong they are. My mind came *alive* the moment I accepted Him into my very being!"

He stood and danced several steps in a circle, waving his arms around, quite a sight for such a large one as he.

"I look at the soil beneath my feet, and I know that I have a relationship with the one who created it!" Nahum exclaimed, unmoving now, but still standing. "I turn my eyes toward the sky and comprehend that the Creator of the stars and the sun and the moon has come to reside within me."

Just as quickly as he had sprung to his feet, the big man settled back on the dusty, rocky ground again.

"I have never known such excitement before, Fabius, and such peace, all at the same time," he added. "Has it been that way with you?"

"It has," Scipio acknowledged. "But for some of the apostles, it is not the same as with you and me."

Nahum waited for Scipio to tell him more.

"I saw that their faith affected certain apostles in very different ways," the younger man continued.

"You were with *them!*" Nahum exclaimed, having had no idea previously that this was the case.

"For a few years, yes."

"How I would like to spend an hour or a day or a week with just one of those men. They could tell me so much about Jesus. They could—"

Nahum was shaking from the very thought.

"You said that the apostles were affected differently," he continued. "Can you tell me more, Fabius?"

"Some were of naturally quieter demeanor, not gregarious like Peter, for example. They often preferred to be off by themselves in serious contemplation before God as they offered up their praise and their prayers for guidance daily to Him. Others were more outgoing, fellowshiping with anyone who was to come along, as you have been doing with me. It was the same with the gifts that God gave them."

"I thought all of them had the gift of language!" Nahum spoke earnestly. "Were there other gifts as well? I have not heard of these."

"That is one of the problems. But, first, let me ask how it is that you have come by this information?"

"Again and again, travelers would tell me that it transforms the lives of those upon whom it is bestowed. Many had been there in Jerusalem where, as I heard of it, the gift was given for the first time."

"You are right, my friend. That was the *first* time. And all of them had it, and continue with it. And, yes, it does fill them with wonder, with awe each time it is manifested."

"Then what I hear is correct!"

"Perhaps, Nahum, perhaps."

"Explain to me what you mean by this."

"It is a gift given to minister to *others*. Though the one receiving it gains pleasure from this very communication, that should not be its essential purpose, as far as I can see. The stories you have heard, as well as the ones that I, too, know of, seem to suggest that this pleasure in itself is the only purpose for a very large number of those who seek it."

"Go on," the other man pressed.

"On the Day of Pentecost, speaking in tongues meant that the apostles could form a precious bond with a great multitude from many different lands and be understood by each and every individual. But then that is the very basis for *all* such gifts that God bestows: prophecy, teaching, the rest—to open the eyes of those around us, to lead them from spiritual darkness.

"No gift should be coveted for the sake of whatever personal ecstasy it might bring, for that only distorts and cheapens the very value of what God has bestowed. It turns us inward, which is not at all what God had in mind from the start. He wants those with gifts to reach out instead."

Nahum pondered that, saying nothing in reply just then.

"My dear comrade Decimus, who was a legionnaire as well, has the gift of prophecy. You should see the change in him. Though he cannot speak in any languages other than his own, he accepts this without reservation. As he told me once, 'Should I regret the will of God, Fabius? Who would be so foolish to do that?'"

"Are you saying that whatever God chooses to bestow should be considered a blessing, and we need not be concerned with one being greater than the other—in fact, that to do so is to be guilty of covetousness?" Nahum asked. "Am I putting it properly?"

A broad smile crossed Scipio's youthful face.

"That is so!" he exclaimed, continuing to be impressed by the other man. "I have known of jealousy besetting some of those who have come to follow Jesus. They lust after the gift another has over their own. That is so very wrong-spirited, a way that Satan has of—"

"I fear the devil still," Nahum admitted, not happy with himself.

"Please, my brother, you do not have to let that fear go on strangling you," Scipio spoke persuasively.

"But I cannot help this."

"Let me tell you why you should not feel as you do, why it can only be destructive. Trust me when I say that I saw much of that sort of thing during the years I was with the apostles, for Satan is known to attack all the more strongly where faith has proved most vibrant. It is such strongholds of redemption that he wants to destroy. He has little time for the Pharisees and the Sadducees and pompous fools like them, since they are already aiding him far, far more than they are achieving any good for Almighty God.

"I can help you vanquish the one who endeavors to keep you chained to the bonds of fear that are among the greatest of his weapons, even though he can no longer drag you screaming to Gehenna. You should be enjoying the freedom from his domination that your fresh, wonderful, vibrant faith has the power of bringing to you."

Nahum was completely captivated.

"Yes, yes, I will listen to you further," he promised, "I will listen this evening to every word you offer."

The two men ceased talking only when dinner was ready, and then, afterward, under the clear Middle Eastern night sky, they continued until both had fallen asleep and Nahum's wife had brought ample coverings to drape over them to protect against the chill air, while one of his sons started a fire nearby so its heat would provide additional security, not only from the temperature but from marauding, hungry beasts of the night.

XXVII

Scipio felt very much at peace with Nahum and his loved ones, but after three full days in their presence, and long, fruitful hours of discussion about matters spiritual as well as political—the latter focused on Gaius Julius Caesar Augustus Germanicus, also known as Caligula, who had just that same year become emperor upon the death of Tiberius—it was time for Scipio to take up the journey again on the following morning.

"Your family reminds me of my own in some ways," Scipio admitted. "But then staying with you makes my heart yearn for them all the more."

So the young former legionnaire departed up the same dusty, rock-strewn road that he had been traveling for weeks already, carrying with him only a large brown leather sack crammed full of clothes and pairs of fresh walking sandals, along with a small provision of food from which he would have to partake in disciplined fashion.

Scipio had no money left at that point, and he prayed for God's intervention in this respect as he continued toward Antioch, for this was the longest stretch of the journey. Between Bethlehem and Antioch, he had been able to stop for a time in Caesarea as well as Ptolemais and Tyre, which were major cities of that period. But after Tyre, no such places existed, only the tiniest of villages, and but few of those.

He passed by one settlement where the people lived not in simple huts or canvas tents or the finished two-story buildings that were in abundance at Jerusalem or any of the other cities, but in natural caves that dotted the side of a chalk-white mountain.

At first he felt pity toward those inside, and then he realized that they were probably more fortunate than, say, Nahum and his family. Huts were subject to weather conditions, such as the heavy rains that began in mid-Tishri, on through Marchesvan, Kislev, and Tevet. These increased in frequency and duration the further north poor families lived, and it was not uncommon for huts to be washed away in a sudden, violent river, carrying entire families with them.

From a distance, the caves reminded Scipio just a little of the tomb where Jesus' body lay until the resurrection. He thought of stopping for the day to see if anyone would take him in, but he decided against it, though he was not sure why.

It was hot that day, as were others during the month of Av, which was now coming to a close. He had taken off the upper part of his garment and was walking bare-chested along the side of the road.

Abruptly he heard someone calling to him.

"Young man!" the voice said. "Would you please stop for a moment? I should like to speak with you."

Scipio saw a rather coarse-looking and extremely large man in his late-fifties being pulled in a chariot-like carriage by four black slaves.

"What is it that you want, sir?" he asked.

"I saw you walk just ahead of me, and I wanted to stop and ask if you would spend some time with me," the man replied in a matter-of-fact way. "You have a good body, and I thought perhaps I might do a nice sculpture of it."

Scipio's stomach tightened as he heard those words and saw that he was facing an aristocrat, someone who could afford fine, imported clothes and a household of servants and whatever else he might desire.

It was not unknown for men like him to have legionnaires they fancied transferred to private guard duty at their residences, the safety and security of the household hardly what they had in mind.

Young, slim, strong-looking, Scipio had never personally encountered a situation of that sort, for which he considered himself fortunate, since none of the men who left the battlefield in that manner ever returned, although stories about what had happened later reached their former comrades, stirring them to disgust.

"Thank you, sir," he said with forced politeness. "I have no such moments of leisure to spare. You see, I must be in Antioch as soon as I can manage, for I am intent on returning to my family at Puteoli."

The man's eyes widened for a moment.

"Ah, yes, I know that area well," he remarked. "It so happens that one of my ships is leaving for Syracuse early next month. I could easily arrange for you to be on it as my special guest, young man."

Scipio hesitated, knowing how much he needed to find space on such a vessel heading in that general direction. He had been aiming for Rhegium, yes, but Syracuse was only a relatively few miles directly south, and Roman roads were in superlative shape between both cities, and on up through Rome itself.

"Your offer is tempting but—," he started to say.

"But why am I making it to a young stranger?" the man interrupted knowingly. "I can drag in anyone I please, upon the order of Imperial Rome itself. Why should I be speaking to you as I have? Are you not asking yourself this now?"

Scipio nodded.

"Because I never expected to find a fellow Roman such as yourself walking this primitive road in this strange land," the other replied. "The Jews, by and large, look like a grubby lot, unpleasant to anyone outside their own country."

"How could you know this about me, that I share a Roman heritage with you?" Scipio asked, greatly puzzled.

"You walk a certain way. You have a certain manner about you. Your face is a Roman's even after a few years of letting the elements in this land abuse it, as they do with everything else they touch, which *is* everything.

"I cannot tell how long you have lived an apparently nomad sort of life but, fortunately, it has not been of such duration that you have entirely shed the valued Roman demeanor of your upbringing."

Scipio knew that he would have continued on his journey, under ordinary circumstances, and, therefore, dismissed with polite finality any offer that seemed suspicious by virtue of its generosity.

Even if he had been inclined to go with this man, it certainly would not have been to pose so that some piece of stone could be chiseled away to form his likeness, but rather to witness for Jesus the Christ to someone of regal Roman station, an opportunity in itself that could only be called rare.

He realized that the expression on his face must have been more revealing than he had intended.

"I want nothing from you except a few days of your time," the man said, grinning slightly. "I have a rather pleasant residence nearby to which I try to retreat as frequently as I can manage, away from the various demands of life in Rome itself, away from the political intrigues, especially since this fatuous but dangerous Caligula has assumed the very throne upon which once sat the great Julius Caesar.

"Yes, I suppose I could have gone to a dozen other places with more celebrated status, of course, but out of sheer recklessness or stupidity or whatever else, I ended up here among the Jews. But then who can explain anything of life?"

"I do not want to pose as you have asked," Scipio countered, half-hoping that that would end the encounter.

"Then it will be only for a visit, I assure you," the man persisted. "I wish you would believe me when I say this."

Still, Scipio shook his head and continued walking.

The stranger threw up his large hands in a gesture of futility that indicated he thought he might have made a mistake being so friendly with the handsome young man, but having done so, decided to stick with it, at least for a bit longer.

"Please," he called after Scipio. "I beg you to reconsider. I have no one but Jews to talk with these days."

"The proconsul-governor of Judea would surely welcome you," Scipio spoke over his shoulder.

"He seldom talks to anyone. Since he sent his poor mad wife back to Rome, he has become something of a recluse."

Scipio stopped and turned sharply.

"Can you be sure of that?" he asked, deeply distressed by this sudden news.

"I am in a land that lies in the midst of nowhere, yes, but I determined from the beginning not to be so isolated from contact with Rome that I knew little or nothing of what transpires there," the man told him. "I get some form of communication every so often from those whom I pay generously to inform me."

Scipio studied him for a moment or two, wanting to know more about what had happened regarding the fate of Procula Pilatus but not eager to contemplate what he might be forced to encounter in order to do so.

The stranger was a short man, with considerably more weight on his frame than was healthy, his face round, with a dimpled chin. His voice quite deep, he spoke slowly, as though he was fighting a speech impediment of some sort.

He was wearing a pure white toga, for that was the required color of Imperial Rome, with no deviation permitted at all, such bland clothing, even the lighter weight tunic, a singularly proud and unchangeable proclamation of Roman citizenship existing from the beginning of the empire onward.

Women, with more colors available to them, dressed in something similar that was called a palla, but in either case, the garment was little more than a large blanket wrapped with some flair around the body of each individual, its material of varying thickness to go with the respective seasons of the year.

This man's toga was held together by a fibula—a kind of safety pin—but the garment did not necessarily require anything like that if it were worn properly. Anything more elaborate was well-nigh impossible, at least as far as the stitching process was concerned, since Roman needles proved to be clumsy instruments made of bone or bronze. Those needles, coupled with the heavy, coarse thread that was available, were not conducive to elegant stitching.

"Where *is* your home?" Scipio asked.

"A few miles from here, near the shore. I built it there because in all of this land there is no more beautiful a place," the man replied. "The sunsets reflecting off the Mediterranean are especially captivating."

"What is your name, sir?"

"It is Quintus Egnatius Javolenus Tidus Germanicus, I am afraid."

Germanicus! The same last name as the new emperor!

"Are you related to . . . to—?" Scipio stuttered, awkward over posing that possibility to someone whose contempt for the new emperor had been made apparent.

"The one nicknamed Caligula, of whom I have spoken in such condemnatory terms? Is that what you were about to ask?"

Scipio nodded, a remnant of his Roman nervousness around the rulers of his nation suddenly surfacing.

"I must confess that I am as you suspected. The overrated toad of whom we speak presently is my much-loathed younger brother, you see, though I have never been acknowledged by a single member of that household.

"I suppose you could call me the Germanicus's bastard child, though I may not in fact be the only one, considering the promiscuity that is so endemic of the way they all live these days. They provide endless streams of money for my various needs, undoubtedly to seal my mouth and prevent greater awareness of me. You see, I dare not expect any of their love when I have nothing but their shame."

"But you say that the emperor himself is much loathed. His reign has just begun. So little is known about him. May I ask, sir, by whom he is deemed so loathsome?"

"By anyone who spends five minutes in his presence, but then after a time those who never meet him yet whose lives are affected by his growing madness will think the same or perhaps worse. It is to be hoped that he remains in power only a little while. For he can bring only scandal to a worthy throne!"

He leaned forward.

"Most of all, it is I who hate this monstrosity with the most profound passion, young man, though it is true that I am far from the only one, for the other members of the family have seen his tendencies more intimately than anything I might have witnessed.

"It is I who have seen the reality that has been hidden from the masses, a foul beast who will soon roar forth in all his blasphemous fury. That part of him happens to be hiding for the moment because it serves his unholy purposes, for he is simply consolidating his power, winning so-called friends for whom he cares nothing, and who will be devoured by him the moment they rebel, for rebel they must when they comprehend the true nature of this malignant entity that they ignorantly have been calling a man."

164

XXVIII

The residence of this particular Germanicus was hardly the rather basic one that Scipio somehow had expected, even though "basic" in upper society terms would be considered palatial in the eyes of the average Israelite.

The two men entered the house through what was called a garden court, though it seemed more like a lush fern jungle forty feet long by twenty feet wide. A wall of quarried gray stone had been erected around it, with a large column at each corner, presumably for decoration only since there was no roof to support.

Scipio could see, at various intervals, charcoal burning braziers, now unlit because it was still summer. In less than two months this standard method of heating would be invaluable to any household fortunate enough to possess it.

Nervous-looking slaves, both Caucasian and black, were scurrying about, clipping off dead leaves, adding nutrients to the soil, and otherwise fussing with the attentiveness of fathers looking after their children.

"I imported them all from various places," Germanicus said proudly. "But the climate here, dry as it is, deprives them of what they need the most, a great deal of water. When there is little extra available, I have it sent over from a port in Italy."

"There are so many, sir," Scipio observed. "A dozen families could live in an area as large as this is."

"I do not know a dozen families."

Directly ahead was the main part of the house he had had built. As they reached the doorway, Germanicus asked him to stop and look back at the court. Then he raised his left hand toward a short, thin, black man.

"Let the rains begin!" he bellowed.

Scipio had not noticed the network of small holes that had been burrowed into the plain, white-washed walls. Seconds after his host had given that order, jets of water surged through them, hitting the ferns at every angle, as well as the slaves in attendance.

"I have installed my own aqueduct, draining as much local water into it as I can," Germanicus told him. "The rest comes, as I told you, from other locations."

From there they entered a large reception room. As with all Roman residences, the floor was bare, in this case, made of marble, with alternating rows of black, then white rectangular shapes fanning out from the middle. Rugs were used as curtains in that room, again a custom for upper-class citizens.

Beyond the reception room was the dining area, and then Scipio followed his host to an adjacent and enclosed heated pool.

"I call this my private nymphaeum," Germanicus said as he noticed Scipio glancing with some embarrassment at the montage of unclothed women painted on the walls. "Some guests prefer to say that it is a shrine to indulgence."

Scipio decided that he would stay no longer and turned back toward the dining hall entrance.

Germanicus started laughing coarsely.

"I was sure you would react in this manner," he said. "I was *hoping* that this would be the case."

Suddenly he stopped, his face quite serious, a look of pain on it.

"I lied to you, Fabius Scipio," he went on wearily. "I did not come upon you by accident after all. I have been looking for you for some time. But you move so very quickly, young man, or so it seems. Yes, you do, and there are left behind numerous reports from men and women who have been blessed by your presence. Even the youngest of children seem to light up from within when they recall your visit."

"Have you been testing me?" Scipio ventured.

"I have. There are reports that you are wholly detached from the sinful pleasures of this world, much like the Nazarene whom you love so dearly."

"And you wanted to see how I would react to the women displayed here on the walls of this room?"

"That was part of it, Fabius. If I were the least bit uncertain about you, there would have been much more, I assure you, much more than your young mind could have comprehended perhaps, in other rooms in this building and below, in a private place that would put Pompeii to shame."

"Why did you stop now?"

"Because your spirit is obvious. You have the manner of someone still maintaining his virginity, even if perhaps you may have lost it in some village one memorable evening away from the rigors of battle, I would suppose not more than a few months after you entered the service of Rome. I have heard the stories of those so young as you are. There is no denying the truth!"

Scipio blushed but said nothing for the moment.

"But it is far, far better that you seem as you do," Germanicus added, his mind swirling with images, "than to give yourself to the memories and practices of a perverse past, as these corrupt you from the inside out."

"But I have not done what you are suggesting," Scipio started to protest, unable to remain silent any longer. "I cannot let you think that I have."

"How fortunate if you speak only the truth," Germanicus acknowledged enviously. "How fortunate when you can climb into your bed at night and close your eyes, and the darkness offers only peace."

He indicated the walls and the giant pool with a wave of his left hand.

"Debauchery could be defined from what has taken place in this very spot, Fabius," he said. "My brother has been here though rather briefly, you know. Any place Caligula visits is defiled by the presence of the man."

He put his hands on Scipio's shoulders.

"I shall be dead soon, perhaps in a year or two, the physicians tell me," he added, a lifetime of regret readily apparent in his deep baritone voice. "I want to learn of this Jesus of yours and to shed myself of all the material fruits of my station. I want to die as the poor of whom the Nazarene spoke, bereft of wealth but rich in spirit. Can you help me, my young friend? Can you?"

XXIX

Quintus Egnatius Javolenus Tidus Germanicus tried to convince Fabius Scipio to stay with him for six months longer. The young disciple admitted to no such intention originally, though he later came to feel that God surely had some special plan for him to be in that place, with that particular individual. Nevertheless, a span of six months, probably the remaining time of his host's life, meant a massive realignment of goals he had laid out for himself, along with the schedule they embodied.

What am I to think? he prayed one evening on the shore of the Mediterranean, the luxurious residence of this man Germanicus directly behind him, its bulk outlined in moonlight under a clear sky. *Heavenly Father, what is the purpose here? My spirit leads me on, toward Italy, back to my family. Or am I mistaking the yearnings of my heart for Your gentle nudging?*

What Scipio eventually saw happening was a more than striking change in his very existence, one nearly equal to what had driven him to his knees in humble confession of sin and forgiveness and caused him to accept Jesus the Christ as his Lord and Savior. He had come from a family not poor by Roman standards but hardly of wealthy roots either. He joined the Roman legions while yet in his teen years. From there, he went on to lead the itinerant life of a follower of the extraordinary Nazarene, depending upon the generosity of strangers.

And now I have allowed myself to be on the verge of being dissuaded from visiting my loved ones, Scipio prayed in that place of exquisite quietude, unbroken except by the lapping of waves on the pure white sand only a few yards in front of him, *and to witnessing of my Savior, yea, my Lord along the way as I go from here.*

Not a minor consideration, even in those days of increasingly lax Roman morals, happened to be what others might think if perchance it became widely known that he had spent such time as he had with a man who once seemed of dubious sexual intent.

Finally, Scipio, in confronting these questions, knew that his uncertainty had to be conveyed to Germanicus.

"Sir?" he said as he found his host sitting by the indoor pool, his legs dangling over into its cool water, the walls no longer adorned by suggestive art but painted instead a solid light tannish color.

"What can I do for you, Fabius?"

"I must discuss now the mission for my life as I see it."

"Sit with me, and I shall be glad to do so."

Scipio did as the other had suggested.

"My faith is of such importance to me that—"

"You cannot waste any valuable moments whereby you might be sharing it with some stranger with whom perchance you might meet, is that not what you were about to tell me—with such obvious trepidation, I might add?"

"Yes . . ."

"Do not forget it is the same faith I now hold."

"I have not forgotten."

Truly it could *never* be dismissed from his mind, that evening when the pool in the midst of a place of debauchery became a baptismal, Germanicus being submerged for a second or two in the water, as his slaves watched, and then he rose up, an expression on his face that none had seen before that moment, whispers among them about how peaceful he looked.

"Then what causes you the distress I see on your fresh young face?" Germanicus asked a bit more than a week later as the young man confronted him, urged on by some obviously onerous task.

"I had planned to go so far, and do so much," the reply came.

"So much *more?* Could you not have added that one word and, thereby, shown me truly what is on your mind?"

Scipio was uncomfortable. The older man, well aware of his young friend's nervousness, seemed to be toying with him.

But then Germanicus bowed his head, and muttered, "Forgive me for my manner, Fabius. It is so hard to rid oneself of old habits."

"Old habits, sir?"

"Oh, yes, *very* old ones, I fear. I have been treating you, more often than I want to acknowledge, with condescension that, surely, you of all men with whom I have fellowshiped do not deserve. While my family is steadfastly ashamed of me, nevertheless they have pampered me, hoping by doing so that I would not become an irritant, remaining anonymous to all but them. And in so doing they have created the vain, pompous, self-indulgent monster they were dreading in the first place.

"Furthermore, Fabius, while legionnaires certainly are respected after a fashion, and appreciated for their service to the empire, they are not considered of equal social station to any of Rome's elite, of course, unless one might happen to be an officer, and then, somehow, that overcomes the barriers, though only to a degree.

"So I have fallen into the habitual conduct fostered by my family's breeding and of the common view found toward men who fight on fields

169

of battle; but in your case, there was, I am ashamed to say, also a residue of what Romans tend to think about this new, strange cult of men, women, and children who have given up everything for their stubborn allegiance to a supposedly dead carpenter from Nazareth."

Germanicus saw Scipio starting to object and held up his left hand to silence him for a moment.

"That is not *my* thinking, dear Fabius," he clarified. "Yet it is clearly what you *will* face when you go to Rome."

"But I did not intend to travel as far as that," Scipio abruptly told him. "You see, my family is—"

Germanicus turned, glanced at him, and then looked away.

"What is it?" Scipio asked. "You seem so sad."

"I am not without lines of communication, you know, and these have been active since your arrival, deliberately so, at my instigation. You see, Fabius, when I heard of what had happened with your brother, I rejoiced for you. It was a wonderful story, my young friend, and it spurred me on to learning more."

"But it is not *just* a story!"

"I know that. But, you see, it is hardly complete. There is another chapter of which you are not aware."

Scipio felt perspiration begin on his forehead, his heart gripped as though in a vise that was being tightened.

"You have learned something about my loved ones?"

Germanicus nodded, his hands bound together into a common fist, the knuckles turning white.

"A parchment arrived days ago, in response to one of my own," he acknowledged. "I resisted letting you know of its contents . . . until now."

"What is it that you have to tell me?" Scipio asked with undisguised anxiety. "Please, I must know this without delay."

"Your brother is dead."

Scipio was quiet for a moment, the news so startling that he blocked it out until it came rushing in on him.

"But he was cured. The leprosy left him. He became quite normal."

"It was not that horrible pestilence that took his life."

"What was it then? Tell me, tell me now."

"Your brother was killed by roving bandits."

"Bandits? How could that be?"

"It once would have been impossible, so close to Rome in terms of distance as your family has been. But there are changes happening within the empire, Fabius. The iron hand of Imperial Rome is developing some strains of rust, I fear, and not only here, with such insurrectionists as that

Barabbas, who once seemed nothing other than a gnat on the hide of an elephant, but whose continuing survival has encouraged others to take up the sword and the lance against Rome's occupation of Palestine."

Scipio waved his hand through the air, showing his impatience.

"And my mother, my father, my—?" he asked.

"The intruders would not touch them, Fabius." Germanicus responded though, oddly, without a smile.

For an instant, Scipio breathed a sigh of relief but then he detected in the other man's manner something that gave him cold, sharp chills.

"Why was it that those outlaws would not *touch*—?" he started to say, but as soon as he uttered that one word, he stopped, hugging himself while unwanted images flooded through his mind.

Quintus Egnatius Javolenus Tidus Germanicus nodded slowly in acknowledgment, with great sadness seizing his countenance.

And Fabius Scipio could say nothing for some while, as the two of them sat in silence by the edge of that pool, the young man quietly sobbing to himself.

XXX

The long, relatively flat ship resting in the tiny harbor was an indication of how greatly Roman seafaring vessels had changed during the past hundred years, from the heavily timbered, multibanked galleys used by Mark Antony at the battle of Actium to the smaller, swifter, one- or two-decked ones, known as liburnian, commissioned from Adriatic builders by Octavian. Most of the latter had twenty-five oars on each side though the larger dromon versions were double this in size, each ship armed with catapults designed to hurl heavy lead and stone pieces up to a distance of 700 yards and, at each end of the liburnian, a so-called fighting tower from which a commander could survey the scene of battle, while archers let loose with a flurry of arrows if the action were close enough for that to be effective.

Germanicus's vessel was of much smaller size, while remaining true to the concept of a broad beam down the middle, which increased its stability, particularly for long journeys where conditions might not be as stable as in its home port.

"They are sarcastically called fair-weather ships by some skeptics," he told Scipio as they stood on the dock, waiting to board. "But that is so much nonsense. This design has been so useful, so strong that our warships have been able to reach all the way north to Britain and even to Ireland. That is hardly a route guaranteeing placid waters along the way, would you not agree?"

Scipio knew that such chatter was Germanicus's way of trying to keep his mind off his parents as much as possible.

"Thank you," he said.

"For what, Fabius?"

"For being concerned about people you have never met."

"It is a concern few have ever shown me, I can assure you of that. What is terribly ironic is that I had conditioned myself to being ostracized by every polite social circle until the Nazarene accepted me as one of His own, and yet it is only now that I have bouts of intruding regret that had been buried long before, brought to the surface in an abrupt surge that has left me awake, crying, in the middle of the night."

"I have heard you," Scipio admitted.

"But you are down at the other end of the residence!"

"I have heard you."

"Why is it that I experience these days in the very center of my being agony far greater than before?"

"You have encountered what uncompromising love is. And now you realize how total the emptiness was that had accompanied you for so long."

"I used to be quite a glutton over what was, in earlier times, my favorite fruit, Fabius. I cannot place a name to it anymore, for it is a golden-tinted delicacy that even my borrowed wealth has never allowed me to obtain after decades of my palate being denied the pleasure of it. So I have tended to dismiss recollections of this morsel from my mind. You know, now that I think of it, I cannot even remember the taste, and the yearning has stopped as a result. Is this what you are saying?"

Scipio nodded.

"But one bite some day will bring it all back, the taste that gave you such pleasure," he said, testing the metaphor somewhat tentatively, for he had no desire to mislead his friend. "And you will sit in a grove of trees bearing *only* that fruit, doing nothing but eating it, smelling it, looking at the color of it."

"You are preparing me for heaven, dear Fabius," Germanicus said insightfully. "Admit it, my friend. Is this not what you are doing? You are not speaking of literal fruit in a literal grove—have I not guessed right?"

Scipio squirmed under such an astute observation.

"I am not *sure* what heaven is going to be like," he admitted a bit defensively. "That is why I offered an allegory just now. You are right about this. I wanted only to give you some hint, as best I could."

"Do not be bothered, Fabius," Germanicus went on. "You are wise for one so young but you cannot be expected to have all the answers."

He sighed as some fragments of memories came to mind.

"I wonder if, during special moments, it may be that clues are given from time to time, not to tantalize us, I know, but rather to sustain us as we wait for that moment when it *does* happen, this passage into heaven," the older man went on. "Even when sin did not bother me in the slightest, I read much about the subject of an afterlife. I came upon some parchments that are quite old, you see, writings that speak so beautifully of a place without tears, a place of joy that never ends, flowing like a river and submerging all those who stand in its path. Shiny beings of pure light, shimmering in its multicolored beauty, walk side-by-side with the souls of redeemed men, women, and children."

"Where were these parchments from?" Scipio inquired.

"From Jewish places of worship, I suppose, since each and every one was written in the language of this land, many undoubtedly stolen by callous legionnaires who ignored the dictates of their emperor. Could these scribblings be correct as written, Fabius? Could they be at all close to the mark?"

"I think that they must be as you say, if they conveyed what you have told me," Scipio agreed, sorry that he had not known about the parchments before deciding to leave for Italy, since he would have found reading them as fascinating as Germanicus had. "The Lord said more than once to the many who were listening that one day He would go to prepare a place for those of us who decided to follow in His steps. Jesus was smiling as He spoke. It was almost as though the Nazarene knew that one day He would be standing in the doorway to a certain place, and all we have to do, upon our deaths, is walk right up to Him and wait patiently for Him to take us by the hand and lead us on through."

"What I have described from these writings sounds very much like a place that the Nazarene would have intended as He spoke—it does, I think, yes, it does."

Germanicus glanced at his hand, which was outstretched just then, as though waiting for the Nazarene to take hold of it that very moment. Embarrassed, he put it back into a side pocket of his gold-fringed tunic.

The captain signaled for them to come aboard.

Germanicus hesitated, turning around and looking back toward the expansive home that had been built for him only, its topaz-colored roof visible to the north, sitting on a small hill, reflecting the noon sun.

"I was so safe there," he mused. "I controlled life there. It was there that I had those hapless souls who provided me my every need. I was almost—"

His face flushed red.

"—a god, a human god dominating my little world."

Sighing wearily, he added, "But a god who cannot even heal himself, instead a deluded mortal being whom the one, the true God has seen fit to—"

He turned from that view and looked at Scipio.

"—forgive!" he declared. "I have been washed clean, it seems, Fabius. But *can* that be how I am now, good friend? Or is this . . . this another fanciful delusion . . . born of a dying man's sad and long rejected heart?"

"It is what our Savior has promised," Scipio said simply.

"But it means apparently that I must leave this place to which I have grown accustomed and go into the unknown. Is that truly His wish? What possibly can be in store for me out there once the liburnian leaves, and I am on it, rather than simply standing where I am now and waving good-bye?"

The captain was more insistent.

Scipio started to walk up the plank to the ship.

Germanicus wavered.

"Go to Italy," he called. "See those you love. Offer them whatever comfort you can. I shall remain behind. My courage fails me, Fabius. It runs like water through these fat, well-manicured fingers of mine."

Scipio stopped and called over his shoulder.

"As your *life* has failed you . . ." he said with some passion. "Is that what you want as death begins its approach? Will you be *proud* of what you have to offer to Jesus the Christ? Tell me this, please: Is it better to stand in the midst of majesty, a coward, or to enter the unknown with the knowledge that you have placed yourself at His feet, ready to go where He leads you, with Him by your side, lighting the way?"

Scipio spun around, his gaze meeting the other man's.

"Give me an answer, as surely you must give one to Jesus Himself. Do you choose God as the captain of what remaining time you have left? Or do you choose to return to what once governed your actions? Those walls may have a fresh coating of paint, but how much of what used to be depicted still tugs at your heart?"

Germanicus did nothing, said nothing.

Sorrow flooded Scipio's very soul as he walked the remaining few feet to the top deck of the liburnian.

The captain greeted him with a hearty handshake.

"Is not the master coming?" he asked, looking momentarily past the young man, then hastily added, "Fine, fine, there is no problem now, I see."

Scipio's head shot up, and he turned quickly, saw the massive form of Quintus Egnatius Javolenus Tidus Germanicus charging up the plank, which seemed nearly to buckle under all that weight.

"My dear captain," he spoke, "how many years have you been serving me?"

"More than two decades, as I recall," the other man replied, frowning. "Is there something you wish that perhaps I have not done, regarding this journey or something else? Please tell me and I shall act immediately, sir."

Germanicus hesitated, and Scipio could see a reflection of still-raging indecision on that pudgy face.

"I . . ." he started to say, gulping twice. "I am feeling rather ill right now. Would you be so kind as to pour some wine for me? It is my stomach, I suspect . . . Jewish water in a Roman gut, you know."

The Sicilian-born captain nodded understandingly and hurried below desk.

"Oh, Fabius," spoke Germanicus. "It pulls me back, that old life. I can barely keep from turning around and—"

He held his hands out in front of him.

Trembling.

"It is as though demons have grabbed hold of these hands, and I am trying to break away but . . . but—"

"We pray on our knees then," Scipio told him. "We raise up your hands toward heaven, and we plead with God for strength, for release, for—"

"Freedom," Germanicus interrupted, "freedom for my mind, my heart, my inner soul. If I do not have that freedom, if the chains are not taken from me and the old passions threaten henceforth, I fear that my resolve will not survive this journey. I fear this so much that it is like gall on my tongue, palpable, bitter."

The two of them dropped to their knees on the worn wood of the old liburnian. For a moment, they prayed silently, but soon their supplications came out in an audible flood, their voices vibrant.

The captain rushed back above deck and then stood quite still, listening to the words that were coming from their lips, words of great power. The next moment he too had knelt in sudden prayer, not quite knowing what he was doing but deeply moved by the demonstration being offered before him.

"Oh, Father God, take us now out into this great sea," Germanicus prayed alone, no longer needing the earnest direction of his young friend. "Still the forces of evil that would seek our deaths. Clear the minds of Thy servants and put our feet on solid ground upon the path You would have us take."

He opened his eyes and tilted his head back, looking up at the afternoon sky.

"Let me feel Thy presence this very moment," he begged, "if it be Thy will."

The captain shot to his feet and rushed over to Germanicus.

"Your eyes, sir!" he exclaimed. "The sun, she is very bright. Do not tempt her in this way, I beg you."

"It is not that sun which I see now," Germanicus remarked. "It is not this world I have glimpsed."

The captain thrust his hands in front of the other man's face.

"Do not blind yourself," he pleaded. "Do not destroy this gift that you have, sir. Sight is so precious. The many pathetic beggars along the Appian Way would love to have what you cannot just throw away."

Germanicus smiled as he diverted his gaze and looked instead at the captain.

"Why do you care about me, at least in this manner?" he asked but not unkindly. "I have played the role of your master for so long that surely you must loathe me by now. Being a slave to a repugnant one such as myself cannot predispose you toward harboring even the mildest affection. Tell me I am wrong about this, and I shall not call you a liar."

"There is no hate in my heart," the captain replied. "There was once—"

He bit his lower lip.

"Speak what you want," Germanicus said. "I will not punish you."

"Pity, sir. I saw you as someone with so much more than myself yet with no joy, no peace, no—"

He fell to his knees.

"And now your eyes, they are not blind from the sun, they are alive. Life itself is dancing in the center of them—I can see it, *I can see it!*"

The captain started crying.

"Why do you weep?" Germanicus asked.

"I weep for your joy, sir. I weep because . . . because—"

Germanicus placed his hands on the other man's shoulders.

"Do not hold back," he said. "Let it out now."

"I weep because I feel that same joy, and I know not why I cannot understand what has taken hold of me. Have I gone mad? Am I no longer fit to be in your service?"

"Let me tell you what has happened," Germanicus spoke slowly, with some warmth. "Let my young friend and I introduce you to One you shall serve instead of me from this moment on."

The captain panicked for a moment.

"Is there someone else to come on board now?" he asked, his voice shaking. "I see no one. When will he arrive? The tides are changing, the weather too. We *must* be on our way without fail."

"He is here already," Germanicus said, astonished at the words that were coming with such assurance from his lips. "He was born of a virgin, this One. He died, He was buried, and He arose from the dead, as no other has done."

The captain's eyes widened.

"Not the Nazarene, you say!" he replied. "Not that—"

He tried to get to his feet, but Germanicus maintained a grip on his shoulders.

"You claim to sense my joy, you claim to feel a measure of it yourself. Then listen to why I have come to where I am, here on my knees, for when I have told you the truth, you will fall in worship before the source of it."

Scipio moved over to the two of them.

"We should join hands," he said.

"But the crew," the captain protested. "What will they think?"

"This crew of great experience certainly will get us *to* our destination," Germanicus told him, "but the One of whom I speak can make the journey *safe* for every man on this vessel. Think back over the years, will you, good captain? How many times have we traveled a similar route, you and I, and lost men to the weather, to disease, to unexpected frailty?"

Scipio glanced to his left.

Slaves had come up from below, standing there with great interest and watching the three of them.

"*See!*" the captain whispered. "We have to be careful not to—"

"We cannot do anything but what we are about to do," Germanicus interrupted. "Take my hand, and take Fabius's hand, and let this blessed Jesus deal with the others!"

The captain shrank from Germanicus and Scipio, his eyes widening as he wondered if they had come under the control of strange spirits.

Abruptly, there were sounds in back of them, shuffling sounds, a low murmur or two, a creaking piece of aged timber.

Without speaking, an old slave came, wheezing a bit, and sat near his captain.

A moment later, another, younger, less bowed by years of hard labor, joined him, followed by others; and soon all but a handful of the galley slaves were seated with the three of them, those timid ones who held back retreating to the steps that led down into the belly of that liburnian, shaking their heads as they descended.

Never the brutal master of any ship in his charge, the captain watched men with whom he had developed a bond because of his kindnesses over the years sit with the learned humility of their circumstance, waiting now for more words such as they had just overheard—and no longer did he speak in protest that first day of a new journey's beginning.

XXXI

The sea journey from the westward coast of that section of the land of Judea to the southeastern tip of Italy took several weeks. It was a time of relatively Spartan living for Quintus Egnatius Javolenus Tidus Germanicus, which would have been otherwise intolerable for him except for the purpose of the journey, his need to help the young man who had entered his life with profound impact.

"I think I shall go on to Rome," he told Fabius Scipio toward dusk one day as they sat on the deck of the liburnian. "I think I shall stand before my family and tell them that I have come to stay, that I can no longer be content with exile."

He burst out into laughter at that, his frame shaking like a tub of lard.

"Can you *imagine* the astonishment on their faces, Fabius?" he said. "Can you just imagine *that?*"

As abruptly as it had come, that moment of wistful joviality passed for Germanicus, and his shoulders slumped.

"What is wrong?" Scipio asked.

"I would not live out the week," the other man spoke sadly, tilting his head slightly as the truth of what he had said gripped him.

"They would have you killed?"

"Oh, without doubt, they would do exactly what you say, dear Fabius. My only consolation is that I am certain it would be an altogether quick death. They would want me out of the way—quite permanently and as soon as possible. You know, get the garbage collected and carried off so that the stench—"

He could not continue speaking in this manner for a number of minutes after that. Finally, when words did come, their tone was filled with almost inexpressible sorrow.

"I shall do nothing, I suspect, but return as always to my hide-away, my beautiful place of isolation as soon as I have seen that you have spent the time you want with your loved ones," he ventured. "It is all I have known for so long. But then how could I possibly object to that? Solitude in splendor? Is this such a bad fate for any man?"

He stood, somewhat unsteadily, and looked out over the Mediterranean.

"So calm," he murmured. "That in itself is a miracle. Not a single moment of turbulence since we left."

"The Lord wants us to reach our destination," Scipio offered.

"Thank you for including me. I am only a bystander. I am no less grateful for His safekeeping, but this is a trip for you in your destiny, not mine."

He shivered and hugged himself.

"Your parents have a condition that causes every society to reject them. My family has a son whose very existence must be rejected as well. I wonder who has the worst of it—your mother, your father, or me? To be healthy is wonderful, I agree. To have no financial concerns only helps. But you will soon fellowship with those who gave you life, and there will be only love between you. Those who gave *me* life would gladly sanction my death if they knew how close I will be in a short while."

Scipio was standing beside him now, the two of them leaning against the dark, hand-carved wood railing in front of them.

"You speak as though no one cares," he said. "You speak as though you are alone and will never be other than that."

"Oh, but it is true, good Fabius. I am not a fool, not in matters of this sort, anyway. I can see that I have no one bound to me except through my substantial purse strings. Those who partook of the unmitigated fulfillment of my many lusts in times past subsequently have fled to more accommodating satyrs."

"Who is in charge while you are away?"

"One of the slaves—someone I *think* I can trust."

"How is it that you feel you *can* trust him?"

"Because he has shown no signs that he is given to acts of betrayal."

"Why is this so?"

"He is a decent man."

"But a man who nevertheless wants only what you can give him? Or is this one an exception? Could he be what he is because he saw in you what you have become?"

Germanicus grimaced irritably.

"You are too young," he growled. "You mouth words that surely someone taught you. You cannot have lived long enough to gain any wisdom of your own."

"You are right. It is not *my* wisdom at all."

Germanicus looked up, for he knew what Scipio was implying.

"Forgive me," he said instantly. "I remember a story about the Nazarene. He was only twelve years old at the time, it is said. But He was able to stand in the midst of the temple at Jerusalem, with the scribes and

Pharisees all around him, and confound those men with the depth of His knowledge."

He glanced toward the galley entrance.

"They shall not serve me any longer after this voyage," he said.

Scipio was surprised by that declaration.

"You are freeing them?" he asked.

"That I am. Some have been with me longer than the captain himself. I can no longer assume the right to stand as master over any man."

"But how will you get around? That would mean you would never leave Palestine except by land perhaps."

"I am sure that Jesus the Christ will determine matters of such importance for me from now on."

Three of the slaves had come above deck. One of them shuffled over to him.

"May I speak, master?" the middle-aged, thin, dirt-smeared man asked.

"You may speak, but I am not your master."

The slave seemed flustered.

"You and the others will have the freedom you deserve as soon as this journey ends," Germanicus told him.

He rather expected the man to break out into laughter and dance a step or two in celebration. But that was not the reaction he got at all.

"I cannot reply," the other said, "because I have been a slave since I was a very young man. I served two masters before I was passed on to you. I scarce can imagine what this freedom is that you now offer."

"You will have no more masters," Germanicus reiterated. "I shall make sure the documents are correct so that you and the others need not be confronted with rebuke by any man."

But still the slave seemed reserved, uncomprehending.

Finally he spoke up again, his forehead rippled by a frown. "You have been kind, kind to me and to my comrades in the galley. Though I do not speak for all of the others, I can say, for most of them, that we could not imagine any form of freedom that does not include serving you in some way."

He knelt before Germanicus.

"If you want us to be free, then in freedom we shall decide to be yet in bondage to you," he said.

"I do not deserve—," Germanicus started to object.

The slave turned around and said, "Look at my back, see the scars. These came from the orders of another master."

And then he pointed to his feet.

"These are new," he said, indicating the tough leather sandals that covered them. "You gave them to us just a few weeks ago."

He smiled wisely.

"The one master slashed into our backs with the leather of his whips. You have used the same material to protect our feet. That is a symbol of why we love you. That is why, as long as there is strength within us, we want to go on serving you"—he paused only the briefest moment—"and the God before whom we have seen you fall in worship."

* * *

The harbor was a natural one, small, barely noticeable among the rock-filled barrenness of that dreary isle. Surrounded by cliffs on three sides, it provided entrance for only the smallest vessels, not the large liburnian.

"We cannot move closer than this," the captain, whose name was Pollio Ausonius, told Scipio and Germanicus. "We risk disaster by ignoring the reality of this place."

Germanicus nodded.

"We shall take one of the smaller vessels, then," he remarked, speaking of the tiny boats that were fastened to either side of the liburnian. "I would be pleased to have you accompany us, my captain."

Ausonius recognized the honor that this invitation carried with it. While very much aware of what faced them on the isle, he hesitated for only a moment, compelled by some inner prodding to which he had not been accustomed, but feeling its insistence nevertheless.

"I am pleased to accompany you," he replied, "very pleased indeed, sir."

Germanicus smiled pleasantly.

"Good! We will push off now."

Given his size, Germanicus took up half of the space on the smaller vessel. The captain did the rowing as the two other men sat quietly, awaiting a moment that Scipio could scarcely bear contemplating.

"May I speak?" Ausonius ventured as they were nearly inside the harbor.

Germanicus nodded.

"I have heard you talking during this journey," the captain spoke. "It was not my purpose to listen, but in order to attend my duties, I—"

"We understand that you were not eavesdropping," Germanicus interrupted. "Get on with it, Pollio."

The other man fell into silence.

"I said you could go on," Germanicus repeated. "There is no need to be shy. We are one from now on, my friend, bound together by our faith."

Ausonius' eyes were unusually moist.

"That is why I stopped speaking, sir," he said.

"I do not understand."

"You called me Pollio. That is the first time you have done so. It is a name that my mother gave me. Soon after that, my father was killed on the foreign field, and she had to raise me with no help from anyone."

"Serving Rome?"

"Yes, sir."

"But how is it that you became a slave?" Germanicus inquired.

"Debts, sir. There was no other way."

"Pollio?" Germanicus spoke as he leaned forward.

"Yes, sir?"

"You will soon be a wealthy man."

Ausonius nearly dropped the oar he held in each hand.

"I have accumulated enough of this world's riches to fulfill the needs of ten men."

"But I am unworthy."

Germanicus reached over and patted the captain on his left hand.

"It is I who should be making that statement, dear man. It is I who have spent so much on unbridled living. I did so because that was all I had at the time. My incessant accumulation of wealth gave me a reason for life itself. If I had more baubles, more clothes, more sexual activity, ever more—"

His face reddened.

"—slaves, then I had some reason to bow before the gods and ask them to give me yet another heartbeat."

"We are not so different, you and I," Ausonius responded.

"What do you mean, Pollio?"

"I begged those gods of whom you speak to give me yet another heartbeat if I could find some new way to please you, to serve you well. For you, it was the baubles and such, as you call them. For me, it was only yourself, sir, only a desire of mine to make you happy."

"And I took your desire to please me and made you bring to me whole shiploads of men and women to indulge my . . . appetites."

"I would have cut out my heart for you," Ausonius acknowledged.

"But all I gave to you, Pollio, was a certain kindness from time to time. Can that be so much?"

"You have seen me unclothed, have you not?"

"I have."

"You must have glimpsed the marks on my flesh."

"I did."

"As with the man you saw earlier, these also were ordered by other masters at other times in other places."

"They beat you?" Germanicus reacted, his astonishment immediate. "I can see certainly that this has been the unfortunate lot of countless numbers of galley slaves but surely not ship *captains?*"

"But then, sir, not every man takes his wealth, his power over other men as you yourself have. Some seem to find themselves to be men only through the pain they can cause those in their charge."

The captain was facing the isle, his two passengers sitting with their backs to it. He glanced quickly to their left.

"We are about to pull up to a flat section of beach," he warned. "There are rocks on every side."

This was Ausonius's discreet and kindly way of telling of both of them that he had to stop talking and concentrate on getting everyone safely through what amounted to a treacherous obstacle course.

The two were silent, knowing that the captain's attention could not be distracted.

They could hear the wood of their little boat touch boulders both visible and hidden below water level.

"Snakes!" Scipio exclaimed. "They ride along the surface of the water on every side of this boat!"

"Keep your hands from dangling over," Germanicus warned him. "They are attracted by the sensation of heat."

Scipio heeded that advice instantly.

Odors drifted out to them as they came closer to land, an awful collective stench filling the air.

"What could that be?" Germanicus inquired, momentarily wishing that he was back with his perfumes and colognes and sweet-smelling bath oils.

They were only a few hundred feet away from where they could pull up on land. Scipio looked down into the shallow water.

Skulls.

He jerked back.

"What is it?" Germanicus asked.

"Look over the side."

The answer was apparent. His face turned white.

"These poor souls often lose their fingers and even their hands. They have no way to dig graves, so they dump their dead wherever they can. This harbor must be one of the places," he said slowly, fighting a nauseous sensation. "Look at how many!"

"The odor of death!" Ausonius spoke uneasily. "That is what assaults us. This is a burial ground."

"With more waiting to—," Germanicus started to say, then glimpsed how Scipio was reacting, before adding, "Forgive us, Fabius.

184

We have no restraint. My captain and I should feel ashamed at our lack of restraint. How very much worse it must be for you now!"

Scipio nodded, waiting a few seconds before he spoke. "My brother was healed but died anyway. Now my mother and my father have caught this foul scourge. I wonder if I can become God's instrument of healing this time. Before it was someone else whom He used. Will He do it again, but with me?"

XXXII

The three of them saw a single rope ladder, the end of which dangled just above the sand of a little beach they had found inside the harbor.

"Does anyone know how these people get their food?" Ausonius asked. "I have heard nothing about this place or them before now."

"The emperor, whether in a humanitarian impulse or not, has decreed that, periodically, food be taken over to this isle from the excess of Rome's storehouses," Germanicus replied. "I do not know how often this occurs or how much is given. Perhaps the inhabitants have been able to plant seeds for vegetables to be raised in their own gardens in order to weather the periods between shipments."

Ausonius went first, followed by Scipio. They had decided that that was the best procedure since Germanicus was not accustomed to any such physical labor. There was simply no way that he could make the climb without assistance. Both of them needed to reach down to grab his hands as soon as he was within reach.

After much effort, they were able to pull him up onto the rocky surface above.

Spread out before them was a flat, harsh landscape of nearly inexpressible barrenness. A pallid gray-tinged haze hung over the area. Thistles, thorns, tares, and a few other desert-based plants growing in patches of sandy soil and through cracks in the rock landscape were the only signs at first glance of any kind of life. Several miles ahead they could see the beginning of a mountainous region.

"Any colony of lepers must be there," Ausonius offered. "Perhaps those peaks hide a fertile valley."

The other two looked at him as though he had suddenly become a man without a brain to think rationally.

"I mean, how else could they survive?" he added defensively. "Any little gardens they might plant could scarcely tide them over. Or does leprosy do something to their appetite as well, destroying it along with everything else?"

"We do not know if they are surviving at all," Germanicus commented. "Certainly no records are kept. Fresh boatloads of lepers come in periodically. In time they will all look very much alike, in their common malady."

He regretted saying this, regretted implying that Scipio might not be able to recognize his parents because of the distorting ravages of leprosy. But his young friend said nothing, though the anguish he felt was clear in the troubled look of his eyes.

They started walking south, toward the mountains. Every so often they would have to detour a bit.

Scorpions and snakes, nests of the creatures.

Germanicus shivered fearfully as he looked back again and again, after sidestepping one or the other.

"Just making certain that those . . . those . . . are not following us," he explained out of embarrassment.

The other two felt similarly but were better able to conceal their emotions.

After a bit more than two hours of walking, they had approached the nearest section of mountain and a tiny pass cutting through it.

"A natural prison," Ausonius observed. "It would not be difficult to seal them off if the emperor or anyone else wanted to do so."

"Particularly if any political prisoners were among those who could be punished by exiling them here," Germanicus mumbled. "I have heard that Patmos, for one, has become a spot for that purpose."

"True, true . . . one of my masters was sent there, though I never discovered the nature of the charges responsible."

Another image came to Scipio's mind.

"I wonder if that rabble-rouser Barabbas will end up in a place such as this, or Patmos perhaps," he mused, thinking of how repugnant the man's release was in view of the one who was condemned in his stead.

"I think that that just may be the fate of all such insurrectionists, if, for whatever reason, they are not executed swiftly," Germanicus agreed. "My sources told me some months ago that Barabbas indeed was caught trying to piece together an army with which he could launch an attack against Masada. By exiling him to a leper colony, this or another, they would be deftly calling attention to the scourge he proposed to unleash through the empire itself, one every bit as contagious as endured by those poor souls with whom he would have to keep company for the rest of his miserable life."

"But Masada?" Scipio repeated. "That would have been stupid. That place cannot be wrested from Rome's control. It is impregnable. Herod picked it initially as the site for his palace for that very reason."

"Yes, I know. But this Barabbas can scarcely be called a man of soaring intellectual ability or astute military logistics."

"He could attempt to conquer any *other* garrison and yet he thinks of Masada? What could be his purpose other than some kind of glory for himself?"

"To use Masada as a symbol, I suppose, for if Rome cannot hold onto that fortress, then its days of controlling Palestine overall would be numbered, a message that undoubtedly would spread with the greatest speed. His choice in that light is not inappropriate. It is rather his ability to achieve that end which can be derided."

Going single file, they walked through the pass, and after a few minutes, entered a large valley. At the base of the surrounding mountain peaks, they saw numerous natural caves and pale faces peering out at them from within.

Scipio started crying.

"What is it, lad?" Germanicus asked.

"My mother! I saw her already. I mean, I *think* it was her. But her face was not the same, oh, it was not—!"

He turned away, ashamed that his emotions had shown through in this manner to the other men.

"You are no longer under the judgmental gaze of a Roman commander," Germanicus spoke. "Do not be concerned about those tears of yours. After a while, you may not be the only one shedding them."

Scipio's face had drained of color, his pale skin covered with cold sweat.

"Which cave?" Ausonius inquired. "Do you remember?"

"It was so quick . . . as I was glancing from one to the other!"

"At least we know that she is alive," Germanicus put in.

"But it might have been better if she had died," Scipio said, his voice breaking. "You cannot imagine what I saw, you cannot!"

But they soon had more than a glimpse.

From all of the caves on every side, strange figures stirred forth. At that hour, their misshapen bodies cast even more bizarre shadows against the sides of the mountain peaks that enclosed their little colony, and the noises coming from them were generating the faintest of echoes, little gasps of pain, sniffling sounds from partially blocked nasal passages, wheezing from lungs pressed in by deteriorating bones, coughs that easily drowned out the rest of the noises only to be replaced by a fresh round of the others.

Scipio pressed his hands to his ears, unable to bear the odd cacophony, and retreated with haste into the mountain pass directly behind him, then propped himself against the uneven rock wall.

Many of the afflicted ones were missing fingers, toes, arms, legs —all lost to the damaging effects of leprosy, either dropping off entirely, leaving only raw, diseased stumps or twisted into shapes that looked like miniature versions of the twisted roots of old trees.

It was not difficult to understand why, in that ancient time, lepers were assumed by great masses of people, primarily those who were of modest education, to be possessed of demons, for their outward countenance often became so repulsive that—the conventional wisdom went—they could only be taking on the appearance of the unholy beings inhabiting them.

A woman came up to Germanicus and Ausonius while, for the moment, the others held back.

"What is it that you want?" Germanicus asked, trying very hard not to retreat to the pass as Scipio had done, for her face seemed nothing more than a series of reddish boils, puffed out, and ready to disgorge their diseased contents.

"My son," she said simply, her voice harsh, like the cackling of an old witch in a play. "I am Berenices Scipio. Can you tell me if you have brought him here? I received a message from someone on another vessel that he might be coming."

"It was I who had it sent," Germanicus told her. "Is Fabius's father also here?"

"Back there," she added, sorrow evident in every word. "He cannot come forward. He has no feet. I can no longer hold him upright."

She looked at one to the other.

"Please . . . my son . . . where is he?" she pleaded.

"In there," Ausonius pointed to the narrow pass behind him as he stepped aside.

She hesitated, her eyes darting from side to side.

"He will be ashamed . . ." she muttered. "I cannot go."

Germanicus instinctively reached out and touched her shoulder, then pulled back, gasping in the process.

So hard, he thought. *Not soft skin, pliable . . . a hard crust, dry.*

"Go to your son," he told her. "He has come a very long way in order to be able to see you now."

Nodding after a moment, Berenices Scipio started to shuffle forward unsteadily, her toes gone, making it awkward for her to balance herself.

"Fabius," she called as she noticed him just ahead of her.

He spoke not at all, wrenching sobs the only sounds coming from him.

"It is not so bad as it seems, my son," she said.

He spun around, his cheek wet.

"How can you say—?" he spoke but found any other words lodging in his throat as he saw her so close to him.

"I cannot hold you in my arms, dear Fabius, child of my womb," she told him. "I cannot ask you to take my hand as I did with the stranger who healed your brother. But I still have a son. How many women have sent their sons off to the service of Imperial Rome only to lose them on some foreign battlefield, and never even get a body back to bury."

Scipio's eyes widened with anger.

"You speak of my brother's healing," he blurted. "Healed so that he could die at the hand of robbers? Is that something over which we should rejoice? You once had two sons. Now there is only one. You cannot expect me to agree with you that this is not as bad as it seems!"

"But he was free for a little while. He knew what it was to feel vibrant, to feel young and healthy," she said. "At the end, as he was dying in my arms, he told me about the Nazarene waiting for him, smiling with such joy—"

"No!" he screamed. "I cannot listen. I gave up everything for this Jesus. I convinced others to follow Him. How can He mock me in this way? How can He treat you and Papa so cruelly?"

"Can you not trust Him?" she went on. "It is I who should be bitter, Fabius. What have I left? Think on that, son. My hands are gone. My eyesight is fading. I cannot keep down for very long what meager food we have here. And yet I go to sleep at night singing praises to Almighty God. I wake up each morning thanking Him for heaven, for this might be the day when He takes me there. For others, Fabius, none of this is true. They have only this life, and they degrade even that by the way they live."

She thrust in front of her what was left of both her hands.

"Look at—," he started to say but could not, the pain on her face driving the insensitive, angry words from him.

"The fingers are gone, yes," she said, "but I still have hands. Perhaps later my feet will go, as they have for your father. And my legs—"

She hesitated, thinking of that horrible possibility.

"With the grace of God, even then I will not curse Him and die!" she proclaimed.

Scipio had not been prepared for any of this. He felt overwhelmed, utterly unable to cope.

"I must leave," he said instead. "I have a journey to complete."

"Your father will soon be dead, Fabius," she pleaded. "Will you not see him? Will you not go to his side this final time?"

It was this prospect that caused him the greatest anguish. The elder Scipio had been a brawling sort of man, with a temper as volcanic, it seemed, as Vesuvius itself. Stories of his strength assumed near-legendary proportions in the region of Italy where generations of his family had lived. He had seldom been challenged physically, but when he had, he always won the fight that ensued.

Oh, how I worshiped you, Scipio thought, remembering the times he and his father had spent together. *How I used you as a model for my own life!*

"When I told him that you had come," his mother's voice intruded, "my beloved smiled for the first time in many months, for he had been very worried about you, wondering whether you had been hurt in battle perhaps. But then he became so sad, Fabius. He cried out to me that I should stop you, that you must not see him as he is. He does not want you to be ashamed of him. He said, 'Let my son go to his grave proud of his father, remembering him as he was before God chose to bring this tribulation upon him.'"

She seemed to become weak and started to fall. Scipio rushed forward and grabbed her as gently as he could.

"So you *are* still my son!" she whispered wisely. "You would not hold any other leper in this manner."

She seemed so frail, her weight loss bringing a once vibrant body down to well less than a hundred pounds, and she trembled constantly.

"Mama, Mama," Scipio cried from the depths of his soul, "please forgive me; oh, I beg you to forgive me."

She nodded, a smile curling up her thin, pale lips.

"As God has forgiven each of us," she said, "because of His only begotten Son, my dear Fabius!"

She seemed to revive and was able to stand without aid.

"On that last day I spent at home," Scipio reminded her as they walked back out of the pass, "you still had not believed, despite my brother's healing. What happened in the meantime to change you?"

"It was later, after you had left to be a legionnaire. Another of Jesus' followers came by, and your father and I talked with him for many, many hours. Finally, we knelt in his presence, and told him that we wanted the gift of eternal life so that the two of us would not be forever apart. Such was our love that the very idea of separation for any length of time seemed horrible! And now we have come to love the Nazarene as much as one another."

Germanicus and Ausonius kept their silence as Scipio and his mother slowly walked past them.

"Your father is much worse off than I," she said as they approached one of the caves. "You must prepare yourself before you see him. If you react as you did with me, it will hurt him terribly, Fabius."

"His hands are gone?" he asked, grimacing as he glanced again at her own.

"No, they remain."

The man had enjoyed working with those well-trained hands, continually carving various figures of wood.

"He has something for you," she added. "He began preparing it not long after some soldiers took us to this place. He kept praying that you would return so that he could give it to you before he died."

"A carving?"

She nodded, a certain pride showing on her features.

They stopped in front of one of the caves.

"There is where your father has spent more than a year of his life, usually in the darkness at the very end," his mother explained. "As his condition changed, he could do no more than stay in that one spot and work with his hands."

"Mama . . ." Scipio spoke not unkindly. "What makes him worse off than you? Surely you will tell me before I enter so that I may be prepared."

"His face, my son," she replied, frowning. "It is because of his face. I cannot even speak of it in detail. You will see, you will see."

XXXIII

Papa!"

The creature Fabius Scipio saw gave little visual hint that he was the man who had been a thoughtful and kind father as well as a devoted friend.

His face, my son. It is because of his face. I cannot even speak of it in detail. You will see, you will see.

His mother had not exaggerated.

Livius Scipio was essentially a man without a face.

Substituted for his nose—bridge as well as nostrils—was a grotesque hole.

Lining the sides of it were flaps of skin together with little blood-red bumps. Part of the cheekbone was pressed so tightly against the flesh that the bone seemed nearly ready to poke through. There was bone below where his nose had been and mouth and lower jaw were under that, which meant that he could still talk, since his mouth essentially remained in place. But as the younger Scipio was to find out, the voice that reached his ears was filled with pitiable noises.

The elder Scipio turned away from his son.

"No!" he said, that voice a mockery of what it was once, so strong in earlier days and so rich in tonal qualities that he had been encouraged to enter the political arena, for it was said that he could easily command the attention of any crowd with such gift as he had and could quickly gain wide support. But he preferred a life unencumbered by the many intrigues that were perpetually swirling around anyone who chose that sort of career.

"Go, Fabius," he said, his tongue bloated and pale. "Let me die here without a vision of your shame looming large in my mind."

Scipio realized that the deepening shock he felt had been written on his own face, stark and obvious.

"I cannot go now," he replied. "I cannot go without telling you that I love you."

Livius Scipio tried to move further back into the cave, but he was already up against the hard, uneven, natural wall. A rough-edged section of rock dug into his right arm and tore open a large gash in the flesh.

"You *love* me?" his father blurted, paying no heed to his injury. "There is no one except God Himself who could love the misshapen beast that I have become. But then you did not care about Him when you left. You were interested only in the glory of Rome!"

"Papa!" Scipio cried out in great shock, as he dropped to his knees in front of the man. "You are bleeding!"

"I can feel nothing. I am numb everywhere. My body is dying, and there is so little pain on its surface. Sometimes, in my stomach, I feel it, sometimes around my heart, but I have burnt myself very badly and I cannot sense anything."

Any strength the elder Scipio had left him just then, and he fell forward into his son's arms.

"Do not . . . touch me, Fabius, I beg you," he mumbled. "Do not visit this plague upon yourself, my son."

"If to save myself I must thrust you from me," Fabius Scipio said, "then it is no tragedy that I become like you."

"I am a piece of rotten meat, diseased and loathsome."

"Only your shell, Papa. Only the outer garment has been affected. Your mind is untouched and your soul remains whole and pure and very much alive. Our Lord will allow nothing to stand against it."

His father started sobbing.

"You *believe*, my son? You share this new faith of your mother's and mine?"

"I do, Papa. I have seen the risen Christ with my own eyes!"

"The *Lord?* You have seen the precious Lamb?"

"In the very room where He ate his last supper with the apostles. He spoke to me and another man, a comrade of mine."

The tormented body slumped as though life had suddenly left it.

"O Father God, a little more time, please!" his son spoke fearfully. "Please—do not take Papa just yet."

The elder Scipio coughed once, then spoke with some awe. "I sensed the touch of someone eternal just then, Fabius. There was no numbness! In that instant I could feel Almighty God!"

They sat side-by-side without speaking for a number of minutes until Berenices Scipio was able to join them. Then the trio prayed out loud, the mother first, followed by the father, and lastly their son; trembling, emotional voices clear and forceful, except for Livius Scipio, who could not get past the wheezing and other sounds that made his words barely intelligible. Yet the sound of Livius Scipio praying was enough to attract virtually all the other lepers in that ragtag colony and cause them to stand at the mouth of the cave, listening for as long as their ravished bodies would permit before exhaustion took over and they had to return to the far corners of other caves in that location and huddle wearily in the darkness.

One shriveled old woman, her limbs brittle, her mind nearly gone, was being held in the big arms of Quintus Egnatius Javolenus Tidus Germanicus, while the captain squatted next to a midget leper whose already deformed features were made quite hideous by the inroads of a plague shared by all but the newcomers.

Finally L vius Scipio presented his son with a gift that was all he had to give, a beautiful cross carved out of a piece of oakwood a kindly passerby from another ship had left with him.

"It is so little," he said, "yet my beloved Fabius deserves much more."

"You give me a symbol of our Savior's sacrifice. How could I receive something greater than that, Papa?"

The elder Scipio had a fainting spell and collapsed into his son's arms.

Though leprosy had dulled the man's ability to feel any real degree of pain, counterbalancing that was the havoc played with the immune system in his body, making him susceptible to infection, pneumonia, and a great deal else; all of which brought him ever-deepening anguish, especially during a time in history when little was understood about a vast array of maladies, and the practice of medicine was not much beyond the use of magic potions and the most primitive of so-called remedies.

Later, after the three men had returned to the liburnian for the night, Scipio found that he could not sleep and went above deck to stand under the stars and try to deal with the melancholy thoughts that filled his head.

I prayed for my father to live longer, so that I could have some more time with him, he thought, *and now I have that. But having seen him, having heard the whimpering as I held him, I wonder if giving me such an answer was more a curse than a miracle.*

He sensed someone standing behind him, turned, and saw Germanicus.

"You are thinking about your father?" the other man asked.

Scipio nodded.

"Now that you have been with him, you must ponder what to do next. Is that not what concerns you?" Germanicus pressed.

"I cannot stay and yet I must stay. I cannot leave and yet I must leave. I am torn—oh, I am torn between my love for those who gave me love and . . . and—"

He saw a knowing expression on his friend's face.

"You have some wisdom to bestow?" he asked uncertainly. "What is it that you want me to hear?"

"You were right in that which you spoke at first," Germanicus told him. "You cannot stay here."

"But if I were the one so ill," Scipio protested, "if I had come down with that which afflicts *them*, they would not have to think for even a moment. They would be there by my side, sacrificing everything to bring me as much relief as they were able; and when there was none left, they would still remain, so that I should not die alone."

"But, in that circumstance, neither of *them* would be the one on a sacred odyssey for the Nazarene," Germanicus stated, modulating his voice to be as gentle-sounding as he knew how. "They will be lifted up quite soon from that ghastly place, you know, their poor bodies left behind, for their strength is nearly at its end. All their lives they served those they loved, and now the time has come for—"

"—one they loved to serve *them*," Scipio interrupted.

"Yea, you are correct, but they do love their Savior as passionately as you yourself, Fabius. And that love would *demand* of you that you follow Him *anywhere*, for therein lies the greatest love—to leave father, mother, sister, and brother in order to serve your heavenly Father with all your mind, body, and soul."

"If I do that, I desert them."

"If you do not, you desert *Him*, my dear young friend."

Germanicus waved his large right arm in the direction of the isle.

"How many men, women, and children will miss hearing the message of this Jesus the Christ if you decide to stay?"

"But if they are to be dead in such a short while, what is the harm of a brief delay? Tell me that, if you can."

"No harm if you escape without bringing along with you the malady that entraps them. Can you be sure, Fabius, that you will not become as they are now, unable to beckon to any man without receiving a look of disgust and fear in return?

"You carry in your heart the message of eternal redemption that the Nazarene gave to His followers. But if you cannot put that message into words that others are willing to hear due to your outer countenance, what is the value of your effort? It will have come to naught. And what will then have become of this grand dedication of yours except that it be squandered on the altar of your love for—?"

"No!" Scipio screamed. "I cannot let you confuse me!"

"But you were confused before I ever spoke. That was only minutes ago, Fabius. Do you want me to repeat your very words?"

"No more," Scipio declared. "I have made up my mind."

"You are staying then?"

"God will understand. He will protect me if He wants me to carry on from here, but if He does not, then I still shall be able to hold Mama and Papa in my arms as they die, and the last words they ever hear will be from my lips, telling them both how much I love them, truly how much I *do* love them!"

Germanicus's expression turned sad, his eyes narrowing in despair, and as he walked toward the old, creaky steps leading below, Scipio saw tears beginning to flow down those great, red-tinged cheeks.

XXXIV

A little rectangular window only three inches in width and less than a foot in length let in the morning sun directly over Scipio's head. He had finally been able to fall asleep after returning to his quarters below deck. The touch of light fell against his eyelids, stirring him. He put his left arm over his eyes and was ready to surrender again to the dreams that had been with him throughout the now-faded night, snatches of moments from the years of his childhood, each replayed in a rush, until he noticed how strangely the liburnian was acting—not calmly as it did earlier, in the still waters of that harbor, but swaying in a pronounced manner, perhaps as some wind kicked up. And yet the motion he felt seemed not the same as that, not of a ship at anchor but of one that had been set out in the open sea.

Scipio sat straight up.

Everyone else is still asleep, he told himself, *and yet we have been drifting! How long can it have been?*

He threw on his garment and rushed down the tiny corridor to the steps.

Once above deck, he saw only the waters of the Mediterranean around him. To the south, there was the now-distant isle where he had come upon his parents.

"Captain!" he screamed.

Pollio Ausonius, roused from his own sleep, hurried from the galley area. In each hand was a scroll.

"Look at what has happened!" Scipio said, panic causing his voice to crack. "We must head back. This is terrible!"

The captain did nothing but stand there.

"Have you not heard me, Pollio?" Scipio asked, greatly puzzled —and angry. "Why are you not doing something?"

"It is not as it seems," Ausonius replied, his eyelids fluttering briefly, still half-claimed by sleep.

"But look at where we are!" Scipio persisted. "I must go back, stay with my poor parents! Get Quintus. And hurry!"

He started to brush past the other man, but Ausonius, so much larger than he, stepped squarely in front of him.

"Stand aside!" Scipio demanded.

"He is not below, Fabius," Ausonius said solemnly. "The one you seek remains no longer on this ship."

"But that means he has been left behind. We have to turn back now more than ever. We have to get—!"

"Fabius, Fabius, you must listen to me. Our friend's wish was to remain with the lepers. He *asked* me to push off. This was not an accident. It was what he *wanted!*"

With that, Ausonius's eyes clouded up as he thrust the scrolls toward Scipio.

"In my left hand is a decree that you are to receive the greater measure of the rather substantial wealth that he has amassed. In my right hand is what he wrote to you, to be read by you only."

"What does it say? What could he have been thinking?"

"I know not as much as a single word of its contents, Fabius. He asked me to be familiar only with the other, in which there is some provision for me and my men, and for careful maintenance of regular shipments of food to that isle, but with only these exceptions you are the primary recipient."

Scipio ran to the southern-facing end of the liburnian.

"But why, Pollio? What madness could have driven him to this?"

"Not that, Fabius, not that!" Ausonius said, his voice rising in volume. "Take this scroll, young man. Sit down and read what your friend has written. Do it for him, please!"

Scipio grabbed both parchments and did as the other man had asked, unrolling it, and reading the contents.

Dear Fabius:

The Lord has told me in my spirit that you are not to be dissuaded from your journey, blessed friend.

It is clear to me that my own destiny is right here, to remain behind with your loved ones and so many others who have been abandoned, so I can be doing all that I can to comfort them, crying with them when there can be no other response to this their plight.

But I wonder who will become the comforter after all? They have so little, and yet they continue to give praise to Almighty God. I am very large and well-fed, and they are so thin, and I have lived as they can only dream—not the sin, of course, Fabius—but the silks and the cherrywood and the banquets and the servants at my feet.

I have never truly belonged to anyone, dear friend, as you know. But now they **are** *my family far, far more than those who gave me life and are related to me by blood. I have my brothers and my sisters at last, those who call my name with love and do not turn from me, as I could never turn from them.*

Yet, is it not, in fact, the blood of Another that has drawn us together so remarkably? Without His sacrifice at the hill of the skull, what hope would there be for any of us? My new family and I are here now because of the Nazarene's sacrifice, here to be a blessing to one another as the angels sing in rejoicing from their heavenly station.

Spread the holy words of the precious Son of God to those in and around Rome. Despite my exile, I have numerous friends in the mother of all our cities. They will be shocked by my story. Seize this moment, my dearest Fabius. Charge on to the very feet of the emperor himself—if you can.

In the love of Him who will one day bring us together again before His throne, I bid you good-bye, Fabius. Go—with our Savior and Lord by your side every step of the way.

Quintus Egnatius Javolenus Tidus Germanicus

Scipio looked up at Ausonius after finishing the scroll.

"I shall miss this man," he said.

"No more than I, no more than I."

Scipio stood and walked over to the carved wood railing.

"He will die there, I think, Pollio," he spoke, nearly in a whisper. "He will become one of them and die like the rest."

Ausonius caught his breath, fighting back tears.

"I know. I wish I could be with him. So many of them have no hands. How will they bury him?"

He remembered what they had seen after entering the harbor.

"Oh, that ghastly place, Fabius, his body will end up there, in the shallow water, staring sightlessly up at any who approach, the fish tearing at whatever remains of him."

Part IV

XXXV

Decimus Paetus had been a wayfarer since Fabius Scipio and he had parted. Periodically he managed to come in contact with other Christians and spend time with them, but he did not take to the role of missionary spreading the new faith of Christianity nearly as well as his younger friend was doing.

Often he would drop to his knees and agonize over that striking difference between the two of them. It seemed that Scipio could easily approach any stranger, engage that individual in conversation, and somehow find an opportunity to witness for Jesus the Christ. Of course, there were some few times when he failed, but mostly he seized the moment and, his countenance flashing confidence and joy, launch into a clear-headed, vibrant presentation of what they understood in those days about sin and redemption.

For many weeks, Paetus doubted himself so severely that he despaired of living. He hoped, when the insecurity and the depression hit, that he would simply not awaken in the morning but would instead find himself to have been transported during the night to the side of Jesus Himself.

Always the raucous call of a rooster at sunrise or the plaintive sounds of nearby cows would alert him to the fact that his desperate prayer had not been answered during the night in the manner he had hoped, and he would have to get himself up and face the bleakness of Palestine once again.

The relatively primitive nature of life for the vast majority of the inhabitants of that land was a contrast of no small proportions to what he had seen in Rome and elsewhere. So many worthwhile buildings or other structures had been erected by the Romans and not the Jews. Even Jerusalem seemed backward, architecturally and otherwise, when viewed against the magnificence of the legendary capital of the Roman Empire.

Faced with these thoughts, as well as memories of the past, Paetus had to admit to periods of regret, regret that he had cast off all of what service to Rome offered. And there was the lingering fear that Pontius Pilatus would cease one day to be in a forgiving mood and send some of his former comrades to hunt him down.

Despite repeated, self-imposed comparisons to Scipio's greater effectiveness as a missionary, Paetus had had to admit that he was not without his successes. There were men and women walking the dusty roads and living in their huts and working their fields who were now Christians because of him.

Everytime he would go on a journey past them, if they saw him, they would drop what they were doing and race over and embrace him with great energy.

That was one of the bright spots of his life—seeing other human beings gain some peace and joy in the midst of a threadbare existence that could only have been dreary at best before he was guided into their lives. Even for those who had managed to be happy earlier, who knew how to celebrate over something as small as an extra loaf of bread given to them by a charitable passerby, there were moments when they too wondered what the point was to life.

"We have been told from times past of another life when we die," an ancient one named Lysimmachus told him one hot afternoon as they both sat by the road, resting, even as the stifling heat drained the energy from their bodies.

"Yes, I know," agreed Paetus. "It is the same for Christians."

"But why does *this* existence have to be miserable? Why is it that our oppressors have such wealth, and yet our lot is dust and hunger and rags for clothes?"

Paetus wished Scipio was by his side then.

"It is a circumstance we have brought upon ourselves," he said haltingly, doing his best to respond.

"What is this that you say?" Lysimmachus said indignantly, his voice loud, angry. "I have been poor since my birth. And my parents were poor as well as their parents before them. Am I to pay for what transpired among my ancestors?"

"If you were to place a serpent in the middle of this road in front of us," Paetus continued, "and then went about covering it with a beautiful blanket of dyed wool, ablaze with wondrous colors, red being one of them, and someone, a stranger, were to come along, see it, be attracted to it, pick it up, and be struck by the serpent and die, would that not be unfair? Should he be made to pay for your act?"

"That is not the same. How can you make such comparisons?"

"But it *is* the same, Lysimmachus. What I have spoken of is simply a part of life. It happens. Can we expect God to protect us from everything? If that were the case, then nobody would ever dare to reject Him, for He would eliminate pain, injury, sickness overnight. We would lose nothing by professing our faith."

The other man was quiet, listening to every word that Paetus spoke.

"There would be no need for trust. There would be no need for caution. There would be no need for armies to protect us or rulers to govern us."

"What you describe sounds very appealing, Decimus."

"But it also would mean that we could do whatever we wanted to do, and God would never punish us. For in punishment lies pain, and in pain, the kind of misery of which you have been speaking. But if we once admit the *need* for punishment, then we allow the entry of pain in the lives of those around us and ourselves as well."

"But I have done nothing to deserve *this*," he spoke as he indicated the swathes of soiled and tattered cloth that covered his thin body. "I have not murdered any man. I have not stolen any money from anyone. When my wife was alive, I remained faithful. I have not committed any other acts—"

"Have you ever lied?" Paetus asked.

"Yes, of course. But—"

"Have you ever looked upon a woman with lustful thoughts?"

"I have, I have. But—"

"Have you ever—?"

Lysimmachus waved his hand through the air in a gesture of impatience mixed with embarrassment.

"I understand what you are saying, Decimus," he said. "Your words have great impact. Tell me more about this Jesus who inspires you to such wisdom."

At first Paetus could think of nothing to say. He was not accustomed to anyone reacting so soon and so strongly to his often rather extended attempts at explaining the nature of the Christian faith.

After they had talked a bit, Lysimmachus stood.

"Why do you not join me at my village?" he asked.

"Your village, Lysimmachus?" Paetus repeated. "I thought you had no home."

"I do not."

"Then—"

"But, still, I spoke correctly," Lysimmachus interrupted. "What you will see *is* my village, though I admit that it is nothing to be proud of, has not been anything to be proud of for a very long time now."

"Where it is located?"

"Just a short distance from the Jordan, nestled among the mountain peaks of that region."

"I would be glad to go."

Paetus said that while having no idea what to expect.

XXXVI

The village had been abandoned a long time before as the inhabitants left to work for the Romans or to move in closer to Jerusalem, where they fancied they had a better chance of prospering.

The country of the Jews was not alone in having places like this, for they could be seen in virtually every part of the empire, but it was Judea that had more than the others, the now silent, sad places where village life once filled the air with the sounds of children and animals, the odors of women cooking or talking as they did their wash—in this case, with water brought in from the nearby Jordan.

"We felt the tug of life elsewhere," Lysimmachus said as they stood at the edge of the now-decrepit group of huts. "Where there were gardens, there are now only weeds. Where families lived in love, there are now only empty ruins."

On three sides, tall mountains kept the very existence of the valley unknown to most travelers.

"We did not have much, even when we lived here," he continued, "but in our scarcity we were fortunate to have each other."

Paetus pondered that remark.

It echoed something he had noticed among a number of poor families. Where there were few clothes, and pitiable ones at that, the people held each other to provide some degree of warmth. Where there was little food, they shared. Where there was work to be done, they took part in the various tasks together.

"The Nazarene said something that I have not been able to get out of my mind ever since His words reached my ears," Lysimmachus said.

"What was that?" Paetus asked, greatly interested.

"He spoke of wealth being a source of anguish and not so much pleasure. The Nazarene said that wealth could become something with the ability to corrupt, that the love of it was the root of all evil."

He walked forward and stood in what used to be a kind of village square.

"We gathered here many times during an average week," he recalled. "We would sing and dance and exchange stories about our lives, about what we hoped for as far as the future was concerned. Here is where we brought the lambs that were to be sacrificed in Jerusalem. Here is where our children underwent circumcision. You could almost say that this was the soul of my village. But that soul is gone, and my people are gone and—"

He fell against Paetus, who was standing next to him.

"I cry out for them at night," he said. "But there is no answer except the wind and the wolves and the other creatures who scurry about in the darkness."

He was sobbing.

"The shell of what once was in this place mocks any dreams we ever had. And now we are scattered throughout the land. Many have died. The rest have become like me, beggars at the tables of rich Jewish rulers and the conquering Roman legions. We get crumbs and then are sent on our way."

Lysimmachus swung around and faced Paetus.

"Your Jesus threw the money changers out of the temple during the last week of His life," he added. "They came right back in after He left, but at the very least Jesus was able to embarrass the high priest and his hangers-on."

Abruptly he got down on his knees.

"It is not possible for me to follow anyone I cannot respect," Lysimmachus spoke, his voice trembling slightly. "That is why I want to become one of His disciples this day. For He does have my respect, and now I also want to pledge to the Nazarene my devotion."

* * *

Though old in body and slight of frame, his bones brittle, Lysimmachus seemed far younger in his mental abilities.

"I have tried to feed my mind even when I could not feed my body," he said as they stood at dusk in the shell of what was left of one of the huts in that village, a musty, sour odor of decay coming from its barely standing walls of dried mud and thatched straw. "Since food has been so paltry over the years, my mind has grown even as my body has deteriorated."

Lysimmachus sighed wistfully as he glanced up at the clear sky and saw stars in particular abundance.

"There was once a roof on this little home," he told Paetus. "We could see those stars only if we walked outside."

He touched his forehead and closed his eyes.

"Are you in pain?" Paetus asked.

"Yes . . . I am," Lysimmachus spoke weakly. "But it is not just of the body, I suspect. My soul is in pain, Decimus, over what has been left behind. Everyone is gone. They may not be dead, though I know my wife is. My children? I cannot say what has happened to them. Are they poor like their father? Do they wander the dusty roads of this land, grabbing scraps from the tables of other men?"

The old one's shoulders fell forward and his chest sank in, a great sigh of weariness escaping his lips.

"Am I to see them again only in this heaven of which you speak?" he asked. "Is there no way God can bring them back to this spot?"

Paetus knew that the truth would be devastating to frail Lysimmachus, the truth proclaiming that those who accepted Jesus the Christ into their lives as their Savior and their Lord would be welcomed into God's heavenly kingdom when they died, but that those who did not—who rejected Him—would spend time and eternity in hell.

How can I tell him that, Lord? he asked. *There is yet some hope to which he can cling, hope that, somehow, even before he dies, his children will be able to gather around him. How can I say that that is the only hope he has left, hope for this life only, if they have failed to embrace blessed Jesus?*

"Your expression tells me much," Lysimmachus observed.

"Much about what?" Paetus asked dumbly.

"I had heard what this Nazarene was saying before He became a prisoner. He spoke of being the light of the world. He said that only through Him could there be gained entry into heaven. Is that not so?"

With sadness descending upon his face, Paetus spoke as honestly as he knew how when he said, "Yes, it is as you say."

"So I am to see my loved ones and my friends only if they have been told of Jesus and only if they accept Him as I now have?"

"That is so, old man."

"Then we have to bring them back. We have to rebuild this village. We have to make it a place to which they would want to return."

Paetus might have scoffed openly at the notion if the absolute wisdom of it had not hit him as profoundly as it did.

"But then how do we start?" spoke Lysimmachus, his rising weariness becoming apparent once again. "I have not a single denarius, nor do you, if I am not mistaken. It is a dream that will remain nothing more than that, to be trotted out when we are alone, such as now, and given to ravings."

"I know but two persons of wealth and it is unlikely that one of them could ever be persuaded to help," Paetus said.

"Who is that?"

"Pontius Pilatus!"

Lysimmachus chuckled at the unintended cynicism of that thought.

"There is another," Paetus said as he brushed his chin in sudden recollection.

"Caiphas?"

Now it was the former legionnaire's turn to appreciate a sardonic comment by the other man.

"*Not* Caiphas," he acknowledged, "but, rather, someone else, the kind man in whose tomb Jesus was buried."

"I have heard of him, I believe. He passes by me on the road every so often, never failing to give me a coin."

"Joseph of Arimathea—is he the one of whom you are thinking?"

"He *is!*" Lysimmachus agreed.

"I have never met him, but his very good friend Nicodaemus—he and I spent an interesting few minutes together."

Eyes widening, lower jaw dropping down suddenly, the old man looked at Paetus and seemed to be groping for words.

"What is it?" Paetus asked, alarmed.

"I know him!" Lysimmachus replied.

"How is it that you do?"

"He tried some months ago to witness to me about the Nazarene. Just came up to me, and spoke of being born again, as Jesus had done to him years ago."

You told me that I must be born again. Yet now You lie in this tomb that belongs to Joseph and me, as cold and dead as any man who has passed from life. When I die, my body shall be placed opposite Your own, and that is where it all ends, both of us in the same grave. What is the difference between us, then, Jesus called the Christ? My body will decay as will yours and become the food of worms. How can You talk with any honesty of a resurrection when there is nothing of the sort?

That had been Nicodaemus speaking in front of the sealed tomb.

In the time that passed since then, he had gone from wanting to believe, to being disillusioned, to redemption.

"We must get to him, must tell him what we have in mind," Lysimmachus said excitedly. "He may reject us, but then again he may not."

"I shall try," Paetus pledged, his emotions scarcely contained. "With the help of Almighty God, I shall try."

He knew that it would require a great deal of good fortune even to find out where Nicodaemus had a residence, assuming he still remained in the area, and to gain some time with the man. Most difficult of all would be somehow convincing him to help out, possibly along with Joseph of Arimathea.

"How can I leave you alone?" he asked Lysimmachus. "I know that you cannot make any such journey. And yet how will you be able to—?"

"*Survive*, my new friend? I know that that was what you were going to say or what you meant in your heart, even if you had other words instead, words not intended to remind me of this plight in which I have found myself.

"But it is a life I have lived, however feebly, for a great many years now. Yes, I do weary of it often but, at the same time, I am well adapted to it, I must confess, perhaps as well as any man could be, and have managed to ignore the hunger and the cold and the great and terrible loneliness more often than not."

Lysimmachus smiled with a warmth he had not felt in a very long time and added, "If I am to die while you, dear Decimus, are gone, it will not be as a result of your departure that this came about. So, please, harbor no guilt should this happen. Remember this: Because of you, I am no longer to die alone. I shall now have One by my side who will take me into the arms of the Almighty Father."

XXXVII

Paetus spent the next week talking to passersby on his dust-clouded travels in and around Jerusalem.

Many could not be bothered and brushed on by, paying no heed to his entreaties.

Most had never heard of either Nicodaemus or Joseph of Arimathea. The few who had some knowledge of one or the other looked at him, at his tattered clothes, and at his dirt-smudged face and spit in contempt at his feet.

Paetus realized that, in his zeal, he had allowed himself to forget his appearance and had come to look hardly better than the worst of the common beggars he himself had once viewed with contempt. Since he had thought of them in the manner the people he now approached viewed him, how, with any honesty, could he condemn anyone for reactions that so mirrored his own?

I must clean up. I must be a better example to those whom I encounter. It is not only my quest that is at stake but my witness for Jesus the Christ.

He knew that the Nazarene spoke sadly of the tendency to look on the outward appearance and not bother to pay attention to what a man was like inside. Yet until such people could be redeemed, that *was* how they conducted themselves, so he had to be presentable in order to gain their attention.

But where will I go? Paetus thought with some anxiety. *Who will let me bathe myself? And give me fresh clothes?*

To have anybody regard him seriously, he had to be clean before he could expect them to consider anything else.

So Paetus decided to go to the Jordan and bathe in it and ask for guidance from that point on. It was only a short distance from the Sea of Galilee where he had stopped momentarily to beg some scraps of fish from returning fishermen.

After he had been fed through the generosity of one of them, he set off toward the historic river.

The Jordan traveled a total of a one hundred fifty-five miles from Mount Hermon in the north of Israel to the Dead Sea, or Lake Asphaltitus, at the extreme south. The Jordan Valley northward was fertile land, but as the river wound south, the desert took over, except for a few acres on either side of the Jordan itself where near jungle-like growth rose in striking contrast to the parched conditions everywhere else.

Much had happened in and around this river over the centuries. Joshua had led the Israelites across the Jordan into the Promised Land. When Absalom rebelled, King David was able to escape across the Jordan. It was this river that Elijah and Elisha crossed before Elijah was caught up into heaven. And there were the many baptisms conducted in it by John the Baptist.

Finally, as Paetus stood on its shore, he looked up toward the cloudless sky, the sun shimmering through trees and thick, hanging vines that formed a half-arch over the river. He had heard that, when Jesus was baptized in the Jordan, a pure white dove descended from heaven and stood for a moment on the Nazarene's shoulder. At that instant, John the Baptist heard a voice saying, "This is my beloved Son, in whom I am well-pleased."

Paetus went to his knees, bowing his head, as he started to pray, overcome by the significance of the spot.

He could not tell how much time had passed since his arrival. He thought perhaps that he might have fallen half-asleep, so intense, so draining was his prayer, for when a hand was placed on his shoulder he was so startled that he jumped, screaming, to his feet, his hands clenched into fists.

A man just into the middle years of life, his white, cottony hair and beard making him seem older.

"I was coming here, as I frequently do, to sit and meditate," he said. "I am very sorry to have startled you."

Paetus was embarrassed that he had reacted so strongly.

"Why do we not sit down together for a moment?" the man suggested. "This is a blessed place. Or are you here by chance, unaware of what it means?"

"Not by chance. I know much about it. I myself came here to pray and also to clean my body."

"Why would someone of Rome—as I perceive you to be—be at all interested?"

"Why would someone of wealth from this land be interested in the place where the Nazarene was baptized?"

"Because—," the man started to say, then bit his lower lip as he hesitated.

"You do not have to be concerned about me," Paetus assured him. "I am not an agent of the empire, posing this day as a poor man in order to entrap the unsuspecting in seditious conversation."

The man looked intently at him and then spoke, "I do not suppose you are, for I now see that you wear your poverty too convincingly."

"Are you offended by the poor?"

"Do I act as though I am?"

Paetus smiled.

"Forgive me," he asked sincerely. "I am so intent on a singular mission that I have forgotten to be polite."

"You are forgiven, though there is little need to be, and I wish you the best of good fortune in whatever it is that makes you so intent."

"I have been utterly unsuccessful thus far. I need to find someone, someone who might help me."

"I have a few denarii on my person just now. I would be very glad to give these coins to you if that would help."

"Your generosity is appreciated. But my present mission encompasses more than that, I am afraid."

"What is the extent of your need?"

Paetus found it odd that this stranger was so attentive, which both pleased him and made him feel apprehensive.

"There is an abandoned village," he started to say.

"Near the Sea of Galilee?"

"Yes, do you know it?"

"I do. I periodically consider the waste that it represents, the abandonment of so much that once kept the inhabitants together."

"I have thought of rebuilding it," Paetus went on, "hut by hut, stone by stone, with men, women, and children once again living within it."

The expression on the other man's face was hardly unexpected.

"Yes, I know how strange that sounds," Paetus admitted, "coming as it does from someone with nothing but these tattered clothes. How could I possibly hope to put such a village back together when I seem almost a symptom of its decline?"

The stranger's answer was surprising.

"I have found that dreamers are stupid only when they dream with utter and total selfishness. The dreams of such men are offensive, benefiting them, yes, but few others, dreams aimed at their power, their prestige, their money—and always the greater accumulation of these, day after day."

He smiled as he added, "What you hope to do sounds wholly impractical, I might admit, yet it is hardly what I would call stupid. But this I ask if I may: What is the reason behind your desire to accomplish this task?"

"For the village to serve as a kindly place for the poor to gather, to live with respect, to work productively, to eat nourishingly, to be sheltered from the terrible derision and insensitivity of others."

"And the one whom you seek? What part would he play?"

Paetus felt uncomfortable, for now he would have to admit that he sought Nicodaemus to ask for money, to ask for supplies, to seek whatever support he could give.

"I feel that he might be persuaded to help," he said simply, "in some manner that he might decide. At least that is my prayer."

The stranger stood abruptly.

"And by what name is this individual known?" he asked.

"Nicodaemus is that name," Paetus answered.

The stranger looked at him with an expression of great surprise.

"I can take you to this one now," he said, his voice unsteady. "I can take you right to his doorstep."

"How is that so?" Paetus asked a bit skeptically, though his heart had begun to beat faster, the palms of his hands sweaty.

"I know this Nicodaemus. The two of us were those who carried the body of the Nazarene from Golgotha, after my friend had appealed to Pilatus for it. It was we who placed it in a tomb directly in the side of that mount, where it rested until He arose from the dead."

He smiled again, even more warmly this time.

"My name is Joseph," he said. "I come from Arimathea. Let me pledge to help you as I suspect Nicodaemus also will."

XXXVIII

The Nicodaemus who stood before them seemed a bit weaker perhaps, more stooped, but otherwise not so terribly different from that night when, for the first time, Decimus Paetus encountered him at the tomb where the cold and lifeless body of Jesus the Christ rested, covered only by a gauze-like shroud.

"Welcome to my home," he said with a robustness that belied his aged appearance as he greeted Paetus and Joseph at the ornate, hand-carved wood front door of his residence just outside Jerusalem, near the Mount of Olives. "I received the good word that you sent by messenger and am so glad that you came upon my brother here."

He was looking at Joseph when he said that.

"You call me brother," Paetus noted a bit querulously. "But this is only the second time we have met."

"What you say is true, of course, but even if that earlier encounter between us had proven to be the only one, I would still greet you as a brother once we stood side-by-side before our heavenly Father."

"But you do it now."

"Because—"

Nicodaemus cut himself off, and turned from them.

"What is it, friend?" Joseph asked, alarmed.

"I was filled with so much doubt as I stood there before that large round stone sealing off the entrance," Nicodaemus muttered. "I had helped to bury my Savior and in doing so, I could no longer bring myself to think of Him as anyone more than an ordinary man whose ordinary body of flesh and bone and blood rested in that humble tomb, destined to stay within those bleak walls until it turned to dust."

He coughed self-consciously, trying to bring his turmoil under control.

"When I later came to believe the startling truth, that Jesus was truly the Messiah, and I accepted Him also as my Savior, I remembered how many people had seen me in the same state as you did, Decimus Paetus—doubtful as I confess I was, forlorn, feeling betrayed by a man who obviously was no longer able to fulfill any of the promises that He had made to so many who had come to believe in Him, to trust Him. He

214

seemed then nothing more than a papyrus tiger, all sound and fury but no real substance.

"So there I was, someone blessed indescribably by being able to spend some precious private moments with this Jesus, someone who had been exposed to His teachings again and again, at my home and on the road, yet I could see in my mind and sense in my hardening heart only that cold, bruised, punctured body, ignoring what He had clearly foretold, the beautiful prophecy that He was destined not to remain long on that hard slab but would rise up on the third day, and, later, after tarrying a bit with his apostles and others, would ascend back into heaven to be with His Father."

Nicodaemus's back straightened and he brushed the sleeve of his long white toga-like garment over his eyes.

"When I got the message that you yourself were redeemed and my abysmal witness had not slammed the gates of heaven in your face, I rejoiced as never before. I acted like a child, full of life and hope and innocent joy."

He reached out to Paetus and Joseph, who were still standing outside, and rested a hand on each of them.

"You are my brothers, you are my brothers in the blood of Jesus the Christ, and nothing will ever come between us. Though distance or death separate us for a time, we will eventually stand united before our Holy God. May He one day tell us as we look up at Him, 'Well-done, my good and faithful servants.'

"When this happens, as undeserving as we are, we leave our tears behind, my brothers, we leave our pain, we leave death and the grave behind forever. May that hope be a light in any darkness that ever threatens to overtake us."

★ ★ ★

Nicodaemus did not have to be convinced about the idea of rebuilding that village as a place for the poor.

"It is wonderful, what you have thought of," he told Paetus as the three of them sat together on the veranda of his residence, the cool evening breezes touching their faces. "With Joseph and myself cooperating, I think it is a dream that can come true."

His eyes flashed with excitement.

"In the morning perhaps we could leave here and journey to the site," he suggested. "I am anxious to see it for myself. Certainly there are other places like it throughout our land. If this rebuilding succeeds, we might be able to try again and again with the others, turning each over to the needy."

Paetus nodded enthusiastically.

"But first you must have some better clothes to wear," Nicodaemus said, looking at him a bit disdainfully. "I shall provide a reasonable wardrobe for everyone who comes to reside in the village. Not far from where you say it is located, I know of a quarry. The Roman officer in charge has shown himself to be a rather kindly sort. I believe he would be willing to let us take some of the stone and slate, which can be used for buildings more permanent than simple mud huts! It is a question as to whether he will also lend out carts and oxen to transport the materials but he just may."

Joseph spoke up next.

"Either the Jordan or the Sea of Galilee or both could provide the water that will be needed," he said. "We have seen what the Romans do with their aqueducts. Once again we might solicit help from any who are sympathetic to what we have in mind."

"Is it foolish to think that Pontius Pilatus himself could become interested?" asked Nicodaemus. "Now might be the time for him to show that he has a benevolent side."

"You could be correct," Joseph replied. "I do not assume, as so many do, that he is totally a cold and inhumane man."

Paetus echoed this possibility.

"He seems one torn between serving his wanton emperor and his sense of decency," he offered.

"Then why did he commit his wife to exile and isolation?" Joseph speculated. "Despite my stated hopes for Pilatus, it remains true that he *is* given to such behavior as he has shown with Jesus and with Procula."

Paetus had thought about this more than once over the past four years. Having seen both husband and wife, having glimpsed a hint of the relationship between them, he could not doubt that Pilatus loved the woman deeply.

"Political expediency," he suggested to the others. "I think it was that he saw Procula as a threat."

"That mad soul a threat?" Nicodaemus blurted out, astonished at the possibility, though not convinced that Paetus knew what he was talking about.

"She *could* have slipped into madness," Paetus responded, "but she did not."

"What stopped her?" Nicodaemus asked.

"She became as we are."

"She accepted Jesus?" Joseph said. "Is that what you mean?"

"It is. And she did so with such fervor that I think Pilatus thought she would convince too many others to follow her."

"So he considered this woman a threat not to himself, in some petty way, but to the empire?" Joseph probed.

"That is how I see it."

"May the Lord Himself comfort her," Nicodaemus prayed aloud.

Paetus surprised them both when he added, "And we should pray for the proconsul himself, that his conscience not become entirely hardened. If it does, while he remains here in Judah, the tough times thus far will seem almost pleasant in comparison."

XXXIX

During the previous day, Joseph had journeyed to the Jordan alone, riding on a sleek, brown Arabian steed that he had purchased years before. Now, one day later, he was returning, but not alone, but instead was coveyed there in an an elaborate chariot-like carriage, with a round front inlaid with various kinds of wood set in an ancient pattern. He rested on a wide, goose-down packed seat cushion with Nicodaemus and Paetus, a heavy awning of aged leather above them, supported by a strong, light-tan colored bamboo pole at each corner. Four horses pulled the carriage along the road that led past the Sea of Galilee, to their destination, which was just east of the Jordan—a conveyance used by Nicodaemus primarily during the hotter times of the year, one that he did not consider an unreasonable luxury under such conditions.

"We spend so much time together," Joseph said, "I suppose people are wondering about what sort of relationship two old men are having."

"It was the same for King David and Jonathan," Nicodaemus added. "Their enemies tried anything they could to destroy that friendship."

Paetus spoke sadly, "Unfortunately, that sort of thing is spreading among many social and governmental circles in Rome at this very moment. The more I hear of it being defended as acceptable, yea, even as normal and desirable, the more recognition is given to these corrupt and perverse people among the power centers, the more I fear for the health of the entire empire. When Rome falls, and fall it must, a decade from now, a century, a millennium perhaps, the resulting stench will spill over on everyone."

"What you say is true, Paetus," pronounced Joseph solemnly. "Any society that tolerates immorality of that sort or any other is destined to be drowned by it. Look at the number of loathsome practices that Caligula encourages, behavior that would not be tolerated if Julius Caesar were alive today."

"This creature tries to be so charming," Nicodaemus added, "but he is like a very rotten melon just before it collapses in on itself."

Paetus got to his feet and walked the two steps to the front of the carriage, squinting his eyes as he stood beside the tall black man who had the reins.

"We are coming to the spot," he called back to the others. "We shall be there in just a few minutes."

Ahead was a series of mountain peaks. The abandoned village was partially surrounded by them. There was now only a small stretch of Galilean desert left before they would be pulling up to the gap that served as an entrance.

"*Look!*" Paetus called back to the others.

Nicodaemus and Joseph both stood, trying to see what it was that he was pointing out to them.

A small caravan.

To their left, heading apparently toward the same destination. It was made up entirely of people, no animals except a pair of straggly dogs.

And waiting for them was someone whose features they could not as yet make out but which became cleared in a moment or two.

An ancient, bearded man, very thin, bent-over.

Lysimmachus!

"I know him," Paetus said.

"Lysimmachus?" asked Joseph. "Is this the Lysimmachus of whom you spoke earlier, Decimus?"

"It is he, a dear man, as I said. But, I wonder, how did those people beyond us find out so quickly?"

"I am very glad we decided to bring along some food for him, plus some little amount for ourselves."

"I would be pleased to give up my share," Nicodaemus offered.

"And I too," Joseph of Arimathea agreed.

"Let me be the one to feed the old man from what has been allotted of the food for me," asked Paetus.

His two new friends agreed, smiling, with Nicodaemus adding, "When you are done, you can help us with the others. I shall tell Onesimus to return to my house and gather together more food from the pantry, as much of it as he can possibly manage."

Onesimus was the black man who held the reins of the chariot. He was smiling broadly as Nicodaemus turned to him.

"My dear Onesimus, you seem quite happy," Nicodaemus observed.

"I am," came the reply.

"And why is that so?"

"Before I started to serve you, I saw nothing but cruelty in this life, back in Africa and, now, here in the midst of civilization. Men filled with a brutal and nasty spirit spitting on other men, beating them, kicking them, denying them food as punishment."

"But that is not my way, Onesimus, especially so now that I have become a Jew who is also a Christian."

"I see that. I see that in your desire to help these poor ones. I remember hearing the Nazarene speaking to a crowd about giving of their bread to beggars, helping the needy with actions and not only words."

Paetus whispered to Joseph, "He speaks so well, I am amazed!"

Onesimus overheard this and ventured a response.

"I speak well, as you say, because of him," he said, pointing to Nicodaemus, whose face turned red. "I was dirty, and he gave me water to bathe myself. I was hungry, and he gave me food to fill my stomach. I was cold, and he clothed me not out of old, spent, tattered rags but from a closet of his finest garments.

"But there was something else that he gave me. He gave me knowledge. I have spent many long hours with his scrolls and the various parchments he has collected. I have read every one of them and devoted much time to thinking about what I have learned. Whenever I needed help to understand, he was there, teaching me with patience that seemed unending, no matter how far into the night this often required of him."

He stopped for a moment, tears streaking his pitch-black cheeks.

"For all that he has given to me, I love this old man," Onesimus added, "and I shall serve him all the days of my life."

"Sometime, when you are ready, I would like to have you accept the greatest gift of all," Nicodaemus told him. "You know, from our times together over the past months, to what it is that I refer."

"Could that be now," Onesimus asked readily, "if I perceive what it is that you want to bestow?"

"I think you do, my dear man, and I shall be glad to oblige, but you must understand that I am not the one who can give it to you. Only Almighty God Himself can provide what you desire through His precious Son."

"There . . ." Onesimus spoke, barely able to see through the flowing tears. "Ahead, in that village which is our destination . . . that is where I want to proclaim this new life, this new Savior . . . to you, to the poor He loved . . . to anyone who will listen from now on."

Nicodaemus nodded, tears of his own commencing.

"It *shall* be," he assured the tall, strong black man whose face seemed as finely chiseled as that of any Greek statue, "it shall be, Onesimus, while we and those needy ones stand by . . . and the angels themselves rejoice unseen."

XL

nd the angels themselves rejoice unseen . . .

$\mathbf{A}$ That provided a striking explanation for the rapid dissemination of the news about the village.

One ancient woman, her spine and other bones twisted by a then-unknown disease, so badly that she was not able to stand straight up and see in a straight line ahead but had to walk with as much care as she could manage by looking down at the ground directly in front of her.

"What is your name?" he asked.

"Lydia," she told him.

"How old are you?"

"More than eighty years."

He heard her whimper a bit as a spasm of pain traveled freely through her ravaged and defenseless body.

"How much of your life has been like this?" he spoke, trying to keep pity from clouding his voice, for he knew how offensive that would be.

"Since I was very young," she told him sadly. "I have spent nearly seven decades in the manner you see now."

She asked him if they could stop for a short while.

"I tire," she said.

They stood quite still for a few moments. Paetus's sympathy for Lydia was growing by the second.

I have been strong and healthy all my life, he thought. *In training as a legionnaire, I surpassed so many others. I even received a commendation from the emperor himself, who said that I was an example to the other men!*

Paetus remembered those mornings when he glimpsed reflections of himself in a stream or a lake or the grand old Mediterranean—the strong face, the muscular torso looking as though it had been chiseled by a master sculptor of the time, the blue eyes, the even white teeth.

I felt that I harbored no need of Thee then, Lord. I had my own strength, I was serving Imperial Rome, before which the whole world cowered. I worshiped many other gods from my days as a child, and my family before that, generation after generation. Though I knew about Thee through some idle stories around campfires at night, shared by profane men in the midst of their vulgar derision, I cared not. I—

The old woman stirred.

"You are crying, dear man," she observed perceptively. "Be you in some pain also?"

"Not of the body," he confessed. "It is something far deeper, I am afraid."

"Are there memories at fault?" she offered.

He gasped at that.

"How could you know?" Paetus asked.

"The way you sounded just then," she said, smiling though he could not see her doing this. "For I too have felt as you must now. I sometimes am burdened by my memories. I yet recall those wondrous days when I was unaffected by this foul affliction, when I could stand tall, and look at the sky at night, and reach up toward the glorious stars, pretending that I could almost touch them.

"I kept doing that periodically, Decimus. Each new time I could stretch less and less toward the heavens, until finally it is as you see me now. And few over the years have taken the time to hold me so that I could look again."

"How have you managed to survive at all?" Paetus asked. "You have not been run over by chariots or been trampled by crowds or fallen off cliffs. Tell me, Lydia, tell me how this could have been."

"I pay attention to shadows," she spoke. "Shadows tell me a great deal. If there is a shadow across my path, I know I must be careful. And I can tell by its direction and its length where the object is, and how big. My life without shadows would be so much harder to endure. I would have one less compass by which to guide myself."

She was holding onto Decimus Paetus's arm as she walked, her left hand clamped on a crude cane fashioned out of gopher wood.

"I am going through a pass, am I not?" she asked.

"Yes," Paetus told her.

"There are people in front of us. I hear their voices but I see by their shadows that there are a great deal of them even now."

"But how did they find out?" he asked, deeply puzzled. "I cannot perceive how this could have happened in so short a period of time."

"I cannot speak for the others, only for myself. With me, it was an angel who came to me when I was asleep last night."

"Where was that?"

"Not far from Jerusalem, in a ditch beside the road."

Inexpressible sorrow enveloped Paetus then as he thought of this woman, like a rejected mongrel, having to find whatever spot she could, no matter how wretched, and lie down in it, closing her eyes and trying to sleep.

"Someone galloping by on a stallion stopped for a moment and dismounted," she said, "He approached me, jabbed my body with a finger once, twice, a third time. When I awakened, groaning, he cursed at me, and I could feel his spit on my cheek."

"He spat at you?" Paetus repeated, appalled.

"He did. By the stillness of my form, he must have thought me dead, and was intending to take from me whatever seemed of value. When he found me living and so poor, he regretted wasting his time and effort and started to walk away."

"*Started* to walk away? How do you mean that?"

"I heard him gasp, and suddenly there was a bright light all around. I heard him scream in fear, get back on his horse, and leave in great haste."

She touched his hand with her own.

"That is what the angel did, Decimus. He touched me so gently that I started to weep with joy, that feeling of such great tenderness that I longed for more of it, longed to see his face, longed to look into the angel's face."

"But it could have been a very gentle *man*," Paetus suggested, wanting to believe Lydia but also knowing that she could have imagined or misinterpreted whatever had happened, as was typical of those her age, particularly the old poor who never had the medical care or the comfortable surroundings that would have eased their lives.

"But others here have experienced the same thing," she retorted, though not angrily. "How could that be unless Jehovah Himself be involved?"

Paetus had no answer but simply another question.

"What did this angel *do?*" he asked.

"He told me that something great and wonderful was going to happen where we are now, that the village and the whole area around it would come to life again."

Paetus was about to respond with his amazement over this happening when Joseph of Arimathea came running up to him.

"I have met someone just ahead who wants to become a follower of the Nazarene!" he exclaimed.

"That is wonderful to hear," Paetus replied.

But Joseph bowed his head.

"What is it?" Paetus asked, ignoring for a moment Lydia, who had started pulling at his clothing.

"And there are others, Decimus. They seem almost eager to do this, Decimus. But it is more than that."

"What could be more?"

"They claim an angel told them to come."

Now Paetus paid some attention to the old woman!

"I know," he said before she could speak, thinking he knew her reason. "You are trying to tell me that I should have listened to you after all."

"I want to become one too," she said.

"A disciple of Jesus the Christ?"

"Yes, Decimus. I want Him at the center of my life while I yet have life left to turn over to Him."

Paetus tried to imagine what it was like to live as many decades as Lydia had, but his mind failed at the task.

"Do you know what this means?" he asked her tenderly, not wanting her apparent eagerness to give her a false picture of what was involved in accepting the Nazarene into her life as her Savior, her Lord.

"That I believe He is God Incarnate, that He died so that my sins could be forgiven, and that He will forgive my sins. When I die, I shall die and be with Him and the Father in Heaven for all eternity."

She paused, then added, "Is that right, Decimus? Am I speaking correctly? It is what the angel told me and I have accepted all of it eagerly."

He lifted her frail body up in his arms so that she could see his face.

"You are already one of His sheep, dear Lydia," he said, tears flowing. "And He shall never leave you nor forsake you."

"In heaven will I have this same miserable body?"

"*No!*" he assured her. "You will stand straight. There will be no more pain at all, no more sorrow. Ah, Lydia, you will run like a gazelle or an ibex perhaps, light of foot as a wild roe. You will jump, and bend, and lift yourself, and do everything that your present body will not allow."

"And shall I be young again?" Lydia exclaimed. "I pray that you can say yes, for I have been old far too long."

"You shall be young and healthy—and eternal."

Joseph had been listening to all of this. He was becoming impatient.

"We must tend to the others now," he said anxiously. "We must hurry before the moment passes and we have lost them perhaps forever."

Paetus paused, the colossal significance of what he was embarking upon hitting him like the back-slinging branch of a wet palm tree branch, for what he would soon find himself surrounded by was epitomized in the countenance of poor old Lydia.

Until he had met her just moments before, he had been caught up in the *idea*, notable that it was, undaunted by what would be required of him once that idea was brought to the edge of reality.

224

But this ancient one, this Lydia was now that very reality, the dozen odds and ends of human beings waiting for him were other manifestations of it.

All of them were rapidly becoming his responsibility.

His insides quivered at that.

My responsibility! he thought, with some panic. *It is one matter to witness to someone about Jesus the Christ and become His instrument in leading them to salvation. In nearly every instance, that is the end of it. I turn a convert over to Him, and then I leave, for thereafter they are His responsibility.*

Paetus gulped twice, the encroaching sounds of awaiting men and women reaching his reluctant ears.

But it is going to be so very different. I won't be leaving anytime soon. And my burden will be more than just their redemption, which deals with their soul, but now it is to be also their immediate survival, bound up in their flesh-and-blood presence, bodies needing to be fed, nourished, bathed and—

He considered with a bit of wistfulness memories of young Fabius Scipio, of their travels together, and how much help his friend would have been.

Lord, I truly do not have him with me anymore. But there are others— Onesimus, Nicodaemus, Joseph—men who will be surely of even greater help for the greater challenge that is before me.

He glanced at Lydia, waiting patiently for him, either to lead her along or pick her up and take her with him.

Everything else he had done bore little comparison to seeing her misery and wanting her to have a place of rest until she died.

You are already one of His sheep . . . And He shall never leave you nor forsake you . . .

Sheep.

He never had *been* a shepherd. He left behind souls headed for heaven but he did not stay to tend his flock.

And yet now—

His own soul cried out, silent to the ears of those around him, audible to the only one who mattered, cried out in desperation, not certain of his worthiness, doubtful indeed of his ability, and, thus, such a cry was born of fear and doubt.

That was when Paetus felt the strangest peace, bestowed upon him in an instant. One minute he wore his insecurity wrapped around him like a shroud, the next he flung it away like a thing despised. It seemed as though he had been asleep, his body resting, and now he was in the process of awakening, the new day bright and promising, his energy reborn a thousandfold, his mind as clear as he could ever want it.

Paetus decided to carry fragile little Lydia, whose body was scarcely a burden, the rest of the way into the center of the once-village.

A dozen other unfortunate wanderers from that region near Jerusalem were now gathered next to Nicodaemus and Lysimmachus.

"They want to become as us," Lysimmachus told him with such great excitement that he seemed shorn of some of those many years of his that had become an abiding burden. "Is that not wonderful?"

Wonderful was not the strongest word that the old man could have used. Surely there were others to convey more fully the strange majesty of that sight, men and women who had been shunted aside by Israel as well as Rome.

And they apparently claim that an angel led the way! Paetus exclaimed to himself, bewildered and yet inspired by the very prospect.

Three of the men were comparatively youthful, older than his former comrade Fabius Scipio but younger than veteran legionnaire Marcus Vibenna, whose own age would pale next to that of Lysimmachus and Lydia. One was blind; another was missing a leg; and the third seemed to be not right in the head, rambling intermittently, his speech incoherent, his eyes rheumy.

Two of the women were in advanced stages of leprosy and stood of their own accord far off to one side, their pathetic bodies covered with large, raw, red sores that had become puffed up with spreading infection, boil-like, ready to burst.

The rest were "simply" poor, the skin on their faces stretched tight against their skulls and rib cages, their bodies showing the effects of malnutrition and dehydration, each movement of a hand or leg like an awkward and distorted ballet.

All had come based upon the promises of a being they thought to be an angel sent by Almighty God!

Paetus rested Lydia gently on the ground and stood before them.

"This village is going to be rebuilt," he spoke slowly, not certain of what words would come from his mouth. "It is to become a safe haven for you. There will be food provided for you, but you also shall be shown how to raise your own."

He had discussed such matters with Nicodaemus and Joseph but, still, he worried about promising too much. And yet he knew that whatever worries he indulged in were not of how he should exercise his mind or his emotions. He had heard Jesus the Christ admonishing His followers not to worry over the concerns of tomorrow, "for sufficient unto the day are the evils thereof."

For the village to serve as a kindly place for the poor to gather, to live with respect, to work productively, to eat nourishing food, to be sheltered from the terrible derision and insensitivity of others.

Those original words came back to him, as though whispered into his ear, the sensation so vivid that he jerked his head to the side to see if someone had actually done just that.

They are before you, Decimus Paetus. Reach them now or reach them not at all.

Whisperer or not, he saw the people awaiting some further word from him. He had no idea how many had accepted Jesus the Christ as their Savior, their Lord. There had been others during his travels but one at a time, caught here or there for a moment, and then gone.

Never such a group in such a way, gathered with hope that seemed to leap from their decrepit frames and stand before him, begging with their infirmities, *You have us here now. Help us, please. If an angel has sent us, how can you dither?*

. . . to be sheltered from the terrible derision and insensitivity of others.

That was as much a part of their lives as the pain they faced. These people deserved none of it.

And I shall listen to Your leading! Paetus declared within himself. *This village will stand once again, this time in tribute to Your mercy.*

XLI

None of the original structures could be saved. All had to be demolished, and new ones substituted. Each would contain a single room, the floor of which was smoothed out in two levels, one for the human occupants and the other for any livestock that had been brought in by Nicodaemus and Joseph, who tried with some success to provide at least one goat per home and several oxen for the village as a whole.

Very roughly assembled steps led from one level to the other. On each side was a fodder trough or a crib, depending upon the circumstances. At the beginning, all such sections were used only as troughs, due to the inability of anyone from the initial group to be fathers or mothers, either due to their age or the havoc to their bodies caused by leprosy or whatever their ailment happened to be.

Set in the middle of the higher of the two levels was a small round loam ring several inches high, inside which a fire would glow, a place for cooking, and one other use, at night and during the Middle Eastern winters: heat. Anyone living in that small structure would place the soles of his feet as close to the loam as possible, with as many as half a dozen people sleeping in this manner.

The outer wall of each house was made of dried mud and stone, covered by a layer of plaster composed of mud and chalk; in the ancient Scriptures from the days of Ezekiel, this was referred to as building up "a wall and daubing it with untempered mortar."

While the building process continued, a number of tents were erected. The material used was canvas, stretched over three sets of poles, the longer ones in a line down the center, with the shorter ones radiating out from these on each side, the poles tied to one another by strong but narrow ropes.

Finally the tent was fastened by cords, as referred to in Jeremiah 10:20, to stakes made of especially hard wood, two feet long, which were driven into the ground where it was other than sandy or hard flat rocks. The canvas was then laden, for insulation purposes, with cloth woven of black goat's hair.

But before *any* serious building could be accomplished, a labor pool had to be gathered together. Only three or four of the assembled poor were able to engage in activity that required heavy work, such as lifting stones or hammering in the stakes.

Getting the strong backs necessary proved to be one of the more difficult tasks. Many families simply were not available to spend time away from their farms, though some sent bread, tools, even some livestock as their gesture of support.

The other roaming poor of that mostly barren land who could benefit from the wages being paid were seldom in any better shape than those for whom the village was being reconstructed in the first place.

And then a man named Nahum stopped by with his sons and offered to help.

"How did you find out?" Paetus asked.

"Oh, the news of what you are attempting is spreading throughout the region," Nahum replied. "Do not lose heart. The Lord will provide for you. My sons and I will work without remuneration for as long as we can. Use the money to get more workers, supplies, whatever may be necessary."

"The Lord? Are you a Christian?"

Nahum smiled broadly.

"Yes, I am, and your dear friend is responsible."

"Fabius?" exclaimed Paetus. "Are you saying that you and my brother in the Spirit have spent time together?"

"We have, we have. He is a wonderful young man. When I saw him off, as he continued on his journey, he was quite healthy, quite happy."

"Bless you, friend, bless you throughout eternity."

Nahum reached out and hugged him exuberantly.

"That is the gift young Scipio brought to me and the members of my family," Nahum replied, his voice nearly at a shout. "Giving you in return the strong backs and hands of my sons and myself is little enough."

"Do you know where he took off to?" Paetus asked.

"North, toward one of the seaports there. He seemed headed back to his family. I would have tried to persuade him not to go but I knew the Lord's hand was upon him, and I dare not interfere, even for a moment."

★ ★ ★

It took weeks for the village to be built up again and longer than that for the new community of men and women to function harmoniously. Any hope that everybody would get along with one another from the start and that there would be no mishaps vanished quickly enough.

But one by one the homes were finished, and one by one the people learned to live together. What helped them was a singular miracle one afternoon in the River Jordan.

Both Lydia and Lysimmachus were tired.

Though they could not do the truly strenuous tasks, they helped out in whatever other ways they could, filling earthen bowls with food, pouring beverages for the workers brought in by Nicodaemus and Joseph, trying to keep the other old and poor ones occupied by exchanging stories with them, and daydreaming out loud about what it would be like to live in one place without drifting aimlessly from town to village to farmhouse to wherever else they happened to go, since there had not been a single spot during a bleak and useless chain of years that they could sit down in and call home.

Once, in the midst of a break when all the strong young men had stopped working and were resting for a bit, Lydia and Lysimmachus broke away from the group and went off by themselves, hobbling on over to the Jordan, which was only a few hundred yards from the entrance to the village, stepping through the dense growth at the edge, and finally, just standing there, listening to the sound of the water rushing over rocks, as it had done for centuries, the river an ancient one at the center of Jewish history, smelling the clear air laced with a variety of scents coming from the vegetation directly in back of them, Lydia leaning against Lysimmachus or, perhaps, more accurately, the two of them leaning against one another, their old, battered, tired bodies gaining some modicum of strength together.

They talked about how some of the new villagers seemed to be resisting any acceptance of Jesus the Christ into their lives, despite the appearance of what seemed to have been an angel to them.

"They are so stubborn," Lydia sighed, wondering how people as close to death as most of them were could be so careless about their destiny after death.

"They are deluded, my dear Lydia," Lysimmachus added sadly, "and their stubbornness grows out of that. Unfortunately, Decimus, you, me, Nicodaemus, Joseph, none of us can press too hard with any of them, or they will surely resort to claiming that those two good men have tried to bribe them by offering them a home and food in return for their faith. Years of rejection have made them cynical."

"But you and I have not escaped the very same rejection," she correctly pointed out. "Yet we both have come in faith, believing. Why is that so? Why is it that some are as we, and others as they?"

Lysimmachus shook his head, unable to supply the answer.

"Rather than commiserating over such matters, we should be rejoicing over the fact that you and I are no longer lost, as we once had been, now that we share the very same redemption. I, for one, look forward to seeing you in heaven, Lydia, in a brand new body. I should like that very much."

230

Lydia blushed as she replied. "I cannot say what that body will be like, nor can you, of course, but I *do* favor disposing of this wretched one, and taking on *any* other that Almighty God has in mind."

"I wish I could see a dove this day," he told her as he glanced at their surroundings. "How wonderful that would be, its feathers glistening under the rays of the sun, its peaceful countenance warming my soul. It must have been wonderful being here when Jesus was, watching the dove descend, seeing the Son of Man arise from the clear, pure waters."

Lydia surprised him with her answer.

"I cannot say that it would have been so wonderful," she spoke.

"What do you mean by that?" he inquired.

"We look back, from what we know now, and, yes, we see it that way. The Nazarene had not begun His ministry as yet, we must remember. Other people who were also being baptized that afternoon or who were gathered in idle curiosity probably puzzled about the dove and the voice that spoke, but no one could be sure who it was or whence it came, and most, I think, simply decided that they had somehow imagined it."

The old man had laid Lydia on her side so that she could see the Jordan in front of her, and beyond its banks, the lush growth on the other side. He was sitting next to that bent old body, holding her right hand in his own.

"So we may have the more fortunate moment in time just now, you and me," Lysimmachus suggested, "as we think back and appreciate what was happening perhaps in this very spot less than a decade ago. We did not see that most precious encounter between the Baptist and the Nazarene, but we know what it is that we have missed. Others came and saw, and it might be that few or none of them ever realized what it was that they were privileged to witness. How sad, Lydia, how very sad to have witnessed the Father's recognition of His only Son, and not know how holy that event was!"

She tightened her hand on his, and said, "I feel His Presence, my friend, I feel it so strongly. Tell me that I imagine this, and I shall believe you. I do not want to deceive myself. I am too old to live captive to any delusions. With so little time left, I want my mind as clear as it can be before senility creeps in and robs me of my sense."

Lysimmachus did not immediately answer her but threw his head back and closed his eyes as though listening for a moment.

"I hear the sounds of nature," he said. "There are many in this region who worship the land and the moon and the sun. I can see why they do this, for whatever else changes, these are always the same. And yet they are blinded by the beauty of a sunrise or a sunset, bowing down before it in adoration."

"They ignore the Creator," Lydia spoke. "They take creation and put it on a pedestal, and make it a god."

"It would be easy to blame the Roman influence, at least in part, but such worship goes back thousands of years in Israel."

Abruptly she asked, "Dear man, would you kindly help me to stand? I should like to bathe in the waters of this Jordan. I want to feel the waters that caressed our Lord's body cover this wrenched flesh of mine."

Lysimmachus took hold of Lydia's arm and lifted her with great gentleness to a standing position.

"I go so slowly," she sighed.

"Not much more so than I," he reminded her.

They walked forward, these aged two, step-by-step, approaching the cool, clear waters an inch at a time.

"I am frightened," she told him. "I do not know why but I am very frightened."

"Perhaps this is where Jesus was baptized. Perhaps you sense this. Other than that, I cannot say, Lydia. Would you rather not go after all?"

"No, no, it is something I must do, Lysimmachus."

Her toe touched the water's edge.

"Oh!" she said, closing her eyes.

"Are you suffering?" Lysimmachus asked in concern.

"I do not suffer," she said. "I was reacting to this water in that way because it is so fine against my skin. I can almost feel it against my poor bones as well."

They walked a bit further into the Jordan.

"Stop here, please," Lydia requested.

"Our clothes are wet," he remarked uncomfortably.

"They will dry. Enjoy this moment with me."

His foot kicked against a stone.

As Lysimmachus was forced to pull back in sudden pain, he staggered and fell, losing his gentle grip on Lydia who slipped away from him, her body hitting the surface, splashing it up around her.

Gone.

For a moment she had disappeared beneath the water, though he could see strands of her brittle gray hair floating on the surface.

Panic instantly took hold of Lysimmachus, and he struggled painfully to his feet, cursing the slowness with which he was forced to move.

Lord, please, he prayed, *please help me to reach her in time.*

He could see Lydia's form through the clear water. She seemed so still, no appearance of having struggled, eyes closed as though taking a little nap from which she would awaken, smiling, and looking quite rested.

"Oh, my dear, my dear!" Lysimmachus sobbed as he approached that shriveled old body. "I wanted to know you for just a while longer."

He fell to his knees in the Jordan, the water above his waist.

"Jesus, Jesus, my Savior, my Lord!" he cried out. "I have come to like this woman very much. It might be that I could love her in time. There has been so much loneliness for so long now. For her, for me. Father, I beg you—"

There was the faintest of ripples, almost indiscernible from the normal flow of that river.

And then Lydia's head broke through, beads of water glistening on her forehead and cheeks and chin.

A momentary look of confusion became one of joy, and she was smiling as she stood up straight and turned in his direction.

XLII

No one noticed Lydia at first, walking without help from Lysimmachus, her head held high, her steps as firm as those of a much younger woman.

And when she called out, a strong, firm voice commanded their attention, but none recognized it.

Every head turned in that direction.

An astonished murmur arose from the group of hired workers —strong men, hardened men, not given to much display of their emotions as they tried to survive the brutally hard times of a hard land.

They all dropped whatever they had been holding—bunches of stones, the mud and chalk mixture used as plaster, and the basic tools needed for building; other men, who had been assigned the task of carefully smoothing down the plaster that had been applied with tools of lava rock, stopped their work and gawked unashamedly, none able to speak, more than a few with tears rolling down their cheeks.

Nahum stepped forward.

"God has spoken to us this day!" he declared, his voice echoing off the sides of the mountain sheltering the village. "The Almighty has blessed what we are doing by showing us that He is yet capable of bestowing miracles."

Everyone approached Lydia with awe, except the lepers who maintained their customary distance. They were the least productive members of that group but no one questioned this, both out of pity for them and a pervasive fear of being infected. Any benefits of living in the community being established would be enjoyed by the lepers as much as possible, without rancor from the others. Only later would it become apparent exactly what they could in fact add to everybody else's life.

"Where did it happen?" asked one of the poor women whose limbs had become severely twisted through an especially destructive form of arthritis, though not recognized as such in those days.

Lydia described the spot.

"We must all go there," the woman remarked with much excitement. "We must bathe in the waters of the Jordan, and we too shall be healed."

Lydia, enjoying the newfound ability to do so, stretched her muscles, and stood straight, speaking with firmness, "I think that that may not be so."

A cry of despair arose from the crowd.

"But you were touched," several spoke out, "your affliction removed. Are we any less worthy of His healing touch?"

Feeling helpless, Lydia glanced at Lysimmachus, remembering that, as the two of them had walked back from the river, they began to talk about what might be the reactions among the other men and women at the village site.

Lysimmachus guessed correctly when he suggested that that presented the only problem they would face but a problem that, in itself, could become the destructive source of turmoil within the community.

"In the midst of the joy you feel, and that which I feel now *for* you," he said, "you will have to realize that the others will look at you as you are and want the same powerful healing that you received."

"What is wrong with that?" she asked, not certain of where he was heading with this statement.

"Those times that I was part of the masses swirling around Him, the Nazarene did not necessarily heal *everyone*."

His expression was a kindly one.

"Do not forget that singular fact, dear Lydia. He healed blind men, lepers, maniacs; he raised Lazarus. He healed many. But he usually healed one individual at a time, and not every day and not in every place. He walked away from countless others, leaving them as they had been from birth.

"I think the Nazarene wanted no pageantry of any kind in such simple but profoundly beautiful moments between Himself and whomever He *did* heal or bring back to life. He knew that these could seldom be private, of course—the swelling crowds precluded that—but it *could* be achieved with some dignity, this temporary transfer of a bit of divine power in its passage through mortal flesh.

"Anything else, like one of those gaudy productions by a troupe of actors, would smack of the tawdry, indulged in almost for the show of it, done for the praise of men, not the glory of God the Father.

"Often, when He touched someone and gave him sight or sanity or words from a once mute throat, only those other men and women in His immediate vicinity were even aware that He had done so. He did what He did and moved on."

"But, surely, the Nazarene must have been moved with compassion for whoever was sick of mind or body," she pointed out.

"Yes, yes, His compassion envelops all of mankind, Lydia, but *not* everybody will elect to receive the gift of eternal life that He offers. Also, not everyone will be healed. I cannot explain why this is so, but I know that it is. I have seen with my own eyes."

Lydia smiled with appreciation as she considered what Lysimmachus had just revealed to her.

"You are so wise," she said. "I admire you."

"Some have said that even before my redemption, I did have some measure of wisdom. I am only sorry that during those years of my lost condition all of it was thrown away, treated carelessly, the ravings of a man without God.

"For long hours, I would reason with endless numbers of those very much like myself, ruminating about this world, the stars, the nature of man, the gods of the Romans and the Greeks and others. And it all sounded so empty, I see now, with little meaning, reducing life to the futile scurryings of mindless ants."

Lydia was becoming more and more impressed with this old man's mind.

"You should not be wandering from place to place, dear Lysimmachus," she said. "What a pity that this was ever so."

"And now that my life is nearly over, I will soon have a home and—"

"I have an idea," she said as they approached the mountain pass that led into the village area. "You could be a teacher, a counselor, a wise man to the others."

"I am not worthy," Lysimmachus protested.

"But we all will need someone of that sort. None of us, I suspect, has the gift that you do. God could use you mightily."

He stopped walking for a moment.

. . . . *God could use you mightily.*

"To be an instrument of His divine plan," he mused out loud. "If only that could be, dear Lydia."

"I cannot read the mind of our heavenly Father," she admitted, "but I do know that something extraordinary has happened with me this day. I can talk about it with scores or hundreds or thousands perhaps. I can do that, yes, and from my experience alone, I shall express a powerful message; but you, Lysimmachus, can take my healing and present it in a way that would challenge the mind as well as the soul.

"For me, it would be only their hearts, and I rejoice that I can do even as much as this. But, I think, I can bring them only up to the gates of heaven. It is for you to help the lost gain entrance, dear man."

And so it went as they walked the distance back to the village site.

XLIII

W e must all go there," the woman remarked with much excitement. "We must bathe in the waters of the Jordan, and we, too, shall be healed."

That was how it began.

Men and women started to rush forward, trying to get past Lydia and Lysimmachus as well as Nahum and Paetus, who had come to stand with them.

Lydia yelled at them.

"It may be that healing will *not* be for everyone!" she told them plaintively. "Please, please, do not force our blessed heavenly Father to have to disappoint some of you or all of you. Do not pass to Him that terrible burden."

But they did not listen.

As a group they rushed from the village site, through the pass, on toward the Jordan, gesturing excitedly, their voices raised as they anticipated the healing of ghastly maladies that had been with them for many years.

Only the lepers remained.

"Why are you not going with them?" Paetus asked.

One was named Zedekiah, a young man who had progressed further in the condition than the others despite the fact that he was not of their more advanced age.

"We have learned not to follow the latest cries of 'Here, healing!' 'There, healing!'" he confessed to them. "Charlatans abound in the cruel aftermath of the Great Healer Himself. It is often difficult to distinguish the fake from the genuine. And so those like me and the others have learned never to seek again that healing we crave so much, except to understand that our heavenly Father will bless us fully when we go to be with Him in His kingdom. That moment will not be so long hence for some of us."

"Aye, that is correct," a middle-aged, leprosy-ravaged woman who was called Hannah interjected. "It is not that we have seldom tried. Oh, it is not that at all, for we surely have, from this healer or that one. Usually they perform in front of a great crowd. Not a one would have anything to do with us."

"Why is that so?" Nahum inquired.

"Because *our* healing cannot be faked before the eyes of any witnesses," Hannah replied. "The twisted bones, the open sores, the disfigured faces. We are either healed or we are not. There can be no playacting with us."

"Are you saying that some healings have been staged?" Nahum spoke again, incredulous at the insinuation.

"Without conscience, and for only one purpose: More coins in the pockets of those who proclaim their falsehoods. They have shifted attention from the Nazarene to their own so-called powers. Some stand before large numbers of onlookers and prance about like fools—but fools giving the crowds that which they demand, a gaudy show and, for some, the promise of freedom from disability and pain."

Her anger was beginning to explode.

"I remember one especially," she continued. "He stood before one after the other, *breathing* on each one, for he had told them that he had the very breath of our Lord. Many deluded themselves into believing this man. When he did what he did, they almost always fell back against the ground, overcome by their anticipations and seduced by his claims. Yet when they came to their senses, they were as they had been earlier, untouched by healing of any kind. They went away, embittered against God, turning their backs on faith altogether."

Hannah's misshapen frame was shaking with anger.

"I know of what I speak because I *believed* that they could do what they were promising, but none even tried with me or any of my friends here. The only so-called healings were the ones that were rehearsed, as well as those whose ailments were but in their heads, for whom the promise of healing was the same as the healing itself."

Her face was reddening with the fury of her emotions.

"The danger is that those disappointed, those exposed to the emptiness of his claims will never again be interested in salvation, thinking that all Christians are as this man!"

Zedekiah spoke up.

"The woman is right," he said. "Even the Nazarene did not heal us."

Paetus was stunned by that statement.

"You asked Him to do so, and he refused?"

"I stood before Him, and He smiled at me."

"Was there nothing else?" Paetus pressed.

"Strange words from His lips."

"What did He say?"

"'Your healing is not for now. It will come later, Hannah.' And then He was gone, down the road, with His apostles, as the multitudes followed Him."

238

She closed her eyes.

"I have repeated those very words in my mind many times a day in the years since He spoke them to me. I have gone to the glory-seekers, yes, I have, thinking one of them might be His instrument after all. But it has not been so, and, thus, I am left with those words only, from His lips, and my body as despicable as ever—no, *worse,* because whatever is wrong progresses unabated."

Hannah opened her eyes and looked up toward the clear sky.

"The Nazarene is standing there right now," she said, "looking at each of us, listening to those words that we utter, peering into our minds, our hearts. He sees what the multitudes around us do not see. As far as He is concerned, this battered flesh means nothing. In time it will be shed. In time, it—"

Other words seemed to catch in her throat.

Zedekiah reached out and touched her twisted arm with his own.

"Can I help?" he said, knowing some of what she must have been feeling at that precise moment.

She shook her head but not brusquely, not ignoring his kind offer.

"I was just thinking how wonderful it would be to know healing in *this* life," she went on, "not as those we detest would have it, but *real,* not demanded by those with an audience but given willingly by a merciful Creator."

She turned to Lydia.

"I do not look at you with jealousy. Oh, I do not do that in any way, praise His holy name. I look at you with the rejoicing of all my being, for I share your joy, dear one. You have been favored by our Lord, and that is something to be happy about, a sister in Him given a miracle that He saw fit in His infinite mercy to bestow!"

Lydia walked over to Hannah, reaching out and starting to put her arms around the other woman's body.

Hannah stepped back.

"No, no—you will become as I," she protested. "You must not risk this malady with your affection."

Lydia stopped, dropping her arms by her side.

"Forgive me," she said, realizing the sense of what Hannah had said, but ashamed of her reluctant submission to it.

Paetus spoke up.

"I think we should go to where the others are," he said. "They might hurt themselves in their frenzy."

"We will stay here," Zedekiah declared, speaking for all the lepers.

Paetus nodded sadly as Nahum, Lysimmachus and Lydia fell in line behind him.

As the four of them reached the mountain pass, they heard some sounds behind them, and all turned to see what it was. One of the roughest-looking of the hired workers had offered a cup of water to Lydia who seemed especially weary. He said something to her, smiled, and then went back to his work.

XLIV

People were sprawled out on their backs in the more shallow portions of the Jordan River, letting its clear, cool waters cover them. Others were standing after having splashed water over their bodies.

"Listen!" Paetus said.

Ecstatic sounds could be heard coming from everyone there, mixing together in a cacophony that frightened Lydia, as well as Nahum, Lysimmachus, and even Paetus, though none were so honest as she in admitting this.

"It disturbs me," she told them. "They sound—"

"Like those who are quite mad," Lysimmachus acknowledged, anticipating what she was going to say.

"Yes!" she agreed. "They are frantic in their desire to be healed."

Some were on the verge of drowning, so desperate were they in wanting the Jordan to touch every inch of their bodies.

"We must help," Nahum spoke anxiously. "They will surely die."

Paetus nodded in agreement as the two of them rushed forward into the river, each grabbing a different man or woman.

"*No!*" an elderly man screamed at Nahum. "You must leave me here. I want the healing touch of these blessed waters."

"You will die," Nahum told him. "You will drown."

"I have not been living, *truly* living for many years. What is the difference?"

He fought with surprising ferocity, considering his age, long fingernails digging into Nahum's arms, a wild expression on his face.

"You are possessed!" Nahum shouted, letting go, staring at the cuts and scratches he had sustained, as he stumbled back to shore.

"If that is the only way I can be healed, then that is what must be," the old man said, his voice barely discernible.

"But how can you claim the healing of the Lord?"

"Whoever can give this to me, that is whom I shall follow, man or god or devil it matters not!"

Nahum became frightened, as Lydia had seemed a moment ago. He looked at Paetus, who was stumbling away from the woman he had tried to rescue.

"She is—," Paetus started to say.

"Mad?" Nahum spoke.

"Yes! You encountered this, too?"

"I did, Decimus, I did. It was almost as though the legions of hell had stepped between us."

"If a man had come to them, with his arms outstretched, and blown upon them, claiming their healing, they would have embraced him as from God directly."

"Or perhaps God Himself, incarnated once again!"

The two men hugged themselves, shivering, feeling a cold that was not altogether of that time and place.

"Desperate people seek any means they can to be freed from the cause of their despair, their pain," Lysimmachus said as he approached them, Lydia by his side. "If someone has a better smile, a smoother manner, if someone speaks with words that they want to hear, they will turn to him, and when he disappoints them, there will be another in his place, this going on and on until they die.

"They are willing to settle for a futile pursuit of false apostles in an endless chain of these. As long as they have hope, no matter how doomed, they feel they can endure the pain that hounds them."

Paetus, Nahum, Lydia, and Lysimmachus stood away from the edge of the river, close to the trees on that side, watching men and women drown themselves. Two tripped and fell, hitting their head on rocks.

Those remaining, unhealed, started screaming as they ran from the water, saw the quartet observing them, and approached.

"How can God taunt us like this?" an old man who had been in a condition akin to Lydia's demanded. "We are in pain. We know nothing but despair and shame. How could He stand over us, up there in heaven, and do *nothing?*"

He raised his head as much as he was able and pointed to her.

"You are whole," he said with great envy. "You can see a sunrise and a sunset now without having to contort your body. Why *you* and yet *not* the rest of us? What has earned you this favor from the Almighty?"

Lydia stepped forward.

"I went to the river earlier but not out of a quest for healing," she spoke. "I wanted to be where my Lord was on the day of His baptism by John from the wilderness. I wanted to feel those waters on my body, touching my flesh as His own had been touched. I was honoring Him by my devotion, not making demands that He do what I wanted.

"If He had *not* healed me, I would have accepted it because I did not expect it in the first place. Accepting the will of God, whatever its manifestation, can be the most wonderful blessing of all!"

242

Upon hearing this, several of the people spat on the ground, their contempt quickly turning to rage.

"Words!" one of the men shouted. "It costs nothing to say them. You have your health, you have new strength. We cannot partake even of a few pitiable crumbs from the table of the Almighty!"

Lydia walked up to him.

"I *have* known what pain is, the pain you and the others here face daily, for I faced it myself. I *have* allowed the despair to swallow me up. And yet, I still accepted the Nazarene into my very soul as my Savior, accepted Him without conditions, without *expecting* anything but the promise of eternal life with Him in the Father's kingdom."

She stretched out her arms.

"I can rejoice, yes, as you cannot, and that is very hard for me to endure, my joy so newly bestowed confronted by your suffering," she said, her expression so intent that it seemed to freeze, for a moment, any words her listeners might have spoken. "For the anguish this has caused you, anguish that my love for you finds difficult to countenance, I would ask that the Lord make me as I once was for so long, that I am no longer a stumbling block to any of you. If He will not honor this petition of mine, then there is nothing I can do to help your flesh. Let me, though, help you in your own souls, let me be His instrument in bringing you to—"

The man reached out and slapped her across the face.

"No *woman* dares to speak to me in this manner!" he yelled, having heard only a portion of what she had spoken, the rest lost on the sea of anger that was swallowing him up.

Paetus strode up to him, grabbed his frail body.

"You may be old, and you may be filled with pain," he declared, "but *nothing* gives you the right to treat her as you have."

The man, his body little more than a skeleton from lack of food and the ravages of his affliction, fell to the ground, sobbing.

"I *am* ashamed," he admitted. "Oh, I am very ashamed but I cannot bear what this life has become any longer. I cannot bear the days nor the nights, for these are the same, every part of this poor body crying out, every moment that passes worse than the others before it. I just need mercy, that is all, merely the mercy of God, a little cup of it, just a fragment. Is that so much to ask for—can you tell me this?"

Lydia got on her knees in front of him.

"I pray with every breath I take, with every beat of my heart that the Lord will take my healing and give it to you instead, sir," she said. "I ask Him to transfer it now so that your bitterness be ended, and there is no longer a barrier between you and Him."

Eyes widening in shock, the man pulled back from her.

"How could you ask for this?" he groaned. "How could you ever give up something so precious? It is what I crave most in life, and yet you are willing to have it given over to me, knowing what you were like before healing was bestowed?"

Lydia smiled serenely, her expression in considerable contrast to that of the one in front of her and those like him who were standing around, trying to comprehend just what was taking place.

"My healing is a blessed gift, it is surely that, and I would clutch it to me until the last of these my days if it were not at the expense of your most precious salvation," Lydia replied. "Yet what has been gained if I were to stay in this state while you and others here go to hell because of me? Is that how I should seek to bring honor to the name of the One whose healing I have received? Is that what I am to confess to Him this day as I kneel before Him in prayer? How could I face the Nazarene without shame if this were so?"

The man could not speak for several moments.

Lydia fell on her chest, crying out to God, begging Him to remove His hand from her body, and remold it into the wretchedness of only hours earlier.

None doubted her intent. None could find even a fragment of cynicism in themselves to negate the extraordinary sacrifice she was intent on making.

The man crawled to her, put his hand on her shoulder.

"You must stop this, woman," he demanded. "You cannot give up your wholeness. That would be a tragedy!"

She sat up, her cheeks moist.

"The tragedy is yours, not mine. The tragedy lies not in my desire to have this healing that has transformed my body revoked but in your stubbornness. Confronted with a miracle, you turn your back on the God of miracles."

Lydia then flung herself against the rock-strewn ground, cutting her skin in several places, and murmuring in pain.

"*No!*" the man screamed, his old thin voice momentarily stronger. "I cannot allow myself to be healed if it means that you are denied that very gift!"

Suddenly he flung his head back, looking up toward the sky, and stretching out both hands in front of him.

"I want to accept this Lord of yours into my life," he said. "I want Him without conditions. Even as I daily become worse, more crippled than the day before, more in pain, less able to walk, I shall worship Him all the more if it is because of Him that you are compelled to such sacrifice for a stranger."

244

As everyone watched, his body shook with great tremors of feeling, so much so that it seemed he would burst into pieces.

Just as quickly as it had befallen him, all this passed and he turned to Lydia, tapping her once, twice, a third time.

"Look, dear lady!" he asked of her. "Raise your head and look! Witness what your faith has wrought!"

Lydia did this, slowly, and saw the other poor and crippled ones kneeling as they bowed their heads.

"Speak to us," the man begged. "We are poor and ignorant, and we need to have you show us the way."

They waited for whatever wisdom she had for them.

"Clasp your hands in front of you," Lydia told them, "and ask Jesus the Christ to come into your souls as your Savior, your precious Lord."

They did that, as one, tears rolling down their pale and wrinkled cheeks.

And when they had finished, suddenly filled with great joy, not healed of the body, but healed of the mind and the heart and, truly, the soul, they jumped up, most of them staggering in the process, eager to rush over to Lydia and hug this woman who had spoken so uncommonly.

"No one has ever offered to do what you have," one of them told her. "You are blessed before God."

At first, she could not seem to move. Suddenly her limbs felt frozen in place.

"God must be accepting her offer," Lysimmachus observed with gathering sorrow at what seemed to be unfolding before his eyes. "In His wisdom, the Nazarene has begun to pass to them the healing she alone had enjoyed."

"Wait," Paetus pleaded. "It may not be so. Our eyes perhaps deceive us. Please, you must not speak loud enough for the rest to hear, lest their disappointment do fatal injury to their new faith."

Nodding, Lysimmachus walked as fast as he could to the old woman, and bent down beside her.

"I am so very sorry," he whispered. "You must believe this, dear Lydia. Please know that I grieve with you."

For some moments Lydia did not, could not move. Finally she did so, sitting up and facing him.

Still whole!

God had blessed Lydia for her willing spirit of sacrifice—and also bestowed healing on another.

She frowned as she said, "If it were as you had feared, Lysimmachus, I would yet rejoice because it still would be an answer to this most recent prayer of mine. But it is not what you fear, my dear friend."

There was the hint of a smile, not for herself but for the dear man whose concern was so strong in her regard.

"I have some cramps," Lydia told him. "But, you see, I am not accustomed to being prostrate on the ground as I have been this short while. I was healed of being crippled but my age is still upon me."

With some effort, Lysimmachus's arms around her waist, she stood.

Everyone there, beggar, crippled, old, young, applauded this lady named Lydia, and it was not difficult to envision angels from heaven joining in as they hovered, unseen, in the midst of that holy place where the feet of the Nazarene once trod its fertile soil.

Part V

XLV

For a number of weeks, the rebuilding work at the village site continued, with old structures torn down, and new ones erected. Poor people from all over the region became aware of what was going on, and thus the village drew them in great numbers, hordes of people making the trip from wherever they were, throughout the whole of Israel, far more than the location could assimilate. Many had to be turned away, even after the village had been completely rebuilt, because its capacity was sorely limited.

Disappointed, and feeling scorned, those who were not accepted spread a different kind of word, grumbling that soon reached the ears of proconsul Pontius Pilatus, brought to him by one Marcus Vibenna . . .

Marcus Vibenna could not have been aware, at first, who was behind the erection of that once deserted village. But he rather admired the initiative that it represented. He was not unsympathetic to the plight of the poor, even if they were Jewish, and he thought the idea of rebuilding a village to make it suitable for housing them was quite brilliant.

When some passersby told a fellow legionnaire, and this had been passed on to him, he knew from the sound of it that Pilatus would be immediately interested, not necessarily out of any charitable impulses on the proconsul's part but simply because it was something new and unusual happening amid the dreary sameness of the land he ruled in Rome's name.

Vibenna had been taken from the many battlefields of his past service, and transferred, for a limited time, to being in charge of the now-substantial guard that was ordered to surround the Judean residences of Pontius Pilatus. This was directly as a result of how Vibenna had come to distinguish himself as a tactical expert and adviser along those lines to various Roman generals in a number of locales through the empire, but it was also due, not incidentally, to his notable ability to ensure that those very generals were protected as much as feasible from harm, a degree of protection that none of their men would ever enjoy.

Pilatus had grown concerned about possible attempts on his life, including outright threats that had been received from one or more of the persistent groups of insurrectionist-rebels that were continuing to be active in Judea at the time. After consulting with his superiors in Rome, the proconsul-governor decided that veteran Marcus Vibenna seemed the perfect candidate to serve him.

Until that assignment, Vibenna had lived amidst typically primitive battlefield conditions, with seldom any kind of real bed on which to sleep, and the most basic of food rations, though Imperial Rome's treatment of its soldiers represented an honest attempt to be as fair and generous as often difficult circumstances permitted.

There was nothing of wealth in Vibenna's background either, since his family had never been other than tenuously middle-class at best. As such, he found himself unaccustomed to the level of splendor with which he was confronted when he moved into Pilatus's Jerusalem palace.

He was lounging in the courtyard where Jesus the Christ had faced Pilatus.

It is almost as though I feel Your presence here, he thought, *as though what the Jews are saying is true.*

"If you *are* here," he said, mockingly, "say something to me this very moment, or you shall have lost forever any interest that I might have."

Vibenna chuckled at the very notion.

"Here I am," he said out loud, "talking to a dead man about a gift He must never have had in the first place!"

"Yes, that is extraordinary, I shall have to admit," a familiar voice intruded.

Vibenna spun around, at attention.

Pontius Pilatus stood a few feet away, leaning against one of the thick columns that encircled the open space of the courtyard.

"I am sorry, proconsul Pilatus," Vibenna spoke, sounding awkward and embarrassed.

"Your words were neither seditious nor insulting and certainly not blasphemous to any god, theirs or ours," Pilatus told him. "You have no reason to offer an apology or to be acting as though I have stumbled upon some guilty secret."

"Thank you, sir," Vibenna replied dutifully.

"You see, I too have thought often about this man. There is no reason for me to do so. He was a rather common type, a—"

Pilatus stopped himself.

"Now I am the one to feel some degree of embarrassment, for we both know that the Nazarene was far from being common, else I would scarcely have devoted another moment of my time after His crucifixion to this matter. He was not an ordinary wanderer, quite forgettable, like so many others in this wretched land, a pathetic Jew, outcast even by those others of His kind who demanded the shedding of His blood."

He sighed with some exasperation, and more than a little weariness.

"Since the Jews sought to eject Him and succeeded in fact through me, then surely I, the instrument of that rejection, should be able to do the very same, right now—cast Him from my consciousness and be done with the matter."

"But you cannot," Vibenna ventured a bit tentatively.

"I cannot," Pilatus agreed. "Is madness contagious?"

"Sir?"

"Have I caught that which infected my dear Procula? Has that woman's condition become mine, though not as full-blown in me as in her?"

Vibenna did not know what to say, so he offered nothing.

Pilatus strode forward, standing before the legionnaire.

"Can you, Marcus Vibenna?" the proconsul asked pointedly. "Are you any better at this than I am?"

Vibenna knew that words spoken in honesty would provide the only response that Pontius Pilatus would accept.

"It is impossible," he admitted. "The Nazarene's image stays in my mind, as though I have no power over Him."

He tapped his forehead.

"I cannot get Him to leave."

"You speak as though He still exists, here-and-now."

Vibenna felt increasingly awkward.

"That is how it seems, yes, proconsul," he said with utter candor. "And yet how can that be true of such a Man, a wandering Jew?"

Pilatus grimaced, not speaking for several seconds. Vibenna waited patiently, knowing the protocol of the moment.

"The man knew a great deal, it seems," Pilatus finally spoke. "One wonders how that could possibly be. He was merely a carpenter from the tiny village of Nazareth, certainly not a learned man at all, and yet He confounded the scribes and others who have been schooled all their lives, it would seem."

"May I speak, proconsul?" Vibenna ventured.

"Go right ahead."

"I have heard that this Jesus was able to engage in this sort of activity even at the age of a very young child."

Pilatus's eyes widened.

"I am listening . . ." he prompted.

"He broke away from his parents at one point and stood among the religious leaders in their temple right here in Jerusalem, as He seemed to be dealing with various points of their law and their history."

"How old was He?"

250

"I cannot say, sir, but I believe the Nazarene was no more than twelve or thirteen."

"And no formal schooling, such as it exists in this barbaric country?"

"None of which I have heard," Vibenna assured him.

"So how is it that He would know so much?"

"That is the mystery."

"We never had offspring, Procula and I, though there have been some mistresses in my life whom, I understand, have given birth to children that I have fathered," Pilatus said, a wistful tone in his voice as he sat down on a hand-carved sandstone bench, indicating that the legionnaire could join him on the one next to it. "But if we had, perhaps our lives, Procula's and mine, would have been different. Perhaps she would not now be in Rome, kept away from the rest of Roman society in a world of her own."

"That *is* sad," Vibenna agreed.

The two men did not speak for a number of minutes, each dealing with the most private of thoughts.

"You wanted to speak with me about a certain other matter," Pilatus finally reminded Vibenna.

"Yes, sir, I did," the legionnaire answered.

He then informed Pilatus of what he had been privy to about the village.

"And you understand that this is happening not far from the Sea of Galilee?" the proconsul asked.

"That is what I have heard, sir."

Pilatus slapped his thigh.

"It is, I must say, a rather interesting concept. Who is behind it? Who is providing the finances for such an enterprise? Surely anyone who is must be rather wealthy. They *have* to be in order to sustain such as this."

"I believe that two men are responsible, sir, though it may not have been their idea, as far as I can tell."

"Which men? Who are they? Their names, please," Pilatus prompted, obviously very interested in what was going on.

"Nicodaemus and Joseph who comes from Arimathea."

He was not sure how Pilatus would react since both had been so intimately involved in the aftermath of the crucifixion of the Nazarene.

"I see . . ." the proconsul pondered that revelation.

"Should I check more into this matter?" Vibenna inquired.

"Yes! Seek out the truth about this village," Pilatus continued. "Is it all that it appears to be, or is it just camouflage for something else? It is the latter that most concerns me."

A moment later, both men stood.

"I hope," Pilatus told him, "that someday you and I are free of the Nazarene. I hope that someday we can cut His image from our brains as completely as though some knife had been applied. Would not it be wonderful to have Him gone?"

Vibenna nodded assent.

"That it would, pronconsul, that it would . . ." he agreed.

Pilatus reached out, clapped his right hand on the legionnaire's shoulder in a gesture of support, and then he was left alone in that courtyard as Marcus Vibenna went from it to his own quarters at the other end of the massive building.

"And as for me," Pilatus spoke, "I sit alone in a place where I condemned a man who should have been set free."

. . . *I hope that someday we can cut His image from our brains as completely as though some knife had been applied.*

He laughed cynically to himself, knowing that this wish might never become reality, that the moments involving Jesus the Christ were perhaps far too vivid ever to be exorcised, bits and pieces of them scattered throughout his consciousness, like some malignant growth.

He recalled, in particular, the encounter at Calvary.

Pilatus raised his head and saw heaven open but for that single instant, the Nazarene newly surrounded not by a mob of sweaty, dirty, common people but by a multitude of dazzling creatures of inexpressible beauty. One of these turned toward him, with an expression of such beckoning love that the proconsul-governor of Judea was tempted to reach out for it, and let whatever it was take him as well, if that were at all possible.

He reached up and wiped away a tear that was starting down his left cheek.

"Now He indeed is free, and it is I who remains the prisoner," Pontius Pilatus sighed, looking from side to side, seeing only the old columns, the imported ferns and other plants, the inlaid Italian white marble floor, a mausoleum for the living, no one but himself present, alone with those memories, oh, those memories.

XLVI

Marcus Vibenna decided to go on to the Jordan River area alone, and in plain street clothes, rather than display his military gear. He wanted no attention to accrue to himself. He used only one horse, older, less sleek-looking, not one of the grand stallions from the proconsul's personal stable.

He rode around the Sea of Galilee, intending not to stop at all, but when he was most of the way to the other side, stop was what he did, dismounting and walking up to the edge of that ancient body of water.

So cool to the touch this day . . .

He tried to sort out just what it was that caused him to do that which he had had no intention of doing.

"I have heard that there was a storm years ago," Vibenna said out loud, "and that You caused it to cease."

The seeming foolishness of that possibility made him wince as he spoke those words, and yet there was something in that story that he could not dismiss so readily.

Including another miracle in a long list of those that seemed to follow the Nazarene everywhere He went.

"It is also said that here You walked on the water," he went on. "Two absurdities, one on top of the other."

Except that the Nazarene was seen doing it, was seen stepping out on the surface of the Sea of Galilee.

And not by just His apostles and others who would have been eager for a so-called miracle but also by some at the shore, fishermen and passersby, none of whom had the slightest interest in becoming one of His followers or perpetuating the legend that seemed to be springing up around Him even as He lived.

"Verified in the presence of witnesses," Vibenna said. "I talked to some of them myself, was told about the rest. Two dozen men and a few children saw it all. First, the calming of the storm, and then, later, the—"

He took off his sandals and placed his feet in the water. At noontime, it was neither hot or cold, but just right to the touch, caressing his skin.

"If I walked directly ahead, inch by inch, this very moment, would my own feet stay on the ground beneath them, the water rising higher and higher up my legs? Or would I too float on the surface?"

He chuckled at the thought, and started to turn away.

But You did, they say, he told himself. *Are you a better man than I?*

Instead of returning to his horse, Vibenna continued walking forward, holding up his modified toga-like outfit so that it would not become wet.

How far did you go before—?

The water was up to his knees before he stopped, not out of any sense of making a fool of himself, not that at all.

"I may not believe that You did this," he spoke suddenly, "but I shall not mock You in the meantime."

Vibenna turned around and started back to shore.

Only accept Me . . .

He stopped immediately. Those words came to him just as surely as though someone were standing next to him and speaking directly into his ear.

"Where are You, Nazarene?" he asked, looking in all directions. *"Where have You hidden Yourself?"*

The contradiction became as real as the words seemed to have been.

A dead man is unable to hide except in the grave, and yet Your body was gone by the morning of that third day, he told himself, knowing that he was starting to ramble. *Am I now, so close to retirement, becoming as one of the madmen I have seen over the years, screaming out their lives to anyone who would listen but none do? And yet on they go, begging to be heard, their mouths spouting the babble of the deranged.*

He was back on shore, finally. Rather than dry off his legs, he just stood there, looking out over the Sea of Galilee.

"I was there at Your tomb!" he shouted. "I *saw*—"

Jesus the Christ stood before them but He was not alone. A multitude of those shining, translucent beings formed an outline around Him.

Vibenna shook his head, not wanting to recall any of what had happened, having spent years trying very hard to dismiss all of it from his mind.

Vibenna's eyes opened wide as the figure took his head in his hands and looked straight into his very soul, or so it seemed. Then he crumpled to the ground not far from Scipio.

One by one, the other legionnaires fell without injury, Jesus the Christ walking past them, still surrounded by those extraordinary beings, even the sound of their wings like music in the still night air.

254

"All this time I have told myself that it was some kind of fantasy," Vibenna said, "that I was actually quite asleep, and my mind tricked me into seeing—"

The tomb.

Always it forced its way into the very center of those memories from years before, a literal image, made of dirt and rock, and standing boldly before him, the large, heavy stone having been rolled aside, the entrance stark and real, no cold, still, torn body inside, not even a vagrant trace of it left.

Except the shroud.

"No one knew," he spoke. "No one knew that I took it. I took it and hid it and did nothing with it for a very long while."

He brought his left hand to his mouth, gasping.

"I could no longer stand to have it anywhere near my presence. So I retrieved the old, bloody thing and gave it to a roaming band of Christians I was able to locate. To a man, those riff-raff all fell down before the shroud, as though a simple length of fabric was something to be worshiped in itself.

"When I was turning to leave, one of that group grabbed my arm, and cried with some passion, 'Bless you, legionnaire. May the Lord Himself protect you throughout all the days of your life.'"

Vibenna had stalked away in anger from those men, though electing not to say anything in rebuke.

I had the power of Rome to protect me, he thought. *What could a dead carpenter from Nazareth do?*

As he stood before the Sea of Galilee, he started laughing hysterically, so hard that cramps filled his stomach.

"I am talking to no one about anything that makes any sense," he said.

He saw only the horse who was eyeing him with a modicum of curiosity but nothing more than that.

At least I am alone in this crazed state of mine, he reassured himself. *I am but a fool before no one.*

As Marcus Vibenna climbed onto the horse, he wondered about the truth of that.

★ ★ ★

Ahead stood a cluster of mountain peaks. The village was supposed to be at their base, surrounded by them.

As Vibenna approached, he saw activity.

A handful of people were filing into a pass that led through the mountains, apparently the only entrance to the village.

255

He found that it was wide enough to accommodate his horse, and so he rode on through, careful not to injure anyone who was on foot.

What he saw was a revelation.

Dozens of small but functional huts were built into the sides of the mountains surrounding them. The back wall of each was mountain rock, the three remaining sides made up of clay, dirt, and stone walls. A myriad of people stood in doorways or sat on the ground, some weaving apparel, some tending to a variety of foods they were preparing, and others bowing their heads in prayer or engaging in hearty conversation.

At the other end of the village was a second pass, one that apparently led to the Jordan River, women carrying earthen jugs on their heads or shoulders as they walked back from it or out toward it.

And he saw Decimus Paetus.

"Decimus!" he started to shout as he dismounted the horse, then shut his mouth in an instant, not from the shock of seeing his old friend so suddenly but out of recognition of who it was Paetus happened to be talking to just then.

Vibenna remounted and rode immediately in the other direction, back through the pass, away from the village, not stopping until he had left the mountains around it nearly a mile behind him.

Then he got off the horse, and knelt beside it, trying to control the trembling that had grabbed hold of his body.

How could this be? he thought, confusion colliding with growing rage. *How could you leave the service of Rome and take up with a criminal such as that one? You have betrayed all of us at the same time you have betrayed the emperor to whom you swore allegiance!*

Tears appeared in his eyes as he said a name that brought a sick taste to his tongue.

Barabbas! The insurrectionist—the one who had been released instead of the Nazarene!

Vibenna looked back at the mountains, and as he did so, he knew what report must be given to Pontius Pilatus upon his return to the proconsul's Jerusalem residence, only the truth of what he had seen, for he could never lie about something of this sort, not even to save the life of a former comrade.

XLVII

Pontius Pilatus could imagine the kind of ordeal the legionnaire had been facing.

"Do you feel that you have betrayed your friend?" he asked not unsympathetically of Marcus Vibenna.

"I do," the other man answered with candor that seemed to have been coaxed from him, "but the greater betrayal would have been dealt Rome if I had said nothing or given you a report founded on lies."

Pilatus nodded appreciatively.

"I have dared to think, over these many years, that the empire was always turning out men like yourself," he remarked, "that Rome always inspired the kind of integrity that you are displaying."

He sighed with more than a little weariness.

"It would be madness to hold to that notion any longer. Everything is slipping: the quality of our government, politicians committing unethical acts, more and more giving in to their baser instincts; and along with this, the quality of our military forces has suffered to an accelerating extent."

Pilatus could see Vibenna wince.

"I believe I know what you are thinking," he suggested. "Will you tell me if I have guessed correctly?"

"I will do just that, sir," the other man replied.

"You are concerned, as I myself am, about discipline, about the morale of our troops if certain men with, shall we say, bizarre proclivities, are allowed to serve, instead of being merely playthings for corrupt politicians."

Vibenna was impressed with Pilatus's observation.

"That is my greatest source of concern," he admitted.

"More so than if certain legionnaires are converted to the doctrines of Christianity and become proselytizers for their faith, within the very ranks of our legions?"

Vibenna began to sweat. It was not possible to tell from Pilatus's manner what his intentions were by posing such a question.

"I think, in the one instance, we would have moral degeneracy," he spoke, realizing how dangerous the moment was.

"And in the other—?"

"Another kind of degeneracy, proconsul, a refusal to have the emperor as the ultimate source of their devotion, their worship, in fact."

"Do you feel that these are equally a threat?" Pilatus continued to probe.

"If it were something over which I had control," Vibenna continued, his trepidation almost a palpable thing by now, "I would have to elect that neither should be spreading their influence throughout the ranks of my comrades."

"But if you had to choose, which would you pick to remain: the homosexuals or the Christians?"

Vibenna's throat was dry, his vocal chords seeming paralyzed for an instant.

"I . . . I—," he stuttered.

"I realize that you have come to me with this news about Barabbas," Pilatus said, "as well as your friend and, therefore, your emotions are rough-edged. Please, calm down, speak your mind without fear."

Vibenna felt oddly emboldened.

"Proconsul, I would keep the Christians," he spoke finally.

"Can you explain why?" Pilatus inquired.

"While their allegiance has been switched from the emperor to their god, it is true that their faith also admonishes them to remain in obedience to their earthly leaders."

Pilatus's eyebrows shot up.

"So that would mean that such as Barabbas could never become Christians?"

"If they *as* Christians are to remain true to the doctrines of their faith, that is correct, proconsul."

Finally, though both had been subconsciously trying to delay it as much as possible, the moment had arrived for the legionnaire to be given his superior's command for the crisis immediately at hand.

"Get Barabbas," Pilatus told him. "Alive or dead, he must be brought to me. He is yet another cancer alongside those we have been discussing."

"And Decimus Paetus?"

"He will be judged. If he is in knowing allegiance with any insurrectionists, I shall have to put him to death as well."

"By hanging, sir?"

"Or—"

Sweat appearing now on his own brow, Pilatus left the alternative unspoken.

XLVIII

Marcus Vibenna was to be allowed as many men as he deemed necessary to accomplish the certain capture of Barabbas, Paetus, and anyone else involved. After careful rumination, he chose to ask for only a dozen or so, thinking that Barabbas had traveled alone this time and not deeming anyone else at that site capable of offering any substantial resistance.

They began the march to the village site only a few hours after the order was given by Pontius Pilatus.

Decimus Paetus had never anticipated, even remotely, coming into any contact with Barabbas or any of his band of rebels. Though the former legionnaire had become a Christian, he still retained a special loathing for the insurrectionist, perhaps more so since his conversion than before, for reasons that seemed valid.

It was Barabbas who was given freedom instead of the Nazarene. It was Barabbas who could be seen in the vicinity of Golgotha, drinking wine and laughing, as he pointed toward the three crosses. It was Barabbas who remained a crude man committed to violence, whereas Paetus had gone completely the other way, becoming a Christian, which meant being Christ-like, and, therefore, someone who eschewed violence and embraced the role of peacemaker.

When Paetus was told that he had a visitor who needed to talk with him, he could not have guessed who it was, but he noticed how nervous Nahum had been in approaching him about the matter.

"You are on edge," he said.

"I am," Nahum admitted, speaking in a voice so low that Paetus had to strain to hear him. "This man will not please you."

"How do you know? Who is it, my friend?"

The other man stepped aside, and the visitor brushed past him.

As soon as Barabbas entered the hut where Paetus had come to live, recognition hit with great force.

"You!" he said as he saw the bearded individual standing in the doorway.

Paetus sprang to his feet and started to lunge toward the other man.

"And you call yourself a Christian!" Barabbas exclaimed. "I see that I have come to the wrong place and the wrong man!"

As he turned to leave, Paetus's entire body seemed to freeze, nearly in midair.

"*You* lived instead of the Nazarene," he snarled. "How can you show your face here before me, before any of us?"

"If I had gone to the cross instead, what would have happened to *you?*" Barabbas asked pointedly. "This Jesus would remain alive, and all anyone would have had was another itinerant, self-appointed wise man, if He can be called that."

Barabbas rubbed his chin.

"That was wrong," he added. "The Nazarene could be called just that, a wise *man*, but I wonder if it ends there, what we might say about Him."

Paetus looked at him in puzzlement.

"You speak in circles," he said impatiently.

"And you act stupidly," Barabbas spoke, looking genuinely disappointed. "The reason I am here is you, for without you there is no reason, and I might as well return to the motley group from which I came!"

"*Again!*" Paetus shouted in frustration. "Leave this village before I forget what I am doing in this place and give in to what my emotions are demanding."

"I, for one, am here because I was *not* picked to die, do you not understand that? And because I was not picked to die, with the Nazarene going to Golgotha in my stead, He died, quite horribly, I know, was buried and it is said, rose from the dead. Without that resurrection, you have nothing, only a delusion, and a pathetic one at that."

Paetus clenched and unclenched his hands, trying to restrain them from somehow springing forward of their own volition and closing around the man's neck, giving him the death sentence he deserved.

. . . . without that resurrection.

He swallowed hard as those three words refused to leave his mind.

. . . . you have nothing, only a delusion and a pathetic one at that.

Vibenna shook his head, the drone of Barabbas's baritone voice breaking through his introspection.

"Without His death, the rest of it would never have happened. I would hope that you see this, and that you do not cast me out of this place."

Paetus looked hard at this infamous Barabbas, an accused murderer, insurrectionist, robber. He saw a big man, someone an inch or two taller than himself and considerably broader, with a wide, full beard, his body clothed in animal skins.

"You look like the Baptist," Paetus muttered.

"Others have said that," Barabbas acknowledged.

A moment of silence followed, each man sizing up the other.

"Sit down," Paetus offered, his reluctance hardly hidden.

Barabbas nodded, and did so.

"I want to become a Christian," he said.

Paetus did not speak at first in reaction to this, unsure as to whether he should be pleased or greatly offended.

"Your loathing is apparent," Barabbas commented, "the very expression on your face, the way you hold your body."

He sighed, then added, "I can scarce blame you for the way you see me now. Think of this, though: It is dangerous for me to be here, in this place that has been gaining so much attention. I come at great risk—"

His eyes widened, words spoken deliberately.

"—for so great a salvation."

Paetus would not trust or accept the man so easily, though.

"Why now?" he demanded of the intruder. "The Nazarene has been gone for more than four long years. What is it that brings you to Him *today*, and not earlier, a month perhaps, or a year ago?"

"Because I can turn to no one else. Because there is no hope that my efforts to overthrow the Romans will ever be successful. Because all that I can do with these hands and with this brain of mine has reached an end. There is no more to this my life if there can be no revolution which I lead."

Suddenly, looking more like a very big child than a thug, Barabbas turned quite pale, as though possessed of a chill to the very marrow of his bones.

"I have lived to die, if necessary, for the freedom of my oppressed friends and neighbors and even those who may be strangers to me but are still born of the ancient blood of the twelve families of Israel," he said, his voice trembling. "And now that that freedom seems as far away as ever it was, there is little to keep me alive. I fight for a futile cause, and there is no way that I can deny the truth of this.

"How much better that I had been the one to endure crucifixion that awful day. At least death would then have come to embrace me in but a few hours, and there would be no more of this misery I face without end."

Barabbas seemed on the verge of collapse.

"I come here, to this village, to you, seeking some way of obtaining the forgiveness of this Nazarene you Christians worship, however you might help me to achieve my goal, for there is no other road to travel anymore for someone such as myself. It is here now that I shall somehow begin a new life or—"

He took out a crude knife made of sharpened bone from a leather sheath at his waist and swung it toward his chest.

"—spill the blood of the present one on the dirt here beneath my feet."

Paetus reached out, in an instant, and closed his fingers around Barabbas's thick, rough-skinned wrist.

"I *will* introduce you to the Nazarene," he said. "Put away your knife, and listen to words of peace and joy instead."

"Peace and joy, you say?" Barabbas repeated. "Is that ever possible? Is that ever a gift He would give to me, let alone a gift I can accept, knowing how much blood these hands of mine have shed?"

"I am the one who drove a spear into His side," Paetus told him. "I have shed His own blood. But before this ever happened, I shed far more than just His own, on a dozen battlefields for the glory of Rome."

Paetus's eyes were bloodshot.

"I have nearly drowned in what seemed like lakes of blood, I suspect as high as my knees perhaps. I have sent those who were unbelieving to hell without ever giving them a last chance to embrace God. The guilt of their damnation lays on my shoulders far more than your own."

It was Paetus's turn to seem like a troubled child.

"And still He forgave me! Still He could take my hands in His own, *physically* take them and *physically* lift me up from my sin, and—"

Paetus fell forward into the arms of a startled Barabbas.

"—and call me one of His own!"

They stood like that for some while before Paetus finally pulled away, and began, with great power, to speak to Barabbas of the saving grace of Jesus the Christ.

XLIX

The intrusion was a swift one, against which there could be no initial resistance because everyone was completely unprepared for what was happening, but still it failed in its objective because Marcus Vibenna did not take into account that there was, at the opposite end of the site, another pass through the mountains.

Accustomed to running in order to save his life, Barabbas was able to escape through it, along with the small band of men who had accompanied him, once again failing to pay the mandated Roman penalty for his many attempts at insurrection.

After discovering that Barabbas had fled, Vibenna became enraged as he stood before the villagers, hired workers, and Decimus Paetus, as well as a special visitor, Joseph of Arimathea, who was unaware that Barabbas had been at the site since his attention was on directing the workers in the final stages of an irrigation system that was designed to divert some water from the Jordan into the village, where it was to be used for drinking, cooking, bathing, and raising vegetables and some fruits.

"How could you allow this to happen?" Vibenna confronted Paetus. "Of all men, you should have been sensitive to the need for this Barabbas's capture. Instead, you welcomed him into this village!"

"How could I turn him away?" Paetus spoke, trying to keep his anger in control. "He came here for food, for counsel, for—"

"Counsel?" Vibenna spat out the word. "What sort of counsel could you give such a criminal as this?"

Paetus started to answer but his former comrade interrupted him. "Unless he realized that you had spent many years in service to Rome and knew—"

Of *course!* Vibenna realized. *Barabbas was here to get whatever he could from Decimus about how Rome—?*

He put his hands as his hips as he tapped one foot on the ground, a knowing expression on his face.

"So that is the root of all this!" he exclaimed, secure in the assumption that he knew what Paetus had not as yet admitted. "Barabbas wanted information about our forces that only you could provide."

Paetus stepped forward.

"He was not aware of me when he came to this village," he said. "I never told him about my former life. We spoke only of spiritual matters."

Vibenna hesitated as he recalled what Paetus, Scipio, Accius, and he had shared that night at the tomb of the Nazarene. But this lasted only seconds. To allow it to affect him any longer than that would make him seem indecisive, weak to everyone there, and such a thing could not be allowed.

"I am concerned with sedition only," Vibenna stated. "You are guilty of consorting with a well-known rabble-rouser, a man dedicated to the overthrow of the empire that is my master, to which you yourself once pledged your very life."

Joseph of Arimathea spoke up.

"You cannot take this man simply because he spoke with Barabbas," he said. "Since you have no idea what they discussed, and no way of obtaining proof, Roman law—"

"Roman law is for me to interpret, old man," he shouted.

"Roman law has a measure of justice to it," Joseph persisted, "and you cannot call your actions just. Nor can you escape condemnation if you persist in this. For we all are witnesses, and even Pontius Pilatus would have to give their testimonies the weight that is deserved. You must not take an innocent man *once again!*"

Despite himself, Vibenna winced at those words, for he knew well enough their intent, and that intent was having its way with him.

As he started to respond, a rock was thrown, hitting him on the side of his head. He fell, not knocked unconscious but only momentarily stunned.

One of the workers, a younger man whose hatred for the Romans caused him to lose his restraint, had thrown the rock and was now picking up another. In a moment he was joined by several others doing the same thing.

The soldiers reacted in the absence of any command by a dazed Vibenna and counter-attacked, charging forward and knocking villagers and workers alike to one side or the other. Pathetic screams filled the air.

Lydia herself was hit by another rock, this one also intended for the Romans. She crumpled to the ground.

Lysimmachus rushed over to her, bent down, and slid his arms around her body, lifting her up and sobbing as he screamed at the soldiers, "Look at what you have done! Are you never satisfied? How much more old blood, innocent blood must you spill before you stop?"

One of the soldiers swung at Lysimmachus with a spear. By now

Vibenna had gotten, unsteadily, to his feet, and had time only to shout, *"No!* You must not—"

The edge of the blade hit the old man's neck, killing him instantly.

Paetus jumped, knocking the soldier over and, grabbing him by the neck, started to choke him.

"Stop it, Decimus!" Vibenna shouted as he managed to stand and run over to them, intercepting the other soldiers. "If you kill him, no one will be able to defend you. By tomorrow you will be hanging from a cross just as the Nazarene did!"

"And then I shall follow Him into the place that He has prepared for me!" Paetus shouted as Vibenna tried to pull him away from the struggling soldier.

"With more blood on your hands! Is that what you want Him to see? The hands of a murderer?"

Paetus released his hold and staggered to his feet.

"What about the men under your command here, now?" he demanded. "Will you allow them to shed the blood of people who are not far from the grave anyway? Is it a matter of honor to crunch their bones, their flesh, under the merciless heavy feet of mighty Rome? We have faced *warriors* in the past. Is this now the level to which we are stooping?"

He stood nearly nose-to-nose with his one-time friend.

"You and I both have hands that dealt oblivion in a wide swath around us, but at least any lives we took were of those who opposed us in battle, sometimes in greater number than our own, and often *they* were the aggressors."

Paetus indicated the villagers.

"What is so dangerous about *them?*" he demanded. "They were peaceful until moments ago when you descended upon this place."

"I could leave them alone, and I may do that, but now I have no choice but to take you back with me," Vibenna acknowledged. "Else I myself would become a traitor to the Rome I have been serving all my adult life."

"I will go with you, Marcus," Paetus assured him, "but only if you will acknowledge to Pilatus that there were witnesses to this matter, people who saw Barabbas come here on his own and can verify that I did not even know that he had arrived until I was told."

Paetus knew that he was asking the veteran legionnaire to do something extraordinary and could not be sure even that single condition would be met.

Vibenna looked around at the scene, men and women held back by the soldiers he had brought with him.

Not an even match, he told himself rather cynically. *The might of*

*Rome against people so old, so ill, so decrepit that they offered no real chal-
lenge to seasoned warriors, despite the rocks that already had been thrown.*

Another legionnaire tapped Vibenna on the shoulder and asked
him if he would step aside for a moment. The two of them walked up to
the pass on that side and stepped into it because the other man did not
want anyone to overhear.

"We cannot allow this to go before the proconsul," he said, looking very nervous. "We have killed one of them, someone unarmed, and
quite innocent, I suppose. That will not please Pilatus, you know. He is a
man of great rectitude. The irony is that one or more of us might be
imprisoned while this one you have known would go free!"

"What would you propose that we do?" Vibenna asked, not at all
sure he wanted to hear the answer.

The expression on the other man's face made him look away.

"They all have to die," the legionnaire spoke. "We must kill every
one of them. There can be no witnesses."

Vibenna spun around.

"You have taken leave of your senses!" he said, trying to keep his
voice as low as he could manage.

"It has to be every single one of them," the other persisted, "especially this old friend of yours. Nobody can be left behind."

Vibenna knew the sense of what he was being told, the cold, literal
truth of it. Killing was an easy act for him after so many years, and yet
now he could see only the objects of brutality—suffering, poor, ancient
human beings in most cases, those who had come to the village for the
final months or years of their lives.

And now we give them only death, he thought.

Vibenna suddenly felt sick, his face turning pale.

"We must—," the other legionnaire went on.

"Yes, yes!" Vibenna murmured. "I hear what you are saying."

He wrapped his fingers around the handle of the sword that had
been strapped to his side for all of his adult life.

"We should hurry!" admonished the other man.

"You seem so eager," Vibenna observed. "Are you entering into
this infamy because it is of tragic necessity or because you are eager to
slaughter the defenseless?"

The man avoided looking at him.

"Does it matter?" he replied. "Is not the end result all that has any
worth?"

Vibenna felt great sorrow then for this fellow soldier of Imperial
Rome.

How many are like this one? came the chilling thought. *How many*

266

exist only to satisfy their bloodlust cravings? What is to become of us if his kind are allowed to infest the battlefields that lie ahead?

He looked at his hands.

But am I any different? he asked himself. *What hypocrisy smothers my reason this day as I cast my scorn at this fellow soldier and ignore my own guilt?*

He stood up straight.

I must choose between the lives of these men and women or the outrage of my proconsul, my commander. There was a time when I would not have done the dishonorable and filthy deed that now I must!

He was wearing his full battle dress, with its Roman insignia.

But this empire, this Rome served by me so well for so long, has taken from me any innocence, any decency, any sympathy for the weak and the ill that once I might have had, for they are now the enemy, my enemy, if not of Rome itself, and they must be cut down.

Vibenna nodded at the other legionnaire, and both men grabbed hold of their swords as they emerged from the mountain pass.

L

Decimus Paetus sensed what was about to happen as he saw the stride of the stern-faced Marcus Vibenna and the legionnaire who was next to him, emerging after several minutes from the pass.

One-by-one, the villagers and the hired workers, along with Joseph of Arimathea, were taken aside by the legionnaires.

The group of the soldiers stood in front of the detainees.

Vibenna approached Paetus.

"This is all your doing!" he declared in a tone that chilled the other man. "Any blood that is shed must be laid at your feet, and your feet only."

"What will you tell your wife and your sons when you return to them after you leave the service of Rome?" Paetus asked sharply. "They will hang on your every word, after so long a time away from them. Will your stories be only of glorious battles whereby the enemy was defeated because of the bravery of yourself and men like you? Yet what about *this* moment, Marcus? How can you *ever* tell your family? That is impossible, of course, for they would never recognize the monster that it makes of you!"

Vibenna slapped him across the cheek with the back of his left hand, sending Paetus sprawling on the rocky ground.

"We *all* are monsters!" he said, losing some control of himself. "Is that not what I have heard this Nazarene and some of His apostles teach? We all have sinned, they say; we all come short of the glory of God."

He grunted as he added, "If such ravings are true, from the lips of God Himself, then the way I am should not surprise you, for what I do now, you also are capable of sometime, somewhere, at some other point in your miserable life! For how can either of us act otherwise if that is what we are, enslaved to our natures?"

"But you saw Him after He had arisen!" Paetus cried out. "How could you not fall on your knees before such a man?"

"What I saw—," Vibenna started to say, and then shook his head violently, not wanting to stir up those memories again.

He stood over Paetus, held the edge of his sword against his former comrade's throat.

"Kill them!" he shouted to the others. "Kill them all as I shall do to this traitorous swine who once fought side-by-side with us!"

Just then something *swooshed* through the air.

An arrow!

It entered Vibenna's shoulder and came out his back.

He groaned in pain and stumbled away from Paetus.

Other arrows rained down on the soldiers, but not before several of the villagers had been killed, along with one other individual.

Joseph of Arimathea.

He had been hit a glancing blow with a lance, and now his attacker was starting to jam it into his side.

Paetus lurched to his feet and grappled with the soldier. The two rolled over and over on the ground, Paetus closing his strong hands around the other man's head and twisting it sharply to one side, snapping his neck.

Joseph lay dying, his white garment rapidly being stained red.

Paetus dropped to his knees beside his friend.

"I have but one request," the old man muttered, his face contorted, one hand reaching out toward him.

"Anything within my power," Paetus told him.

"To lie where the Nazarene rested until His blessed resurrection —that is where I want to be put."

Joseph started coughing, blood seeping between his lips.

"Will you do this for an old man?" he pleaded.

"Yes, yes, I will," Paetus spoke.

He felt a hand on his shoulder.

Barabbas.

"You!" Paetus said, startled.

"I knew what they would do, those men of Rome who are supposed to be so very civilized. It was not something I could allow."

He looked at the fallen bodies of some of the villagers.

"I did not act in time to save all of them," he observed sadly. "That is a regret I shall carry with me to my grave."

"Joseph wants to—," Paetus said.

"I overheard," interrupted Barabbas. "This man may die before we can ever get him to where he wishes."

"But must we not try? I think we have to do at least that."

After hesitating briefly, Barabbas frowned as he replied, "You are right. The years have made me cruel. Forgive me for that."

He looked at poor, dying Joseph.

"It is far more dangerous for me than for you. But, of course, we are obliged to make the attempt. I will send four of my men with you, but

I can spare no more than that. Besides, the fewer the better—far less attention attracted that way."

Paetus nodded, patting the insurrectionist on the shoulder and thanking him.

"You spoke to me of the Nazarene," Barabbas reminded the other man. "We shall continue after you return."

"To here?"

"No, that cannot be. When these legionnaires do not return, they will be sought out. And this will be the first place Pontius Pilatus commands that they look. My men will help you settle elsewhere."

The old ones groaned nearly as a group when they were made aware of this.

"We came from nowhere," one of the old men shouted. "Where do we go now? With this place taken away from us, it will be only a matter of time until we must ply the dusty, lonely roads again, begging for food or a few coins from passersby."

"But you have no choice," Barabbas tried to reason with them. "You will be cut down for certain if—"

"We do," the old man replied. "We can stay right here, place ourselves at the mercy of the proconsul. He did try to release the Nazarene instead of Barabbas. He may be a moral coward, but he is not a man without some kind of feeling for the likes of us, you know."

"How do you know?" Barabbas probed.

"He has, from time to time, taken money from his own treasury and given it to us, or bought food with it, which he has had his private guard distribute."

"But who has heard of this?" Paetus interjected. "It is something unknown to me and others, I suspect."

"He wanted no recognition. It surely would mean that he risked becoming besieged by great masses of the poor, the elderly, the sick. He did not want that, for even he would have to spend every coin in trying to satisfy such numbers, and then there be left with nothing for himself."

"So you feel that, learning of this site, he might not elect to raze it to the ground and scatter all of you throughout the land? Barabbas asked.

"It is the one earthly hope we have! You yourself have become a wanderer over the years, driven from one corner of Judea to the other. We would be no different then if we were to join you. And you are still young, still strong, still able to bear the arduous life your rebellion has forced upon you."

"But what of the fallen bodies of the others, their deaths brought about by Pilatus's own men? What will you say to him about that, old man? Can you tell me—?"

He was interrupted by another voice.

Vibenna had stood, weakly, the arrow remaining in his shoulder.

"I will see to it that they are not harmed," he spoke. "It may be that Pontius Pilatus will allow this place to remain and not punish the innocent."

Barabbas walked over to him, every movement of his body and the expression on his face projecting his cynicism.

"And why are you given to this benevolence, may I speak, legionnaire?" he demanded.

"Because of him," Vibenna replied, pointing to Paetus, "because of what we experienced together the morning of the Nazarene's resurrection, as Christians have been calling it."

"And what do you say about it?" Barabbas asked.

"That *something* happened, yes, I will acknowledge that, for to say that it did not would be another kind of deception. I am not a man of faith, but whatever it was, whoever I saw, though I cannot understand or explain any of this, I also must confess that it was strange and not a little beautiful."

Those last words spread a hush throughout the village, even among the other legionnaires who were trying to stand—some wounded, others merely stunned.

"But you wanted to kill everyone here so that they would not be around to witness to the murder of that old woman and the old man who rushed to her side," Barabbas persisted, as yet unconvinced.

"The woman was hit accidentally by one of the other villagers," Vibenna told him. "The blame about her death cannot be laid at my feet, or my men's. But it is the old man, who had no part in this, who grieves me."

One of the women in the village shouted, "I will say nothing. If the rest of us agree, then we can no longer be called witnesses."

Upon hearing this, Paetus walked over to his former comrade, and asked him directly, "And what will you say?"

"I will blame all of it on the insurrectionist," Vibenna said.

Surprisingly, Barabbas did not object.

"I must lie every day," he spoke. "One more lie will not matter, I am sure."

Paetus was not comfortable with this.

"How can good come from deception?" he muttered. "Can a lie ever be—?"

"But, Decimus, it is my sin, and not yours," Vibenna reminded him. "Let this God of yours deal with me, if He does exist. Leave this place and think no more of it."

Though he was still disturbed, Paetus's attention was interrupted by the cries coming from Joseph.

"If we do not leave now," Barabbas said, "your friend has no chance of achieving what he wants."

Paetus nodded with great reluctance.

Barabbas waved over four men.

"You are to carry Joseph here where my friend Decimus tells you," he ordered. "Whatever he instructs you to do, consider that his words come from me. Is this understood?"

The four nodded, two of them bending down and starting to pick up Joseph as gently as they could.

"Not that way," Barabbas admonished them.

Then, turning to Paetus, he asked, "Do you have some material normally used for tents perhaps?"

"I think so!" Paetus exclaimed. "For a stretcher, no doubt?"

"For a stretcher, yes."

It took only minutes for one to be rigged up, makeshift though it was.

"Thank you . . ." Joseph said in a raspy voice that was growing ever weaker. "May the Lord bless you always."

Barabbas smiled as he replied, glancing briefly at Paetus, "If your friend here has his way, that may be what happens, old man."

LI

The little caravan was more than halfway to its destination when Joseph of Arimathea cried out in a sudden spasm of pain.

The two men carrying him on the stretcher stopped, gently laid him on the ground, and stepped aside.

Paetus sat next to Joseph.

"Can you go on?" he asked. "We could stop here. It is not helping you to be carried like this. No matter how careful—"

"I want to die where Jesus was put . . ." Joseph insisted. "I want to enter His kingdom at that very place."

"But that can happen anywhere," Paetus tried to convince him. "Why subject yourself to this extra strain?"

"I do not know. It is something in here telling me to go on. I pray that it is His Spirit guiding my way."

Joseph tapped his chest with a thin, vein-lined hand, the bones of which had been twisted by age.

"Can you understand me?" he asked. "Can you see why I must try?"

"We will go on then," Paetus agreed, greatly moved.

"I will tell you if I no longer think that I can make it," Joseph said.

And so they continued on, until hours later they approached Jerusalem and the Place of the Skull.

Golgotha.

All were tired.

And Joseph himself was but minutes away from death.

He had not spoken for some time, had not moved to any extent. More than once, Paetus thought that he had died along the way, but then, examining him closely and seeing that the old man was still breathing, Paetus sighed with relief that he yet hung on to life, though that very life was surely leaving him moment by moment.

The roads were primitive since the conquering Romans had done little to impose on Israel any of the physical improvements they customarily made in a country ruled by them. The Romans had little appreciation for Jewish culture and no desire to spend the money and effort needed to make the land more "civilized," with the exception of the palatial residences for proconsuls such as Pontius Pilatus.

So the way the little party of six men traveled was clouded in the coarse dust kicked by their feet, their discomfort compounded by the heat of midday.

Finally though they saw Golgotha just ahead of them and walked around the side of that hill, often misnamed "mount," and came upon their destination.

The tomb.

Only a few feet away.

Paetus stood without moving, his thoughts going back to that night years before.

And then the night sky seemed to open up.

Light poured forth over Golgotha.

And they saw a multitude of iridescent creatures with transparent wings coming in a vast wave!

Golgotha and the land for miles all around them was filled with countless numbers of these beings until the scene was like that of daylight, bright almost to the point of blinding the legionnaires.

Then came the voices, the most beautiful that Paetus had heard in his lifetime . . .

"If only that could happen now, when I would be able to appreciate it far, far more," he said, though low enough that no one could hear him.

Joseph's eyes opened after being closed for nearly two hours.

"We are here," he said weakly, "we are here . . ."

He struggled to lift himself from the stretcher.

"Praise His holy name . . . ," the old man spoke.

"We will carry you to the entrance and—," Paetus tried to tell him.

"No!" Joseph exclaimed. "I will walk to it and go inside of my own accord."

"You cannot! You are far too weak to do so. You have lost a great amount of blood. You will not be able to—"

"Help me up, please."

Paetus knew that any argument, no matter how sensible, would be futile. So, after the stretcher had been lowered, he and one of Barabbas's men assisted Joseph to his feet, prepared to stand on either side of him.

"I will go alone," that tired, weak old voice told them.

Joseph was standing, unaided, but barely so.

He started toward the still open tomb.

One inch at a time, he approached the entrance.

"Blessed Savior," he said. "Take me now, I beg of Thee, into Thy presence. This my tomb which was turned over to Your incarnate form must now be where I will lie at last but only for an instant, I pray."

274

He paused at the semicircular entranceway, leaning against it, nearly all his strength spent. Paetus rushed over to him.

"Let me help," he said.

"Yes, I think I shall need your help after all, dear friend," Joseph admitted.

A second or two later, they both were inside.

"That was where Nicodaemus and I put Him," the old man spoke. "We carried His body from the top of this hill and down the side. He was not very heavy, you know. To touch that flesh, to feel how cold it was, no beating of His heart, no—"

He started crying unashamedly.

"We felt so lost then, so terribly sad, forsaken, momentarily forgetting what He had promised with such great passion," he went on, his voice oddly sounding stronger. "The very faith my friend and I once had seemed to *end* . . . oh, how awful that was . . . at the entrance to this merciless place. We had the Nazarene's flesh and bones in our hands, the breath of life having vanished, and nothing else seemed as real, as irrefutable as that."

He pointed to the stone slab to their right.

"I took that precious head of His and Nicodaemus the feet, and we laid Him for a few moments on the ground where you and I stand now before putting Him there," he said. "We each had a basket of burial spices and ointments with us, and we rubbed His body with those after cleaning Him of blood and other fluids as best as we could. I am quite sure we both missed some spots, especially at His side, but the wound there was so very ugly that neither of us had the willpower to approach it."

Now it was Paetus who could do nothing about the tears that started flowing.

"And it was I who made that wound," he sobbed. "I took my lance and jammed it up into Him and . . . and—"

He covered his face with his hands, his entire body shaking.

"But you are forgiven . . ." came words as to a man in a desert for whom a single cup of water was a precious offering.

"Yes, I know. But the memory is still there. How can I ever rid myself of that image? How can I—?"

He felt a hand on his shoulder.

"Because the Father has commanded it, Decimus Paetus."

His eyes shot open.

Joseph had crumpled to the floor of the tomb.

"Who spoke?" Paetus asked. "Who touched my shoulder just now?"

The interior was small, with no place for anyone to hide.

He sat next to Joseph, whose heart was yet beating.

"Did you hear?" he asked.

"Yes . . . and I saw . . ." Joseph murmured.

"Was it He?" Paetus implored.

The old man smiled as he spoke, "It was He, my brother . . . I see Him even now . . . surrounded by angels. I can hear the music they make, the hosannas they sing in overflowing joy!"

Joseph's eyes sparkled in witness of a scene that Paetus could not share.

"They are rejoicing over *me!*" he exclaimed. "They are saying my voice, again and again, all of heaven in exultation!"

His eyelids closed, and his body went limp.

Paetus bent over him, an inch from his chest, trying to hear a heartbeat. He thought for a moment that he detected one, and then it was gone, a single sigh escaping that frail body.

"Oh, Lord!" Paetus cried out as he extended his arms in front of him. "I hunger for a glimpse of Thee again as You have granted me before. I was shrouded in my unbelief then, but now that is no longer so. Let me see just a measure of what this old man has seen, and I shall be content for the remainder of my days."

Suddenly, as he looked toward the entrance, he saw the round stone being rolled across it and then stopping!

All light was sealed out.

He was now in total darkness.

"What is it that you want to tell me, Lord?" Paetus asked, his eyes darting from side to side. "What is it that I am to see in this place?"

He stood as straight as he could, his head just touching the rough-hewn ceiling.

Cold.

A wave of cold seemed to sweep through the tomb, chilling every inch of his body, even to the extent of making his teeth chatter unstoppably.

And then heat pummeled him, drenching his skin in perspiration.

Paetus stopped hugging himself and extended his arms.

"What is it that I am to know, Lord?" he begged.

Sounds next.

He heard these unmistakably, the sounds of a great battle, men dying, their cries rising up in great, swelling waves, not unlike what he had heard often before, during his service to Imperial Rome, a crashing, discordant symphony of death.

And then something else.

Flames.

276

Their crackling, hissing cacophony was also familiar, for he had seen whole villages belonging to the enemy of the moment, whoever and wherever that happened to be, burned to the ground by his fellow legionnaires and himself, as they stood by afterward and raised their clenched fists in a show of triumph, a roar of self-acclamation accompanying this sudden gesture.

"I do not want to be reminded of what once was, Lord," he said as he stumbled to the entrance, and tried somehow to push the stone away.

I cannot, he thought, *and yet for Jesus it was thrust aside as though it were a tiny pebble.*

He stopped, turned around, closed his eyes, his head throbbing, echoes of those sounds of battle still inside his brain, not so easily extinguished, hanging on like unwelcome phantoms.

"Not the past . . . ," he thought he heard someone speak.

His eyelids shot open.

"Tell me the rest of it, Lord," he entreated.

But there was nothing further, the voice silent, the sounds gone, the cold dissipated, and he was alone with the body of Joseph of Arimathea as the four men outside finally rolled the large stone aside, and saw him on his knees, praying for a answer that God in His wisdom withheld at that time and in that place.

Part VI

*P*ontius Pilatus personally headed the regiment of soldiers whose mission was to surround the village site and seal off the escape of any criminals who might have remained there. All he did find upon his arrival were the villagers themselves along with the surviving legionnaires, including Marcus Vibenna.

As it turned out, Vibenna was required to say very little, either truth or lies, Pilatus immediately surmising out loud that an ambush was responsible for the toll of dead and wounded and that the ragged band of largely old people had been caught in the middle, for they could hardly have been of use to one side or the other.

None of the other legionnaires contradicted this assessment, for it freed them of any complicity in starting the violence that had occurred. But it was not only that that made them feel relieved. In the interim, those civilians who were able attended to the wounded and witnessed to them of Jesus the Christ. As a result, a mighty reconciling spirit was felt by everyone.

Vibenna had prepared himself to present an impassioned appeal to the proconsul about maintaining the village in its present state but even this proved unnecessary. Alerted to what had happened, Nicodaemus, though gripped by intense grief over what had happened to Joseph of Arimathea, managed to get to Pilatus before the proconsul's trip to the village, guaranteeing his own continued sponsorship of the settlement.

With this in mind, Pilatus agreed to let the villagers remain and, additionally, to include a regular patrol of the site in the event any special needs were present to which he could attend, upon being advised of these. It was unlikely, he decided, that Barabbas would ever return, so capturing him at the site was no longer a motivation.

But there was more.

The next day, inexplicably, Pilatus, without entreaty on the part of anyone, sent a very large supply of fresh fruit and vegetables, along with various materials that could be used to fashion new garments for the entire group of villagers and several ointments and salves to help them with infections and the like.

As the population of the village grew to rather substantial numbers, the proconsul went on to handpick men who were experienced in irrigation and other practical matters, to ensure that the water supply was consistent and that the ability of the villagers to raise crops and be self-sustaining would never diminish, even though that meant bringing some of these experts, at consider-

able expense, from Rome itself. More than one of them happened to be serving on the staff of the emperor himself, but Pilatus encountered no resistance.

Women were taught to card and spin wool, dye the threads, and weave them on vertical looms. Old and new clothes were trod in the nearby Jordan. Several of the men had been potters, and their old, long-dormant skills gradually surfaced again. Using red clay, they became busy making various items, such as pots and dishes and pottery for other commonplace needs.

On several occasions, near Jerusalem and at Caesarea, while the proconsul and Nicodaemus met alone, such meetings in themselves a departure from the proconsul's routine, Nicodaemus tried to get some indication from the man as to what was behind these displays of generosity, so unusual as they were. No answers were ever given by the proconsul and the subject was always changed to something altogether different.

Though deeply curious, Nicodaemus nevertheless failed in his mission of discovery each time and, ultimately, gave up, not wanting to risk alienating such a man or spoiling the rapport that had been growing between them.

And in Rome, so many miles away, the mad wife of the proconsul, oddly inclined as he was toward such paradoxical behavior, continued her forced isolation from the rest of the world until the day Fabius Scipio came upon her.

A dozen years later, after Caligula was assassinated and following the rather beneficent reign of Claudius, the worst of all the emperors, assumed the throne of Imperial Rome, accelerating events that would lead directly to a fortress known as Masada . . .

LII

Fabius Scipio got to Rome without mishap and found that, using the set of papers dealing with the financial and related matters—including letters of introduction—left for him by Quintus Egnatius Javolenus Tidus Germanicus, he had no difficulty locating and paying for a residence with a full complement of servants, starting out with a veteran cook, two maids, and three gardeners—the latter needed because of the lush growth on the property, which was relatively small but well-furnished with green plants, flowers, vines, and trees.

But increasingly he was under conviction about this, thinking that a Christian who had been freed from slavery to sin and damnation could not ask another man or woman to be in subjection to him.

So, he set the slaves free only a few months after his arrival, but not before he had gotten to know them reasonably well and had listened to stories from them about the lives they had led with other slave masters.

The cook told Scipio of one occasion when he produced a meal that his previous master disliked, calling it substandard. The not-at-all-rare punishment: being stripped of his clothes and subjected to a flogging in front of the dinner guests until blood ran down his back. Another slave had escaped anything like that but told of her sister who had been clumsy with a water pot and who was taken to the back of her master's residence and brutalized with a long, sharp hairpin. Another of the slaves now with Scipio would have to carry a set of scars on his forehead that spelled "FUG" for the word "fugitivus."

Slaves who were confined to work in a city such as Rome or one of the towns in the Italian countryside, as rough as their lives proved to be, had it considerably better than those who labored in the fields or the mines, many of whom were worked to death, those in the countryside through bringing in crops for marketing by their owners and those in the mines through hunger and exposure to freezing temperatures as they dug out lead, iron, copper, and silver.

But one of them had worked for the distinguished Seneca, whose philosophy was quite different from that of the majority of other Romans. "Please reflect that the man you call your slave was born of the same seed, has the same good sky above him, breathes the air you do, lives as you do, and dies as you do," he would tell those whom he managed to get to listen to him. "Treat your slave with kindness and with courtesy too; let him share your various conversations, your deliberations, and your company."

After being with Seneca for a number of years, that slave was released,
only to become a slave again when he found himself starving in the streets.

At this slave's instigation, four of the six individuals offered to stay on
with Scipio for a reasonable wage, the other two simply desiring to return to
their families in northern Italy.

★ ★ ★

The Rome Fabius Scipio encountered had changed from what he had remembered from brief visits during his youth. With Gaius Julius Caesar Germanicus at the helm of empire, the Roman treasury was close to bankruptcy. Everyday discussion about this beast nicknamed Caligula came down to a tripartite question: Was he mad, bad, or ill?

One aspect of his behavior was not debatable: his unbridled sexual appetite, though the second emperor after him, Lucius Domitius Aheno-barbus Nero, made Caligula seem almost spartan in comparison.

The supposed morality and decency of any earlier period of Rome's rulers and Roman life had been giving way for some time. Caligula's assumption of the throne was but a precursor of what was to follow, hastening the eradication of conscience and temperance even as concepts among the aristocracy of the ancient city.

And yet how decent had the Romans been, at some previous stage in their history? The growing Christian community, some of whom were historians, would not call their earthly rulers decent at all, by any standards that they, as followers of Jesus the Christ, would tolerate. For Christians were confronted by a society that was supposed to be lauded because it sanctioned an emperor or a senator or anyone else from the highest levels of Roman life having a wife and "only" one mistress, but if he had two mistresses, and it was discovered, he was condemned.

Prior to the advent of Christianity, this marital standard was considered circumspect, for it had the virtue of avoiding the excesses of a thoroughly promiscuous lifestyle.

But from the Christian standpoint, to have even a single woman as a sexual partner other one's wife was a sin in the eyes of Almighty God. Adultery and the Roman tolerance of "boy toys" for men so inclined brought cries of outrage from the Nazarene's increasingly large circle of converts, not to mention the convert's condemnation of the many gods worshiped by Romans at every level of society.

Any growth in the numbers of Christians represented a growth in the potential influence of this sect. While there were few of them, they were of little consequence and could be ignored, more suited to snide comments at banquets or at the communal baths where their spartan view of life was derided.

Later, though, this was no longer the case, and even if they gained no real governmental sway, the doctrines they were spreading threatened the lifestyles of those who put the pursuit of sexual pastimes at the very center of their existence.

Scipio, though still a virgin, was all-too-familiar with the erotic antics of other legionnaires. But, naively, he had always chalked these up to the randy nature of men kept away from their hometown women for long periods of time and therefore desperate for some kind of sexual gratification. Homosexual conduct, however, was not tolerated among legionnaires to the extent that it was in civilian Roman society.

Any such activity could result in punishment that was nothing less than severe, since the legions were the pride of an essentially masculine Rome, and intercourse between men was considered counterproductive.

Yet Fabius Scipio, still a young man, witnessed, and at times overheard, as he began to live within the environs of Rome itself, behavior that frequently seemed extreme and offensive, even by battlefield standards, particularly now that his sensibilities were no longer purely Roman but largely Christian.

One aspect of the conduct of the privileged came to his attention when he left his own residence on a quiet little street near the Forum to see someone who Germanicus said would be helpful to him.

Her name was Tullia, married to Gaius Gallienus, one of the wealthy men at the center of Roman society, whose governmental contacts were extraordinary.

Both of them, wife and husband, had become Christians.

Germanicus, before his conversion, had expressed contempt of what they had done, especially since they were continually writing to him and trying to get him to become a follower of the Nazarene, as they now were.

"Tullia and Gaius will be delighted to learn of my decision to take their advice and submit to that for which they have been pleading for longer than any of us undoubtedly can remember," Germanicus's note announced. "Give them my love, Fabius. They have been sympathetic to the plight of this bastard-child for many years. Their sensitivities were, I think, Christian for a very long time before they ever invited Him into their lives."

Scipio had been able to purchase a *biga,* a small chariot pulled by two horses. Germanicus's fortune actually provided him with the financial ability to go all the way up to a *quadriga,* a much larger chariot and one that required twice the number of horses, but a combination of his soldiering days with his period of being a traveling disciple for the Nazarene had taught Scipio the need for frugality, and he was determined to follow these lessons throughout the course of the rest of his life.

The residence he sought was near the outskirts of Rome, where more land was available and numerous estates thus had been built. He found it without difficulty and stopped the horses directly in front.

It was one of the more elaborate private buildings he had seen, though all Roman homes seemed to have more or less the same design. The front had been partitioned and divided into cubicles of various sizes, each one a place of business run by a different merchant, with wares ranging from leather items to pottery and some bakery goods.

Walking through an entranceway in the middle, between the shops, he approached the atrium area in front, with its *impluvium*, a pool that collected rainwater coming in through a large opening in the roof called a *compluvium*.

Scipio was greeted by a quite dignified-looking elderly male servant who guided him through the *tablinum*, a reception room of sorts, and into the *peristyle*, a bright and cheery open-air space at the rear of the house, essentially a pleasant little garden with a small fountain in the middle.

As soon as he entered, he witnessed, on a stone bench at the far end, a sight for which he was not prepared: a quite beautiful woman with very long blonde hair not curled upward and sitting on the top of her head, as was the custom for women in Rome at that time, but flowing over her shoulders.

Her eyes, he thought. *Her blue eyes . . . she is so at peace!*

Scipio stopped, captivated by the rest of her appearance—the delicate cheekbones, the pale skin, the tiny, perfectly formed nose.

She must be Tullio, he told himself, with some appreciation. *I shall be very glad to meet her formally in a moment or two.*

Then, looking more closely, he saw what she was doing out in the open, as naturally as the sunshine that caught her doll-like face in its glow.

Nursing a baby.

It was hardly this that embarrassed him, but rather, that after she had nursed the one baby and it was taken away, another was brought to her a second or two later, and she commenced giving her milk to it as well.

Curious, thinking that she must have been the mother of twins, Scipio stood back, not wishing to interrupt her. But finally, as she was finishing with the second little one, and Scipio was ready to step forward to introduce himself, armed with Germanicus's letter, he saw that yet a third was brought to her, and another after that.

Such a large family, he remarked to himself, as he considered, wistfully, his own unmarried status. *How happy she and her husband must be!*

Finally the suckling had to be stopped, for he heard the woman complain that her nipples were becoming sore.

Each baby had been brought by a different female servant. He overheard the last one tell her, "Will you feel like others tomorrow?"

The woman with the long hair smiled sweetly as she remarked, "If Jesus gives me more milk, I shall."

"I am sorry that so many of us have young babies at this one time," the servant told her. "You must become very tired."

"There will be a day when I have no more to give. Whatever I have until then is yours, for as long as you wish."

Scipio rubbed his eyes as well as his ears.

This fragile-looking female before him was allowing the children of *other* couples to feed freely from her breasts!

He was so startled by this that he stumbled over a small rock and tripped, falling forward onto his face.

The woman gasped and stood, ready to rush back into her home and plead urgently for help, fearing the intentions of any intruder, especially at a time when lawlessness was generally increasing.

"Please—do not be afraid!" Scipio called out. "I have a letter from Quintus—a letter of introduction. It is for you, Tullio Gallienus."

She hesitated, still uncertain, but then, seeing Scipio as he stood, how handsome he was, well-groomed, hardly someone who looked like a common robber from the streets or the countryside, she replied, "If that dear man has sent you, as you say, then, stranger, you are welcome in this home."

Scipio's amazement over the sight of the wife of a wealthy aristocrat nursing her servants' young babies must have shown through in the expression on his face, for Tullio started laughing rather uproariously.

He blushed, realizing that there was much he did not know about customs and such within upper-crust Roman society.

"It is something that we are expected to do, women like myself," she said, trying to make him feel less awkward at the same time she calmed herself down. "It establishes a bond with our servants and with their children, so that they all have a natural affection for the members of my own family."

As he stepped forward at last, Tullio added, "It does not embarrass me that you have seen this. It has always been one of the privileges God gives us as women, surely nothing to be ashamed of."

Her manner in the presence of a stranger continued to be so nonchalant, so sweet-natured, that Scipio began to feel at ease far more quickly than he could have imagined under the circumstances.

LIII

Fabius Scipio became very much at ease with Tullio and Gaius Gallienus. And they felt the same with him.

"There is something about our faith that makes brothers and sisters of strangers," spoke Gaius, a large, muscular man, who seemed in stark contrast to his small, delicate-looking wife. "But then I sense that this spirit of community felt between us will be very necessary over the coming years."

The three had finished, moments ago, a dinner that was certainly the very best Scipio had eaten in some time, even better than what Germanicus and he had shared. There was no meat, due to a scarcity of cattle in those days, with the animals used primarily to work the fields and not to be eaten. But figpeckers and roebucks were in great demand, and both were on the table that first evening. The provided vegetables were cardoons, rutabagas, mallow, chicory—and a plentiful pile of mushrooms as well.

"I remember what Martial said," Gaius Gallienus remarked. "It is easy to send a gift of silver or gold, a cloak or a toga; but it is difficult to send mushrooms."

Scipio nodded in agreement, not having had the delicacy for years.

His hosts included as part of the cheeses those that were made from the milk of younger goats and sheep and brought in from Vestino and Trebula, as well as a particularly fine Etrurian variety from Luni and a smoked cheese from the Velabrum, all of these regions in close proximity to Rome itself.

But no meal served in a household of aristocrats truly fit the description of *av ovo usque ad malum* unless a multitude of fruits were on the menu, and Tullio had made certain that pomegranates, azarolres, quinces, and mulberries were on the table, together with cherries from the Black Sea, apricots from Armenia, peaches from Persia, as well as muskmelons from a farm they owned that was only a few miles away.

"What we have here is wonderful," Gallienus observed, sighing with slightly exaggerated contentment, "but since we have become Christians, somehow little of it—the food, our property, our slaves, whatever else that we possess of the good things of our station in life—seems to hold our affections anymore."

He had just finished dipping his fingers in a bowl of lemon water and was passing the bowl to his guest.

"Have you ever felt that way?" he asked.

"Yes, I have," Scipio acknowledged. "I have never had the abundance that is yours but I began to feel my outlook changing in more ways than one."

"Tell me about this, Fabius, if you please."

Scipio nodded agreeably.

"I am able to deal with lust more effectively," he replied. "I no longer feel that I must have a woman, and I will not have one until God shows me who it should be."

"No sex outside of marriage then?" Gallienus probed.

"Not even for one night or a single hour."

The other man groaned.

"What is it?" Scipio asked.

"My life before the Nazarene took up residence within it . . . ," Gallienus muttered, his voice trailing off momentarily.

Tullio came back from the kitchen area just then, after making sure that everything was tidied up properly. She had a passion for cleanliness, and yet the way foods were cooked in those days—charcoal stored in an arch under a hearth, with small fires shooting through holes on top—produced considerable smoke and grease, running counter to her goal of having a spotless kitchen as much as she could help it.

"I am amazed at how filthy Caligula's kitchen is," she remarked after rejoining them. "But then it may be that it is but a mirror to his soul!"

Her husband grimaced at the recollection.

"No one would eat in the palace if they knew the truth," he said.

"You were talking with great seriousness when I intruded," Tullio observed. "Please continue."

"I was starting to share with our brother here some of what my life, dearest, was like before Christ."

"And mine too," she reminded him. "I was very much a part of that."

Scipio looked intently at this woman, who seemed to embody only innocence and decency, and he could not imagine someone such as she ever living any sort of life that was decadent in any respect.

Tullio saw the expression of disbelief that he failed to mask.

"I know what you are thinking," she said, chuckling. "But, it is true, my husband and I were once very much the products of well-bred Roman social mores."

The two of them went on to tell the story of how Tullio had been little better than a prostitute, Gallienus's secret weapon in his dealings with senators and others.

"I made her available to so many," he whispered.

"And I chose to obey my husband's wishes, no matter what this involved," she added, her cheeks taking on a reddish hue as she recalled the levels of depravity to which she once had lowered herself. "We wanted 'opportunities' and we got a great many of these because I was very good at what I did."

Gallienus reached out and took her hand in his own.

"And I was not above being 'available' to a few who were uninterested in women," he said. "Tullio and I had to be careful about our behavior. Everything we did needed to be in a discreet manner. Word could not be allowed to get out, you know. We were successful at this, and my influence grew along with my wealth."

Tears were streaking Tullio's smooth cheeks.

"It made salvation all the more miraculous," she went on. "We had done so very much that we eventually saw as repulsive to a holy God, and yet, even with all that filth, nothing stood in the way of our acceptance by Him through His Son."

"What were the circumstances?" Scipio asked.

Tullio and Gaius Gallienus launched into some personal recollections that were among the most remarkable Scipio had ever heard.

"We enjoyed the games," both admitted. "Watching them was an obsession that it seemed we could not break."

He cleared his throat before continuing: "From time to time, we would stage miniature versions of these at our home, with two gladiators fighting to the death in front of dozens of dinner guests. The bloodier it became, the more they would eat and drink! And when one of the gladiators was finally victorious, most of the guests would get to their feet, waving some food still clutched between their fingers and cheering mightily."

We both enjoyed the games . . .

This man and his wife were not alone, for in the gladiators were symbolized what was called "the sorrows of the Romans," their acknowledgment of an innate bloodlust in their natures, together with a hopelessness that provoked an "eat, drink, and be merry" philosophy that was becoming pervasive.

"Man is killed for the pleasure of man," Gallienus spoke. "To be able to kill is a skill, an employment, an art. The gladiator undergoes a discipline to shed blood, and when he does kill, it is a glory. They adorn themselves for death, and, miserable as they are, they even glory in their sufferings."

He winced, a variety of emotions playing across his face.

"Each gladiator is obliged to repeat a binding oath that has been the *sacramentum gladiatorium*."

"What were they pledging?" Scipio asked.

"*Uri, vinciri, vernerari, ferroque necari patior*," Gallienus replied solemnly. "To be burned, bound, beaten, and slain by the sword." It is a point of honor among them that they die eventually. To die is an act that will endear them to the gods."

"Is it so different from what our generals pledge on fields of battle?" Scipio suggested. "In the *devotio*, they will consecrate themselves to a violent death at the hands of the enemy and to the *dii inferi*."

The *dii inferi*—gods of the underworld—those demonic entities who were part of the landscape of Roman religious worship.

"Very astute, Fabius. But there is a major difference. As far as the gladiator is concerned, the crowds gathering for a spectacle of blood and pain and death are not his enemies. For he is but their servant, giving them what they crave; and in so doing, he finds his own fulfillment, whatever the costs of purchasing that fulfillment."

Gladiators were trained in schools and always they were given a specific admonition: "What difference will it make if you gain a few more days or years by avoiding your duty? We are born into a world in which no quarter is given."

Gallienus leaned back in his chair.

Tullio spoke up then.

"We shouted as loud as anyone: 'Kill him, beat him, burn him!' And we spoke among ourselves: 'Why does he run on the steel too timidly? Why does he slay with so little verve? Why is he such a miser about dying?'"

"What changed you?" Scipio asked.

"Scaevola was the start of it," Gallienus responded. "We had always admired this remarkable man, as well as his father who was an eminent orator and jurist and the teacher of Cicero. But then even this fine man, with such a wonderful heritage, came to be seduced, to a degree, by what was going on with those barbaric games."

Tullio stood slowly and proceeded to walk back and forth in that large, rectangular dining room.

"Absentmindedly, I left in the open the scroll upon which contained a statement he had written, a statement favoring the games, one that compared them to slavery, in the sense that dying before a crowd while fighting your opponent was preferable to any slavery," she said. "One of the women whose child you saw me nursing came upon it and in the process of gathering it up, noticed those words which I had specially marked. She was disturbed by them, greatly so, and came to me to assure me that the slaves believe them not, that a great man such as Scaevola was terribly wrong, and that she did not consider having my husband and I as masters worse than dying during the bloody games."

Tullio stopped pacing.

"I was moved by the woman's words," she confessed. "And I was disturbed that Seneca would become so debased that he could not see such a twisted difference between serving as a slave and as a gladiator. It is true that there are some cruel masters, but it is not true that all are beasts degrading those whom they own."

"Sit down, my dear," Gallienus asked. "Let me put my arm around you, and we shall share this pain. Will you do that for me, please?"

Tullio nodded, and once again she occupied the chair beside her husband.

"A curious conviction came over both of us," he continued. "What that man stated gnawed at both of us, the awful corruption it showed of one so intelligent, so given to the most beautiful writings and profoundest musings, who was now doing little more than ennobling the cruelest of carnage.

"But if his words on a mere scroll given to the privileged spoke loudly of his debasement, then our actions every bit as well, for we were at every game, for we shouted until our voices were hoarse, for we voted our support by our obvious presence. Were we not guilty of the same debasement as Scaevola?"

Gallienus felt Tullio trembling and put his arm around her shoulders.

"We attended what would prove to be our final game," he said, "just two days before we fell prostrate before Almighty God and begged Him to pay heed to our cries."

"What happened?" Scipio asked, fascinated.

"We were leaving and saw one of the carts where the bodies of the dead gladiators were tossed. Tullio thought she heard someone crying. We both stopped walking and listened; then I too noticed the sounds.

"It was coming from among that miserable pile of bodies. We realized that one of the gladiators was not quite dead and rushed over to the very large slave who was about to close up the sides of the cart and jump onto the back of the horse assigned to pull it to its destination—a grave site of sorts, where bodies were burned and their ashes dumped into a large hole that was rapidly filling up.

"You cannot leave," I demanded of him. "One of the fighters still lives." This ox of a man looked at me, at Tullio, saw our fine clothes, and surely thought that we were accusing him of negligence. Showing his fear, he inspected the bodies with great haste, and found the one that was yet breathing.

"Then this slave swiftly took a long-bladed knife from a sheath attached to his waist. The poor gladiator's eyes opened for an instant, and he had time to utter only seven words: *Dear Savior . . . please receive my soul now.* Hesitating less than a second perhaps, the burly-looking slave slit his throat in one cut with that knife and returned the weapon to its sheath, the blade quite bloody."

Gallienus banged his fists down on the white marble dinner table.

"I assaulted him, Fabius. I reached out and grabbed him by the neck and knocked him to the ground, despite his greater size, and beat him. He dare not raise a hand against me, for to do that to someone such as myself would mean long imprisonment for him, possibly torture and, not inconceivably, his own death.

"Tullio finally succeeded in getting me to step away from him. And then the two of us hurried back home, though we did not sleep that entire night but just sat in bed, shivering in one another's arms."

Neither Gallienus or Tullio spoke again until several minutes had passed. Scipio waited patiently, understanding the depths of what they were recounting and the newly stirred emotions that were surfacing.

"Two days later, through the efforts of an apostle named Stephen, someone my wife and I met periodically become a Christian. A cousin of one of the more prominent senators, this acquaintance of ours saw that Tullio and I were deeply troubled and took it upon himself to tell us of the faith that had altered his life forever."

A slight smile curled up the edges of his lips.

"Tullio and I were vulnerable then and we surrendered to what he was telling us, becoming Christians in a matter of minutes."

The anger and revulsion Gallienus had felt was passing and he opened his clenched hands, resting the backs of them on the table, Tullio doing likewise.

"Will you join us in prayer, our brother?" he asked.

Smiling with obvious appreciation, Scipio bowed his head as he moved to their side of the table and joined hands with both.

The three of them did not stop praying until the first light of morning.

LIV

Through his new friends, Fabius Scipio met a number of other Christians in Rome and also the provinces. Meetings had to be held in secret, usually at night, since Caligula still ruled, an emperor with a special loathing for anyone who followed the Nazarene, though persecution during his decadent reign did not compare with what was to come some twenty years later during the period when Nero was in power.

"Why?" Scipio asked one evening at the now-familiar home of Tullio and Gaius Gallienus. "What is there about us that makes him feel as he does?"

"We are a reminder of all that he is by virtue of what we are," Tullio told him. "Where there is darkness and depravity, he stands in the midst of it, reveling in strange flesh. In the distance, he hears our voices calling him like dreaded sirens, trying to pull him away from such decadence. He hears, yes, but he refuses to listen, and yet the voices do not stop.

"He realizes that even within his own palace there are Christians. He can sense this. He can feel their eyes locking upon him, passing a judgment upon him that he knows he deserves. If he is able to find out their identity, he would banish them from his presence."

"Some say that he is a brilliant man," Scipio observed, fascinated by the intelligence of the woman at a time when wives and lovers and mothers were seldom given much credit for having any abilities in areas other than the bedroom and the kitchen.

"He may be as you say," Tullio replied, "but it is a mind that has been ruled by debauchery for so long and so intently that he knows little else. His life is the pursuit of pleasure, nothing more."

"Together with the need for power, my dear," Gallienus reminded her.

"Power is but another pleasure for this man," she suggested. "For with it, he pursues greater abandonment of restraint. Power liberates him to do whatever he wants, while making him a slave to his passions."

"I wonder how much longer Caligula is to be in power," Scipio speculated. "Can the Senate tolerate his depravity for very much longer?"

"Some within the Senate are a part of that depravity," Gallienus observed. "Yet many more cling to the faded dream of Roman idealism, which we all know was a myth in the first place. But it is *their* myth, so long believed that it seems like reality. And they see it dissipating before their eyes the longer this obscenity named Caligula rules."

They were sitting on pillows that had been placed on the bare floor of a room at the rear of the large residence. Tullio reached over to a small, round, teakwood table next to her and retrieved a little parchment.

"Suetonius has recently written, 'There is nobody in all of Rome —however low his rank and condition—whose happiness has not been disturbed by Caligula,'" she read carefully. "'Who can avoid great inner turmoil as to what is portended for the future when made aware of the depths to which this creature of madness sinks with wild cries of unfettered ecstasy, often arising not from healthy intercourse alone but from acts of such cruelty and sadism as to make the very gods of darkness recoil.'"

Scipio had already heard elsewhere of one such instance. A noted playwright who had written a single line of double entendre in Caligula's regard was burned alive, but his cries were so pathetic that even Caligula could not endure them, so he ordered that the man's tongue be ripped out of his mouth before the fire had spread beyond his legs up through his torso; and then Caligula continued sitting through the rest of the spectacle, watching as the blackened figure writhed in final agonies.

"How long do we remain silent?" Gallienus spoke. "By being quiet about our beliefs, do we not let Caligula assume that he has no opposition?"

"It is not our duty to oppose tyrants—save one," Scipio countered. "It is only Satan we are to resist so that he flees from us."

"But in Caligula we have a man who is living the life of the damned, I suspect, with demons instead of angels at his side. Does not Satan work through human emissaries, and can there be any doubt that the emperor is one of these?"

"We are told to be in subjection to the government, Gaius, to render to Caesar that which is his. Caligula is the latest Caesar. We have no choice."

Gallienus could not accept this notion.

"If we sit back and do nothing," he said, raising his voice, "letting evil run like a roaring pride of quite ravenous lions throughout the land, whom do we serve then?"

Scipio hesitated, then said, "Our concern is for the human soul. There is to be no other mission for us."

"But I think that God wants us to use our good judgment," Gallienus replied. "How many *unredeemed* souls are we condemning to eternal punishment by conducting our little meetings behind closed doors and letting the rest of the world suffer the grotesque behavior of someone who views death as part of a game for his personal fulfillment, perverse that it is?

"When the victims of Caligula die without accepting Jesus the

Christ as their Savior, their Lord, they will spend eternity with beasts like the very one responsible for their deaths. That thought is so repellent I cannot believe for an instant that it reflects even the tiniest part of what God could possibly intend."

Tullio had been silent for a bit, her head cocked to one side, her eyes closed, listening to the conversation between her husband and their new friend.

Finally she spoke, when there was a lull, and said, "This creature will be taken from us soon, and we will have some peace for awhile."

"That sounds like a prophecy," Gallienus told her, his manner not altogether serious.

"Can women tell of the future?" she replied with some sarcasm. "I thought the only prophets were men."

. . . and we will have some peace for awhile.

Scipio repeated those words in his mind.

"Is that what you have given us, Tullio?" he asked. "Has Almighty God entered your soul and passed to you some precious word?"

Her voice softened almost to a whisper.

"Perhaps not God Himself, I think," she said. "It was but a touch . . . I felt no more than a touch just then."

"What sort of touch?" Gallienus inquired, puzzled about such a comment from someone who was usually direct and clear in what she said.

"It was as though the wing of an angel brushed my cheek."

Scipio remembered his encounter at the tomb.

"They are quite beautiful," he spoke eagerly, happy for a reason to enlighten them. "I have seen a few, you know."

"Tell me about them," Tullio asked, a curious urgency present in her voice. "Tell us what you can, dear Scipio."

Scipio recounted what he had witnessed at Golgotha, and both were spellbound by his description. Then he went on to reveal the experience Decimus Paetus and he had had years earlier in the upper room of a little inn where not many days before the last earthly supper had been shared by the Nazarene and His apostles.

"How blessed you have been!" Tullio exclaimed. "How very blessed!"

She brought her hand to her mouth.

"Was there something else?" Gallienus asked.

She looked at her husband and touched his cheek with her fingers.

"You seem so sad now," he observed, sensitive to her manner. "How can you feel that way if it is true that Caligula will be gone soon?"

"Because you and I—," she started to say.

"What about us?"

She did not answer, and Gallienus decided not to pursue the matter in front of their guest.

296

LV

A number of years passed while Fabius Scipio remained in Rome. He had no need to work, since the fortune Germanicus had placed in his hands was more than adequate to support even one as young as he for the rest of his life.

So he spent his time discreetly witnessing for Jesus the Christ, working with Tullio and Gaius Gallienus to expand the circle of Christian influence in Rome.

During the year A.D. 41, Caligula was murdered, along with his then-wife Caesonia and their little daughter. Just before this degenerate ruler died, he was castrated by one of his attackers.

Tiberius Claudius Drusus became emperor at the age of fifty years. While possessing some sexual obsessions of his own, he was hardly the monster that his predecessor had been and was given to acts of kindness that would have been alien to Caligula, including the publishing of a decree that sick and abandoned slaves should have their freedom and that the killing of such a slave should count as murder.

Claudius reigned for more than a decade before Lucius Domitus Aheno-barbus Nero took over the throne when he was but sixteen years old. Until Nero became emperor, the Christian community in Rome and elsewhere experienced a period of relative peace. Persecution was not a primary goal sought by Claudius, and he tended to look the other way when charges arose against men and women simply because they were followers of what he viewed as a misguided carpenter from the tiny village of Nazareth.

It was during this oasis of more than a decade's duration that Fabius Scipio happened upon someone he had not seen for many years.

Procula Pilatus . . .

★ ★ ★

It was early morning.

Since Scipio no longer had slaves—a subject that had been discussed often and heatedly between him and some Christian friends who did own slaves—he had to get up, pull a robe around himself, and answer the door without anyone interceding for him.

Tullio!

"What is it?" he asked, trying to be cordial but not at all certain that she could justify awakening him at such an hour.

"I have gotten some news that may be of interest to you," she said excitedly. "It is about Pontius Pilatus."

Scipio had not thought about the man for a very long time, nor had any information come to him, except one comment from a senator that Pilatus had retired from service and was finding his inactivity not at all pleasant.

That was it, with no further time given to any thought about Pilatus.

Until Tullio Gallienus's visit to him at six in the morning that day.

"There have been numerous attempts to involve Pilatus in one conspiratorial plot or another," Tullio said. "One of those involved Caligula, but that beast was no match for a man as inherently brilliant as Pilatus, who outmaneuvered him so badly that an apology of sorts was forthcoming from the emperor!

"Ironically, Caligula invited him to a special banquet, and it was there that Pilatus witnessed the death of one so despised by all and murdered by those whom he thought he could trust. Pilatus did nothing to help Caligula and secretly rejoiced that such a loathsome thing was finally being eradicated."

"Pilatus was attacked some time after that," Tullio continued, "and was castrated. He was to die not long afterward, it is said, by his own hand, unable to cope with his loss of—"

She blushed over her entire face.

"What reason could there have been for this?" Scipio interjected, wanting to mitigate her embarrassment. "Whatever his shortcomings, Pilatus was hardly less than a loyal patriot of Imperial Rome."

"From what I hear, not everyone in the government accepted him as you have mentioned," Tullio answered.

"What basis could they have had for thinking otherwise?"

"I can only guess that it was his favorable stance toward the Jews as well as Christians both in Judea and elsewhere. He seemed almost their advocate in his final years as proconsul and governor."

Scipio's expression was one of total astonishment.

"Why have I heard nothing of the sort prior to now?" he asked.

"Because that was the way he wished it. He did what he did without attribution, partly out of fear of Caligula, partly because he did not want his motives to be impugned and suspicions to arise among those he was trying to help. He sought no glory in this. He helped, I think, out of guilt over washing his hands of the blood of Jesus."

Scipio thanked her for letting him know about what had happened, although he was still not at all satisfied as to why Tullio thought that such news was important enough to get him up as early as she had.

298

He was about to close the door when she pressed the palm of her hand against it.

"There is more, Fabius," she told him.

He waited for whatever revelation she had next.

"We found out everything I have told you from just one person," Tullio added. "Pontius Pilatus's wife, Procula."

Scipio's sleep-faltering eyelids shot up instantly.

"You have been in contact with her?" he asked. "You know where she is?"

Tullio nodded, smiling.

"Among her first words, after we were introduced, was an inquiry about you and someone else, someone named Decimus Paetus," she remarked. "She had apparently been told by a visitor that you were in Rome. But she could not leave in order to find you because of her husband's orders, conveyed through a decree by the emperor himself."

"But now that Pilatus is dead, surely she is able to go anywhere she wants," Scipio pointed out.

"It is not as simple as that, Fabius, believe me. Would you see her? She has asked that you come. Are you willing to do this?"

"Of course I am," he replied without an instant of hesitation. "Where is she? I will go immediately."

"My driver will drop me off at my house, and then he will take you to the place where she has spent the past ten years."

"Where is Gaius?" he asked, concerned.

"At a senate meeting. Those he advises need him."

"A crisis?"

"Something about a man named Nero."

Scipio reached out and hugged her.

"Bless you for doing this for me, for taking leave of your own rest to let me know."

"You must have wondered, at first, why I did so," she said, a knowing smile on her yet-perfect face.

"No longer, dear friend, no longer."

* * *

Scipio washed, threw on a fresh garment, which was like all the other men of the time wore, fashion changes being nonexistent for men in that ancient city (and it was not much different for the women), and hurried outside to begin the journey to the outskirts of Rome where Procula Pilatus had been kept for so long.

"Is she well?" he asked of Tullio Gallienus as the two of them sat on a wood bench covered by a scarlet-colored pillow, while the driver headed the horses through the maze of narrow Roman streets.

"This woman is remarkably strong in her faith, you know," she answered.

"I am not surprised, and that is good to hear. But my inquiry was regarding her physical health."

Tullio did not reply, her silence telling.

"So that is it!" he exclaimed, confident that he had stumbled upon some measure of the truth. "She has not left because of health reasons, even though the man who imprisoned her a decade ago is dead."

He took Tullio's right hand in both of his own.

"Is Procula dying?" Scipio asked.

Tears came to her eyes.

"Yes . . . ," she nearly whispered.

"How long does she have?" he probed.

"There is no way of knowing."

A chill hit his spine.

"What is her condition, Tullio?"

She hesitated, biting her lower lip and frowning.

Scipio placed his hands on her shoulders and gently made her face him.

"Does this dear woman now have leprosy?" he asked, his voice of a tender and sympathetic tone.

"Yes!" Tullio blurted. "It has progressed quite terribly, Decimus. She is no longer the beautiful woman she was but still she shines, still she talks of the Savior with a great love that is evident in spite of her pain."

"But why did she not want me to know before I saw her?"

"She was afraid that you would not come. Fabius, she is so very hungry for the companionship of people she knew from her days in Judea, especially those who were blessed by encounters with the risen Christ."

Scipio was reminded of his father, on that barren isle in the Mediterranean, trying so desperately to avoid facing him so that the son he loved would not see what leprosy had wrought with such devastation, especially on his face.

"All these years—alone!" he exclaimed.

"Not entirely. Before she was stricken, there were servants who came and went, and it was from them that she was able to get some fragments of information about what had been happening beyond the confines of her little world."

"Did not Pilatus later lift the ban on her confinement? Surely he could not have harbored those original feelings for so long as this?"

"He tried, yes, but since it had been imposed by the emperor, no other man could overrule it. And since Tiberius's successor was Caligula, the circumstances proved hardly favorable for any cooperation or compassion, in view of Procula's never-wavering protestations of Christian faith."

"But now that Claudius is on the throne . . . ?"

"Procula cannot leave. Her leprosy dictates her continued confinement."

"How could this have happened, Tullio? I wonder how she ever came in contact with other lepers?"

"Before the crucifixion she had spent more time following Jesus than anyone would ever have guessed. She was greatly moved by His ceaseless compassion for the blind, the deaf, the lame, the demon-possessed . . . the lepers. She appropriated food from the imperial storehouse, swearing her servants to secrecy. But they went only so far into the various leper colonies. It was Procula herself who came into closest contact with those who were afflicted."

Abruptly, Tullio pointed to a location just a mile or so beyond the chariot.

"That building on a hill," she indicated. "Procula has spent all of these years there, imprisoned by the man she loved so completely."

"It looks like a prison!" gasped Scipio. "Poor, poor Procula!"

"On the outside, it does, oh, it does, Decimus. But on the grounds those bare white walls encompass, you will be amazed at what she has done, at how God has been glorified."

LVI

*O*n the grounds those bare white walls encompass, you will be amazed at
what she has done, at how God has been glorified . . .

As Fabius Scipio approached those bare white walls, walking a
winding pathway lined on both sides with large bushes topped by tiny,
pungent-scented crimson flowers he did not recognize, he had to deal
with feelings of anticipation that collided with a chilly dread that gnawed
at every joint in his body.

Tullio joined him briefly as the driver waited.

Scipio asked if perhaps she wanted to stay with him after he was
admitted inside.

"No," she replied. "It is important for you and that noble, fine
lady to be sharing these moments only between the two of you, with no
one else present. She will want to speak with you in a most private
manner."

"Tell me, please, how bad is she?" he asked, insecurity tightening
its hold on him.

"Leprosy has not reached that beautiful face, though it has ravaged her hands and her feet. Poor Procula has no toes left, and several of
her fingers are gone. She walks with a limp, a slight one, but it is getting
worse, I can tell that it is, worse almost daily, it seems. And she cannot
hold herself as straight as she once did. Something is wrong with her spine."

"Who waits on her now? Who provides for her needs?"

"I think all the slaves have left. No one is permitted to stay with
her, for fear of spreading that which afflicts her."

"You say you think the slaves have left," Scipio noted. "How long
has it been since you were here?"

She hesitated, suddenly avoiding his eyes, whereas before she had
looked at him directly.

Tullio wiped one eye with a finger.

"Despite all this, her spirit shines!" she exclaimed. "Procula knows
what is coming, what she will end up being like, for she need only remember the others from whom she became infected, but that has not
dimmed the light in her eyes, Decimus. If anything, as she comes closer
to God, and feels the touch of His Spirit, she seems happier."

Scipio hugged her.

"I wonder how Gaius and I will endure hardship," she whispered.

"But, Tullio, you do not have any of that right now, do you? Or are there difficulties that you have chosen to keep from me?"

"Nothing for the moment, but I fear it is coming. I sense that the torment of which Jesus spoke is not far off."

They heard the sound of movement filtering over a high, whitewashed wall.

Abruptly the solid wood door in front of them was swung open.

Procula Pilatus was framed in the doorway which was half-circled at the top. Although it was true that leprosy had not as yet claimed her face, and its ravages of her hands and feet were hidden by the apparel she wore, Scipio could see that the strain of her life was showing up in other ways, through lines on her forehead and under her eyes and along the sides of her cheeks and a certain pastiness to the skin that made her seem even more frail than undoubtedly she was at that stage of her condition.

"Oh!" she exclaimed. "It is so good to see you, dear Fabius. Come, I would like to show you something."

Procula asked him to follow her to the rear of the property, and then she stepped aside to let him past.

. . . you will be amazed at what she has done.

He was faced with at least part of that to which Tullio was referring when he looked ahead and saw what Procula had ordered built in the middle of the large open space next to the house in which she had lived since she had been sent away by her husband.

A replica of Golgotha, very nearly as tall, though not as wide, with three crosses on top and a tomblike hole in the side.

Scipio approached it in awe.

"The same!" he spoke. "The very same!"

"It is my memorial to Him," she explained. "Not a statue like those of the gods Romans bow before and worship. It reminds me of His death and His burial. And in my mind and my soul are also memories of being with Him that night after His resurrection."

"I too," Scipio added. "Right at the tomb and in the room where He supped for the last time."

He walked up to the entrance that led inside this stone reproduction and stood there, admiring the detail, which seemed so exact.

"Once you have been there," she said behind him, "once you have experienced what we did, how is it possible to forget, Fabius?"

He nodded in agreement.

"No one could do that," he assured her softly. "I suspect not even Pilatus himself."

He spun around, ready to cry but wanting very much to appear strong and resolute in her presence.

"How is it that you were allowed to do this?" he asked in wonderment. "I can understand it happening with Claudius in power, and, therefore you would not be having any great problems. But what about Caligula?"

Procula smiled as she replied, "The monster of Rome was assassinated less than a week after the work was started. He may have found out what was being planned, but he died before he could do anything."

She started to reach out and touch his shoulder but pulled back quickly.

"Reflex," she muttered, averting her gaze from his own.

Scipio had to acknowledge to himself that he had winced a bit but hoped that she had not seen him do this.

"I understand that your husband was present to witness the death of Caligula," he spoke solemnly.

"Pontius was there, yes, and he helped to plan the act itself," Procula told him.

Scipio's eyes widened, for he had been unprepared for that news.

"Why?" he asked simply.

"My husband's conscience never died. He allowed it to be buried from time to time, but it always came back to assault him."

"Tullio told me that he tried to get you released."

"Pontius did, but keeping in place the decree of Tiberius was an opportunity for Caligula to appear to be honoring the wishes of his predecessor while, at the same time, planning infamies that Tiberius would never have permitted."

She looked at him again.

"By asking to have me released, Pontius incurred the ever-growing suspicions of that beast. If my husband had not assisted the conspirators and been instrumental in their success, he would have become another victim of someone quite mad."

She added hastily, "But I think he would have done what he could anyway to rid Rome of Caligula, even if his own survival were not at stake."

Scipio wanted with all his being to reach out and hug Procula and reassure her but knew that being reckless did no great service to his affection for her.

"You still love him," he observed.

"Despite what he caused to happen to me, oh, I do, Fabius, I do. That love has not diminished one heartbeat now that he is gone."

The serious expression on her aging face gave way to one of joy so profound that Scipio was literally staggered by it, stepping back from her.

"You wonder how I can know such happiness now?" Procula spoke, correctly interpreting his reaction. "Fabius, Fabius, it is because I feel the nearness of our reunion. It will not be long before my beloved and I are rejoined."

"Pontius Pilatus became a Christian?" Scipio asked with astonishment.

"He did, right here, not many days after this memorial was completed."

Procula walked over to the pathway that led to the three crosses on top.

"He climbed up and stood before the center cross," she said. "I followed behind him. After a few moments, Pontius turned, and fell into my arms, and said that he could not bear the thought that we would be separated forever."

She started up that same pathway.

"Come with me, will you, please?" she asked.

Scipio did as she wished.

"We knelt right here," she remarked. "I had not as yet come to be as I am now, and so I could get to my knees easily then."

She groaned as she tried to bend them.

"It is so bad these days. I think the leprosy is spreading quite rapidly now. There is first great pain, and then, when it has taken hold and started to eat away at yet another part of my body, I feel nothing, not even when infection sets in."

Finally she was able to kneel. Scipio got on his knees less than a foot away from her.

"Pontius gave himself to Jesus the Christ by confessing his sins and accepting the Lord into his very soul," she recalled. "It was as though his insides were being torn out of him. He fell forward, sobbing frightfully, Fabius, so much so that I wondered when blood would spew up through his mouth but it did not.

"He knew that he was the only sinner in this world who had such a singular burden on his shoulders, a burden that had been there all this time. 'I caused You to be crucified,' he cried out. 'I tried to believe that I could wash Your blood from my hands as easily as dipping them in a bowl and covering them with water.'

"'But that was never to be. How can You ever welcome one as loathsome as I? Procula tried to stop me from sanctioning Your death, but I did not listen. I can understand her salvation but, surely, not mine. Throw me away, and I shall surrender to this my misery as the punishment I deserve.'"

And then something happened that would change life for this man during the handful of years he was to live afterward.

"Do not touch me any longer, Procula!" he begged, still facedown on the surface of that make-believe mount. "I deserve nothing but your scorn. As much as I love you, I can expect little else from you in return."

"I am not doing so, dearest," she told him in a whisper. "I am not the one whose touch you now sense."

"But a hand is—," he started to say.

Pilatus fell silent with an abruptness that startled Procula and made her wonder if he had not had some kind of fatal attack, for along with the quietness, he was suddenly unmoving, a stiff form there in front of her.

She moved to his side and touched his wrist.

His heart was still beating.

"I held his hand in mine for what seemed an hour, perhaps longer, though I shall never know for certain," Procula remembered. "He said nothing, he moved not a little. I was so frightened, Fabius, so frightened that on the verge of getting him back, and then giving him to Jesus, I might have lost him after all."

Finally he stirred, this man once feared and despised by an entire nation, first with a groan from deep within his soul, it seemed, then a shaking of his entire body, and after more of this, he abruptly sat up, an unaccustomed peace settling upon his countenance.

Head tilted upward, his gaze locked in on the clear sky of that afternoon, Pontius Pilatus, former proconsul-governor of all the land of Judea, started speaking, "I am free, Procula. I need no longer wash my hands of the blood of Jesus as the symbol of my guilt and my shame, for I have allowed that precious crimson flow to cover me. I have bathed in its healing stream, and now I am cleansed, dear, dear Procula. I am *truly* cleansed!"

LVII

Procula and Scipio sat and talked until near dusk.

"Pontius visited me regularly after that," Procula proclaimed to her visitor. "We became closer than ever."

She cocked her head, as though listening, but instead she was running some moment of irony through her mind, before she spoke of it out loud, "We never embraced again, you know, Fabius. I forbade my husband, my only husband to do so. I could not abide even for an instant seeing such a strong man, so tall, and straight, and fine looking, reduced to the plight of being no better than a walking, rotting corpse with a heart still beating but no more of life than that, certainly not a life of vigor as he had known all his years."

Scipio felt an impulse to touch the woman, to show her that he cared not for any risk but more for the need to express his affection with clarity.

"And yet you were so close, as you have said," he spoke instead, deeply regretting his timidity.

"Our emotions reached out and intertwined, it is true," she acknowledged. "Our very souls seemed to merge. Each time, when he had left, to go back to his world of subterfuge and intrigue behind ornate columns of power from which he never totally extricated himself, it was as though he stayed after all, some form of his presence remaining long after his body passed through the open doorway and he was on his way from this solitary place."

"Where is he buried?" Scipio asked.

She smiled at that question as she stood and motioned for him to follow her. They had been sitting on a bare marble bench near the front of the property, and she was now walking around to the rear once again, where she stopped at the painstakingly complete replica of Golgotha.

"Right there," Procula said, pointing to a modest mound of earth just to the left of the tomb entrance.

Scipio had glimpsed that earlier, out of the corner of his eye, together with a tiny, white-painted cross on top, but had been so overwhelmed by the sight of what Procula had duplicated that it did not register, and he soon forgot about it.

"That was what he wanted," she recalled. "He had preferred to be shipped back to Jerusalem and laid to rest in the actual spot but that could not be arranged, and he asked for me to do this instead."

"Was he here when he died?" Scipio inquired.

Procula started shivering. For a third time, he had to force himself not to hug her.

"Is there something that I can do?"

"Nothing, unless you can speak to the Lord and have Him foreshorten the time I have left before the two of us stand before Him in the midst of His eternal kingdom."

She was coughing now.

"Out there," she said, raising an arm, still sheathed in her billowy garb, and pointed toward the entrance.

"He died in front of this estate . . ." Scipio repeated.

"No, he was dead when I found him. I did not have a chance even to kiss Pontius on the lips one last time."

"Did someone help you?"

"I did it all myself. I dragged his poor, beaten, broken body inside, and sat with it for hours, not wanting to let go. How *could* I do that, Fabius?"

"But the grave itself?" Scipio said uncomfortably, not eager to add one whit to her burden by details that were still harsh to her, yet compelled somehow to find out more.

"I did that also. Leprosy was just beginning to attack me then, with little splotches that I never allowed Pontius to see. I had all my fingers. I was a bit weaker than before but I just prayed for strength, and strength was what I was given."

A woman accustomed, in years past, to being pampered, clinging to the material things around her, had changed so drastically, shorn of the old crutches by which she was able to stumble through each day and, now, with nothing to keep her going but a faith and a courage that once would have seemed unlikely.

"Will you stay a bit?" Procula asked as darkness spread. "Tullio and Gaius come as often as they can, but they have so much else to occupy their time these days."

"The groups they have started throughout Rome?" Scipio asked.

"Is it not wonderful, what they are doing? If I were able, I would be so pleased to stand by their side and do what I can."

Procula looked at him with a special fondness apparent in her expression.

"How long will you stay here in Rome?" she inquired of her friend.

"For whatever time the Lord wishes," he replied.

"Will you stop by again?"

"Every day, if you will permit."

"Tell me," she asked, not eager to end their time together, "about what brought you back from Judea."

He was thankful for the sudden opportunity to recall for her those years he had spent traveling as he witnessed for Jesus the Christ and, later, that extraordinary encounter with his soon-to-be-benefactor.

"And Germanicus has been staying with your mother and father ever since then?" Procula repeated in astonishment.

"As far as I know," he told her, "though I have received no letters as yet, with any up-to-date information."

"You have no concerns about lodging, clothes, food, income?"

"None."

"That is so very fine, Fabius. How the Lord has blessed."

She was becoming tired.

He could tell this by the drooping of her eyelids every so often and the way her cultured speech was slowing, now hardly more than an absentminded mumble despite her attempts to stay alert.

"I shall leave now," he said, though not happy about doing so.

"I wish you could stay longer, but I do need some rest," she admitted. "My stamina is not what I enjoyed earlier in this strange life of mine."

She walked with him to the door.

"Other than Gaius, the last man I saw leave was Pontius," she recalled. "I am very sorry you got to know only the one side of him."

"I too regret that," he said warmly. "He must have been so much more than he appeared to any of the rest of us."

"He was, Fabius. If my husband had lived, he might have become emperor. Can you imagine what that could have meant?"

"It is not difficult to do so."

"Or he might have been corrupted as others have been," she spoke, trying to smile but not doing so with any conviction. "I cannot bear the thought of that happening."

After reaching the entrance, Scipio said good-bye and walked outside, then turned and waved back to her. Procula closed the gate slowly, a measure of sadness gathering about her, and then she turned toward Golgotha and the mound of dirt at its base, a last dying flash of golden sun reflecting off the little white-painted cross on top.

LVIII

O ver the next few years, the throne of Imperial Rome changed hands again when, in A.D. 54, Nero succeeded Claudius, who was more tolerant toward Christians but generally an ineffectual ruler as far as Romans were concerned.

At the very beginning of Nero's reign, there was some hope that he might continue the benign policies of Claudius but with more savvy as far as the use of power was concerned. He certainly revealed himself to be of a more artistic bent than his immediate predecessors, with an interest, if not a gift, in poetry, music, and other pursuits.

The most visual manifestation of Nero's self-expression was his unbridled building campaign, new structures created, usually from his own designs, at a rate that ultimately would play a major part in bankrupting the imperial treasury.

But his inability to handle power and money sensibly and gracefully showed up in other ways as well. He used gold threads for his fishing nets, wore a robe once, then threw it away, and shod his mules with silver.

Nero gradually turned malevolent in a vivid display of the truth that "power corrupts, absolute power corrupts absolutely," this and the perverse advice of some close counselors, including members of his family.

It was tragic that this abrogation of the promise embodied in the earliest years of life under Nero occurred, for he was a man who had the potential to bring about a new Golden Age but instead precipitated a descent into an earthly version of hell . . .

★ ★ ★

After years first on the battlefields to which Imperial Rome sent him, and, then, on the mission fields throughout Judea, Fabius Scipio, now in his late forties, lost touch with anyone he had known who came from Rome itself. There were always fellow legionnaires, of course, born and raised there, but these men too had been in only sporadic contact with the city of their youth, and when they were finished with their military service, many went elsewhere. Only a few determined to return to Rome, but then they were invariably men from whom he would hear nothing further.

The sprawling city of Rome reflected the attitudes of its various rulers over the decades that had passed since Scipio had visited it during the youngest years of his life. Under Tiberius, as with Augustus before him, there was a sense of true pride hinted at in the body language of people everywhere, the way they held their heads, the expression on their faces at any given moment, how they walked, what they talked about. But later, with Caligula on the throne, all of that changed drastically, his manic behavior filtered through the rest of Roman society in the same manner as in happier times with emperors who, at the very least, were sane or reasonably so. Under Claudius, conditions and attitudes improved, only to be threatened once again by the increasingly erratic behavior of Nero.

At the very beginning, he seemed to keep his crueler instincts in check, Scipio thought. *Perhaps the influence of his tutor Seneca never told hold.*

He had met the wise old man not long after Nero took over the reins of power. Gaius Gallienus had introduced the two of them.

"Regrettably, any kind of worthwhile philosophy had to fail before the onslaught of monstrosity," Lucius Annaeus Seneca admitted after they all had finished dinner at Tullio and Gaius's residence. "He is all the more dangerous because he has a brilliant mind. I tried to nurture that mind but it is not intellect that gains control of Nero. It is passion. The heart, corrupted at best, takes over, and whatever may be noble, creative, decent is buried, I fear, to an increasingly permanent extent."

"Why does Nero hate the Christians as much as I have heard that he does?" Scipio spoke cautiously, not entirely trusting the philosopher since he was, after all, a favorite of the Roman intelligentsia, and there was no way of perceiving how much loyalty was left for the office of emperor, if not the man himself.

"Because they appeal to whatever conscience the man may have left, although this is only speculation," Seneca opined. "Nero is hardly a moral man, but whereas Caligula's moral slate was *utterly* empty, Nero's can be described as *nearly so.*"

"You are saying that he is afraid of what Christians have been espousing for some time now, is that it?"

"Afraid is not quite the right word, Fabius, though I cannot dismiss it out of hand. There is little that could be called fear as such in his makeup. I would say that he finds any possibility of a resurgent conscience inconvenient, for it would tend to quell his very worst tendencies. I think, frankly, that Nero *enjoys* being what he is. He loves the power over other men. Christians represent boundaries, and he loathes even the *thought* of any restrictions on his power or the behavior that power engenders."

Scipio was impressed by Seneca's wisdom and said so.

The old man chuckled.

"I am now in my sixties," he said, groaning theatrically. "If anyone lives that long in this society, unless he is from the poor classes, he surely must either gain a measure of wisdom, or slip into senility and act the fool."

"The poor cannot be wise?" Scipio probed, with less caution just then. "Is that what you suppose?"

"I do not. I merely offer an indisputable fact—that they have far fewer avenues to dispense their wisdom than you and I do. Mind you, I am not *happy* that this is so. Wisdom is wisdom, from whatever class it comes. To be deprived of it because someone lives in a hut instead of a palace is lamentable.

"If anything, I have found that being wealthy can foster dulling of the mind. You have only to look at Nero to reaffirm this. His money goes where his passions take him, not where his intellect should be guiding him."

Seneca fastened Scipio in a sudden, unrelenting gaze.

"What I admire about these Christians to whom you refer is that their faith in its beguiling simplicity seems very much to prosper among all classes and all ages," he spoke firmly. "Contrary to some of my station, I do not find that their faith engenders the destruction of reason at all. It is only when passion reduces reason to a pleading and insufficient whimper that it is easily ignored because, as we all know, unbridled passion is too often the master of enervated reason. Is that not so, Fabius Scipio?"

Scipio had to applaud the old man. "I have become your student, at my age," he commented.

"At any age, you would be a worthy one," Seneca replied with a gracious manner that had been instilled in him from his childhood spent in Spain and the distinguished Roman parents who were determined that their son be denied nothing that was of value in their goal of shaping a mind that, even early on, showed flashes of effulgent superiority.

"I have seen or read many of your works," Scipio responded. "Ten of your philosophic essays, nine of your tragedies, and that wonderful satire."

"Have you read what some call my essay on heavenly bodies?"

"I have not."

"I shall get a copy to you."

"That would be wonderful."

Later, as Seneca was readying to leave, he paused briefly, and clasped Scipio's hands between his own.

"If only I could believe as you do," he spoke conspiratorially, while Tullio and her husband were otherwise disposed.

312

"As I do?" Scipio repeated, feigning ignorance.

"The Nazarene . . . ," Seneca said without elaboration, an odd expression crossing his face, one of equal parts wistfulness and a certain desperation. Then he added, "Will you have dinner with me at my residence next week?"

"I am happy to accept," replied Scipio.

"Our hosts know the address. They can guide you."

"What day and what time?"

Seneca answered him just as the Gallienuses were entering the vestibule.

"I must go now," the old man told them hastily. "Thank you both for a most enjoyable dinner."

"Our pleasure," Tullio assured him.

Seneca left, his gait slow, not so much from age, it seemed, but rather a gathering dread, perhaps perceiving all too well as he did what would be in the unpromising future for someone such as himself, a man whose intellect had been cultivated so grandly since not long after his birth, but whose soul had hungered throughout the course of his adult life for that which he knew not what.

Four days later, learned and highly moral Lucius Annaeus Seneca committed suicide after being accused by the emperor he once served so personally of an assassination plot, leaving only a little fragment of parchment on which he had written but a few mournful words: "At long last I must pull a final, encompassing shroud around my pitiable frame, and surrender to the hoary darkness that I have feared since first the once virtuous traditions of my beloved Rome gave way to an unspeakable madness seating itself on the noble throne of emperors. Sadly, it is but too late that my redemption draweth nigh."

LIX

Fabius Scipio was becoming restless. He knew he had gone on to Rome because it was part of God's plan for his life that he spend time there. But he sensed not as many avenues for Christian witness as there seemed to be at the beginning.

He knew what Tullio and her husband were doing, theirs being a quiet sort of ministry and an invaluable one because they could reach up into echelons of power to which few other Christians had access.

Scipio possessed the money but not the social position as yet. When he had trod the primitive roads of Judah, he could look forward to numerous immediate opportunities to speak of the death, burial, and resurrection of his Savior. People would either listen or not, but he could at least speak forthrightly, without consideration of social status or senatorial protocol or any other such matters.

Everything is so prim and proper here, he thought as he stood outside his home, wondering what to do that day. *I have no worries about clothes, food, any of that. But I take no thought for these in any event, for my concern is that of saving lost souls who may hear the good news only from my lips.*

He started walking, toward one of the fountain-dominated intersections in Rome. As always, he was assaulted by the noise of the ancient city. Vendors of sausage shouted the virtues of their links above any of the others. And there were the ones who had pease pudding for sale, adding their loud voices to the general din, not to mention the snake charmers, courtesans, street entertainers, and others who clogged the narrow streets.

Roman poet Martial expressed his own consternation: "On one side of the street, there are the money changers idly rattling their coppers on a dirty table, while on the other side goldsmiths are beating gold plate with their mallets. But even this does not speak it all. We as citizens of some note are also faced with the noise caused by an incessant stream of soldiers, high as kites on whatever drug they have procured, shipwrecked soldiers with their bodies swathed in bandages as they moan their agonies . . . and Jewish beggars as well as salesmen selling sulphur with the tears pouring down their cheeks.

In addition to being loud, Rome was a dangerous city, not only because of pickpockets and other robbers, and those who would commit crimes of violence and passion, but for another reason as well. At night, the only sources of light were candles, oil lamps, and smoky torches. Few of the homes had easy access to water, for their needs in this respect could only be satisfied at wells or fountains which were at a distance of up to a mile or more each way.

All of which was why Scipio took his walks mostly in daylight.

A well-to-do man giving a beggar woman a loaf of bread, and then walking on.

He thought nothing more of that until later that day. He was on his way home when he saw the same man give some more food to the same woman.

Scipio stopped this time and watched the wealthy individual talking kindly to her and then leaving.

Scipio approached the beggar woman. Dressed only in a thin, tattered scrap of material, possibly a very old and worn toga she had found in some alley or elsewhere, she could hardly look worse—though she gave no sign of being leprous—smudges of dirt everywhere on a face that showed a large scar across her forehead; thin, pale lips; eyes that constantly shifted from side to side in an obvious attempt at finding more individuals who would contribute something to her survival.

He offered to buy her some food since he had none with him just then.

"That would be wonderful, kind stranger," she replied.

"How often does that gentleman come to you here?" he asked.

"Whenever he passes this way. It seems to me that he brings something to me several times a day."

"Is he the only one who does this regularly?"

She scratched her head, thinking about that for a moment.

"I believe so," she told him.

"You speak well," Scipio observed.

"I was once a woman of means. Then I ran afoul of that wretched Caligula, and I have been on the streets ever since. He took everything of mine."

Instead of buying her food, he had decided to give her a coin so that she could get whatever it was that she preferred.

She thanked him, and Scipio left, returning home a bit later, the old woman lingering in his mind so strongly that he quickly determined to help her as much as the other man seemed to be doing.

★ ★ ★

The next morning Scipio arose earlier than usual, wondering when the beggar woman found it necessary to return to her little spot near the fountain at that intersection from wherever it was that she would spend each night.

He left his residence and started walking in that direction.

As he approached, he saw the woman there as before, and the same man with her, but he had someone else as well at his side this time.

She turned for a moment, saw him and waved him over.

Feeling a bit awkward, Scipio introduced himself, as did the other men.

"I am Publius Cornelius Dolabella," spoke the taller, older one, a man with an almost comically round face.

"And I am Claudius Crassus Inrigillensis Sabinus Appius," the other one added. "It is a name over which I have little control, I am afraid, a long name indeed for one so short as I."

Scipio could see that this little man, with pale skin and a nervous manner, was not comfortable in the company of strangers.

"It is not the longest I have encountered," he spoke reassuringly.

"That is good to hear. What was the other, may I ask?"

"It was so long that I have forgotten it!" Scipio exclaimed.

They all had a laugh over that, and then the three of them turned to the beggar woman.

"You will not starve anytime soon," Dolabella told her. "Perhaps we also can get some shelter for you. It is no good to have a full stomach and die of exposure to the harsh elements when winter comes."

Scipio's eyes widened.

"I would be happy to contribute," he said.

"And I suspect the three of us could find others to house," Appius remarked. "This woman is hardly alone."

"I know of some elderly couples with much idle time and money on their hands who might join us!" Dolabella added. "I heard of some men in that forsaken land of Judea who reconstructed an entire village for a similar purpose. Here, at least, we would be in the center of civilization! As I see it, that gives us quite an advantage."

"There is a building I passed by on the way here," recalled Scipio. "It seems presently abandoned. And it is rather large."

"Will you show us?" Dolabella asked.

Scipio nodded with some enthusiasm.

As they were leaving, he turned back to the beggar woman and said, "We will let you know what we find."

"May the gods guide your every step," she shouted.

Scipio froze at that. The two other men were waiting.

"I believe in but one God," he told her, perspiration running down his back, since he knew nothing about the strangers who were accompanying him.

Am I leading myself into a trap, Lord? he asked silently.

Dolabella and Appius saw drops of perspiration suddenly starting down his forehead and his cheeks.

They both smiled.

"Do not fear your candor," Dolabella assured him. "The three of us are brothers, drawn together no doubt by His Spirit within us."

★ ★ ★

In less than a day, Scipio joined the two other men as they met with elderly individuals within their acquaintance, those who were wealthy as well as not a few who had considerably more modest means but were quite healthy enough to donate much of their time and energies to a cause that caught their fancy.

The immediate object of the labors of this group that Scipio saw expanding daily was the building he had mentioned to them.

"Oh, I see," Appius said, giggling a bit.

"What amuses you?" asked Scipio, not sure whether to join him or be somewhat offended.

"This would be a most apt place in which to start our mission of mercy," the other man went on. "Most apt indeed!"

Then both Appius and Dolabella broke out laughing.

"We would certainly show the change that our faith can bring about!" Dolabella managed to say.

"Please, tell me what is going on," Scipio asked, now becoming irritated.

"This building you have picked was once a brothel!" Appius told him, laughing more uproariously than ever.

Finally, after the two of them calmed down, they told Scipio that it had been abandoned because Nero wanted his whores closer to the palace, so he erected another, grander structure just a few hundred yards away.

"Why was not this building put to some good other use?" Scipio inquired.

"He just forgot about it, I suppose," answered Dolabella. "As you may know, the man spends money needlessly for a score of different purposes, however specious, or no purpose at all but merely to put up another edifice."

"Can we secure permission to use it?"

"I doubt that even Nero would fail to see the value in appearing to have a beneficent side to him."

"Even though Christians are involved?"

"We will try to make sure that he does not find that out until later, and then it will be too late to stop us, for Nero is not so much a fool as was Caligula, and he will realize that he must never seem vindictive toward either the elderly joining us or the poor who are being helped by this enterprise."

"Can one so impetuous be counted on to act rationally?" Scipio posed that most uncomfortable question.

"Is this not where prayer comes in, Fabius?" Dolabella gently reminded him.

"The visual message we give to all of Rome will be wonderful," little Appius said, an expansive smile on his face. "Can you not agree, our brother?"

Scipio admitted that they were right. A few minutes later, the three of them entered the old, ramshackle building and stood in the midst of the rubble inside, joining hands and lifting up their praises to a risen Savior and Lord.

LX

Some elderly couples with much idle time and money on their hands who might join us . . .

Increasingly, it seemed to Scipio a stroke of genius that Dolabella had thought of just the right group of people, for the state of old men and women in Roman society was an ambivalent one. Earlier, before the imperial period of Rome's history, living past a certain age for those who had any elevated position was not all that common, since political assassinations were more commonplace than in successive generations. As Juvenal expressed it, "Growing old has been something of a phenomenon, if one is a nobleman."

But ironically, under the later, often capricious emperors, given to murderous outbursts as they were, older Romans tended to extend their life span and to be more secure in their personal safety. A handful managed to remain at the center of government, with a number of the emperors themselves living into their seventies. Elderly men not occupying the imperial throne itself were often turned to for their much-valued decades of experience and the compelling wisdom this engendered.

A younger man such as Nero left much of the decision making, especially in the military area, to older and, by inference, wiser heads, including Gnaeus Domitus Corbulo, one of the greatest of the Roman generals; plus Lucius Tampius Flavianius, another general; and a variety of others of advanced age were chosen by Nero for various posts, ranging from court doctors even to a woman named Locusta, employed full-time for the purpose of studying various poisons, occasioning one observer to accuse her of running a school for potential poisoners, the talents of which a man such as Nero would find useful.

Yet, despite these exceptions, the elderly of privilege, by and large, had little to do with their ample leisure time except to engage in idle conversation about philosophy, the arts, or any other subject that happened to occur to them. A few stooped to the level of watching the gladiatorial games, but the attendance at these continued to be largely of younger men and women, older ones often repulsed by the bloodshed, since they themselves were closer to death than they wanted to admit and did not need to be reminded of such grisliness.

Those who were in the final years of their lives and infirm, to a greater or lesser degree, were not greeted with any appreciable sympathy in Roman society of those days, which was based, as had been that of the Greeks before them, on the concept of top-flight physical conditioning, the body almost a god in itself, with consequent superior health. A body that was increasingly useless because of one ailment or another became an object of truly heartless scorn, not sympathy, outside the family circle.

One Roman satirist and playwright described advanced age's effects on the body: "Look at this most ugly and hideous thing that was once of human beings loved, now despised and scorned by all, the face of an ugly hide, like that of a dumb beast, somehow passing for skin, the sagging cheeks, and deep, disfiguring wrinkles, a driveling nose, bread now broken but with gums unarmed."

In a society where athletics were worshiped very nearly in the manner of a religion, the elderly who had no real power or influence and who could contribute little to that society came to be discarded in an indifferent fashion.

But, praise God, not those who stay here! Scipio exclaimed to himself a few weeks after permission had been granted by Nero to renovate the building he had spotted, and the work on it was finally completed.

He stood back proudly, along with Dolabella and Appius and the various elderly Romans who had helped them, the group forming quite a crowd outside, which attracted the attention of passersby.

Rotting wood had been replaced, crumbling columns as well, with a new cistern dug in order to provide water, the old one long since collapsed.

Surprisingly, Nero himself contributed some funds from the imperial treasury, a feat in itself since that very treasury was now nearly bankrupt.

"You are now the second former legionnaire to get involved in a charity of this sort," Dolabella remarked later in the day.

Scipio was not aware of whom or what he spoke.

"Remember when I told you about that village in Judea," the other man remarked.

"I recall that now. Was the one you mentioned behind that?"

"As I heard it, yes. His name was Paetus, I believe, yes, that is correct, a chap named Decimus Paetus."

Scipio had been eating a pleasant pastry at Appius's residence. When he heard his former comrade's name, he dropped it on the floor.

"I must have startled you," Dolabella said. "Please forgive me."

"I know this man," Scipio admitted. "We served in the Legion together. We became Christians together."

"And both of you are involved in a similar work. How ironic!"

Appius had been silent for several minutes, which was not at all like him, since he usually was the most loquacious of the three.

"Are you distressed about something, friend?" Dolabella asked.

Appius cleared his throat.

"I have heard another story," he acknowledged.

"Tell us then," urged Dolabella.

"I am uncomfortable about this."

"No need," Scipio assured him. "Spit it out, my brother.

'The story has no happy ending for your friend."

"Has something happened to him? Is he dead?"

"He probably lives, but now he serves the insurrectionists."

Decimus has forsaken the quiet life of being a missionary for Christ! Scipio exclaimed to himself.

"I am sorry to bring such ill tidings to you," Appius spoke, sincerely regretting what he had revealed. "Perhaps the information I have been given is inaccurate. I hope that that is so, my brother."

"Yes, I can always hope that it is," Scipio replied, the shock taking his mind far away from that place, back to Judea and the ministry Paetus and he had been sharing before they parted company. "Do not be concerned that you have said something wrong. Now that I know, I can commence lifting him up in prayer. I owe that to you and am thankful."

He stayed with them and went through the group's plans for getting people into the hospice, but his mind was partially elsewhere, not with them during those moments of distraction but with a man for whom he would have died if the opportunity arose.

Decimus, Decimus, he moaned to himself. *How can you serve the incipient forces of violence and our precious Lord at the same time? How could you ever hope to go through this pretense and not lose that which should be most important to you—His blessing on your mission of bringing lost souls to Him?*

Later, after Scipio had returned to his own residence, he faced a growing concern about what would happen to his friend, especially in view of who had become emperor, a man come to be known for the most brutal punishment of any Romans who gave him the ammunition to call them traitors.

Recognition of the hospice spread throughout Rome and into the countryside. It was to become a model for those that were set up in later years throughout Europe, primarily as a result of the efforts of Christians in the various communities.

Nero himself continued support, with money, supplies, and, notably, a policy of safe passage for any Christians who were involved with the hospice.

For nearly a decade, all went well, and the work of Scipio, Dolabella, and Appius, along with other Romans, including non-Christians, grew mightily, with a second building added in the countryside a mile or two from Rome. It had been bequeathed to them upon the death of one of the supporters of the original hospice.

That all this happened under the reign of emperor Nero was one of the great ironies of those years . . .

Part VII

*N*early *thirty years after the crucifixion, burial, and triumphant resur-rection of Jesus the Christ . . .*

Lucius Domitius Ahenobarbus Nero.

As it turned out, his help with the hospice was a singular quirk of generosity in an otherwise despotic ruler. His more intrinsic loathing of Chris-tians ultimately exceeded that which Caligula had manifested, but since Nero was far more astute, and, therefore, very much aware that this sect routinely practiced the strictest obedience to the laws of Rome, with the exception not allowing of the worship of gods other than their own Jehovah, he could find little opportunity or excuse to take action against them, for whatever his pecu-liarities as a ruler and a man, he had been trying, with some success, to avoid going outside the normal course of Roman law, at least during the first half of his more than twelve years in power, which proved to be little preparation for what he would come to foster during the latter years.

Ironically, even as the seeds of persecution were being sown, this early period in the growth of the Christian church proved a momentous one, with large numbers of converts being added, at the hospice and numerous other loca-tions, in cities and villages and single isolated settlements of a handful of dwell-ers throughout much of the known world.

How many would hold fast and not "fall away" during the coming times of tribulation was not something that mortal man alone could know . . .

LXI

Fabius Scipio had known about Paul the apostle for some time. And he was anxious to meet this extraordinary fellow convert.

I have done so little compared to him, the former legionnaire told himself. *Though I am now middle-aged, yet, over the past twenty years, how many souls have I reached for Christ? There have been a few, here and back in the Holy Lands, but that is all. Paul's impact is being felt over the whole world, it seems.*

He was standing in front of the Mamertine Prison.

You who spread the Light of the world to its darkest corners now must live in a place where so little light intrudes.

Scipio sighed, realizing that getting to see Paul was no small or easy matter, and he should not be wasting time *outside* the prison.

He glanced to his left.

The Forum.

Where learned men spouted philosophies of one sort or another.

Where the blood of assassinations had been spilled.

Where some of the finest structures in all of Rome were located.

Every sane and responsible emperor thus far throughout this century has said that the Forum was built to last forever, for they had deluded themselves into thinking that the Roman Empire itself would never die, Scipio recalled, *and every great civilization needs places where the exchange of ideas can be encouraged. Oh, how they neglected to understand that such men as Caligula, Nero, and others could not prosper in such a climate and were destined to smother it any way they could.*

He looked back at the entrance to the Mamertine.

The most redemptive words of all can be heard within that prison, within its cold, damp bowels of isolation, and yet none of the intellectuals whose voices now reach my ears from the Forum this winter afternoon, none of the senators, none of the philosophers, I suspect, have ever visited this man, for they are weighed down by their pride and the physical majesty of where it is that they speak. Rome they can touch, one another they can hear, food in their stomachs is a reality that satisfies them; but heaven and hell and a resurrected King of Kings—these are beyond their willingness to acknowledge, beyond the ability of great minds to grasp, beyond the smothering, suffocating rationalism and cynicism that wrap around them like a giant serpent, ever more tightly until they can no longer breathe the breath of that free thinking they so readily proclaim from between the towering columns of yonder Forum.

Scipio remembered six words once spoken by the Nazarene as he stood in the midst of a gathering of young ones who had flocked to him that particular afternoon: "Except you come as a child . . ."

They were completely at ease in His presence, accepting Jesus with an instinctive trust in Him missing from their approach to so many adults.

Your conceit dooms you, Scipio thought sadly of the men whose orations seemed to be spellbinding large crowds only a few hundred yards away.

Finally, his nerves as calm as would ever be the case under the circumstances, Scipio walked up to the structure that literally had been carved out of a small, broad hill in the middle of Rome. He paused at the thick, heavy, iron door at the front and knocked.

No answer.

He tried again.

No sounds came from within—the heavy walls of rock kept out all contact with the outside world—and he had no idea if his knocking would be answered.

A third time.

Still nothing.

Discouraged, notwithstanding the fact that he was holding a scroll signed by a senator who had authorized the visit, Scipio halfheartedly tried a final time, and when there was still no response, he started to walk away.

Old hinges creaked, and he spun around.

A Roman soldier of low rank stood in the doorway, blinking, as his eyes adjusted to the light of outdoors.

"What are you doing here?" he asked gruffly. "I am having a meal just now. Come back later, after I—"

"I have to see the prisoner," Scipio interrupted with as much a tone of authority as he could summon.

"Paul—the Christian? Is he the one you seek?"

"Yes, yes, it is he."

"By what authority?"

Scipio mentioned the senator's name as he thrust the scroll in front of the soldier, who took it, unrolling it and skimming the contents.

"Come on in then," he said, his tone softening.

The room into which Scipio followed the other man was quite a bit larger, with a far higher ceiling than expected, the entire space a natural cave.

"This is where we stay, my comrades and I," the soldier spoke, noticing Scipio's transparently hopeful smile. "The prisoner is down there."

He pointed to what was literally a crude hole in the hard rock floor.

"How do I get to him? Are there any steps somewhere?" Scipio asked ignorantly, his outlook changing in an instant.

"No steps. I have a rope. Grab hold of it and I will lower you to the room."

Scipio stood before the small round hole, trying to see down into the murkiness just beyond his feet.

Flickering.

The hint of light.

He could see something flickering.

"Has the prisoner nothing more than a candle?" he spoke.

The soldier was silent for a moment, studying him.

"Is there something wrong?" Scipio inquired a bit irritably, uncomfortable under such scrutiny.

"Are you a friend of his?" the other man asked.

"I have never met him. But I am familiar with some of his writings."

"As I am."

The soldier walked over to a crude wooden table. On top was a parchment. He brought it over to the visitor.

"This is but the latest," he said. "There have been many, you know."

"Yes, I do. May I read it?"

"Be quick. Someone is coming by any moment to send it on its way."

Scipio unrolled the papyrus, skimming the words on one side.

As he was reading, he heard a sound, not from the "room" below but from behind him. He looked up and turned, seeing the soldier, head bowed, shoulders slumped.

"What is wrong?" asked Scipio.

"Those final words. How can he write them? How can that man feel as he does? He writes, he sings ancient melodies, he prays, often loudly, sometimes in the middle of the night. He awakens me at these times, and I hurry over to that hole, and shout at him to stop, that I need to sleep, but when I hear what he is saying, I sit down and listen. And when I finally close my eyes and drift off, it is with what he has been saying still in my mind. Over and over I hear him, long after he too is asleep but I *do* hear him."

His head shot up. His eyes were red-rimmed.

"Praising this God of his!" he said, his voice nearly at a shout. "He does not whimper or moan or rail against anyone except someone called Satan. How can this be? How can he be so happy, so at peace in such miserable conditions?"

He reached out and tapped the final lines on the parchment.

Scipio focused on these.

"I have learned, in whatsoever state I find myself, therewith to be content . . ." he read out loud.

"Down *there!*" the other man told him. "He wrote what you see from that miserable dungeon."

He leaned over so that his nose nearly touched Scipio's and whispered, "They do not feed him well. He is never truly warm enough. The only good thing is that he is a short man, and it is possible for him to stand up straight when he wants to do so. Others have been taller, and that discomfort has been added to everything. Even so, he cannot be other than miserable, this man. Yet he smiles at me when I take him something—"

He broke off.

"What is it?" Scipio asked.

"Nothing. Go now. See the man you came to visit and then be gone."

He grabbed a rope piled next to the hole.

"I shall hold tight," the soldier assured him. "Will you have any trouble?"

Shaking his head, Scipio smiled with great warmth.

"I was once a legionnaire," he remarked.

His eyes widened, and for a second or two, the other man said nothing, as though trying to control his emotions.

"Do for him what you can," he then said slowly, his eyes wide, moisture trickling from them. "I have no power. They listen not to me. But I see your fine clothes. You are well-groomed. They will pay attention to you. Get him some more bread. I give him from my own rations what I can spare. But I know he is hungry. I know he is thirsty. The water here is not enough. A little wine perhaps. Will you try, please?"

"I will do my best, but you know what the emperor thinks about these Christians," Scipio reminded him.

Grabbing the rope, as the soldier held on, he lowered himself down into the chill dampness below.

Paul, formerly Saul of Tarsus, was prostrate on the hard, uneven floor.

Scipio stood quietly, not disturbing the man.

"Not my will, Holy Father, but Thine . . . ," spoke Paul.

His body visibly trembled. It seemed as though he did not realize that he had a visitor, for his utterings were with great passion and with a curiously private feeling to them, part of a stream of communication between him and God.

At one point he seemed to be in pain, and Scipio broke his own silence.

"Are you suffering?" he asked, deeply concerned.

A reply came immediately.

"Yes, I am in agony," the baritone voice, one of a much bigger man, it seemed, told him. "I await my entrance into the kingdom of my Lord, and yet I know there are so many out there who need to learn of Him."

Suddenly he got to his feet, standing quite straight, and looking up into the face of this stranger.

"Are you a Christian?" Paul asked.

"I am," Scipio replied, allowing some pride to manifest itself in his manner.

"You seem pleased with being one."

"I am, praise God, I am."

Paul turned his back to Scipio.

"Your pride is no different than a boast," Paul remarked. "But you should be sorrowing instead."

"Sorrowing? I do not understand."

Paul faced him again, his expression readily discernible even in that semidarkness.

"That you are enjoying salvation while others are still dead in their sins," he intoned, as though he was caught in the midst of an awful tragedy that was unrelenting. "How many within just a mile of this place are headed toward eternal punishment because they have not had the joy of hearing the good news? We should not glory in our successes but cry out in anguish from our failures."

He threw his hands out in a sweeping gesture.

"The mile of which I speak is but one. How many are lost within ten miles of us? A hundred? A thousand? You should not be visiting me, but stay outside, telling the lost about how Jesus suffered, died, was buried, and then arose from the grave so that they would never have to live amid the flames of the damned."

Scipio nodded in agreement with everything that the apostle had said.

"But I want to learn a measure of greater wisdom from you," Scipio told him. "I am convinced that I have so much to learn. And you are the one who can teach me a great deal. Then I will be better equipped to do what you have just said."

Paul paused, for the stranger had spoken quite properly.

"Without a teacher, how is any of us to learn?" Scipio continued rather impetuously. "It is not only learning something new but discarding what we have absorbed in the past that has no place in our new life in Him."

Paul walked up to him, studying his face.

"You are not so old as I," he said, his tone softening. "Yet it is true that I have heard much about you."

Scipio was unprepared for that.

"You have . . . I mean . . . you have heard . . . about me?" he stuttered.

Paul smiled slightly.

"But who should be the teacher?" he said modestly, finally dealing with Scipio's earlier question. "Perhaps I can learn much more from you."

"How could you have heard *anything* about me?"

"From someone named Nicodaemus."

It was true that the old man had become one of his supporters while he remained yet in Judea.

"When did you hear from him?" Scipio asked.

"Quite some time ago. I understand that Nicodaemus has since gone on to his heavenly home."

Paul's eyes narrowed.

"All those years ago, he had written about you and someone who was a former comrade, Decimus Paetus."

"Decimus?" Scipio reacted slowly, still trying to deal with the abrupt news of Nicodaemus's death. "What was there about my friend? It has been a long time since we were together. Please tell me what you know.

"Decimus Paetus has joined the insurrectionists."

Scipio's legs became wobbly. Paul reached out, helping to steady him.

"This surprises you?" Paul asked.

"Greatly. I can scarce accept what you have told me as accurate, though I know you believe it to be so or you would not have mentioned anything."

"Why is it so difficult for you?"

"How can Decimus be a Christian and yet wage the violent acts of that group at the same time?"

"We do not know that Decimus, himself, participates in the violence. I doubt that he does. We do not even know his motive in traveling with the insurrectionists. It may be that he sees opportunities for witness that we do not understand because we don't know the situation firsthand.

"I do know that as Christians we are exhorted not to murder, but there is no admonition against self-defense. The insurrectionists are trying to throw off the yoke of a nation steeped in the worship of strange gods, a nation out of which will proceed the most horrendous persecution of Christians. There was some of this under Caligula but Nero will be much, much worse, Fabius Scipio.

"The Jews have grown accustomed over the centuries to the act of submission, however mournfully, to the servitude imposed by their various conquerors," the apostle said. "I do not think we as a people will ever change in that regard. Like very large lemmings, it seems we are inclined to march straight on to our doom. Rebellion is typically fostered among us, I suspect, only after it is too late to be very effective.

"We are consigned to seeing the truth, yes, but not before our numbers have been cruelly decimated. There is, perhaps you may know, a certain prophecy in this very regard about Jerusalem itself, that most ancient of cities. No Jew should be surprised or offended by words such as these, for they seem commonplace in the prophecies of our past."

"But you are a Christian now?"

"Your words are correct but only partially so. I am *also* a Christian because I have never stopped being a Jew."

Scipio knelt before the shorter man.

"I am not worthy to be in your presence," he said.

"It is I who feel uncertain about being in yours," Paul replied.

Scipio was taken aback.

"How can you compare whatever I have done to your own accomplishments?"

"I shall soon be taken away, my new friend. But you are yet to live. You will have many years ahead of you to bring honor and glory to our Lord."

"But you traveled continents, country after country, I have heard," Scipio spoke. "You have started many churches. I was His instrument in a few lives, that is true, yet nothing like what you have done."

"But there are those who would follow *me*. They lose sight of whom their master should be. I have tried to stop this, but little cults grow like weeds, and I have failed to uproot as many as I would have hoped."

He asked Scipio to stand up.

"You will have people quietly come to you, even from the house of Nero himself. And you will live to such an age that the numbers of those you reach cannot be counted, for they will be so great."

"But some say, you among them, that there will be great persecution. How is it that I am to escape this?"

"You will not escape it," Paul said patiently. "But you will survive it."

Scipio did not argue with him. Finally the two of them settled down awkwardly on that hard floor and for many hours talked about many subjects. One of these was a young man named Stephen.

"I stood by while he was being stoned to death, you know," Paul said honestly. "There was a moment when he turned in my direction, and I thought I heard words of forgiveness from him just before he died."

"You wrote in one of your epistles about a thorn in the flesh," Scipio recalled. "Did that have anything to do with guilt?"

Paul, whose head had been bowed slightly, now looked up suddenly.

"How could you know that, my young brother?" he asked, startled.

"I know that you are a Christian who lives his testimony day after day, so that it could not be a sexual sin of any sort, though I have heard that some of your enemies have attempted to say this about you. And despite your circumstances, you seem healthy enough, as much as you can be, so it is not a physical ailment as others have suspected who have mistaken your fervor for something else."

That the apostle was profoundly impressed seemed obvious in how he spoke, the rather awed tone of his voice.

"You are correct, Fabius," he admitted. "Though I have preached forgiveness for so long now, though I have condemned guilt as one of Satan's most effective weapons, yet still it burdens me to remember standing there as I did before Stephen and watching him die without doing anything to help him because I took the side of the accusers."

"But you were under darkness then," Scipio said. "You did not have your experience on the road to Damascus to open your eyes at the same time as it blinded you."

"I realize that you are right. I *want* to be able to get his image out of my mind, at least in the manner that it has been there for so long. I *want* to be consistent in my thought life as in my prayer life and as I have been writing in my epistles and preaching in my sermons. But it has not been possible all this time. Stephen's words, those kind, forgiving words, sometimes awaken me in the middle of the night when I hear them from the darkness, mocking me."

His cheeks were wet.

"That is why it remains a thorn lodged deep within my flesh, a messenger from Satan that buffets me. I have admitted this to no one but you, Fabius."

Then the apostle shrugged his shoulders.

"We all are afflicted in some way," he said, "because Satan wants only the rank odor of defeat in our lives. Yea, we are afflicted but not crushed; perplexed, but not despairing; persecuted, but not forsaken; struck down, but not destroyed.

"Therefore, we must learn to be content with what we are called upon to face, as with weaknesses, as with insults, as with all manner of distresses, with persecutions, with difficulties, for Christ's sake; for when we are weak, then we are strong."

There were to be other times of fellowship on other days, and the two men would remain alone on all but the last, for it was then that they would find themselves interrupted by an unexpected visitor.

The emperor himself.

LXII

Over the past several months, Scipio had noticed that once-regular contributions from the imperial treasury were being received more and more erratically, this change coinciding with what he was hearing from sources on the street, namely, that emperor Nero was busy spending Rome into financial oblivion and anything that failed to have his specific stamp on it would be cut back severely and then eliminated altogether.

"Many of us are truly scared of the future," a middle-aged senator told him confidentially after lunch one day. "We see all too clearly what this arrogant devil is doing. He is fooling the public by these extravagant gestures of his, with people oh-so-visibly put to work constructing any number of beautiful buildings, and certain specialized groups enjoying support because of his interest in the arts.

"Furthermore, this clever one is still so very young, as I said, even now only twenty-one years old after six years of power, and can be so charming that he retains the ability, of which he is all too aware, to fool people about his true self, with that ready smile of his feigning an affability that is completely foreign to him, and that arrogant, self-confident manner projecting as it does a transcendent competence.

"The emperor does all this while claiming to be an accomplished artist himself, a poet, a lover of music, an aficionado of plays. It is true that he can be very charming and there is some degree of intelligence in the man. He does have great numbers outside the Senate fooled. In time, though, reality will burst the bubble that Nero has spewed forth. I already see the early signs of this happening."

At one point, Scipio was asked by Gaius Gallienus to attend a special meeting of the Senate, as an interested observer.

"I am told to watch out for a certain very brave man who will stand before us and make a statement that is certain to start the gossips working with great frenzy," Gallienus mentioned. "From what I hear through my contacts, Fabius, I think you will be interested in what he is going to be saying."

Scipio agreed, though his friend's manner was hard to read, and he did not know what to expect.

"I should like to pick you up tomorrow," Gallienus spoke rather ominously, "at the noon hour. Will that be convenient, my brother?"

"Fine," Scipio agreed.

Scipio passed the remainder of the day doing battle with a feeling to which he had not been prone for some time.

Dread.

After years of relative calm and the gratifying surge of Christianity that he had witnessed, he wondered if perhaps a time of tribulation would be starting.

Why am I reacting so impulsively? he thought. *Am I worried because I am placing undue attention on the donations, especially those from the emperor?*

He probed his conscience.

Could it be that as long as the money is flowing in, I am happy, but when that flow is reduced or becomes erratic, my sense of stability disappears?

Surrounded as he was at home by numerous signs of substantial wealth, with furnishings and tapestries and clothes speaking clearly of his affluent station, Scipio became concerned with what this might be saying about himself and his Christian testimony. Then he realized that unnecessary guilt was one of the more powerful weapons of the Deceiver's. He knew, once he had finished confessing his concerns to God, that if there was actual sin involved, then there would be immediate and unconditional forgiveness.

Unconditional . . .

He fell to his knees as the reality of that overcame him.

"Father, you know my heart," he spoke. "If there be wrong feelings in it of any kind, please, please wash them away, I beg of Thee, through the shed blood of Your Son, my Savior and my Lord."

He knew a sudden onrush of peace then, which caused him to fall forward on the floor of his bedroom, tears of joy flowing.

"I do not know what lies ahead," he confessed, "but if it is Thy will that I die at the hand of those who are my enemies because they were first Yours, then I shall do so looking forward to entering Your kingdom at last. If it be Thy will that instead of death, I am to survive, I can only promise You, Father, that I will do whatever You enable me to do that will bring honor and glory to Your name."

★ ★ ★

The large, white-toned chamber of the Roman Senate, with a high ceiling and a massive column at each corner, was crowded. All registered senators and their aides were present, together with any authorized guests.

One of the younger men, possessing what might be called an un-blemished baby face, stood before the others, clearing his throat as he surveyed them with a solemn expression.

"His name is Ummidius Nasica Corculum," whispered Gaius Gallienus to Scipio, who was sitting beside him. "An extraordinary fellow, he comes from a family of senators going back over a period of two hundred years. I have to say that it seems he has inherited more than a dollop of their courage as well as their intelligence, not to mention some of the brashness that characterized them for so long."

Corculum started to speak, with no parchment before him.

"I have thought long about what I feel it is that I need to tell you all," he said. "But I have not marked down my words for I wanted them to have the passion that has me in its grip right now, rather than seem as though I am saying something that is little more than a prepared recital, and a boring one at that."

Someone laughed nervously, then, in embarrassment, cut himself off when nobody else was similarly amused.

"I fear for our nation," Corculum continued, narrowing his eyes. "Nearly half of our people receive some form of government subsidy. We have grown weak from too much affluence and too little adversity."

That large room was now quite silent except for the sound of his voice, no coughing, no whispering, no shifting of bodies.

"I fear so greatly that soon we will not be able to defend this beloved country of ours, nor the once-glorious empire, a wonder of the world for a very long time, that sprang so vigorously from it against the sure and certain enemies who are most eagerly waiting for the opportune moment to pounce upon us and wrest from our very grasp that which we have held with the greatest tenacity for centuries."

He leaned forward, frowning deeply.

"Fellow senators," Corculum went on, evidencing with his words and how he spoke them a striking maturity that was belied by his perennially youthful countenance, "we have permitted the debasement of our currency, at one time a symbol of rock-solid stability, yea, we have done so to the point that, at this very moment, even the most loyal of our Roman citizenry are beginning to be skeptical of it."

He raised his right hand which he had clenched into a fist.

"The gods themselves must be planning some judgment against us," he started to shout with ever greater passion. "How long can it be that they will let us live as we have been doing, wallowing in what would once have been judged the most appalling mediocrity and excess, while allowing, unimpeded, forces of decadence to reach the very throne of this once strong, and this once proud empire?"

Corculum's round, broad face was flushing red now.

"On this day now upon us, alas, we have as our emperor someone who seems to believe that government alone can take care of everything, yet he goes on to squander that very government's treasury on such projects that bear only his stamp, and not, instead, on those that are for the long-term good, yea, the stability of this nation.

"By doing so, the emperor cleverly gathers around himself some measure of support from those citizens who do not have at hand all the facts to which you and I have access and who do not bother in the slightest to fathom what his motives might be, for what they see is only the awe-inspiring facades of those edifices that, I myself have to confess, add a measure of outer magnificence to this city.

"It must be admitted that those Roman citizens who are being put to work as a result of the free-spending actions of our sovereign leader are hardly among those given to complaining, loud or otherwise, and have taken instead to shouting Nero's praises, it seems, from every street corner in this city.

"On the other hand, if anyone dares to oppose the emperor, in his despotism, none of you should be surprised to hear me say what you surely have known for some time—that Nero invariably has the protester either executed or imprisoned for a long term, usually to die behind cold, gray walls, or perhaps exiled to a barren little isle somewhere in the expanse of the Mediterranean, another sort of prison, to be sure . . . sadly we must include even the emperor's mother Agrippina the Younger among those subjected fatally to his maniacal ire, which in her case descended *after he had slept with her!*"

It was in his treatment of his mother that Nero's pathological traits were early in evidence. He first tried simple poisoning but, unknown to him, she was alerted by a faithful servant, though she already suspected his intentions. As a result, she began to take the poison herself, but in small dosages, thereby building up an immunity and foiling his plot.

Nero's next attempt involved arranging for the ceiling over her bed to collapse. When that too failed, he sent her on a cruise in a vessel that had been rigged to fall apart once it had pushed off from the harbor, but Agrippina managed to swim ashore.

Finally, impatient to the point of frenzy, Nero accused his mother of treason and had her executed.

Those present in the Senate building knew what a devil the emperor with whom they were dealing had proved to be since he was sixteen years old, and a kind of paralysis had gripped them, for they knew how dangerous it was even to listen to Corculum.

"Our emperor has murdered undisclosed numbers of men, women, and children!" he continued to thunder from the podium. "He cares not about the survival of this nation of ours but rather only that which, in some way, manages to flatter his massive and grotesque conceit. Nero, murderer, incestuous devil, robber of public funds, stands condemned by his own actions this very day and—"

The lance was thrown so quietly and swiftly that when it entered his chest and protruded out his back, no one reacted for a moment. Corculum himself looked dumbly at it, then fell forward, knocking to one side the podium before which he had been standing and falling across the startled, incredulous row of senators in front of him.

Finally everyone turned in the direction from which the lance had come.

A stern-faced centurion was standing there, holding a scroll.

"The execution of traitorous Ummidius Nasica Corculum has been carried out by imperial edict," he said, his voice bellowing rather theatrically throughout the room. "We will now dispose of this scum's miserable remains."

Several of the senators angrily rose to their feet in protest but immediately reseated themselves when other armed soldiers were seen entering the chamber and forcing silence by their very presence.

Scipio continued sitting with Gallienus and the others, silent as they were, until the soldiers were gone, taking along with them poor Corculum's bloody frame, and then everyone began to leave that ancient chamber, words clogged in their throats by the shock that had taken hold, no one daring even to look around himself but gazing straight ahead until they were outside, under the hot rays of a blazing overhead sun, which made the chill submerging every last man of them feel all the more portentous.

LXIII

Scipio struggled with the decision of whether or not he should tell the imprisoned Paul what had happened during the meeting of the Senate. Finally, wavering, he chose to speak to Gaius Galienus about the matter during a lull in their regular duties at the hospice the next afternoon.

As the two of them stood in a little, fragrant garden at the rear of the building, Gallienus spoke first.

"There will be more murders," he said, his voice trembling in the heavy emotional aftermath of what he had witnessed the night before. "None of us should be surprised about this, you know. Nero has gone this route before, with his mother as well as various other enemies, real or imagined, ever since he came to realize what it was that his immense power enabled him to do."

"The man is so young, the youngest ever to be emperor, and yet how much blood does he have on his hands?" Scipio mused.

"I think even Nero has lost count of the deaths."

Finally Scipio blurted out what he had been wrestling with regarding the apostle, with whom both Gallienus and he had become close.

"Should I tell Paul?" he asked, hoping that his friend would say no, that the prisoner's burdens should not be increased.

"Well, he does seem interested in everything that occurs on the outside," Gallienus mused out loud. "I suppose you should, Fabius. But—"

He hesitated, his mind filled with a terrible image.

"I had a dream last night," he said, "born of the murder we witnessed."

"You are fortunate, my brother. I could not sleep more than two or three hours, and fitfully at that."

The expression on the other man's face made Scipio think differently as soon as those words were out of his mouth.

"Was it very bad?" he asked, more intuitive this time.

"Oh, Fabius, Fabius, dreaming as I did was far from being a relief, I must assure you of that. I saw a man's head being cut off. It rolled right up to my feet. I reached down, to turn it over, and find out who it was, but by then I was screaming myself awake when I saw that it was Paul himself."

"Our brother beheaded? What a horrible thought!"

"Nero has done that before. It is a 'special' death which, along with his revival of crucifixions, is being retained for the very worst of his enemies."

"But, surely, he cannot consider Paul to be an enemy."

"To the contrary, Paul is a Christian who has succeeded in drawing empire-wide attention to himself now that he has become a symbol of what Nero has taken to calling 'spiritual resistance.' When people are thinking of the apostle, then Nero does not occupy the center of their thinking, and his ego has become so immense that he simply cannot abide this possibility."

"*Spiritual resistance!*" Scipio blurted in reaction. "I have not heard that description before now."

"It is being bruited about in some circles, I hear, especially among the military and the political factions."

"What is the purpose?"

"I think our dear friend Paul is being set up as a scapegoat for whatever atrocity Nero may decide upon next."

"If that should happen, there will be a Christian uprising," said Scipio, without thinking through his response.

Gallienus snorted.

"Not so!" he spoke. "An uprising that is based upon too few numbers and too much emotion is suicide, and only that. There would be no hope of success."

"What will the Jews do?" Scipio asked.

"That might be another story. After all, our friend once was named Saul of Tarsus. No man was more respected among them than he. Though he has become a Christian as well, few of even his critics would view any execution that Nero might dictate as anything less than an act so cruel, so unwarranted, so intolerable that rebellion in protest of it would not be considered a criminal act."

Gallienus stood, stretching his legs wearily.

"Though we both have spent hours of close fellowship with Paul, it is you who has the best rapport with him," he recognized. "Despite whatever reluctance you feel about telling him everything, I think he deserves all the information we can give. If my dream is perchance a premonition of some sort, then this warrior of our faith must be as prepared as we can possibly make him, lest he be taken by surprise and the shock of what comes is made all the greater because of it."

Scipio was standing now, hugging himself.

"Can you feel it?" he asked, his face pale.

340

"Yes . . ." Gallienus answered. "It will soon not be so, ah, convenient to be a Christian. Is that what you were thinking?"

Scipio said much by his silence.

★ ★ ★

Paul registered no surprise when Scipio told him of the previous day's murder of Ummidius Nasica Corculum.

"He was a Christian, though secretly," the apostle revealed. "Ummidius's argument was that if he held his faith in secret, he would escape the derision with which many of the senators hold us, and that would enable him to be more effective if the true source of his actions, if the true motivation for those, remained unknown."

"But what about hiding our light under a bushel?" Scipio ventured.

"I think our precious Savior, our dear, dear Lord has many of us in many places for many purposes. I will not judge our brother's heart. He died for what he did, and what he did sprang from his walk with Almighty God. What else is there to say, my dear Scipio? He is in heaven now, and we remain here to labor in the fields for the harvest that is to come. Nothing else matters, is that not so?"

Scipio agreed that Paul was right.

"I debated within myself as to whether you should know what happened," he admitted. "I did not want to upset you."

"All things work together for good to those who know and love the Lord," Paul replied. "If we cannot deal with any bad news when we are eventually confronted by it, and can function well only with the good, then we can expect only a dismal life at best, for the bad will come as surely as night follows day."

Tired, plagued by aches caused by the dampness in that place, he stood, with some effort, which Scipio did as well, his own head touching the uneven ceiling of the little carved-out-of-stone room while the apostle's was still several inches below it.

"May I tell you something?" Paul asked with a typical, well-bred politeness that had never been allowed to change into a certain coarseness even though his experiences would have had that effect on many other men.

"Surely, my brother," Scipio replied eagerly.

"I have some pain, yes, and there are moments of loneliness, I must confess, for it would be dishonest of me to say otherwise. And yet—"

He reached out and touched the rough-edged rock above him.

"With a ceiling so low, there are some advantages to being as short as I am," he said, chuckling as he wandered off the subject, but only for an instant, and then he added, "I feel so at peace, Fabius. I feel . . . so happy."

Even in the semidarkness, with a single candle as flickering illumination, Paul's eyes clearly sparkled.

"How can that be?" he went on. "Even I must puzzle at this from time to time. I have felt that way for many months, here in Rome and elsewhere. In the midst of being shipwrecked, I had no real fear, I think, because I had no real doubt. Perfect love has already succeeded in casting out fear. If we love our Lord totally, how can fear assault us? Satan may try, of course, but he can never truly succeed."

"Did you not have a guard chained to you when you first arrived?" Scipio asked, remembering what other Christians had told him.

"Yes, but only because the emperor had no idea what to expect from me. When they saw that I would present no difficulty, such as attempted suicide or whatever else they imagined, the guard was removed by imperial order, and now there are only those who stand guard in their shifts in the room above."

"Have you ever met Nero?"

"No, I have not. I understand he is very young."

"He was but a teenager when he assumed power."

Eyes narrowed, Paul sighed as he spoke further, "To be so young, and so corrupt . . . I wonder who was responsible and what special punishment will be meted out to them by our Father in heaven for corrupting such a brilliant mind, a mind that could have been for the good of Rome, not evil."

"And now the emperor is doing the same thing with others!"

"That has been the way it goes, Fabius, each generation spreading its poison to another, the sins of the one being visited upon the next. Cain's children suffered from their father's obsession that the means fully justify the ends, and their children carried it like a perverse tradition throughout generations to follow."

Paul pointed above him.

"How many human beings are walking around today, in ten thousand upon ten thousand places, still enslaved to the clinging and remorseless wickedness of one man blinded by murderous jealousy?"

"But by Adam, is it not so that all men have sinned and come short of the glory of God?" Scipio asked.

"That began the decline and fall of the human race, Fabius, and every one of us continues to be tainted as a result. But I think it is through Cain and his offspring that Satan, undoubtedly celebrating this, found an endless and willing supply of total depravity that he could gleefully spread everywhere like some awful plague throughout the world.

"The fall of Adam and Eve weakened every human being to follow, opening them up to the propensity to sin. But it is Cain who must forever take responsibility for the introduction of violence, murder, the betrayal of one brother by another, and whatever else he pursued until his death so long ago."

Paul became even more saddened.

"There will come a day, whether in this generation or another, I cannot say, but it will happen that much of this world will be given over to a state of mind so reprobate that Sodom and Gomorrah will seem almost redeemed by comparison."

He saw that Scipio was having to grapple with this and was about to go into it further when they heard the guard above them calling out.

"The emperor is coming!" he said. "His chariot has stopped in front, and he is getting out now."

Startled by the announcement, Paul and Scipio glanced at one another, with no idea of what to expect.

LXIV

When he was very young, Nero could have been called handsome, with a fine prominent brow and deep-set eyes. Not even a pair of oversized ears were able to spoil the pleasing nature of his appearance. He was unbelievably attractive to girls who would flock around him, before and after he became emperor, though he graduated from the virginal ones to a long line of women of some experience.

At the age of twelve, Nero was handed over to the brilliant and famous Seneca, whose duty it was to serve as his tutor. The boy showed real oratorical promise but not that alone, for he had an intellect that, properly harnessed, seemed capable of extraordinary achievements. Only after the advent of power began to change his young charge did Seneca give up in a mixture of disgust and regret.

When he was very young, Nero could be called handsome . . .

But more than six years of gluttony, heavy drinking, and promiscuity ultimately etched lines of dissipation on his once beguiling face, changing it to a startling degree, for it had become bloated, with a fatty area of skin hanging down from his lower jaw and eyelids that were constantly red-rimmed, drooping.

He was young but also old beyond his years, and there was about him a sense of boredom that made the outbursts of violence he was increasingly propagating seem like the acts of a grotesque child trying desperately to amuse himself.

As their emperor, yet looking like the carousing hulk he had become, Lucius Domitius Ahenobarbus Nero stood before Paul and Scipio, though not in the tiny room which could be reached only through a hole in the stone floor of the much larger one. He refused to go below but instead had them brought up to him.

"So this is the giant of Christianity!" bellowed Nero in a voice that had a faintly feminine quality to it.

He had spread his legs apart in a defiant stance, with hands on hips, a scornful expression on his puffy face.

"How could it ever be that I would find myself in competition with a little weasel like you?" he scoffed. "I could envision the lame, the poor, some lepers perhaps, and a few madmen who might find you appealing!"

344

His body puffed up further by a multilayered, hand-stitched, cream-colored silk tunic, he approached Paul, sniffing contemptuously at the apostle.

"You smell," he said.

"It is difficult under the present circumstances to keep as clean as I would like," Paul replied simply.

"Are Jews *ever* as clean as Romans?" Nero added.

Paul said nothing.

"Take this man and bathe him properly," the emperor ordered the two legionnaires who had come with him, "and then return him to me. I shall not conduct a conversation with someone in his present state. And, yes . . . give this *Christian* one of my lesser tunics."

Paul was led away by both soldiers, leaving only the emperor, the regular guard, and Scipio in the room.

Minutes passed, with Nero pacing, grunting now and then, wiping saliva from his lips and chin. The guard and Scipio said nothing, not daring to interrupt whatever momentary reverie into which the man had lapsed.

Abruptly he stopped, looking at Scipio.

"So you are a former legionnaire, I hear," he said bluntly.

"Yes, sir, I once served Rome in that capacity," Scipio replied, not aware of how the emperor could have found out.

"What caused you to leave?" Nero probed.

Scipio hesitated, wondering if he was being set up for a charge of desertion.

"Pontius Pilatus sought and received Tiberius's agreement to release me from any further obligation. As it turned out, six months later, Caligula took over the throne but chose not to countermand any of his predecessor's proclamations."

When Nero smiled, the effect was to exaggerate the deterioration of his features.

"I could certainly overturn the dusty dictates of a dead, failed emperor simply by the snap of my fingers. As easily as that, I could have you also tossed below, to stay by the side of your beloved Paul."

Scipio nodded, without speaking.

"I am very glad you agree," Nero told him. "Disputing me right now is hardly in your best interests."

He chuckled at that.

"Sir, why is it that you have come here to see the apostle Paul?" spoke Scipio, trying to congeal his nervousness but not succeeding, as it turned out.

"I will reply to that question if you first answer one of mine," Nero told him.

"Gladly, sir."

Nero obviously enjoyed seemingly cowing someone who was old enough to be his father and in far better physical condition.

"Why are you, as a Christian, trembling in my presence?" he asked. "Even this Paul here does not."

Scipio's throat tightened, for he knew that this overstuffed almost-child was correct, and a guilty conviction grabbed him.

"If your faith is so strong, and you have, as you claim, the Holy Spirit indwelling you, what is there to fear from *any* mere mortal, even one who happens to be an emperor?" chided Nero, his lips curled up into a sneer.

Scipio had never before found himself in such a situation. He had been called upon to defend his faith, yes, but where rejection might have been the result, not impending danger from someone on the edge of madness.

"I did not—," he started to say.

Someone was banging on the heavy wood door at the entrance to the little prison. The guard answered and allowed Paul and the two legionnaires to re-enter.

"Your friend here fears me," Nero chided Scipio by telling the apostle. "But you do not. Why is one a coward and the other a brave man? What is it about your faith that affects you both so unevenly?"

Paul saw that Scipio was greatly uncomfortable, with beads of perspiration having formed on his forehead and already soaking the front of his tunic.

"My friend is not a coward because he fears the might of the unjust," he pointed out. "If he were truly that, he would run from this place, unable to endure intimidation. Yet he does not. He continues to stand before you.

"If Fabius shows fear at all, it is because this is the first time that he has encountered mindless hostility because of that faith. For me, such a moment has become much more frequent over these many years since my conversion. I am one who knows all too well the wrath of Imperial Rome."

At first, what Paul had said seemed to get by Nero but not for long.

Face nearly beet-red with anger, Nero walked up to the apostle and slapped him across first one cheek and then the other, hard enough that the shorter, thinner man was knocked off his feet, hitting the hard rock painfully.

Scipio stepped forward, fists clenched and raised.

The legionnaires reached for their swords, as did the guard.

"No need!" Nero exclaimed, holding up both hands, palms outward.

346

Paul, unsteadily, managed to get to his feet, and stood between the two men.

"What pleasure do you get from the pain of others?" he asked. "How could someone with such a mind fall to such depths?"

Nero asked the guard as well as the legionnaires to leave.

"But, sir, they—," one of the two who had accompanied him protested.

"It shall be as I said!" Nero demanded sternly, in a tone that told the three men even more than his words.

In a few seconds, Paul and Scipio were alone with him.

"It is obvious how much you both hate me," Nero told them.

"I do not hate you," Paul retorted. "I hate the sin you spread like a horde of devouring locusts, but I love you as a human being and I pray for your very soul."

Nero blinked several times, not at all expecting the apostle to say anything like that.

"You worship the Nazarene," he spoke. "I have heard that you feel his death in some manner I am not able to fathom as one way to ensure that the gods will forgive me whatever my transgressions have been over the years."

"You are correct except for two details," Paul said. "The gods cannot forgive you because they do not exist. Only the God Who Is can and will do that. And accepting Jesus as your personal Savior and Lord is the sole way to gain redemption, not simply one of several from which you can conveniently pick and choose. Ritual will not do it. Nor will giving money to the poor. Nothing but asking Him into your soul is sufficient. Heaven is not a place to be bought but a destination to be received."

"And I have forgiveness as well?" Nero pressed.

"You have it the moment you bow before God in acceptance and confession."

Scipio stood back, holding his breath, as he witnessed this astonishing tableau. Nero was *listening!* The most despotic emperor in Roman history was now being exposed to the good news of Jesus the Christ!

"Are there any limitations on this forgiveness you proclaim?" asked Nero. "Does this God of yours say that everything but this-or-that is included?"

"Nothing is exempted," Paul assured him, the two men only inches from one another, their gazes locked together.

The apostle reached out both hands and placed them around one of the other man's.

"You have no hatred of me now, do you?" Nero observed, not able to keep a degree of wonder from his voice.

"I have only the love that God Himself wants you to accept."

Nero pulled his hand out of the apostle's grasp.

"I think there must be something for which He would turn His back on me," he said. "And I think further that I have done the deed this day."

Paul glanced back at Scipio as Nero suddenly turned away.

"But I can assure you that—," Paul started to say.

"You may *try!*" the emperor spoke with some urgency, sounding as though he was on the verge of sobbing. "But I can never, *never* believe what you or anyone else says in this matter, for I shall not for the length of whatever remains of my life forget that woman's expression nor her words as I stood next to her, my knife covered with her blood. She could say only, 'I forgive you, my emperor . . . in the name of Jesus the Christ.' And then she fell at my feet, the front of her white garment stained with—"

He spun around, facing the two of them.

"All others that I have killed directly or ordered killed have cursed me," he recalled. "They have consigned me to the fires of some nether-world of punishment and pain. But not this one fair creature, not this one woman."

His eyes were bloodshot.

"I saw only love on her face, not hatred. How could that be? Tell me this, please. How could that be?"

Paul sat down on the hard floor and motioned for Nero to join him. Surprisingly the emperor did not object.

"The woman of whom you speak knew a perfect love and gave forth of it herself," Paul said, "for it came from God Himself through her to you. She was but expressing the unchangeable love of your Creator and hers and mine, the Creator of the earth beneath our feet and the heavens above."

"Such joy as well!" Nero exclaimed. "I have unbounded power at my grasp. I have women by the dozens. I can make anyone a slave by taking away his freedom with one signature on a parchment. I have food and drink without end, day and night, if that were my wish at a particular moment. Yet there is not within me today nor has there ever been the smallest measure of what I saw on that perfect face."

"It is without understanding, I agree," Paul said, "but it *is!* There was no deception on her part in the midst of her dying or her living. The deception lies in your thinking that that with which you have been sur-rounding yourself is all that you need to bring to you what you seek and have not found."

"I have spilled the blood of other Christians," Nero, still puzzled, reminded the apostle. "If I am forgiven one death, can it be that I shall be forgiven a score of these others, a hundred perhaps?"

Paul touched the other man's shoulder and saw Nero wince.

"I have never met someone so kind," the emperor muttered. "I wanted another residence, a hideaway where I could go and be alone and think, only one or two of my closest advisers knowing where I was.

"I saw hers, and so I took it. When I visited the property, she was alone. I told her that she would have to leave. She smiled, and said, simply, 'You may have it. I shall live where I can. It does not matter. My true home is not of this world.'"

He reached out in front of him with his left hand.

"I studied her face again. It was without a mark. Though she was an older woman, I found myself attracted to her. I said, 'You will no longer live here because you will be with me in my main residence. Pack up whatever you want to bring with you.'

"She smiled and said that she appreciated the offer but that I did not have to feel obligated in any way toward her. I could not believe her words and assumed that she was trifling with me in a very artful way.

"Nevertheless, with training from me personally, I told her, she would be very adept at the intrigue in which I found it necessary to engage from time to time. If she did not accept my offer, I would be very offended indeed, and she would end up in the street, becoming like any common beggar."

Nero hesitated, sucking in his breath.

"'I will go where the Lord wants me,' she said. I told her that I would be responsible for whatever had happened, not this Lord of hers, and it was insolent of her to suggest otherwise. 'You are His instrument,' she added. 'Whatever pleases you,' I replied. 'Now, please leave this place. I have plans for it.'

"She asked if I could give her a few minutes, to gather some bits of clothing together. 'Some of what I have is very fine but I can carry only so much,' she spoke. 'Would you see that the rest goes to others? The poor perhaps?'

"I assured the woman that I would do so but that she was beginning to try my patience. After she had hurried into the residence, I decided to wander about, examining the rest of what I had just appropriated."

Nero then exclaimed, giving in to some youthful excitement, which made him seem more of a child than a chilling tyrant. "At the very rear of the property, I glimpsed the most extraordinary sight!"

Scipio felt the palms of his hands become sweaty, his heart abruptly beating faster.

"It was a hill, at least that was what I thought until I examined it more closely and saw that it was something else, a re-creation of one perhaps, a hill that possessed the features of a human skull, and on the top were three crosses!"

Nero's voice duplicated the surprise he had felt.

"I heard the woman's voice calling to me, so I turned and saw her standing there, smiling, as she held a pitifully small leather package of belongings. 'Where shall I go now?' she asked with such resignation and simplicity that I began to feel sorry for her.

"'That can wait a moment,' I told her gruffly. 'What is this remarkable *thing* that I see before me?' I greatly appreciated the perfection of its detail. She proceeded to answer in some detail, my astonishment at what she was saying by the minute. And then she walked up to the mound of dirt in front of the entrance to the little tomb, nodding at it and also the cross on top. She told me who it was that she had had buried there in that grave."

Nero clapped his hands together.

"I had admired Pontius Pilatus ever since I learned he was the one to send that wretched Nazarene to death by crucifixion. Though I was born nearly five years afterward, I was later told again and again about the Nazarene, regretting that I did not have the opportunity to witness His agony, for He seemed the worst of those ghastly Jewish insurrectionists who would dare to confront Rome with their ravings.

"I told the woman that I had no idea she was the widow of a great man. 'I did not tell you that because I was trying to convince you to let me say,' she ventured, anticipating what in fact I had been about to tell her. "'I think it must be time for me to go, anyway.' she said. 'I do have one request though.'

"'Ask whatever you wish, widow,' I replied. She wanted only to have that memorial preserved for long as possible. I said that I would see to it that this was so. Then I started to walk toward her, to take her by the arm and escort her to the entrance. She asked that I not touch her. I became quite angry. And then she told me that she was a leper. I refused to believe her, thinking once again that she was toying with me. She immediately dropped the little package and rolled back her garment at the arms."

Nero was trembling now as he went on.

"She had no fingers left. As she kicked off her sandals, I saw that most of her toes were gone as well. She had been wearing a scarf that was wrapped over the top of her head and down around her neck. Clumsily, because of the state of her hands, she pulled it away from her neck, which I saw was little but open sores."

His back to Paul and Scipio, the emperor clutched his hands together until bones pressed hard against flesh.

"I exploded with anger, and withdrawing a dagger from a sheath strapped to my wrist, rushed forward, rage blinding me, making my actions uncontrollable. I plunged the blade once into her chest."

Rage was now threatening to control Scipio as he started to lunge toward the unprepared Nero. But Paul clamped his hand tightly on his friend's wrist, and shook his head as he narrowed his eyes in implicit warning.

"She looked at me," Nero continued, "her expression only of tranquillity as she said, 'I forgive you, my emperor . . . in the name of Jesus the Christ.' I stabbed her over and over, wanting nothing more than to silence her, ignoring the tainted blood that was soaking me."

He faced them yet again and noticed veins that were pronounced across Scipio's forehead and along the side of his neck but chose to ignore what were obviously the other man's rising emotions.

"My men, who had been waiting nearby, rushed me back to my main residence," he recalled. "I spent hours trying to wash myself clean. I kept imagining that more of her blood remained, and bathed yet again, and again, and again.

"I could not sleep that night, as well as the next, and the one after that. For days, I scrutinized myself, looking over every inch of my body, searching for the beginning of any sores, for any other hints that she had infected me. Yet after that fear passed and relief should have taken hold of me, I had to face those few words of hers. For it was they that gave me more torment than any panic I experienced over the prospect of leprosy."

. . . I forgive you, my emperor . . . in the name of Jesus the Christ.

Nero stopped speaking for several minutes.

Paul waited with great patience, but it was Scipio who could not yet control his impulses, either to beat the life out of the obscene, over-aged child in front of him, or to rush from that dismal structure and get to Procula Pilatus's home as soon as possible.

He murdered that blessed woman! he told himself. *I should have visited her more often but, no, I left her so alone, with nobody to help her.*

Nero's words into his thoughts.

"I must go now," he said solemnly. "For one so young as I, the burden of the ages seems to be on my shoulders just now, a single condemning voice shouting at me from the dark corners of my mind. I cannot remain here any longer and make of myself more of a fool than I have done already."

He seemed awkward expressing himself with such candor, more accustomed to the subterfuge that marked the life of an emperor. After having spoken, he started to walk toward the entrance.

"She need not be your accuser," Paul said, raising his voice. "Let her become in death an instrument of righteousness in your life."

"If only it could be as you say, old man," the emperor remarked, pausing in a doorway that been cut through solid rock long years before. "But there are some in this world, it seems, who were doomed from the

351

moment of their birth. And no god or devil can change the course of such a life."

He was stepping through when Scipio anxiously called after him, "Where did you have the woman buried?"

Avoiding the other man's eyes, Nero said brusquely, "Next to Pontius Pilatus. There are two mounds now in that spot. I have ordered that neither of them are ever to be disturbed, nor the memorial she constructed. Remember such a dictum as this, if you will, when you are tempted perhaps to think of your emperor as some loathsome ogre."

"*Two* crosses?" Scipio asked, concerned that the woman's grave might be unmarked while her husband's was not. "Are there—?"

"That is for a *Christian* to do," the emperor interrupted, "not someone who worships gods other than your Jehovah. See to it yourself. I shall not interfere."

And then he was gone.

LXV

fter excusing himself from Paul's presence, Scipio hurried to the residence on the outskirts of Rome and found Procula Pilatus's grave mound. In less than an hour, he had located a carpenter in the trades and crafts section of the ancient city, whom he hired to build a cross identical to the one on Pontius Pilatus's grave.

And then he spent the rest of the afternoon and into the evening in prayer, pouring out his very soul, it seemed.

Less than a week later, a great fire destroyed much of Rome, and along with it, any hope for the redemption of Lucius Domitius Ahenobarbus Nero . . .

★ ★ ★

The conflagration burned for six days, beginning on July 18, A.D. 64.

Of the fourteen sections, or regions, of Rome, only four were unscathed. Three had been reduced completely to ashes. The others escaped little from the flames, though a few structures, damaged, remained.

The fire began at the Circus Maximus. Then it climbed the Palatine and Caelian hills nearby, then spread out to much of the rest of Rome where, as the renowned Tacitus wrote, "The ancient city's narrow winding streets and irregular blocks encouraged its progress."

Those streets became clogged with people seeking escape.

According to the historian Tacitus, "Countless numbers of terrified, shrieking women, helpless old and young, people intent on their own safety, others unselfishly supporting invalids or waiting for them . . . all heightened the confusion . . . menacing flames springing up, and outflanking many Romans. . . . Even districts believed remote proved to be involved. . . . Some citizens who had lost everything could have escaped, as others did, to the country roads but preferred to die and, therefore, stayed as the holocaust claimed them."

Among the innumerable casualties was Nero's splendid palace, the Domus Transitoria, and numerous other buildings he had had erected throughout the whole length and breadth of the city.

To his credit, Nero, who happened to be in Antium when he received news of the fire, returned immediately to Rome and personally directed massive efforts to contain the damage, though these were largely futile. After surveying the damage a week later, he instituted a building program that even those who hated him had to admit was ambitious and saved countless thousands of human survivors from complete homelessness, for he ordered a more orderly design than the original hodgepodge makeup of the city, a design that involved widening the streets, creating more parks as open spaces, and constructing apartment blocks for working families who had lost everything in the fire.

But before any of this could get much beyond the planning stages, his enemies began spreading an absurd rumor, namely, that Nero himself was responsible for starting the fire and could be seen fiddling nonchalantly as the flames spread. This proved to be as spurious as what another group of wealthy and powerful Romans sought to have accepted as fact. Senators who hated Christians as much as the emperor did were behind the allegation that the sect had started the fire in protest against the imprisonment of Paul. It was, sadly, this latter group to which Nero would listen most ardently, eventually buying the lie that they promulgated and feeling betrayed particularly by the apostle Paul.

Enraged even beyond the level of his many other livid outbursts over lesser matters in the past, Nero ordered the immediate imprisonment and soon-crucifixion of any Christian who could be caught.

The Appian Way was lined with the hanging bodies of men and women who had regularly professed their Christian faith, while their youngest children were pressed into slavery. Scavenger birds and other creatures feasted regularly.

Nero reserved a particularly ignominious sentence for Paul, to be carried out in a special arena that came to be known as Nero's Circus.

Decapitation.

He was to be executed in front of a special stand constructed solely for the purpose of allowing Nero to sit in comfort while the apostle died.

"I want the head!" the emperor demanded coarsely. "Preserve it well. I shall keep the thing as a trophy."

Imprisoned along with Paul was Fabius Scipio, arrested while at the hospice he and two others founded, though for the moment Tullio and Gaius Galienus went without capture, perhaps because they were so well connected in the Senate of Rome, and for the short term it would have proven politically unwise for Nero to attempt any sort of action against a married couple more popular than he was, particularly since no one could be made to believe that the two of them would ever become part of something as horrendous as the destruction of the city in which they had lived since birth.

The execution of Paul and Scipio was set for nighttime despite the fact that most such state-mandated killings had been conducted around midday.

"A special surprise," was all that Nero, licking his lips, would say to anybody who inquired about the apparent change of procedure. "You *should* attend. Spread the word! It will be an occasion no one who is fortunate enough to witness it will ever forget. On that you have the word of your emperor!"

And on that final day, before they were to be led a short distance away to Nero's Circus in the very center of Rome, Paul the apostle and Fabius Scipio the former legionnaire sat together in the confines of dismal little Mamertine prison, waiting, but not only that . . .

★ ★ ★

Neither of them could eat so much as a tiny piece of bread, though the guard offered an extra portion from his own food.

"His name is Antias Mettius Valerius," Paul said after the man had left. "His great-grandfather was the much-maligned historian. Such ancestry has been a burden this poor soul has been trying to live down ever since."

"Have you been able to reach him for Christ as yet?" Scipio asked.

"Oh, yes, though he is very shy about discussing his conversion with anyone. Only when he and I have been alone has he been able to do so."

They talked about more subjects as minutes passed through the morning, beyond noon, and into the hours just before dusk.

"You have suffered in one way or another for so long," Scipio said. "I know you must have felt weary sometimes. Yet you talk more about contentment than many I have seen during my time in Rome who lived in the most spacious and beautiful of homes, without ever knowing hunger or thirst or anything like that."

"I have learned to rejoice in suffering," Paul told him.

"How can that be? How can that *ever* be?"

"Because suffering produces perseverance; perseverance, character; and character, hope. And hope does not disappoint us, because God has poured out His love into our hearts by the Holy Spirit. It is the Spirit who has never failed to satisfy my needs."

Scipio had not thought that his appreciation of this man could grow any further, but he was wrong.

"So many today want only what benefits them and them only," he pointed out. "And so few want to work for their goals. The Roman government keeps them happy with handouts."

"Handouts that have driven the treasury into the dust!" Scipio exclaimed.

Paul nodded sadly.

"I could not continue if I felt as many do today," he said. "Even some of those converted to Christ feel such guilt over their sins. What they did before coming to Him haunts them like an oppressive cloud of bleak darkness hanging over them. How they waste the beauty of what has happened to them!"

Scipio smiled as he spoke, "'There is, therefore, no condemnation to them which are in Christ Jesus, which walk not after the flesh but after the Spirit.'"

Paul was pleased.

"You have read my parchment!" he exclaimed.

"It was sent to the community of Christians here in Rome, and they shared the contents with me. It continues to be a great help to everyone."

The apostle groaned then.

"Are you all right?" Scipio asked.

"Yes, dear brother, yes, I am. That sound I made was in anticipation of what awaits me when death comes this evening. I yearn to be absent from this body of flesh and to be present with the Lord."

"You and I shall go together."

"To stand before the throne of God," Paul said. "We have run a good race, you and I. Oh, to hear those words from His lips, 'Well done, you good and faithful servants.' No finer could be uttered."

Valerius called down to them.

"One hour, they are saying," he stated.

"Thank you for telling us," called back Paul. "We will be ready."

Scipio was more nervous than the apostle.

"Forgive me, Lord," he prayed, as he tried unsuccessfully to still a shaking hand.

"Fabius, Fabius, there is no need to ask for forgiveness for that which is not a sin," Paul told him.

"But I feel weak, especially next to your strength."

"You are hardly condemned to death for your cowardice but for your courage in presenting the good news. You would not be here were you a weakling."

Scipio was grateful for the apostle's wisdom.

"I feel ashamed," he confessed forlornly. "How can you stand to be near me? How can the Lord—?"

"No!" Paul said, reaching out and grabbing each shoulder. "Have you not remembered something else that I wrote in my epistle to the Romans? 'Who shall separate us from the love of Christ? Shall tribulation—?'"

"'—or distress, or persecution,'" Scipio continued for him, "'or famine, or nakedness, or peril, or sword?'"

"Yes, yes! Fabius, you repeat the words correctly but you must apply them to your very heart, your very soul, my brother. *Nothing* can separate us from Him, from His love! No power, no man, not Satan himself, *nothing!*"

Paul shook Scipio gently.

"Not even ourselves when we succumb to our worst emotions," he spoke. "Once we experience salvation, it cannot be taken from us by anyone, nor can the love of our Creator who made salvation possible."

He dropped his hands by his sides, his own shoulders slumping.

"Must I go to the grave wondering if you understand this?" he cried out. "Must I do that, my brother?"

This was the first time that Scipio saw Paul conduct himself in any way that seemed defeated.

He put his arms around the apostle, and the two of them shared that moment of tears.

LXVI

I t was not an hour later but several.

The execution of Paul and Scipio was delayed again and again, their guard Valerius giving them a new time once, twice, then yet once more, their emotions and his stretched like three old leather skins with new wine being poured into them, each threatening to burst.

"But why?" Scipio called up anxiously to the other man. "Is Nero trying to break us before we die? Does he get greater pleasure if this happens?"

"It is—," Valerius started to say at the final delay, any other words seeming to choke in his throat.

"You can speak freely," Paul assured him. "We will not betray your confidence."

Unaccountably the guard refused to answer and stepped back from the opening. They could hear him quietly sobbing to himself.

Paul and Scipio joined hands, the damp and chill darkness around them now more than just that of their little cave-like prison, darkness that seemed to be on the verge of reaching into their very souls.

"Father God, You have been with us in our weakness and fear and much trembling," Paul spoke, "giving forth Your strength and Your wisdom, and now we need a special measure of both in this hour as we come so close to the valley of the shadow of death through which we must walk. We are but fragile creations of flesh and blood. As we take one another by the hand, so do we need to have You take us by the hand, O Father God, and lead us through whatever awaits in this mournful night."

Neither could tell whether mere minutes passed or longer. They only knew that, finally, Valerius called to them again.

"I have to take you now," he said, his voice wavering.

He lowered the rope down and pulled up first Paul, then Scipio.

They saw that his cheeks were quite wet.

"I would not let anyone else come to get you," Valerius explained. "I told them that I would be responsible for both of the prisoners."

He went to the heavy, wooden door and swung it open.

Sounds poured in from the street.

"What is it that I hear?" Scipio asked, cocking his head. "It sounds like the cries of people in pain."

Valerius stood in front of the doorway.

"I cannot let you go there," he said, his face contorted with anguish. "I will say that you escaped. I can delay for a few minutes. Find one of the brothers or sisters who will take you in. Hide until it is safe to go to the harbor. Surely we can find a ship that—"

Paul stepped forward.

"Antias . . . ," he spoke softly. "I could not allow that. You have a wife and children. We are alone. You must not sacrifice yourself for us."

"But did not Christ teach that sacrifice was the greatest honor? What greater act than to lay down one's life for another?"

"It is our time to go and be with Him, dear, dear friend. We are in the Lord's will. Surely you believe that He knows what He is doing. Would you deny us the joy of so soon an eternity of rejoicing with the hosts of heaven?"

The guard drew out his sword.

"Then let me do it, and, after that, my own life as well so that we might make the journey together."

"You would be committing first two murders and then your suicide," spoke Paul with great patience. "Is it truly your desire to approach the throne of a holy God with such recent blood on your hands?"

The cries outside seemed to be louder.

"It will be hard on you," Paul added, "if we delay any longer."

Valerius numbly replaced the sword in the sheath strapped to his side.

"Follow me," he said simply.

The cold air refreshed them as they stepped outside. To their right was the Forum, now deserted. To their left, just beyond some buildings untouched by the rampaging fire of a month earlier was the large square where many festivities had been held over the years. Recently it had come to be known as Nero's Circus, since the emperor delighted in staging flamboyant circus acts there, as well as intellectually stimulating plays of a quieter nature written by a favored group of men considered to be Rome's finest satirists and playwrights.

Cries . . . agonizing, pain-drenched cries.

And a sickening odor.

In the night sky, rising from the direction of the square, were clouds of smoke, and just below those the three men could glimpse clearly, as they walked closer, the orange-red colors of individual flickering fires spaced equally apart.

Scipio gasped as he saw the crosses and the writhing, flame-shrouded figures on them.

Ringed around the square.

A different human form on each.

Many were motionless, hands frozen in ghastly death throes while reaching outward with unheeded pleas for mercy from the vengeance-driven young emperor, who was sitting back and stuffing his bloated face with pieces of wild boar torn from a whole cooked carcass set down with some flair in front of him. Whatever was left after he had finished indulging his gluttony would be handed over to the poor, who watched the spectacle from a crowd of rich and poor alike that had gathered at the opposite end of the square.

As Paul and Scipio passed between two of the crosses, a voice shouted down at them.

"I see the Savior now, dear brothers!" the man hanging to their left spoke. "He is taking away my pain. I feel no—"

Paul looked up immediately but could glimpse little of the dying one's features through the flames.

"Lean against me, please . . . ," he whispered to Scipio. "I feel faint."

It was a blessing for Scipio to do this since he himself also was feeling physically weak just then. They walked to the middle of the square, shoulder to shoulder.

Other voices cried out.

"Paul . . . Paul!" the apostle heard, each cry tremulous but also strangely exultant as soon as his arrival became apparent to those who had not yet succumbed.

Straining his eyes as he surveyed the wretched victims, Paul just barely made out the identities of a few.

"Precious Jesus!" he said. "Precious Jesus!"

"So many seem to know you," Scipio managed to utter through the tears that were beginning to choke him.

"I was the Lord's instrument in their salvation," the apostle told him. "I remember baptizing each of these dear souls in the name of the Father and the Son and the Holy Spirit. I remember where it was that this was so and when it was. And I shall carry every detail with me beyond the gates of heaven itself."

Paul's cheeks were streaked with tears as he turned slowly, looking at the grotesque spectacle being played out on every side except where the crowd waited, transfixed, no one murmuring.

"There are flames only now," he announced triumphantly to the several dozen believers, "but once you enter the presence of our blessed

360

Father God, you shall escape them for eternity. Yet not so for those who have caused this brutal infamy."

His attention became focused on Nero with such intensity that, even from that distance, the emperor started to squirm awkwardly in his seat, while hoping no one perceived that he could be affected in such a manner by an itinerant Jew who had been condemned to die the death of a common criminal.

As Paul strode toward Nero, a transformation overtook his small but not so fragile body, as though his entire countenance was in the process of being altered, rage wondrously replaced by something else that could not be fathomed at first.

The crowd noticed and voices shouted, "Look at him! See how different he is after but an instant."

And there came a chill over the entire scene.

It seemed as though a very real canopy of invisible ice had descended abruptly upon everyone present.

"So cold!" someone exclaimed. "I feel so cold!"

"What is happening?" another member of the crowd asked loudly. "What gods doth this moment offend?"

By the time Paul was approaching Nero, guards had formed a line in front of him. But the emperor, needing to seem unafraid of one so small, ordered them aside.

"Do you have some last plea to make to me?" Nero asked with contempt.

"I have one statement only," the apostle spoke.

Even Nero was astonished by the visible change in Paul, from the rage he had manifested seconds earlier to the peace that now settled upon his face, softening his features.

"I speak as the woman did before your blade took her life . . . ," Paul said.

Nero's manner changed as well.

"I do not want to hear those damnable words again!" he declared, a touch of desperation in his voice.

"But you shall," Paul went on, "for it is true that—"

Nero summoned guards with a snap of his fingers. In an instant they were grabbing Paul and starting to drag him back to the center of the square, but not before the apostle spoke what he intended.

"I forgive you, my emperor . . . in the name of Jesus the Christ," Paul said quickly, his voice at a shout above the clamor of the legionnaires around him.

Nero stood, his eyes wide, his cheeks puffed out even more, while he snarled obscenities at the apostle. As Paul walked down the wooden steps in front of him, other voices were piercing the air, dying men on flaming crosses forgiving him in the name of the risen Son of God.

"Disperse the crowd!" the emperor ordered, wincing as their voices reached his ears, his entire face a deep red. "They will not be allowed to witness any more of this!"

He pointed to Paul.

"And off with his head!" he thundered. *"Now!"*

Two of the soldiers held Paul down, and another raised a sword above his neck.

"No, I beg you!" another voice managed to be heard among the din in the square.

The soldier with the sword looked up and recognized a comrade.

Antias Mettius Valerius.

"Get back!" the soon-executioner begged him. "You must not interfere with this, Antias. You must not."

But Valerius would not heed any entreaty. Bigger, stronger than the others, he grabbed the sword and held it against his own neck as he faced Nero.

"Take my life instead, my emperor!" he shouted. "Shed the miserable blood of my pitiable self. But not this noble Paul, this ordained saint to whom you spoke with such feeling just yesterday. Spare his life but not mine, for I could not face another day if I did not ask you to bring the sword upon me instead."

Nero smiled cruelly.

"I see that you wear your mantle of sacrifice well," he said, slapping his thigh, his cynical tone mocking the other man. "Fine, then, I *shall* take your life, as you now request, but I am afraid that you have outsmarted yourself, Antias Mettius Valerius, for your blood will mingle not with that of Paul's hapless companion, as you had hoped, but with Paul himself! How ironic this moment, for the Jew's friend will be the one whose life your death will purchase!"

The next instant, two of the soldiers were able to wrest the sword from Valerius, and then the shorter, younger one decapitated him after the legionnaire had been flung to the ground.

As this was happening, Paul had fallen to his knees in prayer, Scipio beside him, his right hand tightly clutching the apostle's left.

Soldiers pulled him away from Paul.

"My life instead!" Scipio begged of a man who knew so little of the meaning of mercy throughout his young life. "Not this good man's. He must live. Let him live, my emperor!"

"No, I shall not! I tire of this oh-so-noble behavior on the part of Christians," Nero demanded hoarsely as he pointed to the soldier who had executed Valerius. "You there! *Now!*"

The soldier to whom the emperor had pointed quickly raised the heavy sword above the apostle.

Paul looked up at him.

"You send me to my Lord!" he said joyfully. "I see Him now. He stands in welcome. I am ready. Do what you must!"

"Can I be forgiven even this?" the soldier whispered.

"And more," Paul assured the man. "Someday, I think, you will join me by His side."

Suddenly the apostle flung his head back, tilting it slightly at a sound or a scene perhaps, witnessed only by him, his eyes opened wide as he reached one arm out, a single name only escaping his pale old lips, *"Stephen . . ."*

Paul turned, his eyes glistening as he looked again at the soldier, smiled, and then lowered his head obediently.

The sword was swung down in one quick movement. There was time for only a single gasp to escape the apostle's lips.

Another man took the head by its hair and brought it to Nero.

"You asked for this," he said. "Am I now to deliver it to the embalmer?"

The ruler of Imperial Rome turned away without speaking, his lips quivering.

"Shall I take care of this for you?" the soldier persisted, trying to disguise his impatience and his disgust.

"I no longer care," Nero whispered, his voice breaking. "Do with it what you will."

"May I turn it over to his people, and the body as well?"

Nero groaned an exasperated yes and hurried from that place, his entourage of servants and guards following him, more than a few pausing at the edge of the square as they glanced back furtively—even, observers said later, the emperor himself, before he muttered something quite blasphemous and continued on.

As the remaining legionnaires were starting to leave, once nobody lingered from the crowd, one of the soldiers gave Scipio a cloak to wrap around himself against the temperatures of that bleak night, and, his back to the others, made the sign of the cross to identify himself, then rejoined his awaiting comrades who kidded him about his soft and generous heart.

Scipio stayed in the square beside the two bodies, sometimes praying, sometimes sobbing, sleeping only a little, until morning light cast reddish fingers over the melancholy scene.

Someone tapped him on the shoulder.

Gaius Gallenius . . . standing with Claudius Crassus Inrigillensis Sabinus Appius, Publius Cornelius Dolabella, and several others whom Scipio did not recognize.

363

"We were the last to find out," Gallenius whispered. "Please, please forgive us for not coming sooner, my brother."

The torn bodies were then carried solemnly from the square, and later that day there were burial services attended by believers from within the environs of Rome as well as from the countryside in every direction.

Just past midnight, Lucius Domitius Ahenobarbus Nero was to encounter the first of many nightmares that began troubling his sleep, giving him little of what could be called peace, for those gruesome visions were to stay deep and immutable within the soul of the most powerful man of that ancient world, resurrecting themselves again and again, like accusing sirens, until the end of his days and a death that would come by his own trembling hand as he cried out, "How ugly and vulgar my life has become!"

Part VIII

*U*ltimately, the persecution of Christians as scapegoats for the destruction of so much of Rome was not enough for the megalomania of this emperor. His passions drove him on to slaughter other groups which he suspected, in his warped thinking, to be guilty of plotting against him, including the Jews.

But Nero needed, ever cognizant as he was of the political ramifications, some pretext or justification. Together with a trusted group of advisers, he studied the various possibilities and decided that the Jews, after a long period of oppression, would surely rebel in a tumultuous fashion if a Roman governor were installed in Judea whose practices made all the others before him look pristine in comparison.

That was why he decided to send a handpicked, thoroughly corrupt politician named Gessius Florus, a man who could be counted on to be insensitive and arrogant. It was determined that whatever was necessary must be done to bring about what Nero wanted, an excuse to begin an offensive against the Jews.

Florus found the vehicle for this when he instigated a blasphemous pagan sacrifice on some Jewish holy ground in front of a synagogue in Caesarea, prompting a strident protest by a delegation of Jews. The governor arrested these men and, at the same time, appropriated money from the temple at Jerusalem.

After doing so, Florus ordered his obedient troops to raid the various open air markets along the narrow streets of that city, returning to him some of the many jewels, leather goods, rare silks, and other items taken at the point of swords, but keeping the rest as rewards to be divided among themselves.

Shop owners and members of their families as well as other citizens in the vicinity tried to resist this brutal outrage, though they proved to be singularly ill-equipped to do so and could not withstand the armed legionnaires who went on to slaughter more than thirty-six hundred men, women, and children.

News of the atrocity circulated throughout Judea and led directly to a rebellion by thousands of zealots as well as others normally less extreme in their behavior who were startled out of their complacency.

Yet it was true that not everyone was in favor of reacting in such an extreme manner. Moderate rabbis saw through the deliberately provocative actions of Florus and were convinced that it would be far more productive if they did little or nothing of a violent nature, but confined their protests to written communication with the emperor, in whom they had no more confidence than the proconsul-governor himself; yet, they reasoned, having a spotless record of law-abiding behavior even in the face of atrocity would serve them well with whoever Nero's successor would be, if they just waited out his vengefulness.

Three important Roman fortresses in Judea would be marked for an offensive in retaliation: Herodium, Machaerus, and Masada. The insurrectionists and others who had joined them succeeded through the sheer frenzy of their attacks to take over all three. Though the Roman forces quickly retook Herodium and Machaerus, they did not attempt to reach down as far south as Masada, the other former palace-fortress of King Herod.

Two years after this sudden outbreak of warfare began in the land of Judea, Nero was to commit suicide. A succession of three substandard emperors over the next year hampered the Roman response to the rebellion of the Jews. Galba was murdered, while Otho became emperor and committed suicide months later.

Vitellius then occupied the throne, but was clearly the worst of the three, causing a civil war within the empire, but with particular ferocity in Rome itself, ending only after he was put to death by a faction of his own troops, who decided they could no longer stand by and watch Imperial Rome destroyed from within while its enemies waited to rend the corpse.

Finally, brilliant Titus Flavius Vespasianus ended the trinity of mediocrity, becoming the first emperor since Nero to hold the throne for more than a short while. He had been the general in charge of the Roman forces as they fought against the Jews. Upon leaving for Rome, he left his son, Titus, in charge.

The younger Vespasianus moved with special brutality against Jerusalem, virtually destroying the ancient city. The siege was so fierce and effective that hunger ultimately drove the citizens to acts that none would have considered under any other circumstances, including rampant cannibalism, with resultant horrible images of fathers and mothers eating their young children who had died from starvation or injury. Any human or animal corpse came to be considered a food source by a desperate populace.

Masada.

Built by Herod to protect himself and his family from what he imagined were the ambitions—territorial and otherwise—of Queen Cleopatra of Egypt.

It was to this supposedly impregnable location south of Jerusalem that a handful of survivors of the massacre at the Jewish capital fled while a separate group of some three thousand zealots regrouped in a forest called Jardes.

Discovered by a passing shepherd who had secretly been bought and paid for by the younger Vespasianus, all of the insurrectionists were to die when the enemy's cavalry surrounded the entire area and attacked without letup, while the Romans suffered only twelve fatalities and a small number of wounded.

Despite this defeat, the zealots at Masada would enjoy some six years of essentially "safe" encampment there, free from interference by the Roman forces. From that mountain fortress as a central stronghold, they were able to stage marauding expeditions into the area primarily north of the fortress, bedeviling any Roman soldiers with whom they came in contact and angrily executing whatever collaborators they could find, thinking that that was what the victims deserved for giving the enemy even the slightest help.

Among the surviving Jews of Jerusalem were those who tried to stem this tide of blood, reasoning that any such deaths would draw attention to the fact that Masada remained in zealot hands. An "out of sight, out of mind" stance was encouraged, but the vast majority at the fortress scorned it and continued the fearsome vendettas, saddening those who believed, at that point, that the zealots had become little more principled than the Romans themselves.

Standing out among the more than nine hundred Jewish men, women, and children at Masada was a single aging former Roman legionnaire, Decimus Paetus, who remarkably had become an invaluable chief military strategist to the zealots.

LXVII

A large plateau atop an outjutting section of mountain close to one of the most famous bodies of water in the entire region, and nothing for many miles in all directions except the wasteland of a mammoth desert . . .

The clash of battles from forty years earlier rang loudly in Decimus Paetus's mind as he stood at the eastern end of the Herod-built fortress named Masada, moonlight bouncing off Lake Asphaltitus to his left, less than a mile away.

"I am here to vanquish perhaps more than a few of those very men, still young in their service at the time, by the side of whom I fought as a dedicated comrade so long ago," he said wistfully.

Aviram, a burly Jew from Bethlehem who had led the rebel forces against Herodium, which was very near that ancient village, sighed as did most men who had been willing to sacrifice their lives and eventually came to see no good whatever come of their courage.

"I too reflect upon the past in a similar manner," he spoke. "Even now, as I stand beside you, I wonder in my soul how this can be that we are here, you and I, and not opposing one another at sword's length."

"I never killed one of your people," Paetus assured him. "Thank God that that is not another guilt to be heaped upon the others from my past."

Aviram bowed his head.

"I cannot say the same, even before the rebellion," he nearly whispered, embarrassed by his own recollections.

Shaking himself for a moment, as though purging his battle-scarred body of some foul substance, Aviram went on to say, "You are a Christian, I have gathered from talking with the others. Are you not, therefore, uncomfortable being here in such complete isolation with so many Jews who could easily have been part of that mob forty years ago, men shouting their throats bloody as they demanded the death of your Jesus?"

Ironically, that was exactly how Paetus had felt at the beginning. He tried to answer the other man with equal candor.

"It was that way for me once," he admitted, "but no longer, Aviram. We are fighting the same enemy, would you not agree?"

Aviram nodded but raised another matter.

370

"I heard that you were the one who made Barabbas change."

"I did not *make* him, my friend. Barabbas did choose Christ, yes, but out of his own free will."

"But he was a *Jew*, Decimus! How could this man who gave his life for his country surrender the ancestry that Jews as a people have had behind them all these centuries?"

Paetus was not offended by the other man's question, for he had grown to love tough, sometimes crude, Aviram within the span of just a few weeks, though this was the first quiet moment by themselves that either could point to during that period.

"Barabbas gave up nothing," Paetus said. "But he gained a great deal. May I tell you what happened?"

Aviram nodded assent.

The salvation of principal insurrectionist Barabbas occurred some twenty-odd years before. Paetus had lived with the man and his roving band of rebels ever since leaving the village that Nicodaemus, Joseph of Arimathea, and he had succeeded in rebuilding before being confronted by Marcus Vibenna.

"It was on the shores over there," Paetus said as he pointed toward the lake that came to be known as the Dead Sea. "He was baptized in its waters."

"And gave up the fight, I assume," Aviram snorted.

"I am a Christian," Paetus rebuked him, "but can you say that I have, in any way, given up the fight?"

"Where did you all go?" the other man asked, avoiding a direct answer because of embarrassment over how correct Paetus was. "There was a period when the insurrection died down."

This happened as he had understood, with a resignation to their country's domination from Roman being substituted for their previous fanatical nationalism.

"That it did but this was not in any way because of Barabbas's conversion, mine, or anybody else's."

"Others in your group became . . . Christians?"

"All of them, yes. We secretly settled in Petra."

"That is rather near here. How ironic!"

"We had heard that there were a group of the Nabataeans who would be interested in our cause."

"Since many of the Syrians hated the Romans as much as we did, they would surely provide money, equipment, men perhaps," Aviram interjected knowingly. "They could fight as Jews and not draw any attention to the fact that they were actually Arabs. As far as the Romans are concerned, we all look alike, of course!"

"That was exactly how we hoped they would think," Paetus agreed, impressed by how quickly the other man had anticipated what he was going to say. "So, we journeyed to Petra and sought them out."

Petra.

An extraordinary city for any age.

It was a major Arabian caravan stop on the route from India to the Mediterranean. Hidden at the end of a mile-long, thousand-foot deep gorge, it provided a refuge for Christians and others escaping the excesses of Roman rule.

"What happened while you were in Petra?" Aviram asked.

"Since Barabbas was so charismatic, everything was based upon his leadership, for he seemed the only man with the ability to rally sufficient forces to be more than a nuisance to the Romans. Unfortunately, he contracted some disease and died quite painfully, but even in the midst of his pain, he was praising God!"

"And so the Nabataeans lost interest, I assume?"

"Yes—the group of us disbanded. I continued to live in the rose-red city until I learned through a messenger that ben Ya'ir thought I could be helpful. I rejoiced that a new leader had sprung up, but by then the Nabataeans had lost their revolutionary zeal and became content in appeasement."

Aviram fell silent.

"What of the miracles, Decimus?" he asked abruptly.

"By Jesus?"

"Yes . . . I understand that He was capable of almost anything and performed many of these during His lifetime."

"He did, Aviram. Which makes the tragedy of His crucifixion all the more appalling. He embodied only ultimate good, my friend, capable just of those acts that were ordained by His heavenly Father."

A moment later, Aviram spoke again, "What were some of the miracles, Decimus? I was very young at the time. I paid little attention."

"The blind saw, the lame walked, the deaf heard. The dying revived and lived. Food seemed to appear from nowhere in order that thousands might be fed."

"I knew Lazarus," Aviram revealed. "He was a distant cousin."

"The one brought back from death?"

"Yes. But not until after he claimed to have been raised up."

"You did not believe him?"

"How could I? His story was nonsense!"

At that, Aviram turned to walk away, then halted his steps.

"We will talk again about this," he said. "I mean no harm. I have been living by my own hand so long. When I was not fighting the Romans, I was farming. I raised crops, animals. I saw only birth and death.

"It is hard to believe that there is anything different from this scheme of things, Decimus, for I have always witnessed the same cycle day after day, which has, you cannot deny, gone on for centuries. My wife has been dead for many years, and my sons are dead also. That will never change. So what else is there?

"Once their lifeless bodies entered the earth, that was it, I knew, for the rest of my life. I had to go on, yes, I knew that, but it was so hard each time I lost one of them, Decimus. How eager I would have been to see *them* resurrected by the Nazarene! But this Messiah of yours never came our way."

Though never married, Paetus could still understand at least a little of the man's emotions.

"My mother is gone," he acknowledged, "and so is my father. Some dear friends have left too. I know not where most of them are."

He was thinking especially of Fabius Scipio, among others, wondering what would have happened to his brother-in-Christ during those more than thirty years since the two of them had parted company.

So long ago, he thought. *So very long ago.*

"It is hard to say good-bye," Aviram was telling him.

"Yes, it is," Paetus agreed absentmindedly.

"How many has it been that we have lost since all this started? I do not have anything resembling a total. How many were not buried properly because we could not find their bodies underneath the rubble of Jerusalem or one of the other places where those who took this land from us took our relatives I do not know."

Aviram walked away then from the end of the southern bastion, heading toward the northern side and the zealots' living quarters there. Paetus decided to head on to the so-called western palace, which was in the opposite direction.

A new military adviser had arrived in Jerusalem apparently, someone who was quite old but possessed a vast amount of experience. The source of this information mentioned some of the battles in which the man had participated, and Paetus remarked that he too had been involved in those.

Nine hundred of us to their thousands, he thought. *Will we see a miracle of victory as in the times of the patriarchs?*

Paetus was greeted only by the sound of a howling wind, mournful and chill, blowing off the plains, stirring clouds of ancient dust for miles in every direction.

LXVIII

His mouth dry from snoring, Paetus awoke the next morning to the urgent call of Eleazar ben Ya'ir, the boisterous, stocky leader of the band of Jewish zealots. Being one of their most valued members, a Roman military adviser, gave Paetus better quarters than almost anyone else. Herod had built three small palaces at Masada, plus one called his "western palace," the ultimate show of his desire for supreme luxury, a three-tiered palace-villa at the western end, built on top of the plateau and down the side. Other zealot quarters were far more humble, at the northeastern end. But no jealousy developed since everyone seemed to realize how valuable an individual Paetus was.

As he hurried outside from his own quarters, Paetus noticed that the day's temperature was already climbing, despite the early hour, and steeled himself for the kind of heat that gave some hint of what hell would be.

"A wall of one of the cisterns is threatening to collapse," ben Ya'ir spoke urgently to the gathered hundreds standing before him. "If it goes, we will have serious difficulties. Repair must begin immediately, my brothers and sisters."

Cisterns were several huge excavations dug along the northern side by Herod's original workers—all but one situated roughly in the middle of the mountain, at the location of the third level of the spectacular three-terrace palace, showing Herod's tendency to place his own welfare and that of his family above all else.

The remaining cisterns, by far the largest of the group, were just below the uneven surface on which Masada had been built. These averaged one hundred forty thousand cubic feet of water, for a total of close to a million and a half—all carved into the rock by Herod's team of slave laborers.

Much of the water came from adjacent canals that fed from a nearby wadi through which a mountain stream had been flowing for perhaps thousands of years, the rest coming from those occasional rainstorms that hit the area, which though scarce were severe, enabling all of the cisterns to fill up in a matter of hours.

Herod had figured on everything but time, Paetus told himself. *Erosion can undermine whatever man builds.*

Everyone in the community pitched in to shore up the entrance of the damaged cistern. But ben Ya'ir called Paetus aside, in the midst of loud voices and some sense of panic, and spoke to him about another matter altogether.

"Since the occupying enemy has not as yet attacked us," he said, "that must mean that they are experiencing some difficulties elsewhere. I have heard of nothing special in Judea, so I can only assume that other groups in some other conquered land in their empire are bedeviling them. But I think we should send down some scouts and try to find out more clearly what has been happening."

Paetus nodded as he replied. "The Roman strategy is not to spread their forces too thin. Even though they have generally had unlimited manpower, that principle still has invariably held true. They would plan to defeat our forces at, say, Herodium first, then move on to Machaerus or simply the reverse. Then, regrouping, and with just one objective in that case, they would be able to concentrate everything on Masada."

Speaking the name "Machaerus" brought to Paetus's mind another tragedy, the murder of John the Baptist, which occurred at that fortress, located on the other side of the Dead Sea northeast of Masada.

Ben Ya'ir rubbed his arm, sharing the melancholy of that moment.

"We are doomed, are we not, Decimus?" he said wearily, his very full beard looking a bit more straggly than usual.

"I can come to no other conclusion," Paetus agreed with great and uncomfortable solemnity. "Our only alternative, it seems, is to flee this location and somehow seek another, wherever that might be."

"And we would be pursued as Moses was but with no guarantee that God will part the waters again for His people."

"Even if that were the case," Paetus pointed out, "the enemy forces at Machaerus would be sent to head us off when we crossed over."

Ben Ya'ir looked at Paetus intently.

"Besides, both the near and the far shores of Lake Asphaltitus are controlled by the Romans anyway. We would have no destination to which we could ever escape. We die here, we die there, little does it matter."

"Whatever happens will hardly be immediate, since we still have much of the rest of summer with us," Paetus reminded him. "Only the nights are cold, and the Romans could never successfully attack then. With the days as hot as we have seen, the physical exertion would crush them, with so many soldiers collapsing that all of us up here would be able to sit back and watch the whole lot defeat themselves!"

"Autumn then?"

"I see no other time, Eleazar."

The other man's eyes nearly shut, and he touched his sweaty temple with the fingers of his left hand.

"Head aching?" Paetus inquired.

"If it were only that, I would be blessed."

"What is it then?"

"I have been dreaming of late."

"About what?" Paetus asked in a kindly manner.

Ben Ya'ir's manner betrayed a touch of exasperation.

"Whom, Decimus, whom?" he asked gruffly.

"Which man?"

"If I listened to you, not a man at all."

"Jesus?" Paetus probed hopefully.

"Yes."

Ben Ya'ir was obviously uncomfortable, but Paetus knew that he could not let this revelation pass without asking more about it.

"Forgive me, but would you tell—?" he started to say.

"Another time, my friend, another time."

"But we are alone now. Everyone else is working on the cistern."

Ben Ya'ir was grinding his teeth.

"The Nazarene stood before me," he said finally. "He wanted me to come to Him so that He could give me rest."

"What did you tell Him, in this dream?"

"That He was just a man, however courageous he had been. But, I said, only Almighty God Himself could give me the rest of which He spoke."

"What happened at that point, Eleazar?"

"I awoke . . ."

Ben Ya'ir's manner made Paetus think that there was more to it. The rebel leader saw the questioning expression that could not be hidden.

"You are perceptive, my favorite Roman," he commented.

"Then you have something else to tell me perhaps."

"I awoke, Decimus, with tears running down my cheek. Now why would I be crying, can you tell me?"

Paetus started to do just that when ben Ya'ir held up his hand.

"Not now. Perhaps never. I cannot say. Let me sort it out in my own mind before I hear what is on yours."

Paetus spoke no more about the dream, choosing to accede to the man's wishes but still praying, in his own private moments alone, that Eleazar ben Ya'ir would not simply retreat without raising the subject again.

LXIX

With so few men available inside it, the fortress could not be adequately defended strictly by them alone because its near-two thousand foot length and six hundred-fifty foot width would spread their forces far too thin along the perimeter; but that was where the natural makeup of the plateau provided considerable help.

Masada was thirteen hundred feet above sea level!

Only a long series of narrow, little, primitive steps of rock dug into the side of the promontory from the bottom and winding around to the top led directly to it, hardly a viable route for burly legionnaires burdened by armor, weapons, and whatever other necessary items they would have had to lug.

The soil on the plateau at that time was the most fertile imaginable, any farmer's fantasy, and the zealots could hold out indefinitely by raising their own extensive crops, though this hardly pleased men who were accustomed to diets that included a great deal of meat. What with the regular water supply awaiting them in the network of cisterns, they had a classically perfect situation if only for the short term.

But no one believed that the Romans would simply allow the Sicarii, as the zealots were sneeringly named, to stay where they were indefinitely, for as the glaring inability of the occupying forces to do anything to dislodge them became more and more apparent, mighty Rome would be reduced to the level of public impotence and consequent disgrace . . .

★ ★ ★

Marcus Vibenna was tired.

"I am too old to be facing anyone in war," he said to the empty room of his small home near Pompeii, "even though I shall be well enough away from the edge of battle, and others will be doing the fighting for me this time."

An astonishing idea hit him.

"A general!" he exclaimed. "I shall be like a general without the medals and the money but with *some* of the power."

He stretched his legs and walked to the window on that second floor.

A view that never ceased to take his breath away.

Straight ahead was Vesuvius, an impressive dormant volcano.

Dormant, yes, Vibenna thought. *But I wonder about the little spurts of steam that can be seen from time to time at your base, majestic mount. Perhaps there is no connection, but I do wonder, for I have viewed them myself.*

He turned from Vesuvius to the Bay of Naples at his left and sighed as he saw large boats owned by wealthy men and political figures being docked.

They come here because of the pleasures that await them, pleasures of which I have not partaken for a long time now.

Vibenna knew that age had something to do with his disdain, physical performance having decreased along with carnal desire, but he also sensed that there was something else, the ready availability of pornographic images on temple walls, male and female prostitutes, the worship of various gods sanctioning orgies that would have made Caligula look prissy—all this and other widespread practices generated in him a certain loathing that was not his alone but shared by others in his acquaintance.

"That which is done in private becomes obscene and disgusting when it is offered to the public for a price," he mused out loud. "But then I come from another generation, and my values are no longer in favor."

His right cheek started twitching as he remembered the whoring of his own youth, and along with that, his encounter with Mary Magdalene at the tomb.

She was looking up at the darkening sky.

"Angels are poised tonight," she said, with utter conviction. "They will swoop down on this place, and roll the rock aside, and Jesus' resurrected body will come forth."

"You seem so certain," Paetus pointed out, "but others, including the fisherman and Nicodaemus, have been here, and displayed hardly a measure of your earnestness."

"Those forgiven the most should have the most gratitude, and the greatest awe," she said. "Peter and the rest never considered themselves such sinners as I have been. Except for Matthew, they sought to make a living in what could only be called an honorable manner.

"Yet I had been mired in lust and its utter shame and decadence most of my life, even from my youngest years. I allowed my body to be abused for the satisfaction of those who paid me. And I did this often in the temples of our gods! For me, it was the sin of illicit intercourse often in league with blasphemy."

"You speak with the cultivation of someone learned," Paetus observed, "and yet you are a product of the streets. Did this Jesus aid you in that way also?"

378

"He did," she replied, her eyes luminous. *"He cleansed my mind as well as my soul. He spoke with great precision. He taught with great joy that which is the beauty of language, not vulgar, debased talk. It is little enough that I follow His example."*

All four legionnaires had been listening to her for some minutes, and witnessing the extraordinary transformation of a woman whom they had known carnally.

"I have to go now," she told them. *"But before I do, will you permit me to kneel before that great rock and pray briefly?"*

They stepped aside without hesitation.

Mary Magdalene walked up to the sealed tomb entrance, and knelt as she spoke, her voice just above a whisper.

"You called Lazarus forth," she said. *"When will the heavenly Father bring Your body from this grave, O Lord?"*

The five men waited respectfully for her to finish. After saying, *"Your broken and humble servant offers this prayer to Thee with the wish that, somehow, she could be here when the angels descend upon this spot tonight . . . Amen,"* Mary Magdalene stood, and turned in their direction.

"Look at her face!" Scipio said.

But the others already had seen the glow on it, the absolute and total peace.

. . . *those forgiven the most should have the most gratitude, and the greatest awe.*

She was smiling as she walked past them.

"You are an intelligent woman," Vibenna called after her. *"How can you hope for these angels to come? They are creatures of imagination, nothing more."*

At the top of the walkway, Mary Magdalene turned, glanced at him for a moment, and said only, *"Tell me this in the morning, Marcus Vibenna . . . if you can,"* before she walked away into the gathering night.

Vibenna smiled, remembering how different that moment was from the ones he had spent in her bed years before.

The woman had changed so much, he thought ruefully, *and she managed to wear her new life well.*

Then there were Paetus and Scipio, both sharing the same faith that had transformed the harlot.

How could they have been so stupid. I could suppose a Jewish tax collector and a fisherman or two, that sort of man perhaps, but not Romans like those two.

He recalled someone else.

Accius.

A nice little man, brave, intelligent, Vibenna told himself. *I suppose no one has heard from him since those years. He seems to have disappeared from the face of the earth. Have the gods of the netherworld gotten the poor soul?*

Three men, the lot of them gone.

It may be that I am the only one to survive, and for that I should be grateful, he thought, *while not failing to mourn the others, and yet I have survived only to face the greatest loneliness a man can know.*

A great sadness overcame him then, and he leaned against the edge of the window to support himself.

"I thought I would be free to live in peace and not stand in bloody battle once again," Vibenna whispered in rumination to no one in that empty room or the street just below, his voice strained. "But here I am, being drawn back into some carnage somewhere yet one more time. I did tell the courier that I would do what they had asked on their secret little parchment handed to me just hours ago, and, alas, I cannot back out, short of suffering disgrace, but my heart is heavy, and I do not know why."

Three hours later, a *biga* drawn by two horses pulled up in front. Vibenna was outside, waiting for it.

The legionnaire who greeted him was a stranger.

"It is an honor to meet you!" the man exclaimed.

"You must be quite desperate if an aging relic such as myself can be an honor," he responded both modestly and cynically.

"Have they told you what the mission will be?"

"Nothing, except that my services seem to them invaluable."

"Masada, sir, you will be assisting in the retaking of Masada."

"How is it that you know and I do not, young man?"

The legionnaire blushed as he replied, "I am part of the legions. You know how few secrets there are."

Vibenna nodded in agreement, recalling how word had spread quickly when he was serving actively.

"I had forgotten . . ." he mumbled. "It has been many years."

The other man patted him sympathetically on the shoulder.

"I can face an enemy's lance or sword far more easily than I can face age, sir," he spoke honestly.

"When we are young, we think as you do. When we are old, we recall our youth with great regret, for it passes far too quickly."

"And death, sir, so soon it seems ready to come, without warning, and then all is done for us."

"The Christians have an answer, it is said," Vibenna reminded him.

"Yes, that is what is said."

Vibenna detected something in his manner.

"What is your name?" he asked.

"Mavortius, sir, Quintus Mavortius."

"Are you a Christian?" Vibenna asked him directly.

Mavoritus sucked in his breath without answering.

"You need not fear anything from me on that score, Quintus."

"How so, sir?"

"Let me tell you why . . ."

Vibenna then launched into a vivid retelling of his startling encounter at the tomb of the Nazarene.

In an instant, the stone at the entrance to the tomb was rolled to one side as though it had been made of papyrus, and, from within, a blinding light shone forth. Their eyes affected, none of the legionnaires could see, for a moment or two, anything but vague shapes distorted into indistinct blurs.

One larger shape . . . surrounded by a myriad of others.

Paetus's vision returned first. Then Vibenna's, followed by the others.

And they dropped to their knees.

They saw the carpenter, the one who had been crucified earlier, the one proclaimed to be the Messiah for whom the Jews had been waiting, not by the respected and powerful religious rulers of Israel but by His small band of followers, the very ones who had largely deserted Him the moment his mortality seemed to be proven.

No one else had believed the message he had been sending forth, as far as any of the legionnaires knew. But then no one had seen the sight that was playing itself out before them in colors of silver, gold, white, and traces of crimson.

Jesus the Christ stood before them but He was not alone. A multitude of those shining, translucent beings formed an outline around Him.

Scipio walked forward, though Vibenna tried to stop him.

As the young legionnaire fell to his knees, Jesus the Christ reached out and touched him on the crown of his head.

Scipio fell forward on the ground and stayed there without moving.

Vibenna's eyes opened wide as the Figure took his head in His hands, and looked straight into his very soul, or so it seemed. Then he crumpled to the ground not far from Scipio.

One by one, the other legionnaires fell without injury, Jesus the Christ walking past them, still surrounded by those extraordinary beings, even the sound of their wings like music in the still night air.

And then He came to Decimus Paetus.

"Give me your hands," He said.

Paetus thrust them forward without hesitation.

"I see no longer any blood on them," spoke Jesus the Christ. "You are free. You have been cleansed, for now, for eternity."

Paetus burst out crying again.

Jesus the Christ took the sleeve of His garment and wiped the tears from his eyes and from his cheeks.

"Save them, beloved Decimus," He said. "Save them for the end of your days when they will be felt more deeply."

"Are You the one they call the Messiah?" Paetus asked, his voice trembling with the emotion of the moment.

"I am the one of whom you speak, but only of those who believe," that voice, as those words were spoken, radiating not through his ears only but every inch of his body.

"But what do You want me to do?" Paetus asked. "I know nothing but the will of Imperial Rome. I know no commander but Caesar."

"From this moment on, you will listen only to Almighty God," Jesus the Christ told him.

"And my comrades?"

"They will be with you for part of the way but for the rest, you will know only the company of the Jews."

"The Jews!"

"Yes, Decimus Paetus, you will die with them, your enemy surrounding you, your comrades' bodies on every side, when you are very old, and there is no one else left, for you will be the last."

By the time Vibenna was finished, the younger man asked for permission to have the horses stop by the side of the road.

"I *am* a Christian, sir," Mavortius confessed somewhat tremulously after the *biga* had come to a halt.

Vibenna rubbed his chin.

"Why?" he asked earnestly. "You seem intelligent enough. Why should *you* fall for this nonsense?"

"May I speak freely, sir?"

"You may indeed."

Mavortius faced him squarely.

"Was not what you saw a miracle?" he asked.

"It *was* unusual, and the others may regard it as a miracle. As for me, I have never been able to decide."

"Have you not looked at your life and searched for purpose in it?"

"When I was serving Rome, I scarce had time to think about such matters. Rome's purpose was my own."

"But now that you have been inactive, with time to sit back and ponder?"

"You are perceptive, I see, but, frankly, I tire of this now. We really should be getting on our way."

The look of sorrow that raced across Quintus Mavortius's youthful face, with its suntanned skin and blue eyes, was so genuine, seemingly coming from so deep within him, that Vibenna had to look away from its intensity, and not again did their gazes cross until, just over two hours later, the utilitarian biga, a common sight in those days, had been pulled up in front of one of the more elaborate multicolumned buildings in Rome.

From within came the strident sounds of a tense meeting in process, a meeting destined to change the old legionnaire's life to a degree that he would have thought incomprehensible just days before.

"Good-bye, sir," the younger man said. "I shall pray for you."

"And I thank you for that. Masada will not be an easy challenge."

"I meant—"

"Yes, I know what you meant. Now watch your tongue, young man. Others would find your words offensive, even seditious."

Mavortius waved once, and then the horses took him away from that place. Vibenna nearly called out to him but stopped as a fragment from the recollection that he had shared with the legionnaire lingered yet a bit longer.

"Yes, Decimus Paetus, you will die with them, your enemy surrounding you, your comrades' bodies on every side, when you are very old, and there is no one else left, for you will be the last."

He had not considered that statement for nearly thirty years, keeping it buried because its significance seemed unfathomable, and he could not waste his time contending with idle speculation.

. . . your enemy surrounding you.

Unable to dismiss those words easily, Marcus Vibenna walked with marked slowness into that imposing building as they continued to echo strangely in his mind, and he realized that never before had he felt so old as he did at that moment.

LXX

F abius Scipio was to survive the persecution wrought by Nero, though Tullio and Gaius Gallienus did not. Shortly after the death of Paul at Nero's Circus, all three had ended up together in one of the nearly thirty catacombs that could be found ringing Rome—from Bassilla, Thraso, and Pamphilus to the north; just off the Tiber to Timotheus, Commodilla, and Nunziatella in the south; also near that fabled river flowing past the northwestern end of the city, their total length numbering at least sixty-five miles.

For a long while, Roman soldiers and the commanders ordering them thought not to look at any of these miserable locations, but eventually an alert was sounded when a few less than careful Christians were spotted entering Preatextatus, a catacomb southeast of Rome, near the Via Appia. As a result, these once-safe, albeit miserable, havens consequently became tombs in more ways than one, though the sheer number of catacombs delayed the business of discovery by a matter of weeks for some groups of believers.

★ ★ ★

Terra-cotta oil lamps provided the only illumination, some of these engraved on one side with the form of Jesus, who had come to be known as the Good Shepherd, and on the other, with the initials of the Christian potter who had made each one.

Along the earth and rock walls of that catacomb were occasional painted scenes created by bored and weary Christians with little else to do. Just across from Fabius Scipio was artwork that showed a baptismal scene, and to his right, another depicting the cross as an anchor that had "caught" two *pisciculi*, or little fish.

"Because of the *institum Neronianum*, we are hunted like animals," Tullio remarked somberly as the three of them huddled in one of the dank and foul-smelling underground grave sites, which was, as all the others, simply an earth-walled tunnel lined with excavations that were rapidly filling up with bodies where there had been very few before. "Little children are dying from hunger and disease!"

Tullio's only child had died of an infectious disease while still an infant not long after Scipio had seen her nursing the babies of her slaves, and so she knew all too well the pain of a mother's tragic loss.

"Their parents slaughtered by the devils who pledge their allegiance to a mad beast!" she went on. "We saw the flayer's yard as we headed for this place. The flesh was being whipped off men's bones well into the night. I heard that where the Cloaca Maxima flows into the Tiber, the waters could be seen turning red with blood."

"We have lost everything except our mortal lives and our eternal souls," Gaius Gallienus added. "Yet I feel more at peace now than when we both had a residence that many would have called a small palace. Is that not extraordinary, Fabius?"

Scipio had to agree.

"We had so much then to eat that obesity became a problem," he replied, chuckling at some of the memories. "Yet, now, why do I feel so little hunger?"

Others had not been blessed with that sort of self-control. Many were moaning further down that particular tunnel, crying out, "If only I could have some bread."

Some believers had to be refused, especially those suffering from leprosy, and were not allowed to hide among the others, even in such primitive sites as the catacombs. Their rejection took a devastating emotional toll on the ones put to the task of enforcing it on desperate people who surely would go on to torture or death, but the health of those remaining Christians hiding in each catacomb had to be considered, particularly in such close quarters where contamination seemed a real threat.

The extreme discouragement on the faces of those turned aside was evident. More than one shouted, "Christ is supposed to have said, 'Come unto Me, all ye who labor and are heavy-laden, and I shall give you rest.' Yet you do not allow us the very refuge that you have managed to claim for yourselves."

None of this was lost on Tullio, who had witnessed such moments outside the very catacomb where they were hiding.

"You know," she spoke, her expression on that perfect face one of profound wisdom masked by the deepest anguish, "I fear that even after emperor Nero is gone—for he is after all but a puppet in the hands of the arch-enemy of our souls—Christians shall still face persecution again someday, but often, in addition to that, they will be turned aside by their very brothers and sisters in Christ!"

"As long as there is a Rome given to ruthless excesses and with unholy men in charge," Gaius Gallienus added, "the name matters not. It will flare up though there might be passing periods of peace. Only when someone who is committed to Christ takes the throne can, can we as Christians have some assurance that this public persecution of Christians will cease."

"And there may never *be* this sort of man," Scipio suggested. "The church will have to pray about surviving only the assurance of evil rather than the hope of good."

The wailing behind them had stopped momentarily.

Someone had started to sing a melody of joyful worship, another had joined in, and soon the tunnel was filling with the voices of those trapped inside it.

Tullio and Gaius Gallienus glanced at one another and took up the words as well. Scipio hesitated, feeling awkward, since he was not as familiar with the song as they were, but he quickly caught on, and that catacomb became in an instant a place of worship to the glory of God rather than a pit of despair and death.

* * *

Morning.

Normally the only sounds those nearest the entrance to each of the many catacombs heard coming in from outside were of crickets, along with the musical call of an occasional bird. Otherwise, the quietude seemed nearly as eerie as the sight of bones from long-ago interments in the excavations, which were of varying size to accommodate the remains of adults as well as children and infants, eyeless skulls caught in the reflected light of the moon or the first rays of the morning sun.

The silence was part of the isolation, and the isolation had been the greatest single element of their survival. But it also meant hunger, since food could be passed to them only under the most clandestine of circumstances.

That one morning though they all heard more than crickets and birds.

The sound of the military.

Stomping feet and clanging metal and stern orders carried forth by harsh voices in tones missing the slightest touch of emotion.

"We have been discovered!" Tullio whispered the obvious. "We must move further back. We must—"

"If they know about us, they must know everything else about this and other catacombs like it," Gaius Gallienous told her. "They will be waiting at the exit as well as the entrance. There is nothing we can do, my beloved."

Someone else shouted, "Surely we can fight back! Must we be mere lambs collapsing before our slaughterers so that they can do their grisly work unimpeded by anyone lifting so much as a finger in self-defense?"

"In the end," Scipio started to say as he stood up, his head just touching the dirt ceiling of the catacomb, "we guarantee nothing but greater violence. If we are doomed now because we have been discovered, then do we fight our attackers like other men and be mistaken for the criminals they think us to be? Or do we instead come out of this miserable place, singing a hymn of rejoicing and exaltation?"

"But they will cut us down and leave our corpses to be fed upon by the beasts of the night," another man spoke.

"And the murders will be left behind, someday to battle in their consciences an awareness of the cold, awful brutality of the atrocity they have wrought while we walk the streets of heaven, angels at our side!" Scipio rebuked him. "What do we give up when we hand them our lives? What do they gain when they spill our blood? Pilatus could never wash the blood of Jesus from his hands. Nor shall these soldiers succeed where he failed!"

There had been murmuring at first but now it ceased.

"We shall go out there hand in hand," Tullio told the rest. "We shall have smiles on our faces and a song from our lips."

One by one, the sounds of assent filled the musty air of the catacomb.

Tullio reached out for her husband's hand, and Gaius Gallienus took Scipio's, who extended an arm behind him for the person there, and so it went, a human chain, hand in hand, emerging from the tunnel, the morning sun forcing them to shut their eyes briefly. When they opened their eyes again, they saw the Roman cavalry surrounding the entrance, each soldier's sword drawn, a stern-looking commander ready to issue an order as he anticipated their resistance. But none was evident, and he stood, open-mouthed, as they did nothing but stay in one place, singing, a look of unbounded joy on their faces.

If they were to be executed directly in front of that catacomb, it would amount to a significant departure from previous locations. The usual place was at the Ager Esquilinus in front of the Porta Esquilina, where a notorious cemetery had been dug over the years, primarily for the poor but, now, with dead Christians being dumped into one of its large pits. Centuries later, the source of the foulest odors was located and the horrors underground were rediscovered.

"To the lions!" the commander finally shouted. "Give our beloved emperor some thrills this day."

Scipio narrowed his eyes, looking at the man, sensing an ill-disguised sarcasm in those last words, and remembered seeing him at the Senate one day months before, conferring with several members, and heard his name mentioned at least once.

Commander Regalianus.

"We shall die, we know, quite soon, commander Regalianus," he spoke so clearly that none had difficulty understanding him, "but must our deaths be the stuff of a madman's pleasure?"

Regalianus's eyes shot open, showing his surprise at being recognized by a common Christian, and was about to speak again, but before he could, Scipio went on forcefully.

"In time, a year or two perhaps, this emperor will be gone, for he cannot be tolerated for very much longer, but you who have abetted the ungodly perversity of Nero will be left with the memories created by this moment. Why let the horrors that give him such satisfaction rob your nights of peace and keep your hearts enslaved to a devil in human flesh?"

The commander stood completely still for a few seconds, then, his hand on the hilt of a dagger strapped to his side, walked slowly up to Scipio.

"But if we let you escape," he surmised, "our own families could become subject to his monstrous and destructive conceits, for he has not stopped, in the past, from retribution against even the wives of any disobedient legionnaires, thereby hoping to teach the rest of us a lesson that we have learned all too well."

"But such is forbidden by the laws of Imperial Rome itself!" Scipio retorted.

"You may believe in law, I may believe in law, but for this emperor, law is but a plaything of his vanity, to be dispensed with or to be waved in the face of his victims, given his particular whim at any particular moment."

Regalianus leaned forward, toward Scipio, and whispered into his ear, "Will your God forgive me if I order my men to run you through with their weapons?"

Scipio thought he could glimpse a single, tiny stream of water trickling down the man's left cheek.

"And then we shall put your bodies back from whence you came, beyond Nero's grasp. He will be angry at this, I am sure, but not so much so that our loved ones will feel the heat of his wrath."

"Do what you must, but there will be no forgiveness unless you accept as your Savior and your Lord the very Christ whose death purchased that which you seek."

"So I am cornered if I do and cornered if I do not. That is what you are telling me?"

"That is what I must tell you if you want truth, not deception."

Regalianus gave him a surprisingly sympathetic nod.

"We will wait now while you have a last prayer, or whatever it is that you Christians do," he said.

"I pray that it is what you will be doing before very long," Scipio commented, his sincerity undeniable to the other man, cutting through the hard military facade.

The Roman commander winced as he turned and walked back toward his troops.

The dozen Christians got down on their knees and each prayed in turn, more than one of them offering a petition to God for the souls of the men who would be killing them.

One of them shouted, *"Jesus Christus heri et hodie, ipse et in saecula!"*

His meaning was clear: "Jesus Christ, yesterday, and today: and the same forever!"

Finally everyone was silent, and all stood again, facing Regalianus and the contingent of legionnaires with him.

"Have you anything to say?" the commander asked, his voice revealing the slightest shakiness.

"Just one request," Scipio spoke up.

"Ask it."

"May we be sent to our Lord in the manner that the apostle Paul was?"

"Decapitation?"

"Yes."

Regalianus clenched and unclenched both hands.

"It shall be as you wish," he confirmed.

He looked from one Christian to the other, five women and seven men.

"You will kneel again, please," he ordered.

They all did as he had asked.

Three soldiers were picked, each to be responsible for four Christians.

All of them were once again on their knees, heads bowed.

"Identify yourselves one at a time," Regalianus demanded.

"I am Gaius Rabirus Posthumous," the first man said, "and I willingly give up this body of flesh so that my soul can be released for its final journey."

The sword of the first of the three legionnaires was brought down on his neck.

The next Christian, a woman, now spoke, "I am Livia Laertius, and I, too, willingly give up this body of flesh so that my soul can be released for its final journey."

So it went, the first, the second, the third, on, and on, to the seventh, the eighth, and then to the tenth.

Tullio Gallienus.

Nursing a baby . . .

Scipio remembered that first, awkward meeting, the beauty of her face, the peace of it, the act she was performing for the infant children of her slaves. Now, as he heard the *whack* of a Roman sword, he could not force himself to look up.

Tullio! his mind screamed out though his lips were pressed tightly together. *Oh, how I shall reach out for your hand as I follow you past the gates of heaven.*

"I am Gaius Gallenius," spoke the next voice, though barely intelligibly, raging anger together with wrenching sorrow welling up from his very soul, "and I too . . . willingly give up this body of flesh so that my soul can be released for its final journey."

Seconds later, the third legionnaire stood in front of Scipio.

Suddenly, Regalianus shouted, "I shall handle *him* myself."

The legionnaire stepped aside, and the other man stood where he just had.

"Be my intercessor," the commander whispered. "Speak to this God of yours or His self-proclaimed Son or whoever else you must. I cannot commit any more such horrors as this, or I shall lose whatever mind I have left."

Scipio smiled warmly at him, and said, "I shall do this, I surely shall, but you must take the only step that matters."

Regalianus raised the sword above his neck.

"Good-bye, Christian," he said. "If I can believe what I have heard or have read on various parchments passed along to me, you will soon know, yea, in the twinkling of an eye, a peace that has never, ever been mine."

Scipio bowed his head, and repeated, "I am Fabius Scipio, and I, too, willingly give up this body of flesh so that my soul can be released for its final journey."

He steeled himself for the split second of pain that seemed destined to afflict him, followed by—

A hand under his right arm, another under his left.

Lifting him up.

"Lord . . . ," Scipio spoke in anticipation, as he opened his eyes.

The commander.

"I—," he began to speak, startled.

"Say nothing," the other man told him. "You are not to die this day. You have been pardoned by a member of the Senate."

"But who would do that?" Scipio asked, confused.

"You could not know him. Besides, the one I mention was only acting upon the entreaty of somebody else, granting this extraordinary intervention, and at great risk, given who sits on the throne."

"How can I find this man?"

"I am supposed to take you to him."

Regalianus ordered his soldiers to put the remains of the eleven other Christians back in the catacomb, each in a separate excavation that previously had been dug into the damp soil and rock wall on other side.

"Carefully!" he demanded. "These are not some slain animals!"

Then he helped a weary and uncertain Fabius Scipio onto an awaiting *biga* for the brief ride back to Rome, and through the inner districts of the city, to a modest residence just off the Via Flaminia, less than a mile northeast of Nero's Circus.

LXXI

Your benefactor is waiting for you," commander Regalianus told him. "He is in the back, among the flowers."

Scipio was greeted then by a slave who took him through the small house and into the yard. Standing there in the middle of it was a large man whose back was turned to him.

"Sir, I understand that you—," Scipio started to say.

The figure turned and faced him.

Quintus Egnatius Javolenus Tidus Germanicus!

Scipio nearly fainted from the shock of seeing him, thinner, no longer a ruddy look to his cheeks and with the weight of the additional years showing in wrinkles and stooped shoulders and a slight wheezing sound as he breathed.

But otherwise whole, no sign of leprosy.

The two men hugged one another with such force that Scipio, the smaller, was gasping by the time they had finished.

"You are unaffected!" he exclaimed.

"Not a mark, not a hint," concurred Germanicus, "though especially at the end, I was in such close contact with your dear—"

He caught himself, a look of pain on his face.

"Oh, forgive me, Decimus," he said. "I am so stupid, so insensitive."

He bowed his head sadly.

"Your mother and father went to be with the Lord but days apart. They both asked me to send you their deepest and truest love if you and I were to meet again."

Germanicus cleared his throat.

"There was little pain for either of them, Decimus. At the end, I saw nothing but peace on their faces. One by one, the others died as well, and I was left alone, very, very alone. I could no longer stand it. I managed to convince the captain of the next boat bringing its meager food supply to take me back. He was willing, if I made it worthwhile for him."

Scipio felt weak at the news about his parents, stumbling back into a brown leather-covered chair less than a foot behind him.

"Their bodies," he spoke, "were they dumped . . . into the harbor?"

"No!" Germanicus told him, with some pride. "Some of us got together and carved a tomb out of the side of the mountain where so many lived in those caves."

"Just like—," Scipio tried to say without crying but failed.

The other man nodded, his own eyes moist.

"I have gone along without them for so long, and yet I thought about them every day. I wondered what had finally happened and if you had died there. I prayed that somehow you would not, that the Lord would help you."

"Oh, dear Fabius, my brother, my blessed brother, He has helped far, far beyond what I could ever deserve. Your prayers were answered in the way you wanted. Our precious Father kept me from that foul plague. And I am quite well even today, except for the normal ailments, none severe, of my now advanced age."

They sat quietly for quite some time, then Scipio spoke up, "But you were an outcast. How have you managed to come back here at all?"

"The only improvement under Nero is that politicians can be bought," Germanicus told him forthrightly.

"But the money? How could you get any?"

"I gave you a very large percentage of what I had accumulated but some of it did remain in my hands."

Germanicus looked conspiratorially to his left and his right.

"Something wonderful is about to happen," he whispered. "Something we all have prayed for earnestly . . ."

Scipio's manner brightened.

"Is it about—?"

Germanicus nodded in an exaggerated fashion.

"Nero is going to be deposed within the week," he said. "The military cannot stand him. They loathe his policies in just about every area and believe that Rome will suffer irreparably if he stays on the throne any longer. Our devil of an emperor will be either executed or forced to commit suicide."

That was what Scipio needed to lift him briefly out of his despair, until he was plunged almost immediately back into it.

"I have not told you what happened before Regalianus brought me here," he said, pronouncing each word as though it were a separate sentence. "A terrible slaughter took place at the catacombs!"

After Scipio had described the circumstances, Germanicus broke out into an hysterical fit of crying.

"Those good people!" he sobbed. "If only you could have been found sooner, if only I had been able to—"

He leaned forward, his face pressed into Scipio's shoulder, and shook violently from deep inside himself.

"May God have mercy on the day of judgment," the big man muttered. "How feeble these pitiable deeds of mine will seem to Him!"

* * *

Though Nero's death occurred in A.D. 68, the Roman Empire continued in upheaval through the reigns of Galba, Otho, and Vitellius.

Until Vespasianus became emperor.

He was to be on the throne for a full decade. Stability returned to Imperial Rome. Though the Coliseum was built through his sponsorship, no casting of Christians to the lions occurred while he was emperor.

It was the Jews who suffered most at this point.

Though the Jewish War, as it was called in Rome, began when Nero was in power, it continued under Galba, Otho, and Vitellius, though for the Romans it was a sputtering effort at best. During this period the insurrectionists were able to enjoy their greatest successes. Early on, two of the three fortresses were taken back into Roman hands, but Masada remained invulnerable. And it was from Masada that the Sicarii could strike out very effectively against the legions stationed in the countryside between there and Jerusalem.

The fall of Jerusalem in A.D. 70 toughened the resistance of the insurrectionists, but it also destroyed much of what Judaism had been, fostering among Jews the view that there was no hope for them, that they were in the early stages of becoming a dying people.

Nearly all the members of the still-powerful Sanhedrin perished during the Roman siege against Jerusalem. Nearly all were either those who had been involved in the plot against Jesus the Christ or the sons of the original plotters. One of the latter was heard mumbling on his deathbed, "God finally punishes me for the sins of my father!"

One of the few survivors from the inner circle of the Sanhedrin was Rabbi Johanan ben Zakkai, who had tried earlier to get his fellow Jews to arrange a truce with the Romans.

"They will turn this city into rubble if we do not," he warned.

But he was not heeded.

After fleeing Jerusalem by posing as a corpse in a coffin, Zakkai ended up at Jamnia some thirty miles away, where he started a school for rabbis, teaching them what he earnestly believed—that, as clergymen, they should not pursue a warlike stance but should honor God by teaching love to others.

Zakkai adopted at least one of the teachings that he, in his youth, had personally heard the Nazarene expound with great conviction, for he told his students that they should learn to love their enemies and to bless those who would curse them. To this, he added, from Hosea 6:6, "For I desire steadfast love and not sacrifice."

394

But the zealots eschewed any such wisdom or restraint and vowed to maintain control of Masada at whatever cost, which they did for a very long time. After Jerusalem fell, it was that former palace-fortress built by the prolific King Herod that became more than ever a symbol of Jewish defiance . . .

LXXII

Fabius Scipio became quite ill the moment he learned about what had happened to Jerusalem. Nor was Quintus Egnatius Javolenus Tidus Germanicus any less distressed over the tragic news.

"Apart from the tragedy of so much suffering and death, think of all that was of historical importance that is now lost forever, ground under the feet of Rome," Scipio groaned, the blood drained from his no longer youthful-looking face. "How can Vespasianus condone such barbarism?"

"I cannot say that he does," Germanicus told him honestly, as they both sat under a gray-colored canvas awning in front of the new residence that Scipio had been able to obtain after his rights and privileges—not to mention his assets—were restored.

"It was Titus by himself? Is that what you are saying?"

Germanicus grunted with contempt.

"I believe so, Scipio. The emperor can hardly make a public statement that would humiliate his own son. He is not a saint himself, but he seems almost that after such men as we have seen precede him on the throne. He has carefully chosen a new government from bits and pieces of the old *cursus honorum*. He seems interested in being a fair ruler and as just as the circumstances permit."

"The fate of Jerusalem is hardly an indication of that!" Scipio blurted.

"As I said, the emperor must tolerate his son's stupidity. He can do nothing else except in private perhaps. Titus is popular among the troops. Vespasianus *has* to maintain his rule as carefully as possible, and risk no alienation of his supporters, especially those who are among the military."

"But then what about Masada? It has seemed untouchable, with no attacks as yet mounted against it."

Germanicus paused, rubbing his chin.

"That solitary fortress is the only thorn that remains in the side of Rome, at least as far as backward Judea is concerned. Realize this, my dear Fabius: The Jewish War has been won most decisively—*except for Masada!* As long as Masada remains in the hands of less than a mere thousand insurrectionists, it will be an acute embarrassment.

"Vespasianus's prestige surely must soon begin to suffer accordingly in view of the fact that the excesses and weaknesses of his predecessors can no longer be blamed for what is happening, since Masada becomes, as each day passes, a mocking reminder on his watch that Rome may not be quite as all-powerful as it would like to seem, or as it *must* seem, shall we say, if control is to be maintained over its vast map of conquered territories."

"Is Masada so difficult to attack?" Scipio asked naively, never having paid much attention to that isolated place.

"You have not seen it?" Germanicus asked, surprised.

"No, I was never in that vicinity, although there were many stories among us about how legionnaires came to despise their assignments at Masada. It is stifling hot each summer and desperately cold in the winter, with winds that are every bit strong enough at times to knock a man off his feet. And the maddening isolation was another factor, provoking animosities between even the closest comrades."

Showing no surprise at any of what Scipio told him, Germanicus nodded sympathetically after his friend had finished.

"Yes, I was at Masada," he said, "a special guest of the government at that point. Herod's three-tiered palace at the western end was not the only one he had built at Masada but it was by far the most elaborate, and one of the more astonishing sights any of us will see. But by then it had been turned back into just another military building, however beautiful it might have been, with plenty of hints of its past luxury."

He stood, stretching his legs.

"I have learned something that should enrage the Jews," he said.

"What is that, friend?" Scipio asked.

"A Jew named Josephus has deserted the zealots and joined the Roman forces. He can only spell more difficulty for them."

Germanicus was biting his lower lip. Scipio noticed this and asked the other man what else was bothering him.

"Yet the Jews themselves have had a deserter join them as well," he said with manifest reluctance.

"A Roman?"

"Yes, Roman."

"Who is it?"

Germanicus had been looking at him but now turned away.

Scipio stood and placed a hand on his friend's shoulder.

"You can tell me what you know, and I shall not be dismayed," he said reassuringly. "I promise you that this will be so."

"The Roman is an aging former legionnaire," Germanicus muttered, "someone named Decimus Paetus!"

Scipio fell back, almost doubling over.

"How . . . did . . . you . . . find . . . out?" he asked, each word spit from his mouth as a terrible pain seemed to be gripping him.

"I have, shall we say, 'contacts' everywhere, Fabius. There is little I do not know or cannot uncover."

"Decimus . . . ," Scipio whispered soulfully as he recalled an overwhelming moment from decades before.

★ ★ ★

Against the singing that continued as a backdrop, the Nazarene said, "You will be forgotten by the generations to come after you. No man will speak your name. No scroll will contain it. Yet Decimus Paetus, some forty years from this moment, nine hundred and sixty human beings, on a high and isolated place in the midst of the wilderness, will accept you as a brother and as a friend because you will have chosen to devote the remainder of your life to them.

You will be to a handful an instrument of righteousness since you are to bring a message of redemption so strong and so beautiful that, at the end of their days, some of them will turn to you, Decimus Paetus, for the hope of eternity, and you will give forth the very truth that will free them from the flesh and blood domination they fought so hard to overthrow."

"Jesus knew!" Scipio exclaimed. "All those years ago, He *knew* what would be happening *today!*"

"There can be only one outcome," Germanicus spoke grimly. "The insurrectionists either will all die on the spot, slaughtered by their attackers, or they shall suffer capture, and then, frankly, wish that they *had* died atop Masada before going on to experience the vengeful wrath of Rome in its imperial dungeons.

"Everyone there and on the outside knows that they cannot escape and that there is no way that they can defeat the hordes of soldiers surely soon to be sent against them. Those men and, I suppose, not a few women and children are doomed even as we discuss their terrible fate, Decimus."

"And my brother in Christ among them . . . ," Scipio muttered as he broke down, weeping. "Decimus will be giving up his own life in this sin-cursed world that others might know the truth of blessed eternal life."

Germanicus was greatly moved.

"Your tears will always be mine," he said as he took Scipio's anguish upon himself.

LXXIII

Marcus Vibenna was introduced by Vespasianus to the deservedly notable commander who had just been placed in charge of the forthcoming Roman assault against Masada. This individual proved to be
someone other than the emperor's son, which was not entirely a surprise
to Vibenna or anyone else.

It was Flavius Silva, the pronsul-governor of Judea, a tall, thin-
faced man who was also a much-decorated general considered one of the
most capable officers serving Rome at that time, who came to be charged
with the logistical nightmare of breaching a fortress long considered to be
well-nigh impregnable.

"I have great respect for our enemy," Silva admitted at the outset.
"They have been making fools of us for a long time. I cannot ascribe their
success simply to any form of good luck. They have at least one advantage over us, namely, that they are fighting for their very survival. Men in
such a circumstance tend not to be complacent to any degree, whereas
our Roman forces have generally fallen into the trap of regarding the insurrectionists as not much above being annoying but ineffectual and inex-
perienced barbarians and, therefore, quite unequal in manpower as well
as intelligence."

"But those barbarians overran two other fortresses apart from Masada!" Vibenna protested. "Should that not have sent a contrary message, sir?"

"I quite agree," Silva acknowledged, "but the problem is that our
forces took back two of the locations very quickly. With Masada to the
south, conveniently out of the way, there was the delusion before I arrived that we could take care of it whenever the mood struck, if I may put
it that way."

The short, round-faced emperor grumbled his displeasure.

"My son's gross miscalculation!" he exclaimed with bitterness that
could hardly have been more obvious to his visitors. "I hope, if he takes
this throne one day perhaps when I am too feeble to rule, that he will be
smarter here among the luxuries of Rome than he was on the grimy fields
of battle."

. . . *the grimy fields of battle.*

Where the Jewish war was concerned, Titus had turned those fields into bloodier places than usual. He slaughtered prisoners by the hundreds, some of them thrown to wild animals so as to amuse himself and his legionnaires. He set up the Roman eagle in the Holy of Holies and carried off to Rome precious treasures from Herod's temple, including the silver trumpets, the seven-branched candelabrum, the menorah, and much else.

But there was more to the emperor's seething than "just" his son's purely military decisions regarding Jerusalem, for there also had spread abroad considerable gossip over the tawdry revelation that the younger Vespasianus foolishly had engaged in an affair with Berenice, sister of Herod Agrippa II, a dalliance that his father found to be in the worst possible taste. The emperor believed that if it had been anyone but a Jewess, even a Romanized Jewess as she was, that kind of conduct would have been acceptable.

Titus also was given to riotous parties that invariably became the most disgusting of orgies, debauched and perverted, involving sex with homosexual young men and other reckless behavior, all of which was anathema to a father who felt that his imperial mission was to restore decency, honor, and restraint to the Empire.

Silva turned to Vibenna.

"I realize that you have been retired for a number of years," he spoke with a touch of admiration in his manner, "but when you were on active duty, you distinguished yourself by helping to plan some of the most important sieges we have had to mount during this century, as well as providing other generals with tactical advice in other matters that led to numerous successes, successes for which they routinely claimed credit, but which saved countless thousands of Roman lives."

He narrowed his eyes as he held Vibenna in his gaze.

"Unfortunately," he added, "that will have to be the case once again in regard to Masada."

Vibenna tried to show no emotion, and largely succeeded, for he had trained himself to expect no glory for anything that he accomplished in life.

"I should extend to you the courtesy of telling you why this has to be quite deliberately the outcome and no other," Silva explained. "As I have said already, the Jews have made fools of us. We have to take Masada and then do everything possible to make what has happened fade from the public's memory."

The general grimaced at that because Imperial Rome's way was to hold up for public acclaim the valor and the skill of its fighting men after any important victories, and finally retaking the mountain fortress and officially ending the frustrating Jewish War were hardly events unworthy of celebration.

After self-consciously clearing his throat, Silva spoke, "There will be no announcements of victory, no celebrations. We will do what we must, and then it is over."

He shifted his attention away from Vibenna.

"Fortress Masada *cannot* be allowed to become a symbol of defiance any more than it has already."

His tiny eyes narrowed to thin slits.

"We are to face months of hard work ahead of us. There will be death and injury and pain everywhere. The coming battle will be after the summer, because otherwise the heat would defeat us without the Jews lifting a finger.

"There also will be occasional hunger as well as thirst, since the logistics of keeping nearly fifteen thousand soldiers supplied with necessities is going to be a nightmare in and of itself, and, alas, we will not always be as successful as we would want."

He was nearly nose-to-nose with Vibenna.

"The Christians talk about a place called hell," he said. "We will think, after a while, that we have entered it."

Silva backed away then and tried to smile, but the resulting expression proved quite humorless.

"I pledge to have you by my side from the beginning," he declared with some satisfaction. "As far as the troops are concerned, of course, I shall be recognized as their only commander. As far as *I* am concerned, you will be the one man to whom I undoubtedly will be turning the most as the battle progresses, the real intelligence behind any response that we have to the Jews down there at Masada. The success or failure of our efforts against them will be as much on your shoulders as mine.

"I urge you to remember above all else that time is short for us. The calendar is our unyielding master this time, determining our actions as the days and weeks march on. I have never had a taste for beating around the bush, Marcus Vibenna. I can speak no other way than as plainly and as urgently as I have."

"What about this Josephus of whom I have heard?" Vibenna asked abruptly, revealing something he had learned earlier.

Joseph ben Mathias, only thirty-three years old at the time, and a source of enormous satisfaction to the Romans, as well as a bitter symbol of unmitigated betrayal to the Jews, zealots and moderates alike, had been one of the youngest of the various Jewish commanders, his responsibility being the Jotapata fortress in Judea. There were other men with even fewer years of experience, and this was a primary reason that the tides of war turned badly for the Jews, dedicated though they may have been.

After Jotapata fell, Josephus escaped with forty others but was pursued by a contingent of legionnaires. Realizing that they could not avoid capture any longer, thirty-nine of the men entered into a suicide pact. But Josephus and one other decided instead to surrender. In a desperate ploy to save his life, he spoke out to Vespasianus, "I have been sent by God to you . . . for He has told me that you will become Caesar and emperor."

In A.D. 69, that prediction came true, and Josephus was released from prison and quickly enjoyed imperial favor. He was given the Roman name of Flavius Josephus and assigned to Roman forces during the siege of Jerusalem. But his real passion proved not to be that of any military endeavor. Instead, he seemed obsessed by the goal of chronicling the Jewish War in a mammoth volume that he would come to entitle *Bellum Judaicum*.

"You know about him?" Silva remarked, surprised.

"I do, sir," Vibenna replied, unable to conceal his distaste for what he and others considered Josephus's cowardly actions.

Silva nodded knowingly, gleaning from the other man's expression as much as a whole torrent of words could tell him.

"Yes," he acknowledged, "I can sympathize with the way you feel. If it can happen to them, perhaps it can happen with us, though I would hope that Romans know more about loyalty than do these Jews!"

The general waved his hand through the air.

"Nevertheless, this traitor is a not-so-hidden resource because of insights he can provide about any traits his people are accustomed to showing as they conduct warfare. You should feel free to call on him whenever necessary, though I suspect that you will have to fight for the little man's attention at times."

Silva chuckled with rare humor as he spoke those last words.

"How is that, sir?" Vibenna asked stolidly.

"Josephus has rather loudly indicated that he is determined to take notes about everything that occurs, down to the last detail, all for what he passionately calls the sake of history. That could have been one reason why he consented to help us in the first place. He would be in a position that placed himself at the center of the action, surely a fascinating prospect for someone with his intentions.

"Whatever his literary aspirations might be, I am certain, however, that saving his own hide was of far greater importance when he decided to switch from fighting for those rebel Jews to serving Imperial Rome as he is doing now."

Vibenna saw the irony of the situation, irony that would become apparent to Josephus only later.

"And this exhaustive work on which he toils, unknown to him, will be suppressed, for the sake of the Empire?"

"For as long as we can keep it so," Silva told him.

Vibenna nodded, pleased at that.

"I am ready, sir, to serve however I might," he declared unequivocally.

. . . Decimus Paetus, you will die with . . . your enemy surrounding you.

"I may know—," he started to add as that fragment crossed his consciousness, then cut himself off.

"What is it, Vibenna?" Silva asked, not patiently.

"Nothing, sir, I just had an idle thought that was not worthy of repeating to a man such as yourself."

The commander was not convinced but let the matter drop.

My enemy . . . my friend, Vibenna told himself, anguish twisting his insides. *If you are on the other side of whatever wall we breach in perhaps a few weeks or months, may you be found alive so that I can somehow protect you after the battle is no more. But, better still, I pray that you are not there at all, that somehow—*

Pray . . .

To which god he could not be certain.

Part IX

*S*ince the destruction of Jerusalem, the insurrectionists at Masada had gone very much unchallenged. They were able to leave the fortress one by one, down the narrow "snake path" that led from the plateau itself to the desert below. And they would push out into the countryside—north, east, and west —for the purpose of getting dietary supplies, clothes, and suchlike that they could not raise or make themselves, these donated to them by sympathetic villagers.

Sometimes the rebels sent by their leader Eleazar ben Ya'ir would stay too long with relatives and friends, and, thus, narrowly escape patrolling legionnaires, who came uncomfortably close, but in general, the hand of God seemed to be on them because none were ever caught during those furtive missions away from Masada.

Men given this sort of duty fulfilled another purpose as well, for they were able to report what was happening on what came to be called the "Roman front," which encompassed virtually all of the land of Judea.

For more than six years, from early in A.D. 66 through the middle of A.D. 72, the zealots had sanctuary. All that ended when the final group of hardy Jews to leave Masada on a routine patrol returned days later as downcast warriors, carrying with them the long-dreaded report that a well-equipped force of some fifteen thousand Roman soldiers at last had begun a relentless march toward the mountain fortress . . .

LXXIV

Wood . . .

It was at Decimus Paetus's persistent urging that the zealots had started to stockpile an immense quantity of timber during the winter months of A.D. 70. For a time there was grumbling from a great many of them about the effort that was required to do this, along with the danger involved in transporting to the fortress those rough-hewn planks that had been cut from trees found along the mountain range next to them, for this left them vulnerable to discovery by Roman patrols. But there was another source of danger—getting the timber up the winding snake path that remained their only way of reaching the plateau itself. More than once, planks were lost as they tumbled from bruised, splinter-wounded, aching hands suddenly incapable of holding on any longer, and almost taking some strong men to their deaths down the often sharp-edged, rocky side of that plateau.

But, backed by ben Ya'ir himself, the former legionnaire persisted, and then when he was satisfied that they had a large enough supply of wood, he announced this welcome fact to the 959 men, women, and children standing before him at the center of the plateau, directly in front of two of the smaller palaces built by Herod the Great.

A very loud cheer of relief arose from the group of them.

In seconds, so many were approaching him to apologize for their previous anger that it looked, for a short while, as though he would have to embrace everyone there, his muscles starting to ache after the fortieth individual, some of whom were none too gentle as they openly expressed their appreciation.

Finally, though, the suddenly boisterous crowd dispersed, ben Ya'ir also leaving, and Paetus stood alone, somberly looking from one end of Masada to the other, some nineteen hundred feet apart.

At the western side stood the top layer of Herod's three-terrace palace, which had not been kept up to the standard set by the old king nearly a century before. Prior to the zealots capturing it, Roman officers and soldiers had used the palace for basic living quarters, with no regard for maintaining its former opulence. And the more urgent needs of the new conquerors contributed to its continuing decline, with all the imported, hand-woven tapestries and other luxurious material stripped away at one point or another.

Paetus walked the several hundred feet to its entrance, past the second largest of the four palaces on the plateau and the two-story apartment-type building not far to his left, a basic structure where the king's staff of slaves as well as low-level guests had stayed during the years of Herod's occupation of Masada.

The palace itself was more accurately described as a structure composed of a series of unified lesser buildings or compartments than a single building, an early proof-positive of the truism that the "whole is greater than the sum of its parts." There were storerooms, a large bathhouse, a smaller one, an administrative section, and then the actual terraces built down the side of the plateau.

On the upper level were the once-extravagant royal living quarters that faced a semicircular terrace from which the king could look out over Lake Asphaltitus to his right and the mountains of Moab on the other side, and the long, empty stretch of desert that was both bleak and strangely beautiful at the same time, visibility so clear that it seemed possible to see all the way to Jerusalem.

In this entire spacious area, only four dwelling rooms had been included at Herod's insistence, along with the several corridors that adjoined them, leading to the suspicion that all of it had been meant perhaps for only the king and one or two of his many wives.

This first level proved to be the most lavishly decorated of all the terraces. Inlaid mosaics covered every inch of the floors. In one room these were arranged as white stones alternating with black ones in a pattern consisting of hexagonal shapes, a simple design, with the more intricate ones visible in the corridors, for no other purpose than to impress visitors invited to Masada by the king.

The middle terrace below it was an open air pavilion and colonnade for outdoor meals, meetings, and other functions. It was built with only one goal in mind: the relaxation of those fortunate enough to be ushered onto it. Architecturally, though it was the simplest of the three, the mood it helped to create was nevertheless quite pleasant, surrounded as it was by breathtaking vistas.

The lower terrace was similarly of an open air design, the walls on the inner side lined with carefully executed paintings of classical quality that faced an impressive double colonnade at the outer edge.

It was here that the plateau curved to its narrowest point, in fact, to not more than a few yards wide at its extreme end. To accomplish any construction at all here, the engineers commissioned by Herod were driven to devising ingenious methods and unique devices, such as a platform, aided by powerful supporting walls, up to eighty feet in height, that was made to extend over the abyss at the end of that side of the plateau, gaining maneuvering space for the men who worked from this platform over onto the terrace.

Columns were sculptured out of the side of the rock wall just below the middle terrace, the spaces between them smoothed down, and then magnificent frescoes painstakingly painted on these.

The lower part of the wall had been given the appearance of being paneled in stone and marble. At the base of the columns, the stonework was painted to imitate veins of marble. Once again, this final terrace had no other purpose than serving up a colorful environment for leisure enjoyment.

How much of this will be destroyed in the ferocity of any siege? Paetus thought. *Though Herod was extravagant with the treasury of this country, there is no denying even the now somewhat faded beauty of what he had had constructed.*

He walked down the central corridor, past the bedrooms on one side and the storerooms on the other, and on to the exit that led out to the terrace.

Finally, as Paetus reached the edge, he placed his hands on top of the protective, five-foot-high wall that encircled it, leaning forward and ignoring the heat as he took in the vista that spread out before him, cut off only to his left by the mountain range from which the plateau jutted out.

"Lord, Lord," he whispered out loud. "I am more than seventy years old. I feel every last one of them as pain assaults my joints, and my muscles are weary. How long before You take me to be with You in Your holy kingdom?"

His gaze shifted for a moment, and he saw ben Ya'ir on the second terrace just below him. The zealot leader was kneeling in prayer.

Lord, I believe ben Ya'ir is so close now to inviting You into his very soul, despite all his bluster to the contrary. May this brave man, possessed of such great passion for the land of his birth, feel just as strongly about the heavenly home that will become his if he is born again, as Jesus persuaded Nicodaemus.

Gone . . .

As Paetus's thoughts turned to the kind little man, he realized that Nicodaemus had been dead a long time, as had Joseph of Arimathea.

How many others have left me behind and joined You, Lord?

He wondered if headstrong Peter was still alive. And there were John, Andrew, Thomas—once a strong skeptic about the resurrection but later one of the most effective of the apostles—and the other men who had given up such a great deal to spend their lives in the service of Jesus the Christ.

How many more of the original apostles chosen by Jesus at the start of His earthly ministry had somehow survived the sword of persecution?

And Scipio.

What has happened to you, my beloved brother-in-Christ? he added warmly. *Will you be there at the gates of heaven to greet me? We will have so much to tell one another. I look forward to seeing you again.*

He heard a voice coming from the terrace below.

Eleazar Ben Ya'ir.

Paetus was startled out of his reverie.

With no warning the zealot leader, shaking with emotion, had let out a sound that seemed born of shock and alarm.

As he turned in Paetus's direction, he appeared to be staggering a bit before he was able to steady himself.

"What is it?" Paetus called down to him, wondering if the man had had some sort of heart spasm.

"Look ahead!" came the leader's trembling reply, his hand raised and pointing northeast. "There! Toward Jerusalem, Decimus!"

Paetus's gaze turned in that direction.

Figures in the distance were announced by clouds of sand and dust kicked up from the hooves of advancing horses and foot soldiers as well as heavy equipment.

"It *is* time!" Eleazar ben Ya'ir proclaimed simply, confirming the obvious, cold tension straining his normally strong and vibrant tone of voice and twisting the expression on his strong, heavily-lined face.

Roman legions were finally on the way.

LXXV

Paetus again stood before the gathered zealots and their families.

At his back was the fading magnificence of Herod's terraced palace, to his right a small building that had been turned into a synagogue.

"We must now prepare as never before," he told them. "We will need to see exactly what the Romans have brought with them in order to adjust our plans but, for the time being, before they arrive, there is much we can do."

"Such as burning all that wood you have been forcing us to collect for so long!" a tall, very broad-shouldered, heavily bearded zealot shouted sarcastically.

With some effort, Paetus reigned in an otherwise fierce Sicilian temper and replied with marked restraint, "I declare now for all to hear that it will *not* be burned but it *will* be used in the morning."

"How?" the same zealot persisted, his antagonism unleashed. "What fancy plan are you next going to foist upon us?"

"We will use the wood in our storehouses for the task of building another wall!" Paetus proclaimed, glancing at Eleazar ben Ya'ir, who nodded in approval.

"The casemate wall already here is sufficient. It would be yet another waste of time and energy to do what you say."

"No, the existing wall will not be enough," spoke Paetus, finally dealing with an issue that ben Ya'ir and he had decided to withhold from the others until the last minute, though they increasingly regretted that strategy when they both saw the degree of complacency that had been filtering throughout the Masadean community.

Paetus knew that he was talking to a band of people who had had years to become entrenched in a collective delusion that led them to believe their mountain fortress could not be breached even by the resourceful Romans, that as long as they had sufficient food and water and such weapons as arrows, swords, and clubs, plus a certain God-given ingenuity, they would be safe for the foreseeable future.

"I predict that the Romans will be bringing battering rams," he went on, knowing well their tactics after having served many years as a legionnaire.

412

"If they can get up to the plateau here in the first place," the other man retorted vehemently. "How do you propose that they achieve that miracle? By the intervention of their pagan gods perhaps?"

Scattered laughter.

"I heard years ago, long after I had ceased being a legionnaire, that a comrade of mine had become a key planner behind Roman siege strategy," Paetus spoke slowly, as though he were a teacher addressing some students. "Part of what he was to contribute was the idea of building strong siege towers, which were then used to scale the walls of at least two enemy fortresses, though there may have been more of which I am just not aware.

"From each one, the Romans could shoot arrows, hurtle great masses of molten metal or heavy iron balls, to burn or crush the enemy. Then, the other side's defenses weakened, legionnaires would fling themselves from the siege tower onto the fortress walls, and, finally, reach the interior grounds, where the battle would be over quickly enough, the ground strewn mostly with the dead bodies of those who dared to oppose Imperial Rome."

The outspoken zealot lapsed into silence, and no one else spoke up.

"The new wall will be made up of two sections of wood placed several yards apart," Paetus told them. "In between will be simple dirt."

He paused, then added, "So that any rams they manage to bring up will be stopped by the cushion all that earth will provide."

Skeptical expressions on the faces of many of the zealots were changing to outright surprise and then appreciation, grudging or otherwise.

"This is how we will do it," Paetus continued, gaining more confidence that they would not simply ignore him when the time came to get started. "The timber brought here with such effort will serve part of the purpose, but those planks have had to be fairly small or using the snake path to transport them would have been impossible.

"Larger beams, of necessity the stronger ones, since we could not carry any of their size and weight from the mountains, will have to be gotten from the buildings right here on the plateau. This will mean tearing down more than one structure that had been providing many of us with our basic living quarters, forcing a large number to sleep elsewhere, the hardier ones outside, I imagine."

Paetus used his hands in gestures that helped to describe what he had in mind.

"The larger beams must be laid in exact parallel rows to form essentially a double wall," he continued to explain. "It will be essential that these are fastened together at the very ends. To prevent the big timbers from being shaken apart by the force of the rams, which will be enormous, I assure you, smaller ones—which are those that we cut down ourselves—need to be laid as cross-pieces firmly attached to the others."

Some in the crowd started to murmur loudly but this time it was in appreciation, not derision.

"This approach is actually nothing new, for it has been used by Roman forces in the past," he told them, "unfortunately because I was the one who came up with it one day, though I cannot say that they would not have thought of it eventually anyway.

"However, none of the enemy will suspect any such defense because they cannot have any idea that a fellow Roman has joined up with you, whereas we all know about the traitor Josephus, and that reduces greatly any value he might have for them."

The crowd grumbled about the mention of that name.

"As far as I am concerned," Paetus added confidently, "they surely must believe that I perished a long time ago. After all, I see no Sicarii here as old as I am. It is not a life given to great longevity."

Some nervous chuckles this time.

"Thus, since it does seem unlikely that the Roman high command could have any clue that I am with you now, they cannot be prepared for the kind of defense we shall be presenting, which has been a peculiarly Roman invention. What I am hoping is that it will catch them completely off guard."

Someone called out, "They probably think of us as dumb Jews!"

Paetus raised his arm sternly.

"*No!*" he shouted. "Do not ever think that way. The Romans have great respect for us. They would never assume that we are mere barbarians of some sort, as they might call others. And they shall surely send against us only the best that they have at their disposal—men as well as equipment."

After the crowd had dispersed, Eleazar ben Ya'ir approached Paetus, carefully out of hearing of any of the others.

"It is a wonderful idea that you have presented, Decimus, and the people are pleased now," he said sincerely, then lowered his voice. "Can you estimate from we have seen in the distance how big their force is?"

"I think it will be the legion X Fretensis," replied Paetus almost in a whisper, "plus auxiliaries at least equal to that size."

"Many thousands then?"

Paetus frowned, sorry that he could do nothing but confirm ben Ya'ir's guess.

"Not counting any Jewish prisoners forced into service for however long it takes to win back Masada."

"It will not be easy for the enemy, whatever happens, Decimus," ben Ya'ir surmised, "a nightmare of nightmares."

"Not less than that, Eleazar, not one bit less."

The zealot leader's upper body sagged.

"Think of the terrible suffering that will befall our poor enslaved people down there!" ben Ya'ir spoke in anguish. "Valiant Jewish men will be made to take the part of dumb asses, many worked to death by their oppressors . . . God's chosen ones becoming animals of burden carrying the heavy loads of—"

He turned away, not wanting Paetus to see the tears that deep emotions were forcing upon him.

"One day not long from now, Jews will have no homeland upon which to raise our families," ben Ya'ir moaned. "One day—and, make no mistake, a new Diaspora has already started, I believe—we will be completely scattered unto the far corners of the world, living on land that belongs to others, ruled by governments not our own. Ishmael will at last have received the sweet taste of his revenge!"

He pointed northeast.

"Over there, on the other side of Lake Asphaltitus, lies a very special spot for my people," he said with no joy.

"Tell me about it, Eleazar," Paetus asked of his friend.

"It was where Moses was able to view the Promised Land. That great man came up to Mount Pisgah and stood and cast his eyes upon what Jehovah had offered a nation of wanderers. Now, all these centuries afterward, looking out over the same stretch of land much as he did from the other side of that lake, we find ourselves in the final stages of enduring the tragedy of having that very land being ripped from our grasp.

"For the Jews of Moses' day, it was a wonderful beginning to the golden years of this land, this Israel, with David and Solomon and other great kings of our history to follow. However, my Roman friend, for you and me and all the others, it can only be the end, as we stand alone against the coming might of thousands."

A sudden wind had started to howl, adding its own voice of melancholy.

Eleazar ben Ya'ir paused, his words nearly lodging unuttered in his throat, and then he was able to speak though hoarsely, "We are broken and spent. It seems God in His holy judgment has cast us aside, for we have been given no one to take the place of those magnificent rulers so that we can once again be led victorious before our great enemy."

LXXVI

The legion X Fretensis arrived in a great mass of bodies and equipment, the common soldiers known as *milites gregarii*, along with the various seconds-in-command for each group, a class of legionnaire who were called *optio*, and those named *tessarius*, actually sergeant of the guard to the others, such as the *hastatus posterior* and the *primus pilus*, plus nonmilitary support personnel and a large group of Jewish prisoners who were given the heavy labor duties.

Almost from the first day, the encampment at the base of Masada was being put in place. And the massive scale of it, in full view of the defenders of the mountain fortress, was part of Silva's strategy, for he hoped that the display of Roman power and discipline would intimidate the zealots and weaken their resolve.

"But I am not counting on this, Marcus," he told Vibenna. "I think of it more as a piece in a mosaic."

"Agreed," the other man replied, nervously looking up at the plateau, though realizing that neither he or Paetus could recognize one another from such a distance.

"You are acting strangely," Silva observed.

"Some part of us views them with admiration."

It was the commander's response that proved the more surprising.

"You are not alone," he said. "They are there because of a cause. How many of my thousands of legionnaires can say the same thing?"

"They serve Rome," Vibenna ventured. "Is that not cause enough, sir?"

"They serve Rome because it is Rome's treasury that serves them."

Silva looked up at the plateau.

"I went to sleep last night thinking that we should be handing them medals instead of grave sites."

He chuckled as he saw Vibenna's expression.

"It was a fleeting thought—albeit an instinctive one—soon gone, I assure you, from a military man who allowed himself to admire the bravery of his enemy."

He excused himself and disappeared into the organized chaos all around them.

Vibenna knew that he should have felt quite proud of himself as he turned and watched the camp being erected, for he was able to contribute a handful of ideas that would make it a more efficient operation.

The more organized it is to be, he thought, *the more likely we are to win this battle, and the more likely that poor Paetus's body will be among the vanquished.*

A long line of mules was pouring into the area, carrying timber balks and sheet iron. Along with them came the prisoners burdened with canvas for tents, heavy iron balls (which would be among the most fearsome offensive weapons to be used against Masada), food and other supplies, and a great deal else.

The plan was to erect as many as eight separate camps, the largest east of the fortress, with two others close to it, with one at the northern end, three west, and one south. Silva's headquarters were at the largest of the western camps, where he could see what he considered would be the main theater of battle.

The bulk of the troops were to stay in two half-legion camps, the rest in the remaining smaller ones primarily as guards who would not necessarily become engaged in combat. These concentrations of manpower had several purposes: the obvious one of quarters for the troops; cutting off possible escape routes through the various wadis at the base of the plateau; and, finally, the provision of mutual defense if the troops were attacked, for, with one exception, at the least accessible end of Masada, the camps were arranged in groups of two or three, each one, though separated by a short distance, facing one or two others.

But Silva did not stop with the precautionary placement of troops. At Vibenna's suggestion, he added another step—a siege wall.

As Josephus was to write in his chronicle, "At the base of the plateau, the commander also built a wall quite around the entire fortress, that none of the besieged might easily escape; he then set a number of his men to guard the several parts of it."

The wall was nearly four thousand yards in length and six feet thick. Guard towers were placed at intervals of eighty to a hundred yards.

"The emperor ordered me to clean out this nest of rebels once and for all!" Silva exclaimed as Vibenna and he stood in the midst of his command camp. "But first I must make certain that they stay *in* the nest."

The two men were only a few feet away from Josephus, who was sitting on a flat rock, scribbling down notes as he had been doing since he arrived.

"The air here stinks!" Silva spoke loud enough for the Jew to hear. "We should go elsewhere."

Vibenna sought permission to remain. It was clear that the commander had no idea why, but he offered no objection.

"How can you do this?" Vibenna asked after he had walked over to Josephus.

"Record the destruction of my people for all to read?" the little man spoke. "Is that what you mean?"

"It is precisely what I mean. How can you be a traitor *and* the historian preserving this moment?"

"I am still alive, and free, and they shall soon be dead or imprisoned. Is the answer so difficult to grasp?"

"But you may know some of those zealots. You may have fought beside them earlier in the war, before you deserted to the enemy."

"I *do* know a few, yes, but that makes no difference. My life is more important than this madness of theirs."

"More important than honor?"

"Than *anything* else, yes."

"I have great pity for you, Josephus."

"Reserve that pity of which you speak for those on the plateau. It is their blood that will be spilled, not mine."

Vibenna walked away then, as Silva had done, the stench of betrayal too thick for him to endure.

* * *

Each of the largest camps seemed an exact duplication of the others. In the center was a *praetorium*, which had a large center court, and a *tricilinium* holding twelve people, who sat on stone couches that had been arranged on three sides of a square, a place where soldiers could concentrate as they ate meals and simply wanted to fellowship; a *tribunal*, which was a square measuring three by three yards and one yard high, with a ramp where the commander could stand when viewing parades and from which he could address his men; several *arae*, altars for the soldiers' sacrifices to their gods; an *auguratorium*, from which the priests could watch for good and bad omens embodied in the flight of birds as well as the pattern of the stars on a given evening; a forum for the sale of goods; and, finally, a *quaestorium*, which was the camp's treasury.

Even the smallest camps had hundreds of *contubernia*, mess units, each with enough room for as many as nine soldiers. Walls of rubblestone measuring roughly four feet high, these were foundations for tents, the canvas elevated and then attached to them.

Each tent's interior was arranged in the form of a smaller *tricilinium*, the benches used for sleeping at night as well as eating for those not interested in using the public *tricilinium* at the center of the camp.

The sites at the base of Masada attracted many camp followers comprised of beggars, tradesmen, and the simply curious, who were tolerated but watched carefully, with some concern about sabotage.

When the camps had been set up to Silva's satisfaction, Vibenna and he rested for several days, allowing the troops as well to do so.

"I would like to get away from this place for a bit," the commander indicated. "You were stationed here in Judea many years ago. Have you any thoughts about where we might go, Marcus?"

Vibenna thought for a moment.

"We are too far south for what easily comes to mind," he acknowledged, "except for—"

"You have thought of something then?" Silva asked, seeing the expression on the other man's face.

"Perhaps, sir. What I remember is as much as two or three hours from here at a moderate clip, by horseback."

"Tell me the location."

"At the very south end of the lake that is directly across the way from here."

"I have heard it called the Dead Sea, or another name."

"Lake Asphaltitus, sir."

"Nothing can live in there because the water is so salty. This whole area is a place of the dead, never more so than after we leave it. What could be of interest at the south end?"

Vibenna frowned, obviously disappointed.

Noticing this, Silva hesitated but then smiled as he said, "If you can come out of retirement, my dear fellow, and sacrifice months of your time and possible safety, how can I refuse to spend a few hours away from here, based upon your recommendation, particularly if I am willing to submit to your judgment on this field of battle soon before us?"

"There is an element of danger, sir?"

"An ambush by some rebel group?"

"That seems a possibility."

"Negligible at most, I am sure. You have me interested now, Marcus. I shall not be dissuaded by anything like the locals. We can check to see if any of the officers have heard of insurrectionist activity in that region, but it seems to me there has been nothing. I think the only remaining rebels of any consequence or quality in all of this forsaken land are the ones at Masada itself. But, please, what is it that you have in mind?"

"An interesting site, ruins that speak a library of parchments in the lessons that they can offer up," Vibenna told him. "I am told that it has had the most profound effect on those who have gazed upon it."

"I am more than interested," Silva admitted, licking his lips in anticipation. "You have succeeded in intriguing me. All right, here is my plan: We shall take a small number of legionnaires with us, but merely as a precaution, as well as food sufficient for our needs should we end up staying overnight tomorrow and returning here the next day, along with tents for the lot of us. Would that do it, Marcus?"

"It would be more than enough, sir."

"But you have never been to whatever it is that you have in mind for us?"

"That is correct, but I understand that, once you know exactly what it is that we are to be seeing, the implications are rather sobering."

"We shall not be having much fun on this little trip, I gather, Marcus?"

Sweating a bit, Vibenna spoke forthrightly, "It is scarcely a time for fun, would you not say, sir?"

Silva nodded while replying, "I must agree, sadly I must."

The men embraced, as was the custom in those days, and went to their separate quarters for the rest of the day.

Filled with a sudden insecurity, Vibenna slept not at all well that night, as he grappled with the wisdom of his choice or the lack of it.

LXXVII

They could see Lake Asphaltitus to their left, as well as Jebel Usdum to their right, a barren region aptly called the Valley of Salt and referred to in 2 Samuel 8:13.

"This is essentially an area of great victory that had taken place alongside another time of great horror," Vibenna remarked. "It was here that the Jews were victorious over the Syrians. But it was also here that—"

Silva had gotten off his horse and was looking at the site before him.

"Such blackness . . ." spoke the commander in a hushed voice.

"Nothing alive here at all," added Vibenna. "Not a single plant grows. There are no serpents or other such creatures."

"I have seen places with little life," Silva said, "but never before where life has *completely* ceased to exist."

He pointed to the sky.

"No birds overhead, either," he observed. "No vultures looking for bodies upon which to feed because there are none."

He walked up into the valley with mountain peaks north and south of it.

"Up the sides of the cliffs," he murmured, "the same as the ground—nothing but barrenness, tinged with that ghastly black hue."

As Silva stood in the middle of that place, he suddenly spun around on one heel, his face flush.

"Something *was* here!" he exclaimed.

"A city," Vibenna told him excitedly, "a thriving city, together with a sister city some miles away, bound together by a common govern ment and way of life."

"I *see* that!" the commander exclaimed again. "These are not for mations of rock all around us but the remains of buildings."

"Right into the lake, sir. If you go through the valley and stop at the water's edge, you can see their outlines beneath the surface."

Silva walked determinedly down the middle of that valley, past the mountains, and to the shore of that sterile body of water.

Just as Vibenna had said.

"The tops of some just barely pierce the surface," Silva spoke.

He spun around, looked back at the valley, the shapes hinted at across its expanse.

"Streets," he said. "I can see what must have been streets."

"The water claimed part of this place," Vibenna surmised.

"But what took the rest? What awful catastrophe destroyed this city?"

"And the other one, too, near this spot."

"Do you know, Marcus?"

"I know what Jewish records state."

"Then tell me."

"God's judgment. This city was named Sodom, the other was Gomorrah. The citizens of both became exceedingly evil."

"And so their God destroyed everything as a result," he said, "is that what I am to understand?"

"According to the Jewish writings, yes," Vibenna replied.

"I wonder, then, if this Jehovah, as I have heard them call Him, is not worthy of consideration after all, if He did something as wise as that."

"I have long wrestled with that very question in this matter and in others, sir."

The two men turned back toward the valley and retraced their steps.

Abruptly, Silva stopped, his face growing pale. Vibenna's gaze traveled to where the other man's seemed frozen.

In the ground . . . the faint outline of a human skull.

"I have seen much bloodier sights," Silva remarked, "but somehow—"

He pointed to another spot, and another, and still others.

"All over this valley, it seems," the commander said.

"Fire and brimstone are supposed to have destroyed them," Vibenna recalled, "molten rock covering them and then hardening, leaving behind what was left as a—"

He stopped, biting his lower lip.

"Finish your sentence, Marcus," Silva demanded.

"A reminder, sir. We see what we see—those skulls in the ground, the blackness of this place as a reminder."

"A reminder of what? You can speak freely."

"Of a society that, in its decline, warranted only the wrath of this Jehovah in whom the Jews believe so ardently."

Silva saw where the soldiers who had accompanied them on the journey were standing, and waved for Vibenna to go with him some greater distance away so that no one would overhear what was being said.

"Why have you thought of all this?" he asked.

"I live in Pompeii," Vibenna replied in a low voice. "I see the filth there. And so I think of coming judgment from the gods and wonder if it can be long before that city is left as Sodom and as Gomorrah."

422

"You sound as though you have absorbed the morality of the Jews we shall soon be fighting at Masada," Silva said.

"If one man murders another, he is subject to punishment. That is the same in their society and ours. If a man steals from another, he is again the object of punishment. There are many links between Jewish and Roman morality."

The commander nodded after Vibenna had finished.

"I have to agree with you, Marcus," he spoke. "And I too think of the corruption started through that monstrous Caligula as well as Nero, whom I hated with a great passion, and I sometimes must awake in the middle of the night as I consider what might become of Rome if that corruption is not finally rooted out. Will we end up as those poor fools whose skulls look up at us from their very graves?"

"We fight against a people who fight against us because we have sought to impose our way of life on them," Vibenna said sadly. "Yet can we so much blame the insurrectionists if they are simply looking at us as honestly, as clearly as we have just spoken? I must wonder whose cause is righteous."

He was at great risk with that statement, placing his life in the hands of a man who had assured him that he could speak freely.

"You speak those very same thoughts that have been plaguing me," Silva admitted. "When I have battled other enemies, I have done so without qualms, because Imperial Rome demanded this of me. Yet if our government does not pull itself from the moral pit into which it has been sinking for most of this century, must I wave my conscience aside and go on wallowing in the dirt along with it? But then I would be guilty of treason, would I not? And how could I ever allow that to be so, Marcus?"

★ ★ ★

Decimus Paetus knew what the commander of the Roman forces would do next. He had participated in sieges elsewhere. A specific pattern was nearly always followed, and this was so because that pattern had proven invariably successful.

"There . . . ," he told Eleazar ben Ya'ir. "The White Promontory. It is the only possible route for them. Nothing else connects us to the mountain. The slopes are too steep. And they do not go far enough up any side. It has to be the Promontory."

"I think you are right," the zealot leader agreed. "Unless their plan is to starve us from Masada."

"We have the ability to grow enough foods to support ourselves for years. The cisterns take care of any water needs we might have. Even if there is an especially dry year or two, we could still survive if we imposed stringent rationing. Our need of clothes to last throughout the siege is one superficial weak spot in our planning, since we have nothing but that which we brought along with us."

"According to the parchments, it was no problem for Adam and Eve before they left the Garden of Eden," ben Ya'ir said half-jokingly, a rare moment of levity for a man embroiled in thoughts of survival for his followers.

"If we had to stay on here with just rags to cover our poor bodies or nothing at all, I suppose it could be done. But none of this is going to be necessary, Eleazar. They *do* plan to attack eventually. And it must be soon."

"Because of a compelling need to restrict any damage being caused to the reputation of Rome, I suppose."

"The less time it takes to defeat us," Paetus agreed, "the better it will be for them when they return to Rome."

"But then why have they taken so long merely to set up camp?"

"Part of Roman strategy has been to undermine the enemy from inside the enemy's own camp . . . make them nervous . . . cause them to wonder exactly what is going on. And we must not forget that each camp is not placed at all randomly or haphazardly but with a specific objective in mind. I found, when I was a legionnaire, that the best of the Roman commanders are if anything methodical."

Shouts interrupted them as they stood on the eastern side of Masada near one of the snake-path gates in the casemate wall that faced Lake Asphaltitus.

Someone across the width of the plateau from them was jumping up and down and gesturing wildly.

Paetus and ben Ya'ir ran toward him as did others who were gathering around.

"May God help us!" the man gasped.

"What is it?" ben Ya'ir, panting, asked him.

"Look through the wall! *Below!* You were right, Decimus!"

The zealot leader peered through one of the observation slots in the wall, and saw the White Promontory below and slightly to his right.

He stepped back and let Paetus look.

"They have started," ben Ya'ir groaned. "How long will it take them?"

"Half the time they required to set up the camps. We must be ready for them."

The White Promontory was the only link between the plateau and the mountain range. And it was on that very spot that the Romans had begun construction of an earth and rock ramp, the sight of which filled every man, woman, and child with a dread that they had managed to keep subdued until then but which now was springing to diabolical life.

424

LXXVIII

Marcus Vibenna had not been the Roman who had actually invented the siege tower that would be used against Masada, for it preceded him in the Roman arsenal by many years. But he was able to suggest to commander Silva a number of changes in the traditional design that would make it more suited for the particular terrain in front of them: the size of the new one; how many levels it should contain; the type of construction capable of reducing its weight but maintaining its intrinsic strength; the angle of it so as to make pulling the huge structure up the White Promontory less arduous but without sacrificing the stability that the tower had to have or else risk the deaths of scores of legionnaires, if not more.

There was, however, a limitation to its height that proved nettlesome.

"If we build the tower any taller," Vibenna spoke quietly, "it will be subject to an imbalance and be at the mercy of the very severe winds that we have experienced here. And due to the narrowness of what the locals call the White Promontory, we cannot make the ramp any wider to keep it steady. If we build it to the maximum safe height, the tower will be still several hundred feet below the top of the casemate wall that surrounds the entire plateau."

. . . the very severe winds that we have experienced here.

As Silva listened, he could only agree with the other man's assessment, for he had been sharing in misery with his troops the early stages of severe winter weather plaguing the plains of that region of Judea. Tents had been knocked down, more substantial wooden buildings toppled. Rain had washed away supplies and made men and beasts of burden wet and miserable. Ironically, the zealots at Masada were much better off since they could retreat to one of Herod's palaces on the plateau.

Nevertheless, waging the siege during the winter months was preferable to doing so in the summer, where the great enemy of heat could only be on the side of the zealots.

"A solution? Tell me what your thoughts are," the general asked, aware that whatever they were saying would be given a certain permanency because nearby once again was Josephus, continuing his seemingly inexhaustible notes.

As the little bearded man went on writing, he as always seemed oblivious to anything around him but that which was to be preserved as the content of a waxen tablet, several of which had been provided for his use by the Romans. To imprint his outpouring of words, he used a stilus, one end of which was sharp, whereas the other was flattened so that he could rub out on the wax what he wanted to change. Once he was back in Rome, he would duplicate everything on standard parchment.

"Since therefore the Roman commander Silva had now built a wall on the outside, around the base of the plateau," he recorded for ages to come, "and had thereby made a most accurate provision to prevent any one of the besieged running away, he undertook the siege itself, though he found but one single place that would admit of the banks he was to raise. Accordingly he got upon that location, and ordered the army to bring earth; and when they fell to that work with alacrity, the bank was raised, and became solid for thirty feet in height, yet was not this bank sufficiently high for the use of what was to be set upon it; but still another elevated work of great stones compacted together was raised upon the White Promontory, being eighty feet both in breadth and height."

That was the solution Silva sought. They would build up the end of the White Promontory attached to the side of the plateau first by dirt, and then by stones. And it was on this base that the fearsome siege tower itself was built.

★ ★ ★

The zealots were as prepared as the circumstances permitted. The invention put forth by Decimus Paetus—a two-fold inner wall of wood with soil in the middle—had been erected now that they could see the Roman plan of attack taking shape.

The Sicarii arms included arrows, clubs, axes, and the daggers for which they had been named, all brought with them plus a substantial arsenal found at Masada after they had routed the Romans.

"They think they are so clever, so advanced," ben Ya'ir said as he looked through an opening in the casemate wall. "And look at how much trouble they must go to in order to attempt retaking a fortress that we were able to wrestle from their control in the first place."

Paetus had been thinking about that also.

"I came later, of course," he said. "It is remarkable that you were able to sneak up the snake paths without alerting anyone until it was too late for any of them."

At night . . .

One by one, the zealots climbed to the top. Despite the beginnings of the Jewish War, the Roman soldiers on the plateau had become convinced they would be completely safe. How could a simple band of ragtag Jews figure out a way to conquer Masada, a deed that would have taxed even the finest *Roman* military minds?

When certain of ben Ya'ir's men, who had shaved themselves of their beards so as to appear as Roman as possible, reached the top, they picked off the sentries, and donned their outfits, beginning a successful masquerade that lasted until morning. While the other legionnaires slept, a large number drunk with wine after an evening of letting off steam to fight the boredom of being isolated on the plateau, the zealots took up near their barracks, ready to confront the Romans in the morning, victory assured because of the key element of surprise.

Nevertheless, many soldiers who tried to fight back were killed, but with no resulting casualties among the Jews. The surviving legionnaires were allowed to leave by the same snake paths that were the only route up to and down from Masada. A large number of these men died in the desert, only a handful surviving to be picked up by Roman patrols some distance away.

"What we did is denied *them!*" ben Ya'ir exclaimed as he pointed to the men visible through the opening in the wall. "Their attack could never be other than out in the open, as they are starting to do now."

From that the zealot leader drew some satisfaction.

"If we all are to die, those who plunge the killer weapon into our hearts will have to work very hard to do that foul deed," he said, pulling his lamb's wool cloak around himself as a slight but very cold wind kicked up.

Ben Ya'ir grew angry.

"It is more difficult for me to endure *another* disturbing truth. For in the present circumstance, at least I can face my own death with the fullest assurance that we conduct ourselves bravely. Everything we do is for the sake of our homeland."

. . . *another singular truth altogether.*

"That Josephus is free, I suppose you mean," Paetus suggested.

"Again you are right, my Roman friend. At least *you* came over to us for a just cause. It is unbearable that all this may happen while that traitor down there goes on to outlive us, pampered by the very enemy against whom he once fought. Cornered, with no escape, he became a coward, and sold us out that he himself might live."

"Did you know Josephus?" Paetus asked.

"I did, and I trusted him. He was the one who brought to us what had happened to my sister, Mary."

"I did not know about her."

427

"And I would prefer to say nothing more. It is a terrible thing, Decimus, to know that a human being, a precious loved one, has stooped to living like an animal."

Surprised by this revelation, Paetus was curious but saw how troubled his friend was, and turned his attention instead to that double wall, to make sure, for the last time, that it had been constructed properly.

LXXVIX

The mountain behind him, General Silva stood on a slope at one end of the White Promontory, his hands cupped around his lips.

"I must address Eleazar ben Ya'ir!" he shouted.

Silence met his words.

"I want to offer terms of an honorable surrender," he continued. "If it is harsh punishment that you fear, I am empowered to tell you now that should you surrender within the next three days and acknowledge the primacy of Roman rule, you will be imprisoned, yes, but for a period of one year, and, with good behavior, you will be released in six months. This offer is brought by me from Emperor Vespasianus himself!"

Silva waited and was on the verge of deciding that the zealots had chosen to ignore him when the deep voice of their leader carried from the plateau to where he was standing.

"You speak of Vespasianus," called out Eleazar ben Ya'ir. "It is the son of this emperor who attempted to annihilate my people and destroy our holy city. If the son is a monster, can the father be very different?"

Silva glanced at Vibenna who was standing just a few feet away.

"This zealot has seized upon the one point for which I can offer no defense," he acknowledged.

"May the gods give you wisdom," Vibenna replied.

"If I could only believe that the gods themselves were wise," the general whispered cryptically.

He turned back toward the mountain fortress.

"You speak correctly," he said. "What happened at Jerusalem six years ago *was* barbaric. Even the emperor's son has expressed his regret."

"His *regret?* Mere words of recanting cannot dissipate the tragedy," ben Ya'ir retorted, a mixture of sorrow and rage in his voice. "If this man were brought before us and we could deal with him ourselves, that *might* serve."

"You are talking about someone who may succeed his father as emperor one day!" Silva exclaimed incredulously.

"And *you* are talking about the greatest imaginable infamy, for which we are asking that the perpetrator be made to pay with his own life. Thousands died because of the younger Vespasianus. One life for so many—*can that be called unjust?*"

Silva was beginning to perspire despite the just-above-freezing temperature.

"That cannot be done," he lamented. "Yours is such an absurd and pathetic request that I do not have to bother the emperor by asking him, for he obviously would not allow it. Apart from any considerations of familial loyalty, such an action on his part would provoke civil war because there *are* many in the Senate and the military as well as common citizens on the street who think highly of this man. Yea, Titus Vespasianus happens to be viewed as a hero by them, and they could never abide what you ask."

"Do you feel that way? Do *you* give him a hero's wreath?"

Silva grimaced.

"My feelings are not what is at issue—"

"Then we cannot abide the surrender you expect of us!" ben Ya'ir interrupted him, spitting out these words with a contempt that survived even the considerable distance their sound had to travel. "Roman rule has doomed my ancient nation. Roman war and its effects turned my loving and kind sister into a desperate, loathsome creature. She was then found behind the walls of Jerusalem by a contingent of legionnaires who became sickened by what they had caused, while their commander took time off to sleep with pretty boys taken prisoner, as well as the sister of Herod Agrippa.

"Unable to endure the sight of my sister, her deplorable state accusing them every moment she remained alive, they decided to do away with this once dear, dear girl hardly out of her youth, and brutally took her life, burying that poor emaciated body, and then walked away to wash their hands of her in a nearby stream."

A pause—apparently to enable him to control his emotions—and then the zealot leader added, "Neither my people nor I can leave this fortress in peace without something in return. Giving Titus Vespasianus over to us is hardly enough, but we are realists, and not so foolish as you may think us to be, and we know we can expect little else. We shall await your final answer at the end of the truce you have offered."

Eleazar ben Ya'ir apparently left the casemate wall, for he spoke no more that day.

Silva, hardly an amateur in negotiations, stood back, still looking up at the plateau, an astonished expression on his face.

Vibenna hurried over to him.

"Sir?" he asked tentatively, not certain that the veteran military man wanted to speak to anyone just then.

"Do not sound so apprehensive," Silva chided him. "You will not be executed at dawn for interrupting my thoughts."

"What will you do?" Vibenna asked.

"Not what that conniving Jew has asked, I can tell you. Yet—"

He lowered his voice.

"Marcus, this ben Ya'ir has succeeded in making me feel that I should offer *something*. Yet what can that be? I came here to force him to surrender or be wiped out, yet it seems that he has turned matters around completely."

"Perhaps you would be better able to judge that, sir, if you knew what he was talking about when he referred to his sister in such a despairing manner. And there might be one man here who could tell us everything."

Silva's eyelids opened wide.

"Josephus!" he exclaimed. "The little Jew can at last earn his keep by telling us whatever he knows."

"And he may know a great deal since the siege of Jerusalem is presumably an important part of the chronicles he is writing."

Both men turned and saw that Josephus was standing a hundred feet or so away. They raced up to him, their sudden speed making him cringe as they approached.

"How much have you heard?" Silva asked.

"Not everything. Just bits and pieces. I do gather that ben Ya'ir told you about his sister Mary."

"He did," the general admitted. "Can you enlighten us?"

Josephus nodded sadly.

"I have already written about that tragic soul."

He reached down for a leather sachet where he kept the most recent of his wax tablets, and carefully pulled out one of these.

"I will read to you exactly what I have recorded," he told them with some rather theatrical solemnity.

Josephus held the tablet up before his eyes and said, "Among the residents was a woman named Mary, sister of Eleazar. She had fled to Jerusalem, where she became confined by the siege."

Josephus paused, and looked up from the tablet.

"Behind ben Ya'ir's anger is the burden of a certain guilt," he said.

"Guilt?" Vibenna questioned. "How can he feel guilty? That he was not with her to help, is that it?"

"It is much more than what you say. The zealots were aware of secret underground passageways into Jerusalem."

"If into, then surely *out* of the city as well," spoke Silva. "Why then were not more people able to escape?"

"The rebels never told anyone but those from their own group."

The general again registered great surprise, this time with more than a little shock as part of it.

"If they had, not so many would have died."

"You speak the truth," Josephus confirmed.

"But why keep vital information of this sort hidden from your own countrymen?" Silva persisted.

"From your *older* countrymen, yes, and from the women, the children, others who were sick, also yes, but it must be said that many of the able-bodied young and middle-aged men knew, and they were the ones to escape and reinforce the numbers already at Masada or else to flee to hiding places in the countryside, even as far from here as Petra."

"The zealots consciously picked the most combat-able Jews, and left the others behind to their fate?" Vibenna repeated, this time the one to be startled.

"Only those who were unmarried or widowed went with them. They knew the others would not desert their families."

"But surely Eleazar ben Ya'ir would have seen to the safety of his own sister," Silva reasoned.

"If he had known she was in Jerusalem, yes, but the last he heard she was still in the village of Bethezuba where she had spent most of her adult years. You see, there was great panic among the Jews in the countryside. Not everyone acted sensibly. Many thought they surely would be safer in heavily fortified Jerusalem."

Josephus put down the tablet for a moment as he said, "History may well view Eleazar ben Ya'ir and the other zealots as noble and courageous, but the truth is that there are countless numbers of Jews given to viewing them only as the most reckless and self-centered of adventurers who, once the Romans gained an upper hand, turned tail, and ran south, deserting everyone else as they hid behind the walls of Masada, undoubtedly hoping to last on the plateau until the war sputtered out, and then they could emerge reasonably unscathed, and in the process, gain some show of leniency."

"I understand now that ben Ya'ir's sister Mary was in Jerusalem during the siege," Vibenna recounted, "but then what caused her to deteriorate to such a level that soldiers felt compelled to kill her and dispose of the body?"

Josephus held up the tablet again.

"There is more," he said, "and it is much worse than anything you have learned thus far. Listen to this: Most of the property she had packed up and brought with her had been plundered by zealot tyrants—"

432

"You are the one who is mad!" Silva exclaimed. "I have heard none of this before. It sounds as though you are trying to justify your own actions, this betrayal of yours by painting these people as the worst villains!"

"You may think that, if it suits you to do so but what I am describing is every bit the truth as I know it."

"Continue . . . ," Silva said grudgingly.

"—plundered by zealot tyrants, together with such meager food as she had been able to procure."

He closed his eyes briefly, and mumbled, "Jerusalem was being constantly raided during the early stages of the siege, its food stores depleted by zealots who took large quantities of it for their own use, primarily for consumption at Masada. This hastened the end for those trapped citizens who were forced to remain behind the walls of Jerusalem and drove them all to abominable acts of desperation, robbing each one of a civilized humanity and forcing them into the behavior of ravenous beasts."

"The sister of Eleazar ben Ya'ir was no exception . . . ," Vibenna mused.

"In her bitter resentment, the poor woman cursed and spat at the crude extortioners and tried to rally others inside the city to line up against the zealots but she met only the deafest of ears, every citizen she confronted refusing to believe such ugliness as she described. Eventually the hunger of a growing famine began gnawing at her vitals, and the fire of rage within her became even fiercer than famine.

"So, driven by fury and want, she committed a crime against nature. Seizing her child, an infant at the breast, she cried, 'My poor baby, why should I keep you alive in this world of war and hunger? Even if we live until the Romans burst through, they will make slaves of us; and, anyway, hunger will get us before slavery does; and the rebels, should they return, are crueler than both. Come, be food for me.' With these words, she killed her son."

Josephus saw Silva and Vibenna out of the corner of his eye, the blood draining from their faces.

"When some rebels returned for more food, they smelled the roast meat and threatened to kill her instantly if she did not produce it. She assured them that she had saved a share for their appetites and then revealed the remains of her child. The whole city soon rang with the abomination. When people heard of it, they shuddered, as though they had done it themselves."

Silva raised his fists in the air.

"Oh gods, wherever you are, whoever you are, which are the greater barbarians?" he cried out in utter disgust. "The zealots who stole food from their own starving countrymen . . . a woman who tried to satisfy her hunger with the flesh of her helpless infant son or . . . the vaunted forces of Imperial Rome responsible for the horror in the first place, our finest fighting men who, when confronted with such a ghastly aftermath of their actions, conspired to murder and bury a mad creature bereft of her humanity?"

LXXX

T*hree days . . .*

For the Romans and the Jewish zealots, it could have been three
weeks or three months, the time passing snail-like. In those days, truces
had the force of imperial law, and were not broken since the integrity of
both parties was at stake. Even in the midst of war, honor still had its
precarious place.

Finally, the morning of the third day, Flavius Silva stood at the
opposite end of the White Promontory.

"I await your answer, Eleazar ben Ya'ir," he said. "What is it that
you have decided—surrender under the terms I gave you, or face certain
annihilation?"

"I can scarcely hear you this day," called out the now-familiar
voice. "You will have to step closer."

Still bound by the ethics of his station, Silva started walking up the
White Promontory for about fifty yards.

"Can you hear my voice any more clearly?" he asked.

"Yea, I can, and you shall have my answer just as surely!"

In an instant, an arrow had been shot from behind the casemate wall.

"General!" Vibenna shouted at him.

Silva saw the weapon but could not step aside in time to avoid
having the blade gash the top of his left shoulder. Since he was not in
battle gear, but a more ceremonial uniform that had no protective metal
or leather, his decision to wear it essentially a gesture of trust and respect
on his part. The lighter, more colorful material was easily sliced open and
took a chunk of skin along with it.

"You have our answer!" ben Ya'ir screamed at him. "We shall not
surrender to those who rape our land and slaughter helpless, maddened
women."

Vibenna rushed to the general's side.

"It is not serious," he said after examining the wound, "but it
needs to be medicated and bound up."

"How could he do that?" Silva spoke disbelievingly as they walked
back toward camp and the medical tent near the center. "How could he
show such disrespect?"

"Do you have a sister, sir?" Vibenna inquired.

"I do, Marcus."

"How would you react to any man, any group of men who had brutalized the life from her soft young body?"

"I would—!" Silva started to say, clenching his hands at the very thought.

"Ben Ya'ir has faced that very horror, sir, together with the deaths of thousands of his countrymen. Is it hard to understand that he may have . . . lost his mind?"

Part of his uniform now covered with blood, pain not insubstantial, Silva nevertheless stopped walking for a moment.

"I understand you," he said earnestly, his voice a bit weak. "But now understand me, Marcus: For a soldier, there is but one set of complexities with which he must be concerned and by which his actions are governed, those of the battlefield, and no other place or circumstance can be allowed to interfere.

"It is not a matter even of simple morality or politics, it is rather a matter of defeating your opponent, however understandable the reactions that guide his own conduct, especially in this instance. For the truth is that he has no other course himself. He must face the same reality, Marcus. For this Eleazar ben Ya'ir is a general of sorts himself. He must either crush us or hand over to us the opportunity of doing the same to that rebel lot he now commands. Nothing else can be allowed to take up our time and attention or his own."

* * *

Decimus Paetus had protested against what had happened, calling it the act of a mind beyond reason, because wounding or killing the commander of the Roman forces who had come to the scene under the protection of a truce was not an action from which anyone could retreat. Once committed, it could only bind every man, woman, and child to a last, awful clash, with no hope of reprieve.

But he was outvoted. And it was enough of a breach of decency and honor that it became a serious wedge between him and Eleazar ben Ya'ir.

"You argue passionately for keeping this Roman general, oppressor that he is, untouched, as though he is some special being, a god of sorts perhaps," the zealot spoke sarcastically. "I do not hear you voicing as loudly your understanding of why I feel as I do, and why I must act as I *shall* act, Decimus. In fact, your sympathies seem to be undergoing a change that I do not find reassuring."

"What you say is absurd," Paetus replied, every bit as angry as the other man. "I know exactly why you have come to this point. Remember that we have been fighting the battle together ever since it began, and I with Barabbas, before you were old enough to take care of your bodily functions without help."

"Barabbas the *Christian*, you mean."

"So it was his Christianity that seems, now, to render invalid his leadership in those days, are you saying this, Eleazar? Not too long ago, you expressed a desire to learn more about the Nazarene, or have you forgotten?"

"Not too long ago, Decimus, fifteen thousand Roman troops had yet to surround this mountain fortress."

"But you knew they would come eventually."

"Seeing them start to gather below us much as they did around Jerusalem has changed everything."

The pain of that nightmare from two years before was freshly written on ben Ya'ir's heavily bearded face.

"Perhaps some of those same legionnaires participated in that tragic assault against our ancient city and against my beloved Mary. I cannot trust the word of any Roman as a result of what they have done. I can trust only the sword and the arrow which I shall thrust into any Roman who stands before me in combat!"

He held one of each in his hands.

"These are what Jehovah has given us to defend ourselves, together with whatever rocks I am able to use as weapons."

"But how long can you resist," Paetus probed, "before you are forced to go on to another course of action?"

Ben Ya'ir's face froze, as though the chill winds had gotten into his blood and made it like the icy lid on a winter pond.

"I overheard you and some others talking," Paetus went on. "There *is* another plan, is there not? Something you will do if defeat is but certain?"

"We were musing," ben Ya'ir protested, "the idle speculation of desperate men."

"But how is it that such a course could even come to your mind?"

Suicide! Paetus thought. *You would rather take your own lives than admit that you have failed and put your trust in a sovereign Creator.*

"Is it so wrong?" ben Ya'ir demanded. "We would be made helpless slaves, forced to serve the very government that has been smashing our bloody bodies into the parched earth of this our native land.

"Oh, they may offer to us, in apparent sincerity, the olive branch of eventual freedom but once they have disarmed us, once they have imprisoned us in their dungeons or perhaps send us in chains to their rock quarries, we are at the mercy of our ruthless conquerors and then we can no longer hope to resist."

He cleared his throat and spoke even more firmly.

"As Jews, we must accept only the yoke of our heavenly Father, but, on the other hand, *nothing* that is pressed upon us by this heathen emperor, whoever his successor might be or anyone else of their kind."

"But suicide, Eleazar?" persisted Paetus. "Not everyone would want to die in that manner. Surely you must suspect this, whatever the well-rehearsed reasons for engaging in such action. Some doubtless would try to escape upon learning of your intent, and others would *beg* you not to do this terrible thing."

His eyes narrowed as he leaned forward.

"If you were to go ahead anyway, that would make you and the rest who did so murderers! Remember, my brother, you must face a holy God in judgment for your sins. Do you want any of such magnitude to have to confess before Him after you leave this world?"

"You cannot *dare* to call me your brother if you stand in the way of this!" ben Ya'ir declared with welling anger.

Paetus could not believe what he was hearing from a man he had pledged to support through the worst of times.

"It sounds as though you have already decided!" he exclaimed, horrified. "This was not idle banter on anyone's part. It—"

Ben Ya'ir grabbed him by the neck.

"You must tell no one of your suspicions, which are, of course, all that you have, old man," the zealot leader warned.

Nothing in the man's tone left any doubt about the outcome if Paetus chose to ignore him.

LXXXI

The ramp pressed up against the side of the plateau was only to serve as a sturdy foundation for the siege tower that, after more tense weeks, had finally been completed according to Marcus Vibenna's suggestions. It was ninety feet high, extending above the casemate wall by about thirty-five feet.

The tower was built of thick wood, the large timbers overlaid with heavy sheets of iron that had been fitted to them weeks before.

On top of the enormous structure was a quick-loading ballista and a ram, the latter intended to break through the casemate wall. But when it did, the ram collided immediately with the inner wall that Paetus had concocted, reinforced by earth. Each new assault only pounded the dirt tighter, making it all the more impenetrable.

Nor had the zealots made it easy for the Romans to complete the tower. While much of the structure had been built earlier near one of the camps, soldiers still had the task of assembling it into a cohesive unit. Hour-by-hour, rocks would be hurled down upon them from the fortress. Several score soldiers were injured or killed in the midst of the torrent of primitive but potent weapons.

Eventually the defenders ran out of their natural "heavy" weapons, and had to switch to another strategy.

"We will use boiling water next," suggested Paetus, snapping his fingers as the thought occurred to him.

Ben Ya'ir agreed.

"I misjudged you earlier!" he exclaimed.

Paetus avoided looking at him.

After ben Ya'ir gave the order, his men heated large cauldrons of water on top of the casemate wall itself.

"Let them see what we are doing," Paetus had added. "It will send them into a frenzy."

Those below had to deal with the knowledge that any minute, they risked being scalded or worse.

Which was what did happen, a simple defense, primitive at best, but producing a startlingly effective result.

Man after man had to flee in agony.

Some lost their sight, their eyes destroyed, while others would be disfigured for the rest of their lives. More than a few fell to their deaths.

Others found themselves involuntarily gulping down the steaming water, burning their insides and consequently dying in the worst pain any had ever known, even in the midst of a more "normal" battlefield.

Next came the oil.

Paetus had urged that the zealots pool any remaining oil that had been reserved for lamps and other uses, and use it as well. Whatever harm the water had caused was exceeded by the flowing oil which ran out sooner because the supply was more limited—but its devastation was greater among those in its path.

"They must pull back!" Vibenna urged, seeing the chaos and fearing for the lives of those on the siege tower.

"I will *not* do as you suggest," Silva rebuked him. "We *must* burn out the Jews, even if it means annihilating every one of their men, women and—"

He could not bring himself to say "children."

"We will stay the course, Marcus," he added brusquely. "You know what must come next as well as I do."

Vibenna nodded reluctantly, even as the desperate cries of dying legionnaires reached his ears.

The ballista.

This was the principal assault weapon Silva had at his disposal. And he now passed along an order that it be used without delay.

After getting the bodies of their fallen comrades out of the way as best they could, the remaining legionnaires commenced a relentless barrage of stone and iron bolts flung from the ballista.

"The range is limited," Paetus shouted to ben Ya'ir, who was next to him along the newly built wall.

The zealot leader acknowledged this without hesitation and ordered, "Retreat! To the center!"

But several of the men had been hit despite the speed with which the group moved. Not a few died as their skulls were crushed; others died from chests caved in by heavy rocks. Some had legs broken and had to be dragged away by comrades.

It seemed that only seconds passed before the next stage in the assault began. That was when a select number of legionnaires, among the finest marksmen available to Rome, unleashed wave after wave of arrows, the tips of which had been wrapped in special cloth, soaked in oil, and set aflame.

"The wall is giving way!" someone near Paetus shouted.

With the wood burning and soon turning to smoldering pieces, nothing was left to hold back the wall of dirt, and while it remained firm in some spots, it fell apart in others, and soon the zealots' important defensive line no longer existed.

440

But more devastating than that, such an inferno was started along the wall and jumping to nearby structures that the zealots immediately were driven back even farther and were forced to retreat into one or the other of Herod's palaces and any adjacent hiding places.

At that point, Masada became virtually an irresistible open-sesame to the Romans, now very much ready for their brutal intrusion, with all of the zealot defenders stuck at the opposite end from where the breach had been opened.

Yet the very intensity of the flames that contained the enemy proved so great that none of the attackers themselves could grab the abrupt strategic advantage thus created, and they were denied being able to make it over onto the plateau at last.

Silva uttered a rare profanity after he learned what was happening, cursing the stymied opportunity.

Yet the situation deteriorated even further.

Those capricious strong Judean winds had been blowing the fire toward the interior of Masada.

But then—

"Look, sir!" Vibenna said, pointing in horror at the scene.

A change of direction in the winds began sweeping the flames momentarily back toward the tower itself!

Legionnaires, less heavily armored because of the need to move quickly and in cramped quarters, were igniting like stalks of dry wheat. Some dropped where they stood, life scorched from them before they could move. Others ran frantically to the edge of the siege tower, and fell over, plummeting ninety feet to the stone-and-dirt ramp below.

For a brief hellish time, the only people in danger seemed to be none but the Romans!

But, just as erratically, the winds switched yet again and turned against Masada more strongly than before, pushing the flames across nearly the full length of the plateau in a sudden and ferocious initial gust, with others to follow in its path.

The outcome of that initial offensive was quickly reported to Silva.

"Shall . . . we . . . go . . . in . . . after . . . them . . . now?" the breathless messenger asked.

Silva glanced knowingly at Vibenna, then said, "No, we will wait. Let the fire run its deadly course and do much of our work for us. Our attack will continue instead in the morning while, in the meantime, we shall seize the privilege of a full night's sleep. I dare say *they* will not be doing the same!"

A moment later, the general walked off toward his tent, a slight swagger to his step.

LXXXII

Eleazar ben Ya'ir was huddled in a corner of the third terrace of Herod's palace at the far end of Masada.

"The people need you," Decimus Paetus started to plead with him as soon as he had come upon the other man.

"I cannot face them," ben Ya'ir moaned. "All of us are being punished for what we have done."

Paetus could not rebuke the zealot leader for saying that, because he had come to something of the same conclusion.

"For which offense?" he asked, feigning ignorance.

"For all that we have done over the past six years against our countrymen," ben Ya'ir blurted out, "all those horrible actions we have visited upon them during the days after we fled Jerusalem!"

"But some were traitors," Paetus reminded him.

"Some were *thought* to be traitors, Decimus. This was true of Josephus, but I think perhaps that some others were not. I only suspected them. There was not often much proof. They died because I *pretended* to be certain of their guilt, even when I could have been persuaded otherwise about them."

He held out his hands.

"Will Jewish hands never be free of innocent blood?" he cried. "From the death of the Nazarene to the present! This must be why Jehovah is punishing us."

"It may be, but you should consider another cause, if what we are seeing is from the hand of God," Paetus spoke.

"No!" ben Ya'ir screamed. "I will not listen to what I know you cannot prevent yourself from saying!"

"Then it *has* occurred to you. How can you expect God to honor that which only He has the right to perform? You cannot take your own life—and force others into suicide as well—and yet moan over His judgment as though you are a mere victim and not a recipient who has left a just and holy God but little choice!"

Ben Ya'ir jumped unsteadily to his feet.

"We are here *because* of Him!" he declared. "We are His chosen people!"

"Chosen to be His *obedient* people, Eleazar, not to engage in the terrible sin you are obviously bent on becoming guilty of before sunrise."

"We have had this argument before."

"And you are as blind and wrongheaded now as then!"

Ben Ya'ir started to push past him.

"Out of my way, old man!" he growled.

Paetus withdrew a dagger from its sheath at his side.

"Are you now to commit a sin of your own in order to deter me from mine?" ben Ya'ir said sarcastically.

Paetus hesitated.

Suddenly ben Ya'ir grabbed the hand in which the weapon was clasped and swung it around, plunging the blade into Paetus's side.

"Now I can be about the business that has been ordained," he said as he stepped over the fallen body.

"God does not *ordain* atrocity," Paetus managed to say.

"We will do what must be done as a valiant act of sacrifice for a noble cause."

". . . but . . . what . . . of . . . the . . . ones . . . who . . . will . . . not . . ." Paetus groaned before he became too weak even to open his mouth.

Impatient, and angry, Eleazar ben Ya'ir would have no more of this and left him behind on that third terrace of a long-dead king's once-majestic safe haven, now no longer what it was, and never to be so again.

* * *

The date according to the Christian calendar was April 15, 73 A.D.
The time: 3:45 A.M.

Ben Ya'ir knew that he had to inspire his followers, to convince them not to renounce the pact that their leaders, of which he was chief, had decided upon in secret.

"Since we, long ago, my generous friends, resolved never to be servants to the Romans, nor to any other than to God himself," he began as they all stood before him, directly in front of the terraced palace, continued flames at their back but not quite reaching so far, "who alone is the true and just Lord of mankind, the time is now come that obliges us to make that resolution true in practice."

He had been sleeping since he left Paetus but spent this time honing the message now being delivered to nearly 970 doomed human beings.

"We were the very first who revolted against Rome, and we are the last to fight against its legions," he continued. "I cannot but esteem it as a favor that God hath granted us, that it is still in our power to die bravely, and in a state of freedom."

Paetus had been able, though very weak, to walk the steps from the third terrace to the second, and from the second to the first. He had lost so much blood that he himself was amazed that he could do this, but he knew so strongly the presence of his Lord that his surprise turned only to gratitude, as he sat quietly, out of sight, listening to ben Ya'ir.

"It is very plain that we shall be taken within a day's time; but we still have the ability to die after a glorious manner, together with our dearest friends."

Several of the women gasped, for they were beginning to understand the implications of his words.

"Our enemy has no power to hinder us," ben Ya'ir continued. "Since it would be better for the Romans to take us alive, we cannot give them that."

That was the only part with which Paetus could agree, for the rest he considered rank and offensive hypocrisy.

To claim the blessing! he thought. *What blasphemy!*

Ben Ya'ir went on, with other noble phrases spewing from between his lips, until he had concluded the planned part of his speech.

"Let our wives die before they are abused, and our children before they have tasted of slavery, and after we have slain them—"

Small children started to cry then, terrified by such words of death to come by their fathers' hands.

"Finally, let us bestow this glorious end upon one another mutually, and preserve ourselves in our state of freedom as a most excellent funeral monument."

He paused, raised both arms above his head, and added, "Come, while our hands are free and can hold a sword, we must do what has been ordained. Let us not die by our enemies, but instead leave this world as free men in company with those we love so dearly. We must proceed quickly and do what we—"

A roar arose from the gathering, one that chilled Paetus through to his bones.

As Josephus was to write, "They cut him off short and made haste to do the work, as full of an unconquerable ardour of mind, and moved with a demoniacal fury."

Paetus saw it all.

. . . with a demoniacal fury.

That was how, as an eyewitness, he himself would have described the scene before him if he were instead writing the account, in place of a secondhand telling by a man hated by the Jews and, in private, despised by the Romans.

"So great was their zeal that they seemed to be swept along by an eagerness to slay their wives and children," Josephus would add. "Miserable men indeed were they, men whose distress forced them . . . to do those evils that were before them."

Paetus saw the most ghastly of sights—fathers killing their sons and daughters, husbands stabbing their wives.

He could watch no longer without standing in protest.

"You are mad!" he yelled. "Demons have taken up residence within you. How can this be for the sake of Jehovah and your ancient land?"

No one paid him heed.

He saw large, sturdy men who were blood-covered over nearly every inch of their bodies, their eyes wide, their expressions of unrestrained drunkenness, not in any way the noble cause their devout leader had touted.

Ben Ya'ir himself had fallen a short distance away, and Paetus ran to his side.

"Decimus, Decimus," he cried out, "I have started this monstrous evil, and it cannot be stopped."

"You have killed before in battle," Paetus reminded him, sobbing. "Surely you knew how it would be!"

"My son . . . my young son!" ben Ya'ir murmured. "He looked up at me and begged, 'Father, I do not want to die. Please do not do this to me.' But I would not listen, and I cut him straight through."

He struggled to his feet.

"So many are *enjoying* this," he said. "So many have succumbed to bloodlust and are prolonging the dying of some so that they can get greater—"

Ben Ya'ir suddenly became quite sick.

Paetus reached out to steady him but the zealot leader pushed away and stumbled off, half-blinded by the smoke and the heat and the perspiration dripping from his forehead and into his eyes.

"Eleazar! Look out!" Paetus yelled after him.

Too late.

Ben Ya'ir ran right into a back draft of flame, which overwhelmed him in an instant, and after taking only two steps, he fell straight down, screaming.

Some women were fighting their husbands for the lives of their children, but all were beaten down and killed, men raising their bloody swords then against themselves and dropping next to those they had murdered.

Paetus turned away, near death himself and far too weak to intercede for anyone. He managed to reach some steps at the edge of the plateau that led down toward one of the cisterns. He scarcely knew what he was doing, and tripped, then struggled to his feet, and went the rest of the way.

A cavern to his left opposite the cistern.

He thought he saw movement within it and headed toward the mouth.

Huddled inside were two women and five children. They screamed as he entered, seeing only a man drenched in blood, with a wild look about his face.

One of the women grabbed a rock and raced toward him.

"No!" he screamed. "I had no part in this."

She stopped short, eyeing him in sudden recognition, then dropped the stone.

"You once spoke privately to us of the saving grace of Jesus the Christ," she called out to him in gratitude. "We have accepted the truth of what you said, and we are now among His flock—my sister here and our precious children. But our husbands would not listen. They both went on with the madness of the others, the blood of many staining their very souls."

Decimus Paetus, old and weary and in great pain, fell into her arms and died while she held his battered frame, trying somehow to soothe him as, in tender and sweet voice, she sang an ancient song of worship and adoration that followed him to the gates of heaven and beyond.

LXXXIII

The fire was still burning by the time the Roman forces continued their attack, just after sunrise.

All were now armored and with a full complement of weapons. And they ran one man at a time onto the plateau, through the breached casemate wall, over planks that extended from the siege tower, scores of them becoming hundreds, and hundreds becoming a thousand or more in the first wave.

They had to race through the flames, the most treacherous part of the attack thus far, but once that was done, they expected to face an onslaught of arrows and charging zealots also armed with other weapons.

Only silence.

"Ahead!" someone shouted. "Ahead there! Look at the bodies! *All those bodies!*"

The mass of legionnaires moved from that eastern end of the plateau toward the terraced palace. Hundreds of dead men, women, and children were on the ground, the soil stained with their blood.

Several followed the gruesome trail into the palace itself and found many more bodies inside, at least five hundred on the three levels.

A messenger was sent down immediately to General Silva.

"You must see this for yourself, sir," the red-faced soldier told him as he waited, with Vibenna, midway up the White Promontory.

"There was no resistance?" Silva asked incredulously.

"None, sir. We made it over without a single casualty."

"But they are not fools. They must be hiding out, ready to launch an ambush. Be sure that the men are prepared and—"

The soldier did not verbally interrupt him, but the expression on his young face had the same effect.

"I am coming now!" Silva exclaimed with some urgency and motioned for Vibenna to follow him.

He strode up to the tower, climbed the side, and then approached the planks. The legionnaires on either side of him duplicated the look of horror and astonishment that had gripped the messenger a moment earlier.

Once Silva had crossed over onto the plateau, he saw that his men had cleared a less hazardous path through the decreasing flames, anticipating his soon-arrival.

They all stood at attention as he passed them.

Ahead nothing had been touched.

Silva saw exactly what had greeted the legionnaires when they first entered Masada. He walked numbly past piles of bodies, then stopped before two of these—a mother holding her child in her arms.

"Marcus . . . ," he said, his voice trembling.

"Yes, sir, I am right behind you. I see it as well."

Silva continued walking.

Vibenna looked away from the two, and continued following the general.

"In the palace, sir!" a legionnaire exclaimed. "So many! Not one alive. Not one!"

Silva stopped at the entrance. Already he could see the dead, could hear flies buzzing, could smell the stink.

"I shall go inside," Silva muttered.

"You need not do so," Vibenna whispered to him.

"I *shall* go inside!"

Silva walked down the short flight of steps leading to the first level.

"Stay, Marcus," he said firmly. "I will do this alone."

Instinctively Vibenna knew why the general had given this order. An emotional man beneath the tough military veneer, Silva could only become overwhelmed by what would confront him within Herod's palace.

Minutes passed.

No one could move until their commander emerged from within the palace.

And this he did, with a tiny baby in his arms.

"This little one is barely alive," he said, trying very hard to keep his emotions from spilling over. "We must do what we can to save her."

One of the medics rushed over to him.

"You must not let her die," Silva ordered. "She *has* to live."

The man acknowledged what he was told by his commander and gently took the fragile form in his own arms.

"Treat the little one well!" Silva called out as the medic started to hurry toward the siege tower.

The general looked about at his men and had opened his mouth to speak when he was interrupted, a rare occasion.

A centurion had climbed back to the plateau from the area of the largest of the cisterns along the side.

448

"Below!" he shouted, his face red. "Two women and five children. Alive! I thought there was also a dead zealot near them, but the women hastened to tell me that the body is not that of a Jew at all *but a Roman!*"

"I shall go back down with you," Silva told the centurion.

Dreading what he would find, Vibenna's muscles tightened and his face went pale as he fell in line behind them.

The cistern was at the opposite end of Masada from where they had been standing, just across from the siege tower, which had been erected toward the narrowest end of the mammoth plateau.

The three men hurried past one of Herod's other palaces, the second largest, which was on their right and, then, to the left, the smallest, which had been converted into zealot living quarters during the nearly seven years since the fortress had been ripped from the grasp of Imperial Rome. All the major individual fires had now died down and only a few were sputtering among the blackened timber, with the rest having become glowing embers.

They approached the siege tower and, at the centurion's direction, turned away from it toward some crude rock steps leading down the side of the plateau.

"In a rock next to the cistern," the centurion told them.

Two women and five children.

All of them nearly frantic with fear, as well as dirty and, in the case of one of the women, covered with scratches.

"What happened?" Silva asked her.

"We overheard our leader ben Ya'ir, my cousin, order our husbands to take our lives," she said. "But my friend and I did not want to die, nor did we want our children dead. So when the others were not looking, we ran down to this cave and prayed to God that we would not be discovered."

The other woman spoke up.

"So many murdered!" she exclaimed. "We heard their screams. They pleaded for life, for mercy, and were ignored. God would bless what had to be done, they were told. The Romans would treat them horribly. Dying as free Jews was far better!"

She fell to her knees in front of Silva.

"Nothing you could do to us would be worse than what has already happened," she cried out pitifully. "We are at your mercy, sir. Do with us what you wish—but, please, see to it that no harm comes to these our dear children."

Silva bent down, took her shoulders in his hands, and lifted her up.

"You shall not have another moment of fear for the rest of your lives, and it will be the same for the little ones whom you love so much."

She fell into his arms, and the other woman as well came to him.

Finally, after perhaps a minute or two had passed, Silva gave orders to the awaiting centurion; and both mothers, their three sons, and their two daughters were taken up the steps and helped across a plank to the siege tower and then down to the camp where the general himself had been headquartered since the start of the action against the zealots.

Back in the cave, Vibenna had remained silent and was kneeling beside the body of Decimus Paetus.

"A Roman?" asked Silva simply.

"Yes, sir, a Roman," Vibenna replied.

"I can scarce imagine why he was here. A prisoner perhaps?"

Vibenna looked up at him.

"I cannot say so, sir."

His voice quivered as he spoke, something Silva noticed.

"You seem especially distraught," he observed, concerned.

There was no reply.

Grunting, Silva knelt beside Vibenna and gently tapped the back of the other man's right hand.

"I know," he said softly. "Do not be concerned about my reactions. I am not an unfeeling ogre, as some may think."

Vibenna jerked his head toward the general.

"You *know?*" he spoke. "How can that be? I have told no one."

"There was much talk before we left for here. We had our traitor, and the Jews had theirs. It seemed ironic, somewhat perversely amusing, I would say."

He started frowning.

"I wanted to find out what I could about anyone who would be so stupid as to desert the glorious privilege of Roman service and citizenship to join such an unpleasant and backward group as the Jews.

"I discovered a great deal about a certain former legionnaire, someone named Decimus Paetus. The records showed that your path and his crossed more than once, the last time at the tomb of the Nazarene just outside the gates of Jerusalem. He was an interesting man, from what I gather. That village of his near the Sea of Galilee is still standing, still very much in use. A remarkable feat!"

. . . your paths crossed at the tomb of the Nazarene.

"The rest of them are all gone now!" Vibenna said, trying not to break down in front of a man who loathed weakness in other men. "Scipio, Accius, Nicodaemus, Joseph of Arimaetha. I am the last from that time."

"No, no, you are not alone," Silva spoke warmly. "The one called Fabius Scipio is in Rome. The other, Accius, I believe, is in Corinth. He has taken over a Christian church in that city that had been established by the apostle Paul, who died under an unnecessary and unjust execution ordered by Nero."

"Had Scipio become a Christian as well?"

"I understand that he did."

Silva paused, then added, "Marcus, look at me, please."

When he had Vibenna's attention, he went on to say, "You do not owe this imperial empire of Caesar's another moment. I shall take you to Rome with me, if you wish, and after we part, you can seek out Scipio."

"He is a Christian, sir. I would have nothing in common with him."

"There are worse than Christians about in this land and others. We have just now seen the results of the actions of some of these. Marcus, you are alone. You are old. Be a companion to this man, and he shall be one to you so that you may not spend the remainder of your days forgotten and alone."

"But he will doubtless try to convert me."

"Allow it, Marcus . . . do not hesitate in that. I ask you: When have the gods of Rome ever *truly* seemed real to either one of us? Could it be that this Jehovah is the answer to what men like you and me have been seeking all our lives through the ways of the flesh, only to be denied again and again?"

Vibenna wondered if his mind had failed and he was imagining the words that reached his ears.

"Are you a Christian, sir?" he asked with the greatest hesitancy. "Are you seeking to become one?"

"Not as yet," Silva replied. "Nor may it ever be. But when the sirens of my lust seem ever stronger, and I look into the darkest of nights with no comfort, no joy, nothing but my flesh tormenting me, who knows what will happen or to what or whom I shall reach out before it is too late?"

He stood.

"Go, Marcus. Find this man. Do not stop until the two of you have been brought together after so long, and soon thereafter perhaps you will be able to call yourself by the name that he embraces with the greatest passion, perhaps the only passion that matters."

"Until I become, as Fabius . . . a Christian?" Vibenna asked uncertainly, realizing what harm could befall him if he misspoke.

. . . your paths crossed at the tomb of the Nazarene.

"I wish I had been there at the tomb with you and saw what you saw," the general spoke wistfully. "But, of course, I wish for what can never be."

As they walked through the mouth of the cave, Silva remarked, "However, you alone *can* tell me what happened. Will you do that, please? I have always wondered but never spoken with someone who was involved."

He smiled wanly.

"It is a long way that we have ahead of us in our journey back to Rome. There is plenty of time. I shall listen to every word, every word indeed!"

Vibenna turned and looked back toward the body of Decimus Paetus, which was now caught by a morning ray of sun.

"He seems almost to be smiling," Vibenna remarked, nearly whispering.

"The Jews have sometimes called this existence a vale of tears," Silva said sympathetically. "If your friend is beyond its reach at last, why should he not have been smiling?"

"I want him to have a proper burial. I want this comrade of mine who once served Rome so well not to be left as the others will be."

Silva smiled warmly and patted him on the back.

"I shall arrange this matter as you say," he spoke. "Now, let us be gone from such a desolate place and back to a city where there is life abundant."

A moment later, Vibenna slowly followed Silva across the ramp from Masada to the siege tower.

Life abundant . . .

Feeling some cold, awful irony at the sound of those words, the old man wiped a single tear from his left cheek, then descended, the last of his battles for Caesar in its quickly dying embers, and, soon, only the ashes were left behind, before the Judean winds scattered them across the Promised Land.

452

EPILOGUE

After returning to Rome, Marcus Vibenna eventually found Fabius Scipio and, following much entreaty on his friend's part, became a Christian, his baptism carried out in the ancient Tiber and witnessed by dozens of rejoicing fellow believers.

The two men lingered in Rome for some time among the growing, vibrant Christian community in Rome, including some who were of the households of emperors Titus and Domitian, the sons of Vespasianus. Then Scipio and Vibenna decided to go together to Corinth and assist a surprised Severus Accius as best they were able.

The work in that great city considerably benefited from their presence, for Vibenna had undergone a most remarkable transformation and was to become the soul-winning equal of his younger friend, or, as some said, nearly as great in his efforts as the apostle Paul.

Furthermore, both Scipio and Vibenna were to escape the ravages of those periodic outbursts of persecution visited upon Christians during the latter part of that first century A.D. There were several reasons for that. Scipio had made many friends in the Senate and elsewhere; while Vibenna maintained numerous contacts within the Roman military hierarchy, especially with men such as Flavius Silva and others of his stature. And although many of those helped through moments of personal crisis of one sort or another by the two men did not become Christians themselves, their appreciation was undeniably manifested when it became obvious that Scipio and Vibenna were never in the same danger as was faced by those Christians from among the common populace of Roman society.

Yet there was another compelling advantage that the two former legionnaires enjoyed—the extraordinary legacy left by the bastard son of a long-dead Roman emperor.

For Quintus Egnatius Javolenus Tidus Germanicus, who was to die, surrounded by a host of brothers and sisters in Christ, less than a year after the fall of Masada, left everything that he had—an estate found to be larger than anyone could have guessed—to Scipio, his friend of some forty years, for whatever use was deemed most fitting. And so it was that this proved to be the blatant and largely effective "buying" of the lives of large numbers of fellow believers, thus keeping these fortunate ones from the fearsome beasts of Rome's arenas, including those of the newly built Coliseum, as well as the torments of any of the other places of execution or prolonged imprisonment that had sprung up in and around the fabled city.

I want to leave something behind, my dear Fabius . . . something worthy for the kingdom of our precious Lord . . . something that neither moth nor rust doth corrupt.

That had been his desire, his compulsion, as his life drew to a close, and because of it, when his soul ascended at last, freed from its weary body of flesh, angels in glory heralded his coming as they stood in majestic assembly at the gates, awaiting.